INS/
LEE GLI

Insatiable

Lee Glenwright

Published by Dark Corner Press, 2025.

For David M Thompson, for being the first to ask.
Also for Jane D Watson, for having faith.

Also from Lee Glenwright

Mutt
Ripe, and Others
Little Wounds, and Other Dark Tales
Meat Puppets – A Novel of Fragments
The Voices in My Head Will Not Stop: Stories

PROLOGUE

He had no idea how far he had walked, or for how long. Time no longer had any real meaning and hadn't for as far back as he could recall. Its only measurement was the sound of his own uneven footsteps, a series of clumping, hollow crunches that were soon absorbed by his surroundings. It felt like he hadn't tasted the outside air in forever, instead staring at the same four walls for what had so soon become an endless, stretched out agony. He had once thought that he was made of stronger stuff, much stronger stuff, but he had been wrong. He was now paying the price for his pride, his vanity, or whatever it was that had first started him on the path that had led him to where he was right now.

The sun was already red and low in the sky, the breeze that whipped at his face, streaking the tears across his sunken, dirt-smeared cheeks. The back of his throat was caked with the thick, bitter taste of bile and the soles of his feet felt cracked and raw as they scraped across the gravel path that it felt had flayed the flesh away to the meat beneath. The call of the birds in the trees off to the side of the track was more like the sounding of car alarms to his sensitive ears, his hearing so painfully acute that every sound rang in his head until it felt like his skull would swell and burst open to spill his brain out onto the ground in front of him. He almost wished that it would, if only so he could find some measure of peace at last. His other senses felt equally sharpened, the damp, earthy smells of the surrounding woodland masking a fainter underlying scent of mould and decay, of rot and the musky stink of dead things, a reminder that death was something that could never be escaped.

There was a low growling sensation in the pit of his belly that made him want to retch. Nothing, just a dry heave this time. Still, his mouth yawned open in anticipation, a bilious rush of sour gas pushing its way out with little more than a hoarse croak. He wiped at his chin with the back of his sleeve anyway, a frantic rub at the drying vomit that was already there.

He really should have been getting back, before he lost his way. Minutes, hours, days were nothing but a blur, the same way that they had been for what seemed like so long now. All that he could remember was that he had been overtaken by a sudden need to get out, to escape, even if just for a little while. Anything else felt vague, a mix of half-formed thoughts that were no longer important anyway. He turned and looked back along the length of the narrow path down which he had somehow managed to find his way. The first buildings were still just visible in the distance, although they could have been a whole world away, and might as well have been. The gentle gurgle of the stream alongside him was so tranquil, speaking to him as though in tongues, almost tormenting him with the promise of rest that he knew wasn't his to have, at odds with the crowding and choking bustle of the city that he had never quite gotten used to calling his home. He wished that he could just close his eyes and relax, losing himself forever in that sound and in the welcoming darkness. Better yet, he wished that he could just lie down and let the water wash over him, cleansing him and making everything go away forever. He knew that he couldn't. He was far too much of a stupid coward, even for that. Besides, deep down inside he knew that it was already far too late.

There was a sound behind him, and he turned on one foot, the one that was slightly less torn ragged by the gravel. His tattered shirt flapped in the wind as he did so, the same shirt that had strained at the seams just a few weeks earlier. It really had all been *that* fast, far faster than he was ready for, although the speed of things was probably the least of his worries right now.

He strained his sore, tired eyes, picking out a large shape just ahead, blocking the pathway and standing out against the twilight.

As though sensing his surprise, the horse snorted, its breath billowing in clouds that hung in the evening air.

"Ein...*pferd?*" He rubbed at his eyes with his bony fingers, trying to ignore the dull ache swelling behind them. Despite his initial surprise, the creature wasn't an unfamiliar sight. Indeed, he had the vague recollection of being a child on his parents' farm, back home in his native Germany. The country was still divided in those days, split down the middle by concrete and steel, but they didn't live like savages. He had grown around animals for most of his life, a couple of horses kept in the old stables in one of Papa's fields. Back in those days, he would help in their feeding. He refused, even back then though, to have anything to do with the cleaning, probably thanks in no small part to the compulsive disorder that wouldn't end up being diagnosed by a doctor until many years later. The creature standing in his path still seemed out of place somehow, standing little more than a few feet ahead of him, looking as though it had been picked up from somewhere far more suitable and dropped in front of him, probably for no reason than to hinder him, to get in his way, just the same as it felt like everyone and everything else did lately. Perhaps it had just wandered down to the stream, looking for somewhere to drink. There was a pasture just a short walk further up the path, it had probably come from there. His stomach churned again, a sound that stood out far too much in the growing darkness. The creature dragged a hoof across the gravel, as though alerted by the noise, perhaps aware that something wasn't quite right.

"*Mach dir keine sorgen pferd, ich werde nicht-*" the man started to mutter, the words clogging in his throat as he tried to keep from dry heaving again. Weak, far too weak, he fell to his knees as his legs gave out beneath him and he pitched forward, both hands planting flat in the dirt as he struggled to hold himself upright, fresh pain lancing through the numbness in his feet. His stomach lurched as he emptied himself out onto the narrow track. Not just vomit this time, but blood, thick and dark, in an almost solid jet. *"Mein Gott,"* the words sounded as though they were being choked through a mouthful of dirt as he hacked until his chest burned, trying to spit a trail of mucus away from himself, his breath fluttering, shallow and rapid. Then more again, his midriff seeming almost to lock itself into a ball as the muscles contracted, feeling as though they would crush his innards, disgorging himself again as he expelled what felt like it must surely have a chunk of his insides. The stinging in his eyes matching that in his throat and gullet now, he peered through tears at the puddle already soaking into the ground beneath him, his heart pounding faster than should have been possible as he saw the oily, fleshy lump of tissue glistening on the surface. For just a second, it looked almost alive, as though it was moving, trying to nestle between the stones in search of a hiding place. *Schisse,* he thought, *that must be a piece of my stomach lining. What the hell is happening to me?* He knew, deep inside he *knew,* but like some old memory from decades before, he couldn't quite recall it through the hazy delirium of forgetfulness. There was another crunch of hooves against gravel, as the horse took a tentative step closer, curious about this intrusive stranger.

"Nein...nein...keep away from...me," he mumbled as he tried to move back, away from the mess he had made. He panted, trying to bring his breathing back under control as the urge to vomit washed over him again. He pushed himself back on his hands, his knees scraping against the grit with a pain that he barely even noticed. He could feel the muscles in his belly unknotting and relaxing, leaving behind the same sensation as always. An aching need to fill himself up, to somehow rid himself of the near-constant hunger that still gnawed away at him.

He had to get home, he had to at least try to get back. Maybe if he could just make it to somewhere a little more familiar, then he could lie down and get some much-needed sleep. Yes, perhaps he could rest, and it would all get better again, the way it had been before he had been so stupid. With one last, almost superhuman effort, he tensed every muscle in his body as he struggled to his feet, trying to keep some sort of balance. Not here, no, not here, he *couldn't*. He had to try and make it back home, if he could still even remember where home was. He would be safe there, surely? Safe until the morning, then maybe he could try and get some help, the way he should have done much sooner.

As if in protest, his stomach rumbled again, the churning sensation vibrating up into his chest and making his heart rattle behind his ribcage. He was hungry, so very hungry, all the time. If only there was some way to just make it stop, to make *everything* stop. His breath wheezed out in jackknife bursts as he stood wavering, he looked at the horse again, at the full, firm muscles, rippling beneath its taut hide. He wiped the back of his hand over his parched lips, dragging a thick trail of saliva out across the side of his face. The creature snorted again as it took a step back this time, stamping against the gravel and sending stone chips scattering.

"No, no, *no! I can't!*" He sobbed, fresh tears coursing down his cheeks as he bit down on his lower lip, drawing blood, the sharp, bitter taste hitting the back of his throat. He *could* have, and he knew it. In truth, he could have done so without a second thought, except for the problem that he was nowhere near fast or strong enough. Still, he grunted as he stumbled forward in a pathetic lurch, his arms outstretched towards the animal. Instinctively, the horse reared up, whinnying defensively as it did so.

"*Gott!*" Shocked, he almost fell back again, raising his hands ready to shield his face. The spell broken, he turned about and staggered back in the direction from where he thought he had come, sobbing like a lost child as he went, the maddening rumble in his belly matching the droning noise that still filled his head.

9

***

The man was gone soon enough, swallowed up by the darkness, his moans of confusion and pain fading away with him. Once the idea of any threat had passed, the horse stepped forward again, curious. It raked clumsily at the blood-soiled gravel with one hoof, looking for anything that could possibly be of interest. There was the faint odour of something familiar, carrying on the breeze, something rich and inviting.

Bowing its head, it moved its nose closer, almost touching the damp grit, its muzzle twitching, keen to investigate this strange new thing that it had found.

ONE

"Just give me a minute, let's see if I can fix this thing right here," Brad Whitman scrunched his face in disgust as he lifted the sesame-seeded lid of his burger. His thick fingers – he preferred to avoid the use of words such as *fat* - probed their way through a mess of tomato ketchup and relish, to reach the thin layer of lettuce beneath. He picked the clump of soggy green muck between thumb and forefinger, an almost gelatinous, snot-like lump hanging down from his cautious grip. He stared at it with a look of distaste mixed with incredulity before flinging it down onto the faded plastic tray with a limp, wet slap. "How the hell did that stuff even find its way in there, anyway?" He swivelled his head, as he asked the question of no one in particular, his bulging eyes looking to see if anyone was paying him any attention. If he had really wanted to eat any of that vegetarian rubbish, he would have got up and slogged across the road to a place that sold actual pet food. He probably wouldn't have cared that much really, but Betty should have known better than pretty much anybody else. He had told her plenty of times that he couldn't stand anything even slightly green-coloured getting near his food. Satisfied that he had removed all trace of anything even resembling salad, he replaced the top of the bun, squashing it down flat with his palm and admiring the imprint left behind to dimple the surface of the bread. Gripping what was left of the sandwich in both pudgy hands, he raised it up to his face with an almost ritualistic slowness. He closed his eyes as he inhaled a deep breath, taking in and savouring the enticing smell of fresh-cooked meat, or as near to fresh-cooked as Betty's place was prepared to offer at least. His mouth yawned open as he brought the burger forward, ready to take a bite.

"Get away from my food, you dirty *sod!*" His voice was a possessive shriek as the humming drone filled his ears. He opened his eyes to see a bloated fly buzzing around his head, drawn by the rich, sickly odour of beef fat. He swiped his arm out in a wide arc, the palm of his shovel-like hand connecting with the insect with a slap, leaving a greasy, dark smear across the adjacent wall.

"Good - *urrp* - riddance," he mumbled, wafting his hand in front of his face in an effort to dispel the stink of the belch.

Rosa Whitman shuffled on her chair, trying not to look embarrassed as she set her own bacon and egg sandwich down to one side and waved a slender, thread-veined hand in front of her face, the sour smell robbing her of her own desire to eat.

"Do you *have* to do that in here? Especially when I'm trying to eat *my* bloody lunch as well." She looked up from beneath a greying fringe of hair, her brow furrowed. "It sounds disgusting, and it stinks something *awful*, believe me. It smells like you haven't brushed your teeth in days." She glanced around the room, pulling her arms into her sides in a vain effort to make herself look less conspicuous as she tried to gauge whether or not anyone else had noticed the sound or the accompanying odour.

"Days? Who's counting?" She winced as her husband chuckled with that dirty little laugh that he always used when he thought that he'd said something clever. He always did know how to get under her skin, still gaining an almost morbid kick from trying to make her squirm in public. "It's not my fault, burgers always give me wind - you know that." He spat out a fine spray of breadcrumbs as he spoke through a mouthful of bread and meat mush. He wiped his fly swatter hand down the front of his off-white shirt, adding to the collection of stains on the cotton stretched out across his paunch. "It's a real medical thing, anyway. It's discrimination to pick on me over it. They're always talking about *that* stuff on the news, in case you never noticed."

"Oh, bugger off with you and your *discrimination*. *Burgers* give you wind," Rosa hissed through her teeth, not wanting to make a scene. "*Beer* gives you wind, bloody spaghetti hoops on toast gives you wind. Brad, *everything* you eat or drink seems to give you wind these days."

"Yeah, I suppose it does," his voice was still garbled between chewing even as he laughed at his own reply, as though he had just said something really smart again.

Bradley Whitman had never been the kind of man to really care what anyone else might have thought, either about him personally or about anything he did. In total contrast to his wife, in fact, who seemed to almost always walk around with a *whatever did I see in him* expression fixed to her face.

"You spend far too much time out of your day worrying about what other people are going to think about you," he said, leaning forward, his belly pressing against the edge of the table and causing a wave of fat to bulge over the top. "You know, that's the kind of thing that will just take years off of your life if you let it."

"In the same way as your horrible eating habits are going to end up taking years off yours," she replied, already knowing damn well that it was a waste of breath and that he wouldn't listen to a single word she or anyone else said. Anyone who dared to criticise any of his habits was obviously just mean-spirited. There were a lot of nasty people out there, hiding behind half-baked scientific facts in order to pick on him and his way of life. Most folk really just couldn't let him just get on and be happy, could they? Self-righteous arseholes.

"I reckon you need to just stop worrying as much as you do," he said, the burger still gripped between his fingers, hovering in front of his face ready for him to take another huge bite, "both about me and about whatever any other nosey buggers might think. They should all just mind their own bloody business anyway." He looked around again, his sunken, piggy eyes shifting from side to side, as if he was watching those women that he liked to watch playing tennis, only interested in the game of course, along with those funny noises most of them made when they hit the ball. He almost felt a pang of disappointment to see that Betty's other regulars looked as though they were oblivious to him, instead just minding their own business. Or maybe they had just grown so used to his ways over the years, he had been providing his custom to Betty, and her father before her. He never could understand why Rosa got so wound up, why she *always* let herself get so wound up. As much as he liked Betty and her little café, the place was little more than a dump anyway, and it always had been. Exactly the kind of greasy spoon place that would go to the lengths of slapping a handful of limp-as-a-dishcloth lettuce across the top of a beef burger, a beef burger that had probably been cooked from frozen anyway, thinking that doing so somehow made it classier. It was hardly Michelin standard. He could probably let rip and fart out the national bloody anthem and no one would so much as bat an eyelid. No one except Rosa, at least.

They had been coming to the same place for years now, long before their twenty-two years of marriage, when he had been younger and slimmer, someone who really *knew* how to show a lady a good time. Nothing much - very little in fact - had changed in those years, except for the trouser sizes, meaning that he'd had to switch to a bigger waist measurement. He blamed the Europeans, with their stupid bloody clothing regulations. It wasn't enough that the doctor wrote his weight down in kilos now, the labels on his jeans claimed that his waistline had increased by six inches. He knew exactly what a load of old bollocks *that* stuff was as well.

Whitman's mouth yawned open like a tired old hippo as he shovelled in the last of the burger, poking it to the back of his throat and wiping a red smear of relish from his chin before picking it from his fingers. *Waste not, want not.* He put his hand up to his face this time, in a failed effort to stifle yet another belch. Rosa wrinkled her nose in disgust, shoving her own plate further across the table, the last of her appetite swallowed up by the resulting smell.

"Are you sure you're finished with that?" Whitman wheezed as he spoke, already reaching for the leftover bacon while making sure to keep well clear of the side salad, little more than a sad-looking pile of wet moss-textured slop that clung to the side of the plate as though it had been glued into place. *Garnish*, Betty liked to call it, always making sure to put on a deliberately sniffy accent whenever she did so.

"*Really*? Are you serious?" Rosa rolled her eyes, despite not even needing to hear his answer. He just mumbled a response though a mouthful of crisp meat. In reality she had given up trying to change his ways a long time ago. It always seemed that the more she had berated him, reminding him of how much his health was sure to suffer for his slovenly eating habits, the more he had dug his heels in, actually piling more weight on rather than losing it. Nowadays, her not-so-subtle hints were reserved for those rare occasions when she managed to convince herself that he might actually listen.

He smiled a fat, lazy grin, placing both large, stubby hands across his now full belly just beneath the table. He nodded as the owner of the café shuffled over to their table, dragging her left leg in a limp, as though it belonged to someone else.

"Hey Betty," he raised his hand to his mouth again, just in case. "Rosa's been taking one of her pot shots at me again. I think she still reckons that you're overfeeding me."

"Don't you go blaming me," the short, wide woman ran her hands first across the top of her greasy auburn hair, then down the length of her stained, washed-out apron before scooping up both plates. "You're your own person Brad, I've never twisted your arm up your back, ain't none of it my fault."

"Don't worry, I'm not blaming you Betty, really," Rosa was grateful of the opportunity to talk to someone else, even if that someone else was Betty MacKinnon. "I was just reminding my lovely husband here about how he really needs to look after himself a bit better."

"Look after himself a bit better?" Betty repeated, balancing both plates and an empty coffee mug inside the crook of her arm, a roll of hanging flab wobbling as she did so. "What 'you trying to say? Ain't nothing wrong with the food here," her already dour face creased into a defensive scowl as she gestured her free hand towards the door, the crockery teetering in place as she did so. "Anyone what says otherwise, they know where the door is. Besides, old Brad here probably keeps this place going. Ain't my place to talk him out of nothing."

"Hey, what about me over here, Betty? *I* like it here just fine!" An old man sitting in the far corner spoke up, raising his hand as he did so. He looked like a long-haul truck driver on a stopover at a service station, dressed in a scruffy old flannel shirt and faded dungarees, an oil-stained cap covering silver hair that matched several days' growth of stubble.

"Sorry Eddie," Betty said, the attempt at cheer coming across just as forced-sounding as always. "Of course, you can be my other best customer. Don't be telling anyone though, okay? I wouldn't want anyone else getting jealous."

"In that case, can I get another coffee over here, sweetheart?"

"In a few minutes, Ed. I'm busy right now." She nodded her head at Whitman and Rosa, her way of showing that the conversation was over. Either that, or she'd had enough of being in their company, before shuffling back across to the counter, stopping to pick up a steaming coffee pitcher as she did so.

"She's a strange one, she always has been," Rosa kept her voice low, a hoarse whisper, "Especially since Mackie died. Maybe this place is too much for her. It wouldn't surprise me if it was, especially cooking stuff for the likes of you."

"Hmm?" Whitman mumbled, not really listening.

"She doesn't even try to put up a front anymore. She hasn't for a long time, either. It's like she wants to scare people away," Rosa looked down at the table, as though worried that someone might pick up what she was saying. "Perhaps it's just the way she is, I don't know-"

"What are you going on about now woman?"

"*I was talking about Betty!*" Rosa hissed again. Glancing up, she thought she caught old man Eddie Caplin looking across at her, his nose twitching like a rabbit as he caught the smell of something new to gossip about. She lowered her head again, her voice softening. "Either way, she's wrong about you, at least."

"Wrong about me? How?" Whitman picked at his teeth with a ragged, dirty fingernail, trying to dislodge a hard sliver of bacon that had become stuck in there. "She made perfect sense to me."

"You know what I mean, Brad. You're not getting any younger and if you don't start taking better care of yourself, you're probably not going to get much older either. You can do without the likes of Betty MacKinnon pandering to you, shoving that fatty slop down in front of you for you to shovel down your throat like there's no tomorrow."

"Here we go," Whitman drummed his fingers against the table surface. "I was starting to think it's been a while. You only go on like this because you think I'm too fat."

"No Brad, I'm only saying it because I love you, believe it or not."

"I keep telling you, you should just stop your worrying and I'll be fine," he stood up, scraping the chair back against the worn linoleum. "I'm happy and I can get about just as well as I need to. That's good enough, isn't it?"

Rosa didn't answer him, instead just bowing her head as she followed him up and towards the door to leave. As Whitman reached the door he turned around and gave Betty a cheeky wink. She returned the gesture with a lopsided attempt at a grin that looked more like a grimace, almost spilling scalding coffee in Eddie's lap as she did so.

**

Mornings really were the worst part of the day.

Whitman groaned as he moved to try and disentangle himself from the thin cotton sheet, the creak of bedsprings all too telling as his bulk shifted across them. Rosa had always been an early riser, usually up, ready and on her way to work before he had even stirred. Today was no different from the usual daily routine.

She was right and he knew it, of course she was. He had tried in the past, he really had, but patience and willpower had never been two of his strong points and every diet that he had tried had ended up being scrapped when they didn't show definite results within the first few days. *You've got to stick at it for months, not days*, Rosa had always said, in her usual superior way. It was easy for her of course, with her stick-thin figure and appetite like an anorexic sparrow. It was a different story for him altogether though, trying to make do with meals made up of insect-sized portions of the kind of food you would give to a pet rabbit, especially if you were feeling cruel. It didn't help matters that Betty's greasy spoon was just a few minutes' walk away. Well, it used to be a few minutes' walk away, nowadays it wasn't quite so easy to get there in so short a time. He had a tendency to get out of breath a little bit sooner. It was probably just his age, you know, a bit of wear and tear on the old joints, that sort of thing. It happened to everyone sooner or later.

The real problem was that he just loved food. Well, it had never *been* a problem back in the day. He had always been active enough when he was younger, able to burn it off faster than he put it on. The old *cliché* about him being half the man he was now wasn't too far off the mark. The problem was that the slide from middle-age onward had slowed down a great deal of things, including his metabolism, it seemed. Nothing much, just a few extra pounds here and there, Rosa didn't even notice any change to begin with, so there really had been nothing to worry about. Burgers, chips, pizza, and pasta, he kept right on telling himself that they weren't a problem, that he was still in control and the fact that month by month, he could pinch just a little extra around the region of his belly didn't make a difference, it just made sure that there was a little bit more of him to love, especially around his waist area.

Then, without warning, there *was* a difference, a bloody big difference as it turned out, one that came sneaking up on him from out of nowhere.

"You're getting a bit of a paunch there mind, Brad," Rosa had said one day, trying her best not to make it sound quite so much like a criticism and falling just short of the mark. "I think you might have to start watching what you eat a little bit."

"I'm fine, it's nothing to get yourself worried about," he had been caught off-guard, unable to stop himself from sounding defensive.

"We might have to cut back on the number of our trips to MacKinnon's," she had followed up. Whether she hadn't taken his hint to drop the subject or had chosen to ignore it, he couldn't be sure. "It's probably a good idea anyway, Betty's put all of her prices up just a couple of weeks ago. We could do with saving some money as well."

"I'm telling you, there's no problem," he insisted, the mention of it alone enough to fill his head with visions of Betty's generous servings of deep-fried oven chips and grilled beef burgers, smothered in cheese and ketchup and decorated with crispy, fat-dripping bacon, just to bump up the calories that little bit more. He had to struggle to keep himself from drooling at the thought of it. Betty's little place wasn't the best or the classiest around by any stretch of the imagination, it never had been, even when old George was running the place before her. It was still cheaper than anywhere nearby though, and the food servings were generous. That in itself was good enough to keep him going back for more, while keeping him ticking over nicely in between visits. "I can cut down any time I want," he would insist, seeming unaware of just how much he sounded like a stereotypical alcoholic or drug addict when, in reality that was exactly what he had become. He was a food junkie, always craving his next fix of anything calorie-laden and greasy. In his own head though, he was fine. Nope, nothing wrong here, not at all. Shortness of breath, increased sweating and a heart that sounded off like a drum roll every time he walked more than a street length away, they were all just signs that he wasn't getting any younger, of course. None of it had anything to do with the fact that his trousers barely fitted him anymore as they strained beneath his ever-growing belly. Eating was a bit like smoking or drinking, no one else could tell you when it was time to stop; you had to be the one to decide to make the change for yourself. As he hauled himself up into a sitting position, the mattress almost feeling like it was about to give out, he pinched at his part-exposed midriff, grabbing a sizeable chunk of flab between his fingers, kneading it like raw dough, or one of those annoying stress ball things.

The sigh he let out was like the sound of defeat and was far too loud in the otherwise quiet room.

Really, he knew that he was going to have to do *something*. Rosa *was* right, as much as he could never imagine telling her so. He knew that he brushed off half of her comments without a second thought, playing them down as a joke or just her speaking out of turn. The remaining half, he just tried his best to ignore completely. As hard as he tried though, he couldn't fail to notice, on those occasions when Rosa still did question his habits, the look of concern on her face that she could never quite manage to hide. If he spent too long thinking about it then it started to make him feel guilty, which in turn increased his appetite. It was as though he was a fat old hamster stuck in its wheel, going around and around, with nothing ever changing. *Tomorrow*, he would tell himself, *I'll do something about it tomorrow*, knowing that tomorrow was always going to end up being just that, *tomorrow*.

He managed to work himself into a sitting position and turned to swing his legs over his side of the bed, the worn old springs groaning again beneath the strain. It was even later than he had thought, Rosa must have left without resetting the alarm clock. She was usually mindful of the fact that he didn't sleep too well with his breathing difficulties, asthma, or whatever it was. He flung out his arms and arched his back in a yawn, the movement almost stretching the roll of fat at his gut out of sight, doing no such good for the excess flesh that dangled from his upper arms like miniature wings. His stomach churned and growled, reminding him that it was long past breakfast time.

***

He sat at the kitchen table, cradling his second mug of coffee with a plate pushed to one side, a scattering of breadcrumbs and a sticky yolk smear all that was left of the bacon and egg sandwiches he had just demolished. They weren't as good as when Rosa made them, but they had still hit the spot.

Wearing a faded old *Status Quo* t-shirt that had obviously shrunk several times over and a pair of grey jogging bottoms, he hadn't bothered to shave or take a shower, wanting to make sure that he got his priorities in the correct order. Food first, cleanliness second. It wasn't as if he had much planned to justify getting dressed anyway.

TWO

He had experienced better starts to the day. Sure, he'd probably had many worse, but he couldn't remember most of them, not at that precise moment in time at least.

Frank Popper lay as still as his tender head would allow, raking at his crotch area like someone had poured extra hot chilli sauce up inside his pissing slit, his fingertips felt like sandpaper as they scraped across the wiry hairs and loose, turkey-neck flesh of his balls. He tried keeping his eyes shut tight, almost tight enough to make them water, hoping that it would help to stop the movement, or at least slow it down a little bit. It felt as though he had been lying in that same spot for days, frozen in place and trying not to move, doing his best to ignore the suspicious, stale odour of the bed covers. His joints felt like they had rusted and seized up at some point during the course of the last few nights, locking him into a supine position, ready for some well-meaning stranger to stumble in and mistake him for dead. Perhaps it would be for the best if they called someone to cart him away. It would certainly be a better option than festering any longer in his own piss stink.

The last time he had braved it, he had managed to stare at the ceiling for a whole four minutes, watching the crack in the age-yellowed plaster as it moved around the light fitting at a steady rate of five and a half revolutions per minute. He had even bothered to count the seconds out loud, in an attempt at some sort of distraction. Anything to make the encroaching pain go away.

It wasn't a hangover, not a proper one anyway. He guessed that it would be another hour or two before the full-blown pain of *that* kicked in. *It'll give me something to look forward to at least,* he thought, with the same level of sarcasm that had always prevented him from having too many friends. It had been a little while since he had experienced a proper *kick-you-in-the-face* hangover, the

23

symptoms of the morning after usually depending upon the poison of the night before. The last few nights had been fuelled by a binge of cheap whisky and illegally imported cigarettes, which meant that, once he had gathered up the courage to face it, the day probably wasn't going to be pretty. He had sworn off most other drugs quite a few years ago, finally accepting, albeit reluctantly, that he was getting a bit old for his body to tolerate *that* sort of abuse. The last time was about three years ago, a hit of speed, just to keep him awake for long enough to make an already overdue deadline. He had been left an edgy mess for two days straight, a sweaty mass of muscle tremors and chattering teeth, wired up to the eyeballs. He hadn't slept for three nights in a row. Instead, he had sat in place, strung out like a telephone wire, convincing himself that the walls were moving in and out, mainly in, the people behind them just waiting for him to drop his guard so they could come out from their hiding places and get him. At least booze had the advantage that it knocked him out. Sleeping like a baby right through, it was only when he woke that it would all go horribly wrong, gaining the somewhat bizarre superpower of being able to pebble dash an entire house front with his arse.

It was wrong and he knew it. But there was nothing much else to fill his life when work was as slow as it had been of late. That was always the trouble with freelancing, over a regular desk gig.

"Oh, for Christ's sake," He groaned aloud as he tried to force his left arm to move far enough away from the reassuring, warm comfort of his bollocks to reach his watch on the bedside table. Next to it were a dog-eared reporter's notebook and the stump of a pencil, the end that once held an eraser chewed away almost to a jagged, splintered point, so you could just about make out the *H* in *HB*. It helped him to concentrate sometimes, in those moments when he was bothering to try and avoid jamming another cigarette into his mouth. The notebook rarely left the table, the

idea behind it being that it should be used to capture any waking thoughts before they could evaporate away into nothing. It was good practice apparently, but the trouble with that idea was that by the end of most nights between jobs, he ended up too wasted to be able to form coherent dreams, as though even his subconscious mind was pissed off with him. It wasn't a good way to be, not really. Not when pretty much his whole livelihood depended upon his ability to string words together into a more or less sensible order. Even the most down-market of rags needed his stuff to make *some* sense at least. He sometimes wondered how he still managed to keep doing it and, he suspected that he wasn't the only one who did so. Drink, write and drink some more until too drunk to continue with either, most nights it was pretty much the same routine.

Stories: they were the only reason that he had continued to stick around for as long as he had, or at least that was what he usually told himself. It certainly wasn't out of any sort of love for the place. If you could actually find anyone who claimed to love the city, then Frank Popper would be ready to call them a liar straight to their face. He had somehow managed to get by for a long time now, long enough to grow some sort of basic immunity to its disease, the way it burrowed under the skin like a sucking insect, a massive tick, drawing off life so slowly that it usually kept on unnoticed. Instead of being on your guard, you went about your day-to-day drudgery, telling yourself that you were okay, that *everything* was okay, not great perhaps, but at least *okay*. All the time, you turned a blind eye to a whole ton of nasty, *nasty* shit going on right under your nose. Frank Popper had seen plenty of that nastiness in his time. He had seen it, investigated it, and written about it, usually while in an alcoholic haze of righteous anger.

Bare-faced bravado told him, along with anyone who would listen to him, that he was immune at least. He had to be. A bit like parents to their kids, back in the days before all those forward-thinking health crusaders stepped in and tried to suck all the fun away. *A little bit of dirt never hurt anyone.* In small doses, exposing yourself to the muck could be a good thing, it could help to build up the immune system against all the rotten badness that surrounded it. That was how things were. The best way to avoid getting sick was to just roll with it and see where it took you.

Perhaps that was why he currently had a burning sensation down below, the end of his cock feeling like it'd had a whole box of matches stubbed out on it. It had only taken three days after the actual event, or maybe he had just been too wasted to notice the near-constant itching sooner.

He hadn't even bothered with the formality of asking her name at the time, glad that Frank Junior was even getting some action, a rarity in itself. The old *fuck me, I'm a writer* line might have still done the trick sometimes, but not as often as he would have liked. The bloody awful racket that had passed for music would have made it impossible to hear her anyway, never mind the fact that they were both drunk.

If he concentrated hard enough, he could just about remember the inside of the toilet cubicle, with its fishy stink of urine mingled with stale vomit, the broken flush chain hanging down limper than a monk's dick. Despite his having been a chain smoker for most of his adult life, it was just as well that he could still hold his breath for quite a long time when he needed to. She was as drunk as he was, probably more so. Her tight top, just a little too low-cut to be decent and a skirt that her mother would never have let her leave the house in, hitched right up to her belly, her knickers pulled to one side and her legs wrapped tight around his waist as he pumped himself into her, not too bad a performance, considering the amount of the cheapest booze available that he had already put away. He winced, cringing as he could still just about remember the hollow sound of the cubicle door rattling as her bare arse smacked against it in time with his best John Travolta-style pelvic thrusts. He could still feel the taste of stale vodka on her tongue as it wormed its way down his throat, lapping at the roof of his mouth, as though she was trying to search out and remove any gold fillings. He could remember it all, no amount of alcohol could ever be enough to blot the whole sorry three-minute fumble from his memory, no matter how much he might have wished that it would.

Even the part just before he finished, when she promised him that he didn't need any protection. It was all okay, she was on the pill and had just been tested a couple of weeks back anyway.

Tested a couple of weeks back? Tested for what *exactly? General knowledge? Ability to cope in a crisis?* Somehow, he doubted that it was either of those things. As soon as they were done, he had wiped himself off on the hem of his shirt, before stuffing his already softening member back into his pants.

"Ain't this the part where we're supposed to swap 'phone numbers or sumfink?" she had slurred, struggling to stretch her skirt down far enough to cover herself as she hitched her lace-trimmed panties back into place. "I mean, it's not like I always make it a habit, letting meself get shagged off of some bloke half an hour after meeting him, you know." The sound of her voice was almost indignant, despite the slurring effect of those last few cocktails that she had roped him into buying for her, like he could actually afford those fancy-arse things with their deliberately smutty names.

"Only if they tell you that they're a writer, *right?*" As wasted as he was, he couldn't resist making the comment. That had always been one of his many faults, speaking before he had thought everything through properly.

"Why, you cheapskate twat," her cheeks had flushed red through the layered-on foundation, her voice quivering part in burgeoning anger and part in drunken disbelief that she ever could have fallen for such an obvious line in the first place. He soothed any notion of a guilty conscience by telling himself that at least it probably wasn't the first time she had been caught out by something similar. "A writer my arse! I bet you say that to all the girls. It's probably the only way you can ever get your cock sucked," she had bent down in the cramped cubicle, nudging him in the chest with her breasts as she did so Luckily, he never had actually been the most randy of blokes, especially after a few drinks. Nope, definitely a once around the block type of guy, there hadn't even been a follow-up stirring.

"I wasn't spinning you a line," he had protested, unable to let that one lie. "I really am a writer. I'm just not a very nice person with it, maybe, if I'm being completely honest." He had reached his hand behind himself, his fingers fumbling for the lock on the cubicle door and sliding it back with a far too conspicuous *thunk*.

"Whatever. You're *still* a cheapskate twat," she had muttered, perhaps thinking that he hadn't heard her the first time, her eyes shining with a mixture of alcoholic gleam and the realisation that she had been pretty much played like an old fiddle.

"*Umm*...yeah, well, I suppose I'd better be going now," his voice dropped to a mumble as he had edged his way out of the cubicle, squeezing his way around the inward-opening door. "I would love to get to know you better, but I've got, you know, a heavy day tomorrow. Deadlines to hit, that sort of thing."

"Just get out of it, you tight bastard," she slurred. "I prefer women, anyway." She had brought a lipstick out of her bag, smacking her lips together as she applied the deep red colour, trying to look as though she didn't really care. "If I ever see you again, I'm going to cut it off with a broken glass, you lying shitweasel."

He had been called worse things - his job had always made sure of that, but *lying shitweasel* was still a pretty inventive insult. Safe in the knowledge that *whatever-her-name-was* wouldn't be expecting him to turn up at her third floor flat, bearing flowers, chocolates, and a Zeppelin-sized erection any time soon, he had made good his escape, somehow finding his way home and crawling into bed, where he had crashed out until morning, or at least what his mind imagined to pass for morning.

***

Yes indeed, from there it had been downhill all the way.

Fast forward three days of his envy-inspiring life to him stretched out on the bed, the front exit of his boxer shorts gaping open as he scratched at himself. It wasn't just an itch; it was AN ITCH. No, make that A GREAT BIG FUCKING ITCH. Something all too real and deep-seated, as if a swarm of angry fire ants had crawled up through his pisshole while he slept, stomping around inside his groin with wasabi-dipped hobnail boots.

At least he'd gotten a shag out of it though, for the first time in more months than he could remember. That *had* to be worth it, *right?*

He tried telling himself that there was a story tucked away in there somewhere. Perhaps an article on the links between inner-city deprivation and the spread of venereal diseases, or at least a half-decent editorial on the fallout experienced when stupid-arsed journalists opted for a quickie in a club toilet. Just add alcohol, female of name unknown and subtract barrier contraception.

The light from outside was almost non-existent, a thin halo showing around the blackout blind, a thick screen of tattered material that also dampened down the sound of the rain spattering against the windowpane with a *shit-shit-shit* sound that matched the current pattern of his thoughts.

He sat up with a drawn-out groan, his legs from the knees down and his feet tingling as the blood started to flow back into them. He couldn't be sure what was worse, the pins and needles or the infuriating burning feeling in his genitalia. At least he knew that his legs would start working again soon enough. The movement sent a clenching spasm up from his surely diseased crotch up into the base of his gut, making him groan again in discomfort. He looked across at the telephone still off the hook, just as he usually left it, the act of doing so being a prompt of sorts, a reminder to himself to keep away from the damn thing. Besides, hardly anyone ever bothered calling him anyway, not that he ever complained. Perhaps he should be braving it, calling a doctor, although it was often surprising just how many ailments you could usually ride out when the alternative was to embarrass yourself in front of - let's face it - a stranger. Still, it didn't feel too good, not by any stretch of the imagination. A squirming, itching feeling, an almost rippling sensation across the skin of his crotch and testicles, as though maggots were writhing their way through the tangle of his pubes. *Great. Just great. Clear my arse. She's probably gone and given me something to remember her by, a good old dose of nastiness, just to make sure I don't forget her in a hurry. She would probably say that it serves me right for not getting her number. I'll bet that she probably wasn't really on the pill, either. A couple of days to pluck up enough courage to score some antibiotics from the nearest clinic, then another nine months to emigrate to a Tibetan monastery and take a vow of celibacy.*

He looked at the telephone again, at the bright yellow rubber gloves hanging alongside it - for emergency use - the sight of it alone enough to make his stomach turn even more than it already was. He wondered just how bad it would really need to be before he gave in and called a clinic for advice, trying to hide his embarrassment behind his usual journalistic swagger.

INSATIABLE

- Good afternoon, what seems to be the problem, Mister Popper?
- Oh, you know, just the usual. A drunken grope in a bar toilet cubicle with some woman I've never even met before. A few days later and now my dick's just hanging on by a thread. She had a pretty good set of tits on her though, so I guess that kind of makes it all worthwhile. Nothing major, really. I bet you get that all the time, yeah?
- No Mister Popper, we don't get that all of the time. Not at all. Someone your age should really know better than to have unprotected intercourse in a cloakroom. You should try keeping it in your pants, it works better than anything a doctor could ever prescribe for you.

Yeah, that would *really* be a conversation to look forward to. Suddenly, staying in bed, preferably forever, seemed so much like the lesser of two evils. Maybe he could just cocoon himself in his blankets and ignore the world outside, like a petulant kid trying to bunk off on the day of his first exam. With any luck maybe his trigger-happy penis would just wither up and die, making sure that he couldn't make the same mistake ever again.

***

Despite having what he had always liked to think was a pretty decent tolerance threshold for discomfort, after a while the stultifying closeness combined with the sour stink of old sweat ended up being too much, even for him. No matter how bad things could ever get, he never had much fancied the idea of wasting away in bed, left alone to rot, with his only legacy a bloated, festering corpse to be discovered by the neighbours, once they realised that they hadn't heard the strange, dirty-looking guy in the next flat screaming at his typewriter for a few weeks. They probably wouldn't notice anyway. Armenians, or at least he thought they were, they spent most of their days shouting at one another in a language that he didn't understand. Then when they weren't fighting with each other, they were trying to break through the paper-thin wall with the headboard of their bed. The best part about arguing almost constantly was the making up again afterwards, apparently.

Like it or not, he had a living to make. It was no use just lying around waiting for whatever nasty little infection he had picked up to overwhelm him.

***

Just about every bone in his body cracked and popped as he walked to the bathroom, vomiting twice once he got there, emptying himself of the bellyful sloshing around his insides. Still wiping whisky and bile-tasting spittle from his lower lip and chin, he hesitated before stepping into the shower cubicle, rubbing the stubborn leftovers of sleep from the corners of his bleary eyes and turning the tap with a tired creak as he did so. The shower head gave out a brief sputter before disgorging streams of scalding water. He gave the temperature a minute to settle, not wanting to add third-degree burns to his growing list of problems. On tiptoe as he drew the bright-coloured nylon curtain closed behind himself, he winced as the high-pressure jets bounced against his skin, raw and sharp, flaying him like thousands of pinpricks all at once.

After a few seconds, hot clouds of steam billowed up to fill the room with a thick, humid fog. He leaned his head back, groaning again as the neck muscles stretched out, his eyes closed against the stinging torrent.

He held himself under the spray for as long as he could bear to do so, scourging away any trace of the previous few nights, scrubbing at a stubborn, crusted stickiness that still clung to his inner thighs. "*Infected jizz juice,*" he muttered to himself, his own voice sounding unfamiliar, like an alien croak to his ringing ears. The torrent of water seemed to sting even more than usual, to the point of causing actual pain. It really did feel as though layers of his skin could peel off, falling clean away if he stayed still long enough. Hopeful that he had been purged of any remaining sex taint, he leaned forward and turned the tap back to the *off* position. The water slowed to a steady trickle with a rasping hiss, before subsiding to a slow gurgling *drip-drip-drip*. He could almost start to convince himself that if there was no physical evidence then perhaps it didn't really happen after all.

The dull throbbing in the front of his head still refusing to shift, he shoved the gaudy, dripping curtain back and stepped out onto the rug, the threadbare fleece finding its way between his toes like worms squirming and wriggling beneath his feet, in competition with the still-present sensation in his balls.

An ugly churning sound came from his gut, probably in protest after he had voided its contents down the toilet. The problem was that he knew anything he tried to force down would reappear well before he could even digest it. It was usually best just to ride out any hunger pangs until his delicate stomach had settled itself.

He opened the bathroom cabinet, trying to avoid making eye contact with his reflection in the mirror, as much as it stared out like Medusa, just daring him to look back at it. At the front was a half-empty tube of toothpaste, some cough syrup, a packet of paracetamol, and a slim box of condoms, still cased in its protective cellophane wrapping. He almost laughed at the irony as he reached in a hand and fumbled around, almost tipping the cough syrup out to the floor below. He found what he was looking for, a plain, off-white box. The label on the front stated that the contents were *Metronidazole 400mg* and should be taken three times daily until the course was complete. It also read that they were a year and a half out of date. They were probably still fine, they were *antibiotics* and surely, they couldn't go bad, right? What was the worst thing that could happen? Besides, if taking them meant that he wouldn't have to end up visiting a clinic then it was well worth the risk.

"Three days," he said aloud. "I'll give it three more days and if it still feels like my bollocks are going to drop off, then I'll go and see a doctor, honest." He broke two of the tablets free from their aluminium foil and flipped them into his mouth, wincing in distaste as he dry-chewed them to a chalky pulp.

THREE

It was one of the few remaining pleasures that he had in life, one of the few that Rosa didn't object to, at least. The twenty-minute walk from the outskirts of the city could of course be considered as exercise, especially lugging his bait box and old canvas fishing bag, the flimsy fibreglass rod slung over his shoulder bobbing up and down in time with his lumbering steps.

Escaping to the lake was like crossing over into a whole other world, even with a tosser like Mitch Brennan in tow, nagging in his ear almost as much as Rosa could when it suited her. Despite that, their destination was the closest thing to an oasis, tucked away in a neat little corner. It was the sort of place that he could go to hide when he wanted to get away for a little while, something that he just had to do sometimes, leaving the real world behind for a bit; the real world where he was a slow, fat knacker with a food addiction. Instead, he could just be plain old Brad Whitman, and no one could tell him otherwise. His fishing trips were becoming more and more frequent.

He stumbled several footsteps ahead of Brennan, his baggy t-shirt flapping in the light breeze as he almost bounced along.

"Come on, you slow old fart," he called over his shoulder, without turning around, "I thought I was supposed to be the lazy one. At least that's what people keep telling me." He grinned, pleased with himself. "Besides, it's going to be a good one today. The sun's out, the wife's out and I've got a four pack of beer in my bag," he sniffed at the air. "Yep, a good one. I can feel it in my bones."

"In your *big* bones?" Brennan's voice was high and strangled, matching his pinched, weasel-like features. He was one of the few people that had actually known Brad Whitman for long enough -

since they were kids in fact - to make such a comment and expect to get away with it.

"Don't you start, you smart-mouthed sod," Whitman said, "I hear enough of that sort of thing from the old woman. Always bloody pecking at me, she is. I swear she's getting worse. It's just as well I've got this place to come to, or I'd go mad."

"Really?"

"Yeah. Just the other day, she actually suggested that we spend too much time going to Mackie's place and that we – and by *we* she really meant *I* - ought to cut down."

"Perhaps she's got a point though. Betty's not the most accommodating of people, she's usually got a face on her like a smacked backside on a *good* day. Besides, I noticed that she put her prices up not that long ago."

"That's what Rosa said. It sounds to me like she's just thinking of new ways to make me feel miserable. It's always the same, I'm telling you it has been for a long time."

"Or maybe it's because she loves you and just wants you to live a little bit longer," Brennan wheezed, probably the grass seed from the neglected undergrowth flirting with his asthma. It didn't help that despite his bulk, Brad Whitman could still be pretty fast on his feet when the mood actually took him. Even if only over short distances, he was like the world's fattest cheetah.

"Anyway, wait for me, will you?" Brennan croaked, his throat drying out on the clouds of dry, dusty earth the two of them kicked up in their wake, "I'm doing the best I can." Christ, old Whitman was like a steam engine, slow and steady. It was as though he liked to play up to peoples' expectations and, in doing so, somehow managed to turn something that could easily have been a disability to his advantage. In spite of whatever faults he might have had, he managed to get by, most of the criticisms at least seeming to roll right off his broad back.

"What in the *hell*-" Whitman's voice came from just around a bend in the dirt path. Tired of waiting for Brennan to play catch-up, he had struck out ahead, his long shadow bobbing and rippling across the gravel track.

Sighing as he tightened his grip on his own fishing rod, Brennan picked up his pace at the sound, jogging by the edge of the tree line to the narrow stream that led to the lake, where he stopped just behind Whitman, both of their paths blocked by the thing in front of them.

"Bloody hell, Brad. What is it, and what happened to it?" Brennan looked down at the creature at the edge of the water. Stretched out across the dirt path, its head resting just above the surface of the stream.

"It's a horse, what does it *look* like?" Whitman squatted beside it, the movement forcing out a belch as he reached out a spade-like hand, undecided as to whether it was safe to touch.

"I'm not sure you should be doing that," Brennan said, his eyes bulging, unable to take his gaze away from the thing.

"I don't think it's going to be jumping up and kicking me any time soon, if that's what you're getting bothered about." The creature's hide was dry and leathery, as if it had lain out in the sun for several days. It looked emaciated, ribs showing through, as if every ounce of fat and muscle had been stripped away to leave little more than a skin-covered skeleton. Its head was angled down towards the water, its muzzle almost touching, as though it had died in the act of reaching for a drink. The mouth was drawn back, and the gums shrunken away, giving the teeth an even greater illusion of length.

"Poor thing," Brennan muttered. "I wonder how it died."

"It looks as though it starved to death," Whitman ran his hand across the xylophone rib cage, feeling the empty spaces between the bones. "But the way it's lying here, it looks like it happened suddenly. I was here just a couple of days ago and it wasn't here then."

"Are you sure?"

"Jesus Christ, Mitch, I'm pretty sure I would remember seeing something like *this* blocking my bloody path!"

"Perhaps it got sick and just came here to die." Brennan shuffled his feet, still trying to look away. "I'm still not so sure about this. It doesn't look right somehow."

Whitman turned his head to one side, wrinkling his nose in disgust, as if Betty MacKinnon had just waved a handful of her damp dishcloth lettuce in his face. "What's that godawful smell?" At the rear end of the animal, a length of fat, grey intestine snaked away, still glistening in the daylight. It ended in a wet, blood-smeared pile, nestled in the undergrowth, from where the droning buzz of flies could be heard. Brennan cupped a hand over his mouth and stifled a gag.

"Oh, Jesus, it's shit its guts out. I think I'm going to puke mine up. That stink is *disgusting*."

"It *is* pretty weird, isn't it?" Whitman prodded at the carcass again, satisfied that it wasn't going to fight back. "It looks as though it's been dead for ages, but it doesn't feel like it."

"What do you mean, *doesn't feel like it?* Make a habit of prodding dead horses, do you?" Brennan's voice was muffled behind his hand. He took off his faded old baseball cap and waved it in front of his face, trying to shift the odour that seemed to have lodged itself into his nostrils.

"It's still soft. Here, have a feel," Whitman gestured towards the body. Shocked, Brennan shook his head. "Ahh, *shit*," Whitman grimaced, wiping his hand against the leg of his jeans, leaving an oily, tell-tale smear where his fingers had been. "That's just bloody typical. There's a wound there, and I just went and dragged my fingers right through it."

"What? What did you get on you?"

"Nothing really. It's just a bit of pus or something, you know, the usual sort of thing."

"*Nuh-uh*, no way am I touching it." Brennan shook his head, the bones of his neck cracking as he did so, his mind made up.

Whitman groaned, his kneecaps popping as he stood up. "Come on then, you soft old bastard. I suppose we'd better get going then, before it's time to pack up." He kicked at the horse one last time, the remains still spongy and supple, despite their obvious wasting. He lurched forward, bringing his still-bloodied hand up to his face in an effort to stifle a cough.

"'You okay Brad?" Brennan hesitated, still uncertain about getting any closer.

"Yeah. Probably just a bit of grass seed or something, went up my nose. No worries, I'll be okay" He pinched his nostrils together between his thumb and forefinger, trying to dislodge whatever had gotten up there. "Anyway, come on, we'd better get a move on."

"You *are* kidding, right?" Brennan said. "You still want to go to the lake?"

"Why not. The thing isn't going to jump up and come after us or anything. Besides, I don't know about you, but I reckon I've got me some fish to catch."

"Fishing, right." Brennan's face had drained of colour, except for twin spots of red flushing his cheeks, as if he had just been smacked across them. "But that thing has got its head in the water," he pointed along the length of the stream, in the direction of the lake. "It could have died of something catching. Something that fish might catch."

"Maybe, but it's down *here*, and we're going up *that* end," Whitman jabbed a finger upstream, in the direction of the lake.

"Water *flows*. You might fancy your insides dropping out from between your own fat arse cheeks, but I don't."

Whitman narrowed his eyes into slits, pondering the idea while he tried to think of a suitable reply. "You can stay here if you want to, but I'm going on." He started off around the corner, his baggy shirt lifting as he did so, flabby, pale folds of flesh rippling as he walked.

Placing his cap back on his head at an angle, Brennan raked at his stubble with his ragged, nicotine-stained fingernails, pondering his options. After a few seconds he shrugged his shoulders. Follow Whitman, or stay by himself, with nothing for company except that dead *thing*. It was a no-brainer really.

Resigned, he followed along the track.

FOUR

Clack-clack-click-clackety-clack-
"Fuck. Shit. *Fuck.*"

Each individual push of a key was like a tiny hammer, smacking against the inside of his head and setting of a chain of little fireworks in the back of his brain. It wasn't always quite as bad. He preferred to avoid modern word processors, along with a lot of electrical things. Computers, telephones, calculators, with their horrible little germ-collecting, keys and their soft little clicking sound. He had his reasons. Instead, he was happier with his good old-fashioned Royal typewriter, a solid, sturdy thing, the likes of which was hard to come by in the days of modern technology. He had picked it up from a flea market just a few years ago, managing to wrangle the price down to twenty quid, still more than he really wanted to pay, but worth every penny all the same. Among other things, he always found something more real, more reassuring in using it, the repetition of keystrokes almost driving whatever story he was working on out of his head, one word at a time. Of course, it didn't hurt that the noise at all sorts of unsociable hours probably pissed off his neighbours no end. It served the randy bastards right for supergluing their headboard to the adjoining wall, disturbing his train of thought with their noisy, pornographic rutting. The downside was that it soon became a bit of a pisser whenever he made a mistake, but that was a small price to pay for interrupting their post-argument couplings every time they felt the need to make up with one another. The frequency with which he heard them tearing lumps out of one another with their shouting, followed by the conciliatory round of fucking led him to believe it was some sort of miracle that their genitalia wasn't worn out.

It was just as well that he lived alone, it meant that there was no one to complain about the discarded papers strewn across the

41

floor, torn into pieces, crumpled into balls, or sometimes folded up into intricate origami shapes, depending on whatever mood he happened to be in at the time.

Stories. It might have been a tired old cliché, but it was still true, there were a million of them hidden away in the city, all just waiting to be told. That was his job: to find the stories, to sniff them out and pin them down by whatever means it took, to put them out there for other people to read. He wanted people to absorb his words in the same way that so many of them allowed themselves to absorb the filth of their surroundings. The dirt clung like an old layer of skin, slowly working its way into every available place, seeping into the very pores and making people feel like they had somehow become immune to its poison.

He was a self-confessed hack, for want of a better word, but Frank Popper still liked to at least *try* and glamourise what he did by telling anyone who would listen long enough that he was an *investigative journalist,* whatever the hell *that* meant nowadays. The reality of it was that he would sit down in front of his old typewriter, hit whatever bottle of alcohol was on the desk next to him and think of something that riled him up, something that he thought might actually get some reaction out of those other people who still bothered to read. Over the years, he had honed his craft, developing both his own acerbic brand of nastiness and a knack for finding the sort of stories that he believed would cause sufficient outrage in other people. He had always tried to imagine himself as some latter-day Hunter Thompson sort of figure, choosing to ignore the possible reality that he was little more than an often drunk forty-something, still railing in anger against what he saw as all the injustices of the world, whilst making a living selling his point of view to anyone who might be interested in running with it. He tried to write about the sort of stuff that usually got ignored, the poverty, the filth and corruption. He got it out there as much as he could, to try and make sure that at least some people didn't walk around with their eyes quite so tight shut. He might not have come across as the nicest of people and that would most likely never change. He wasn't proud by any means, but it was how he needed to be, in order to see the truth and make it known to the sort of people who probably wouldn't give a damn about it otherwise.

***

He hated the place, but it was a strange, almost paradoxical sort of feeling that stemmed from an almost symbiotic relationship. It was the sort of emotion that still sparked a fire in his belly and kept him going, even when everything else failed. All the same, he didn't think that even he could handle living right in its belly, not anymore. He had once, living in a glorified squat of a flat in *The Reds*, as in Redevelopments, a crowded, squalid, dirty place that he had called home up until about a couple of years before, but that was a whole other story. Instead, he had dragged himself away to a block of flats a little further from the actual city centre and still not all that different, save for fact that he was a little less likely to get a knife between his ribs if he wandered outside after dark. He had swapped one cramped, single-bedroom flat for another cramped, single-bedroom flat. As an added bonus, the new one came with a free pair of argumentative neighbours who would sometimes let him into the audio secrets of their explosive sex life. Of course, he knew that he could never move away from the place completely. He still needed it in order to be able to work. It kept his creativity ticking away, kept everything just bubbling under and ready, just in case he felt the itch of a decent story, as opposed to the itch of a one-night stand.

***

"Aww, *shit*..." Another half-typed sheet of paper found itself pitched to the floor, joining the rest in what looked like a really bad game of French bowls. Maybe it was the itching, not as bad as before but still definitely there. He couldn't quite focus, his mind refusing to stay on the topic. That was never a good thing when you'd promised the editor of the local rag that your next column would be ready in two days, having already shifted the deadline twice. Local press didn't really pay a lot - hell, most of them paid next to nothing in fact - but when you were a writer in Frank Popper's not too lofty position, every little helped. The almost constant rain spattering against the window where he had positioned his desk was usually pretty soothing, a veil of white noise that screened out most distractions, with the exception of the neighbourly banging, perhaps. With his head still full of fuzz and the itching in his crotch though, it *was* the distraction, forcing him to look up from his story of drug-dependent prostitutes and their rich pimps more often than he usually would have liked.

If he leaned his head forward enough, he could look down and see what was going on through the dirt-smeared window. Through the grime that streaked the never-cleaned glass, everything had a faint yellow taint, as if the whole place below was jaundiced, suffering from some sort of weird, collective liver failure. It usually got pretty busy down on the ground most days, even the near-constant rain not enough to keep people from milling about like rats, rushing by, their heads angled towards the ground as they tried to ignore one anothers' problems. Every now and then, raised voices would cut through the background noise, more often than not arguments over the usual things, money or drugs. Just across the road there was an empty pitch from where Little Joe used to do business. Probably somewhere in his early to mid-twenties, Little Joe was a dealer who hung around almost right across the street from Popper's window. Frank had scored some acid off the kid once about four years ago, during one of his experimental phases, shortly before he finally managed to convince himself that he was a bit too old for that sort of thing. He was working on an editorial about the inner-city drug problem and had stupidly decided that he could gain a better understanding of the situation by partaking himself, gonzo-fashion. Never again. The fucking stuff had nearly finished him off. For about a week after, he had kept on seeing eight-foot-high scorpions climbing out from cracks that kept appearing in the walls, leaving rainbow-coloured puddles of scorpion piss behind them, before scuttling back into their hiding places. He still shuddered at the thought. He had gotten a decent story out of that one all right. He was still living in fear of the possibility of flashbacks.

About a month later, Little Joe had tried to sell a wrap of coke to a punter, who didn't take too kindly to his blow having an orange tint from the amount of brick dust it was cut with. Little Joe had probably done the wrong thing by coming over all cocky and telling the punter that it had been left out in the sun too long and had gotten a tan. His smart mouth probably hadn't helped his case too much. *Tanned coke is the best coke,* he had said. *Sun-dried, makes it healthier, you know?* He had spoken in his usual loud, cocksure way, with a wide grin that showed off huge, nicotine-stained teeth that looked like they had been jammed into his mouth. A couple of days after that, a pair of burly guys in black bomber jackets and balaclavas turned up and left Little Joe bloodied and beaten to a pulp in the gutter. It took half an hour of people side-stepping and ignoring him while he rested in a puddle of his own blood, snot and puke, before someone found the time to call an ambulance, have him scraped off the pavement and dumped in a hospital bed. It would be a good while before he could eat, walk or piss unaided, never mind go back to dealing badly-cut drugs on street corners. That was one less pair of eyes and ears for Frank, for a while at least.

Cheating prick that he was, Little Joe had helped supply the gory details for more than one Frank Popper story.

On the plus side for Joe, at least his dental bills weren't quite so high anymore.

The city was a dump, but it fuelled Frank's journalistic anger in a way that he couldn't imagine many other places could, making it almost a certainty that he would never get away from the place completely, unless he died of course.

He paused to look down at the sheet of paper sticking out of the top of the typewriter. He had barely gotten through a page and a half, stopping every couple of sentences to have a good old rake at his balls, wincing every time his ragged fingernails snagged in the wiry brush of his pubes. The paracetamol that he had taken right after the antibiotics had taken the edge off a little, but it still felt as though there was something smouldering down there and not in a good way, either. He narrowed his eyes as he looked at the bottle of bourbon also on his desk, in the same spot as always, the top discarded to make for quicker access whenever needed. Booze didn't make him a better writer, far from it in fact. What it did do though, was make him *think* that he was a better writer and more often than not, that was good enough. Sometimes, it *had* to be.

There were still some days however, when even whisky couldn't help to make the words come into his head and spill themselves out in some order. It was starting to look like it was shaping up to be one of those days.

He gazed out of the window again, to the street below. The rain spattered against the glass, driven by the wind in a constant rhythm that swelled and dropped in turn. Everything outside looked dull and faded, all flat greys and washed-out muted colours, as if in the process of being flushed away by the never-ending downpour. He could hear voices from beneath him, raised and angry-sounding voices, shouting back and forth, those few words that he did recognise made it obvious that whoever it was down there wasn't out collecting for a charity.

"Wheresmyfackinmoney?"

"Gerroffyoucahnt!"

"Dontcallmeacahntyoufackincaaaahnt!"

After a few seconds there was the sound of fist connecting with head, or perhaps some other body part, followed by the hollow noise of body part connecting with concrete.

He rubbed at his temples with his fingers, trying to knead out the aching sensation that had so far refused to budge. There was a stale whisky taste clogging the back of his throat and a tingling on the tip of his tongue that he always got when he needed a cigarette. He felt like he had to get outside, to taste the smog clinging to the air and to feel the rain on his face. Anything was better than the prospect of a day sitting indoors, scratching at himself and probably gathering dead lice beneath his fingernails, while he tried to pull meaningful sentences together from nothing. If he was going to wind up in some sort of burning agony, he would rather that he wasn't stuck in front of his typewriter when it hit him fully.

Besides, it was past eleven, the pubs would be open. His decision made, he looked through the gap in the doorway at the telephone on the wall, rubber gloves hanging from the picture hook alongside. There was a flutter of apprehension in his belly, something that he didn't feel too often, not just at the thought of picking up the receiver and touching the buttons with his fingers.

The pub was waiting for him, and there was someone that he needed to see.

***

"I didn't think you'd show up. I'm bloody glad you did. I was going mental cooped up in that flat and, besides, it's been far too long." He planted a pint of snakebite on the table, the liquid slopping over the side of the glass. Kim Dzanic reached forward, picking it up in one still-gloved hand. "You're looking well, by the way."

"I was *feeling* well, until about five minutes ago at least." She raised the glass to her mouth and took a gulp, wincing at the cold. "I'm still not one hundred percent certain why I actually said yes."

"Maybe it's because you're like me, because you realized that nine years is far too long," Frank sat down opposite, cupping his own drink in one hand and resisting the urge to down it. There was still a chance that it might be needed more in the near future.

"Oh, I could argue that it's nowhere near long enough," she flicked strands of dark blonde hair from her eyes, fixing her gaze upon him as though determined to show him that things *had* changed, show him that she was there out of choice, not out of need. "Besides, it's nearer to ten years now, just in case you lost count. I'm just surprised that you actually managed to call me, what with that stupid phobia of yours."

"It's not a phobia, it's a real thing and I'm working on it. I've found that gloves usually help." He cracked a smile, hoping to thaw the tension that was still noticeable between them. "You haven't changed a bit, have you? Apart from the obvious, of course."

"I fucking well hope I *have* changed, *Franklin Popovich*," Kim interrupted. "You're still the same old smarmy bastard when you want to be, aren't you? You can save the sentimental bollocks though; I can still see through it. *Nine years is far too long*," she mimicked him in a mocking tone. "Piss off, Frank. You've had every single day of those *almost nine* years to reach out the olive branch. That you're just doing so now makes me wary. I *know* you, remember?"

"No one around here's called me Franklin in a long time, Kim, not for ages."

Kim did crack a thin smile this time, recalling, just how difficult it was to stay angry at Frank Popper for too long. Christ, he really hadn't changed at all. Beyond his projected image as some sort of audacious crusader of the people, sticking it to *The Man*, he was still just a lonely, middle-aged drunk, who spent most of his time venting his anger onto paper and the rest of it resorting to ever more desperate measures to fill the empty hole that was his life. At least he was one of the few people who had been there for her when she really needed someone, right up until the point when he wasn't anymore.

"Okay, I'll admit it," she took another swig, raising her hand to her mouth as she let out a belch. "It's probably kind of good to see you again. *Kind of*, you can get the emphasis there, yeah?" Popper nodded. "But I'm still not too sure if I've forgiven you yet," her brows knitted as she frowned at him. "Like the rest of the world, I've moved on, even if you haven't. Don't even try taking the piss out of me, or I mean it, I will be the death of you."

"I wouldn't dream of it," Frank decided that it was time to down his own drink in a single gulp, placing his glass back on the table after. "It *is* good to see you though. I miss having someone as smart as you around to talk to."

"As smart as me?"

"Come on Kim, you know what I mean."

"Now you're just trying to soften me up. What's the matter *Franklin?* Lonely in the big bad city these days, is it?" She took another swig of her pint, wiping her mouth on the back of the sleeve of her thick anorak.

"I'm serious, Kim, I've been struggling lately. I'm starting to worry that I might be losing it. I've got some stories to tell you, for sure."

"Yeah, I'll bet you have."

He shifted his weight on the bar chair, the fake leather-look plastic letting out a squeak as he did so. It felt as though his trousers had moulded themselves to his arse cheeks, thanks to the cheap seating. All he could think was how hard he was trying not to start scratching at himself again.

"That's the third time I've seen you having a good rake at your bollocks. Each time, you've looked up pretty damn quick afterwards. What is it Frank, have you gone and caught crabs or something?" Kim grinned before tipping the rest of her drink down the back of her throat. "You *have*, haven't you? You dirty sod!"

"You're still a regular Sherlock Holmes, aren't you?" Frank had learned to grow a pretty thick skin over the years, but she had always been one of the few people who actually knew how to make him feel self-conscious at least every once in a while. The time they had spent apart certainly didn't seem to have dulled that ability.

"What is it this time Frank? If it's not crabs, then maybe it's something more serious? It wouldn't surprise me. Like I said already, I bet you haven't changed a bit. As for stories, yeah, I've already heard a few about you, believe it or not. Besides," she pushed her empty glass across the table and leaned forward, ready to stand, "your fifteen minutes are up. Cheers for the drink, but it's about time I was going."

"Please, stay. Just a little while longer. I've already said that I've missed you. There, I'll beg, is that better?" He widened his eyes, trying to look pleading, while trying to imagine what it would feel like to dip the end of his cock in chilli sauce, anything that might bring him to tears. With the stubborn irritation that was still down there, it wasn't too difficult.

"Okay. I suppose I was at a bit of a loose end today. Besides, since you begged me *so* politely, and I want to take the time to make you feel like shit for the way you ditched me."

Frank looked down at his empty glass, as through searching for an answer in the dregs of his drink. "There aren't many days go by that I don't regret that. I know I acted like a prick and I'm sorry for that. Trust me, nine – sorry, *ten* - years feels like a lot longer sometimes."

"Penitence really doesn't suit you, Frank, and the maudlin attitude gets annoying pretty quickly. It'd probably make me happier if you just carry on feeling like shit for a little while yet."

"So, you've been stalking me too?" He raised an eyebrow as he tried to deflect from the subject. "Go on then, what have you heard about me? Only the good stuff, I hope."

"That would be telling," Kim said, "but I know you well enough to guess that you probably ventured out for the first time in ages and that, since you're more than likely still the sex-starved arsehole that I remember, you stuck yourself balls-deep into the first woman who looked like she might actually drop her knickers for you." The corners of her mouth turned up in a wry smile. "What I'm wondering is, did you bend her over the toilet bowl so she could puke her overpriced cocktail back out while you shafted her?"

"And people think *I'm* disgusting," Frank wrinkled his nose, the image she had just placed in his mind was one that he would rather forget and probably wasn't too far from the truth, as far as he could remember it. "That's pretty nasty, especially coming from you."

"Don't act like you're offended, *Franklin*. We both know that it's probably true. What I don't get is why, on the rare occasions you decide that you need a shag, you always go for the dirtiest mares around. It's a miracle that your balls haven't been reduced to a rotting mess."

"She called me a lying shitweasel," he said, trying to sound hurt and almost managing it.

"I'm sure that you've been called worse. I have to admit though, she had a good point. It's probably your own fault, knowing the sort of women you always used to get yourself mixed up with."

LEE GLENWRIGHT

"Perhaps I still get mixed up with *those sort of women* because they're the best I can manage to get mixed up with." He stared into the bottom of his empty glass, wishing that it would just refill itself without him having to make the short trip to the bar. His head was already starting to buzz with a faint alcoholic warmth that almost helped him to forget the itching down below at last. "You try telling people that you're a writer and everyone wants to know your business. Tell them that you're a journalist, they suddenly think that you're the worst scum of the earth." He raised the glass up to his lips. "Except for the sort of people who get drunk to the point where they let strangers screw them in a toilet cubicle, that is."

"The trouble with you is that you don't think you deserve any better," Kim fumbled in her jacket pocket for enough loose change to stretch to another two drinks. "You spend far too much time putting yourself down, you know? You have a knack of settling for the first thing that comes along."

"And *your* trouble is that you're always just itching to criticise my lifestyle."

"It's got to be better than itching at your bollocks every five minutes," she smirked, without missing a beat. Frank tutted, she really hadn't changed, on the inside at least. She had always been a rare friend back in the day, something that he hadn't come across very often with his choice of lifestyle or work, and he had always felt proud to be one of the few people that she had trusted, something that had never come easily back then. It had hurt him bad - *really* bad – when they had fallen out and it had taken a long time for him to own his part in it. It really did feel like almost a whole lifetime, but he could still remember every detail, those memories making himself feel ashamed of how long it had taken for him to just swallow his damn pride and try to make a first move. Now he had done it though, that shame was tempered by the stupidity that he felt for leaving it for as long as he had. Things were still more than a little awkward, just a bit short of uncomfortable, but at least they were talking. It was a start, a better one than he could ever have hoped for. He tried not to think about it too much. She was sitting within touching distance, for the first time in years, and that was the important thing.

She placed another drink in front of him, jarring him from his memories as he realised, he hadn't even noticed that she had been back to the bar. She took her seat opposite him again, still holding her own glass.

"Wake up, Frank," she said. "I could've just walked out the front door and you would have been none the wiser."

"Yeah sorry, I was miles away. I haven't even asked you yet, how *are* you doing? I've got to say, you're looking pretty good," Frank nodded, raising his glass to his lips and taking a sip this time, drawing a sharp breath as the bourbon burned its way down into his gullet with a crisp, spreading heat that was almost enough to cheer him up. Almost, but not quite.

"Me? I've never been better. It took a while, but I feel like I'm actually *me* at last, you know?"

"Really?"

"Yeah, *really*. It was hard for a long time, but the operation helped a lot. It cleaned me out good and proper for a while though. Going private isn't cheap."

"Could no one have helped? Parents, anyone?"

"You're kidding me, right?" Kim snorted. "*They* disowned me a long time ago. They never did anything to hide the fact that I was just one big disappointment. Good old God-fearing Catholics, both of them."

"I'm sorry, I shouldn't have said-"

"Don't worry," Kim cleared her throat, "I stopped worrying about them years ago. Anyway, it's your shout next, I reckon. I'll get them, but I'm not paying." Frank reached into his pocket, fumbling for a handful of change that he dropped onto the table between them.

"I'll get them in a few minutes. Anyway, apart from feeling like your cock is hanging on by the last few strings, how *are* things really?" She was a little quicker to smile now, the first couple of drinks starting to ease whatever initial tension there might have been between them.

"I guess I'll find out for sure in the next few months," Frank reached for his glass, his hand wavering as he hesitated. "You know, if some strange woman I hardly recognise turns up looking like she's swallowed a bowling ball, demanding money and arguing that *I told you we should've swapped phone numbers or sumfink.*"

Kim gasped, her jaw almost looking like it was going to fall off and land in her drink. "You *didn't? Please* tell me that you used some protection."

Frank said nothing. Instead, he looked down at the table, his silence speaking for him.

"You really do need to try and find somewhere a bit classier to hang out. Have you ever thought about getting away from this place, even just for a little bit?"

"No, not really. It hasn't crossed my mind in a while, to be honest." He downed the rest of his bourbon in one again, a hissing breath escaping as he put the glass back down. "I've tried it before. I moved away from The Reds a couple of years ago now. Something," he hesitated, not knowing what to say next. "Something bad happened. I just needed to get out of there."

"Bad? Like what?" Kim leaned forward, curious.

"It's a long story. Let's just say that this place might be a shit hole, but it's *my* shit hole, and I *need* to be here. I'll leave it at that." He couldn't tell her about *The Reds*, or why he got away from there. He couldn't tell anyone, not ever. He hated it when people said that some things were best forgotten. Sometimes, there were horrible things that couldn't be pushed out of the memory quite so easily. However, he still went on trying, pretending to himself most of all. Sometimes, he needed to do just that – *pretend*. It was the best way - the *only* way - to make it from one day to the next.

"Oh, that old excuse again." Kim's voice was deliberately mocking. "*Poor me, I'm a tortured journo, I can't write unless I'm in a place that's just as miserable as I am.* It sounds to me like someone needs to step back from his self-pitying horseshit and get laid. I mean *properly* laid, not just a quick shag in a nightclub bog somewhere," Kim smirked. "Trust me, I've heard of some of the stuff you get up to, and I still reckon I know you better than you know yourself."

"It's true," Frank spread his hands outward, not really wanting to put his case forward yet again. "It's weird I know, but if I was happy, I'd probably want to be doing something different."

"Then why do you do it, you stupid prick?"

"Because," he took a deep breath, "it's the only thing I know. I've never been in the right sort of headspace for long enough to be good at anything else."

"That just makes you sound really messed up, Frank. You *do* know that, right? Even more messed up than I ever was at the worst of times."

"Anyway," he shrugged as he pushed the pile of coins across the table towards her with two fingers. "You *did* say you'd get them in if I paid, yeah?"

FIVE

It hurt. No, saying that it hurt was an understatement. It hurt a *lot*. So much that she hadn't been able to get herself together enough to step outside the flat in almost a week. It was *that* bad.

Susanne Walters usually lived for Saturday nights. High heels and a dress short and tight enough to make sure that she got plenty of the wrong sort of attention had long been her regular weekend uniform. Nights spent drinking whatever was on offer as long as it was enough to get her hammered, and preferably paid for by someone else. Hopefully all finished off in the company of someone with enough spare change at the end of the night to fork out for a large Donner kebab with chilli *and* garlic sauce, if they expected anything in return at least. Life really was that straightforward. Well, it was most of the time anyway, just as it should be.

"Susanne? Have you topped yourself in there or something? Hurry up, will you? I'm dying for a piss!"

Even if she had actually heard Alex's protests, she probably would have ignored her. Instead, she was far too focused on clinging to the porcelain rim of the toilet bowl, as if afraid that letting go would lead to her being flung away by the spinning whirlpool that it felt like she was caught up in. Struggling to spit away the trail of bile-tainted drool that dangled from her bottom lip, Susanne groaned as she released her grip on the ceramic edge for just long enough to reach up with one hand and flush, watching as the contents of her stomach were washed away for the third time. No sooner had she done so than she felt a clenching sensation as the muscles in her belly knotted up once again.

"Susanne! Seriously, you'd better have died in there - I'm going to leave a frigging puddle on this floor if you don't get a move on!"

"Piss off! Can't you hear I'm ill, you selfish cow?" her voice sounded muffled and choked, even to her own ears, as though she was talking through a mouthful of rotten, clotted kebab meat, the back of her throat feeling like it was coated with something that she would rather not think about.

"It serves you right! If you can't take it, you shouldn't do it, you dozy bitch! Who was it this time? Some pisshead with his brain in his bollocks as usual? Or did you play the bi card and hit up some random slag you met at the bar? I don't know why I'm still with you, you slapper – you only like minge when it suits you anyway!" Alex rattled the door handle one last time, making sure that her presence was felt, before stomping away, probably outside for a smoke. Susanne had been thinking of looking for somewhere else to live for a while. Saddled with an on-off girlfriend who insisted on treating the place like a frigging ashtray. Bloody hypocrite, she was the one who had been all up for the idea of an open relationship in the first place, claiming that they were both free spirits, like they were stuck in the fucking sixties or something. Yet, here she was again, complaining, just the same as she always did when Susanne at least managed to get out and get herself a seeing to every now and then. Yeah, she would have gladly moved out in a heartbeat, leaving the spiteful mare to fend for herself, except for one small problem: there was no chance in hell that she could ever hope to scrape enough money together to do so.

That was why she had taught herself to spot the sort of people who at least looked as though they had their own place. Each night that she got lucky and spent the night in a bed other than her own was a night that she considered to be a blessing. It was usually worth it, just to get away for a little while. Sometimes however, things didn't work out the way that she hoped.

Just the last time, she thought she had pulled a good one, but the guy had turned out to be some really dirty bastard. It was a surprise that he had even managed to get into the club in the first place and that was saying something. One of the bouncers must have owed him a favour, the scruffy beggar. He had been the kind of bloke she wouldn't have even paid a second glance if she had been sober, he had a good fifteen to twenty years or so on her at least, looking like he had just wandered in from off the street, rather than making any effort for a night on the town. He had promised her that he had his own flat though, and that alone had been enough to make it worth a go. They had ended up in one of the toilet cubicles, with one of his feet braced against the door in place of the broken lock, as he yanked her knickers to one side and slid himself into her from behind, both her hands resting on the chipped, off-white toilet cistern for support. It was all over so quickly; she hardly had enough time to read the graffiti scrawled across the wall - a number to call if *you wanted the best blowjob ever* - before the same old excuses had started. The scruffy prick had cut and run faster than his leftovers could drip back out. At least he'd gone up her from behind, so there would be no chance of pregnancy.

Or at least that was how she remembered things. The dirty bastard had made sure to get her drunk first.

Christ, she *hoped* that he'd slipped it up her arse. She could well be in big trouble if he hadn't. She remembered insisting that he better not pull out too early. She had been wearing her favourite dress and didn't want any of his manky tramp jizz-juice ruining it.

She had told him it was okay, that she was on the pill. Okay, with hindsight, maybe she shouldn't have lied about something like *that*. But then again, maybe he shouldn't have spun her some shitty chat up line about being an investigative journalist, or whatever the hell it was that he'd called himself, either. Honestly, men could be such cunts sometimes, saying anything if they thought it would help them to get their hole. While she couldn't actually remember him promising that he knew people who could get her on page three of one of the rags, she couldn't recall hearing him deny it either. So surely if he was any sort of a real journalist, there would at least be the chance of such an opportunity, *right?*

Her thoughts of elusive fame were interrupted by a tightening in her gut as her stomach locked itself into another spasm. She leaned forward and opened her mouth to retch, only a loud belch of sour breath escaping this time.

It was the third morning in a row that she had woken up feeling worse than shit, spending the best part of an hour hugging the toilet bowl before she could manage to pull herself together.

No, things weren't looking too good.

She thought again about that three-minute fumble in the cubicle. *Three fucking minutes.* Or rather, *three minutes fucking.* Christ, she hoped she wasn't. She *really* hoped she wasn't, not after a three-minute fuck in a seedy, graffiti-covered bog, surely.

She closed her eyes, squeezing tears from them as she braced herself for another round of gripping gut muscles. When it didn't come, she exhaled a slow breath that smelled like rotten cabbage, or something worse. Opening her eyes again, she looked down into the pan, just in time to see the blood as it dispersed in the water.

"What the hell?" Ever since she was a kid, she had always hated the sight of any sort of gore, especially when it was her own. She even remembered being freaked out by that old Stephen King film, the one with the psychic girl having her first period in the shower, even though she knew how unrealistic *that* stuff was, just the sort of rubbish that a bloke with no idea how that sort of thing worked would write. She brought a hand up to her face and wiped the back of it across her mouth, leaving a tell-tale crimson smear on her thin, pale skin. She sniffed, feeling a wad of warm, metallic-tasting liquid moving from inside her nose and hitting the back of her throat. She stood up on her unsteady legs, turning to face the mirror on

the bathroom cabinet. Both of her nostrils were gushing now, thin streams of crimson running down either side of her mouth and coming together below her bottom lip, to drip from her chin.

"*Buh... blood...*" she gagged, the taste warm and sickly in her mouth. "It *must* have been him. What the hell has he *done* to me?"

Closing her eyes once more as she stooped, she fumbled for the rim of the toilet bowl and yawned her mouth open, ready to puke again.

SIX

Frank had ducked out, leaving Kim in the pub to fend off the unwanted advances of some drunken old guy leering at her over his pint of best bitter. The poor old fart really had no idea, none at all. He had trotted out the not-too-far-from-the-truth excuse that he had a whole load of work to catch up on, deadlines biting at his arse, that sort of thing. For a change, it wasn't a lie. The few drinks that he had necked had taken the edge off the itching in his groin, replacing it with a faint, but still preferable buzzing sensation somewhere in the back of his head.

It was raining, but he was just fifteen minutes away from his flat and he usually preferred to walk. Apart from clearing the fog from his head, it gave him time to think, to draw inspiration from the filth all around him, every last drop of it serving as fuel for the creative spark that had been hiding away of late.

Frank Popper had long ago learned that most people turned a blind eye to a lot of things, either out of wilful ignorance or a genuine lack of awareness. It wasn't easy, but if you took a look around, you could usually see what was going on. As long as you knew what you were looking for and you tried hard enough.

Most of the time they could be found gathered at the street corners, beneath the tattered old shop fronts and huddled under bus shelters, as though seeking safety in numbers. The police ignored pretty much most of what went on most of the time, as long as there was no *real* trouble. Of course, when the shit did kick off, there never seemed to be anyone around, like the time Little Joe had wound up getting the crap beaten out of him. Most of them didn't even bother waiting until the cover of darkness, not in this place. It wasn't like they were vampires or something. No, they grouped together against the rain and cold, at any time of day or night. After all, there weren't too many blokes that were

63

too keen on a wet trick. Yeah, they liked to stick together, in an effort to show that there was still such a thing as solidarity. They set the example, showed the lengths to which some people were prepared go for money. Sometimes it was cash for drugs, other times for food, or bills, or just to keep a roof over their head. Or perhaps, it was just to keep their pimping boyfriend from smacking them around quite so often. Everyone had some real, legitimate reason for what they did, whatever reason it might have been. He could still remember one that he had seen only a few days ago, the image still fresh in his memory. She had been in the back lane, just next to the rear fire exit of the family welfare centre of all places. Some bloke, built like a brick shithouse, had pinned her right up against the wall, gripping both of her wrists hard, as if he was worried that she might escape to tell someone just what he was really getting up to. Judging by the force being used it was almost guaranteed that she would be covered in bruises by the morning. Her already short skirt was hoisted above her waist, her panties twisted around her knees as though in a knot, a further attempt at preventing her escape. Her eyes were closed, and she was biting down on her bottom lip as she tried her best to ignore the sound of his grunting as he thrust himself into her. Looking a little longer than he probably should, and hating himself for it, Frank thought that he could make out a graze on her left shin. Perhaps she had scuffed it against the paving stones when she was on her knees sucking the punter off. Or maybe it could have been from earlier in the day, when she was spit-roasted by two city boys, going all out to celebrate their double promotion. After all, what better way to commemorate your big money pay rise than by cheating on your girlfriend, right? She looked as though she might have been trying to focus on the pain, to block it out somehow. Doing that was probably better than any alternative. Hopefully, if she was lucky enough, he wouldn't expect her to take it up the arse at no extra charge.

And then, just like that, it was over with. He didn't even look back at her as he turned away, stuffing his still slick cock back into his jogging bottoms as he broke into a hunched stride, brushing past Frank as he bustled past him. He was probably already trying to figure out what he was going to say to his son and his pregnant wife when they both asked what it was that had taken him so long. He'd only gone to the chemist for some headache tablets, right?

Suddenly, she had started to chase him down, trying to hike her panties up from around her thighs as she demanded the twenty quid that he still owed her. He had paused for just long enough to grab her face in one spade-like hand and shove her back against the wall, calling her out for the money-grubbing, two-bit whore that he knew she was. There had followed a sharp sound and probably an equally sharp pain, as her skull had struck against the brick with a crack, a trickle of blood from her nose pooling just inside her bottom lip.

As he went around the corner back onto the main street, still muttering curses against all the *slack-fannied prossies* making the streets look untidy, she had looked as though she was about to call after him, just to make people see him for what he really was. Not that many of them would have listened to her anyway.

Then maybe she had thought about him going back home to play happy families, and about the infection that she had been carrying around with her for at least six months, ever since she was gang-banged at that party full of rich boys, the one she had ended up shuffling home from, somewhere around three-thirty in the morning, cold and wet, half-naked, alone and afraid. The same party where, to top it all, they hadn't even paid her. She had thought about it and started to laugh, the sound choking its way through a mouthful of bittersweet-tasting blood. The mental image of him having to go and see a doctor, then to explain to his wife why they had to pass on their fortnightly sex, on account of the constant itching in the swollen head of his cock, had suddenly seemed far more entertaining than any simple name-calling could ever have been.

Frank had kept his distance. He preferred to think of himself as a silent observer rather than the far more tawdry-sounding *voyeur*. He hadn't known her name and, to be honest, he had been grateful for that little bit of ignorance at least. Finding it out would have probably humanised her just a little too much, even for his liking. It could have been anything. There were plenty more like her, if you just looked long and hard enough.

He knew that he couldn't do a damn thing to stop it. All that he could do was write about it, making sure that her story and the stories of others like her, were read. That was why he did it. That was what had always inspired him.

***

As he rounded the last corner to the block of flats he called home, a rat scuttled out from the far side of the road, a large, black mass of matted fur with bright, keen eyes. It weaved and darted as though trying to dodge each raindrop and skirted around a large puddle before making it to the oversized bin that stood outside the rear exit of the takeaway, scavenging for leftover junk food.

He almost walked past Batra's General Store before he remembered that his stocks were running low. The alcoholic ringing in the back of his head would probably be wearing off soon enough, leaving just an average headache in its place instead. He pushed the door open, the upper surface knocking against a little brass-coloured bell nailed to the top of the door frame, fixed in place to announce the presence of any potential shoplifters. Faster than a whippet in heat, Hareesh Batra appeared from behind the seventies-style multicolour beaded curtain that partitioned the rear of his shop, his look of usual distrust dissolving into a broad, toothy smile when he saw who had entered.

"Ah, Frank bloody Popper. Has everyone's favourite hack written any more exposés lately then?" he rubbed his hands together before wiping them down the front of the faded blue smock that he always wore. Frank had never actually seen him do it with dirty hands, maybe it was just OCD or something. He didn't like to give it too much thought, it was just a little too close to home.

"You know I don't like that word Harry," he smiled back. "*Hack*, it has that nasty ring to it. Makes me sound kind of dirty."

"Yes, absolutely bloody filthy," Batra's smile didn't waver as he took his position behind the counter. "The usual, is it?"

"No, I reckon I'll have to go with vodka this time around. The cheapest you've got." Frank fumbled in his coat pocket for what little money he had left after placating Kim with an extra round. "Make it a three-quarter bottle. I'm pretty skint right now and I've still got enough left in to last the next day or two. Tell you what though, chuck in a pack of ten king-size as well, will you?" Harry turned to the cabinet behind him, finding the cigarettes and placing a pack on the counter.

"Skint my arse. Those things are going to be the death of you, you know," he rested one hand on the countertop, stroking his bushy, greying beard with the fingers of the other.

"Trust me Harry, lung cancer's probably the last thing on my mind at the moment."

"Problems?"

"Always. Nothing that antibiotics and a pair of garden shears won't fix though."

Harry laughed, his perfect white teeth contrasting against his skin. "Oh dear, it sounds like someone's been a naughty boy again.

To be fair, it's been a while, but aren't you a bit old to be getting into *that* sort of mischief these days?"

"If by *that* sort, you mean landing yourself a dose of something nasty then, yeah, I reckon you're probably right." Frank shrugged his shoulders. "Age is just a number though, ain't it?"

"I bet that's not what your doctor said, right after you dropped 'em for him."

Frank looked straight at him, saying nothing.

"Frank? You have *seen* a doctor, right?"

Still nothing.

"Blimey! Frank Popper, you're not invincible. You should get yourself seen to, before something drops off. Fags and booze aren't the answer to every ailment, you know."

"Says who?"

"Says pretty much anyone with an ounce of bloody common sense! Really, mister journalist man, you're unbelievable."

"For fuck's sake Harry, you're starting to sound like my mother, or worse, Kim."

"Kim? You haven't mentioned *her* for ages. Why now?"

"I've just spent the last hour or so in the pub with her."

"Really? You didn't say she was back down here. When did that happen, and how is she doing these days?"

"In order of asking," Frank looked down at the cigarettes in front of him, "today and she's alive." He picked up the packet from the counter and slid a ragged fingernail around the cellophane wrapping before sliding it off and throwing it back down. Opening the pack, he took out a cigarette and tucked it behind his ear. "She's looking good, finally had the operation, she says she's much happier for it. Anyway, enough about her. I'll be fine, trust me. I've got all the medication I need back at the flat. If it turns green and starts smelling of mushrooms, *then* I'll go and see a doctor, I promise."

Harry laughed, although whether it was genuine or more sarcasm, Frank couldn't quite tell. "Mushrooms, *ha*, you're a funny guy sometimes Frank, you know that? It would be such a shame if you died in agony of something really nasty."

"I'll pretend that you were being sincere there. Seriously Harry, if my penis were to drop off tomorrow, it wouldn't even bother me, never mind kill me." He looked up and down the shop, as though checking to make sure no one else was within earshot.

"Speaking of dying, it's pretty nasty about that guy, isn't it?" Harry's voice was hushed, his way of making it known that he was talking about something a little more serious.

"What guy?" Frank asked, fiddling with the cigarette and resisting the urge to relocate it to between his lips. "At the moment, you've narrowed my guesses down to about half the world's population. I need a little bit more than that to go on, mate."

"Who's being sarcastic now?" Harry asked. "I mean that guy in the flats over at The Reds."

"The Reds? What's happened over there now? Whatever it is, I'm surprised it made the news. Bugger all that happened there did while *I* was living there."

"Maybe that's *because* you were living there," Harry tapped the side of his nose. "Besides, you've still never explained why you upped and left the place for the quieter side."

"That's because I don't want to talk about it," Frank sniffed. "Ever. Anyway, *what* happened there that's so newsworthy?" he asked again.

"Well, maybe *newsworthy* is a bit of an overstatement, Frank," he pointed across to the wire rack of newspapers with one finger, crooked with the beginnings of the arthritis that he liked to complain about on colder days. "If you just grab the local rag there, I'll show you, for what it's worth." Frank followed the direction and scooped up one of the newspapers from the stand, spreading it out on the counter.

"You *do* know that I'm not paying for this, right?" Frank laughed. "Jesus, their writers are even worse than me."

"Yeah, yeah, that's fine. I'll just find the article," Harry pulled out a pair of reading glasses from the breast pocket of his smock and perched them on his nose, low enough that he had to look down through them. He had always convinced himself that doing so made him look clever. He leafed through the pages, stopping with a tutting noise once he had found what he was looking for.

"Here it is," he tapped the page with a finger, "forty-five-year-old man, found dead in the bathroom of his flat."

"How did he die, having a shit? Let me tell you, I reckon if that's the case then I've had a fair few near death experiences myself."

"You insensitive sod," he prodded the tabloid, as if making a point. "The report says that he was undiscovered for about two weeks." Frank wrinkled his nose in mock disgust.

"Grim. Did they say what killed him?"

"No, like I said, the report doesn't really go into too much detail. Perhaps it's for the best."

"That's because it isn't a report, Harry." Frank jabbed a finger at the paper too. "Jesus Christ, it's barely a sidebar." He stroked his chin, his fingernail picking at something in amongst the stubble that might have been a scab. "Now you've gone and made me curious though."

"The great Frank Popper is interested in something other than booze or cigarettes?" Harry stepped back, moving his glasses a little further up the bridge of his nose to keep them from slipping.

"Of course I am," Frank gave a lop-sided grin. "I quite like sex, too."

"Shame that you have to struggle to find anyone who'll let you."

"I'll pretend I didn't hear that. Seriously though, you know me, just as much as you know what I think of that place. It's a dive, the kind of place that gets ignored all too easily, passed over in favour of the people with actual money to burn." Frank scooped up the newspaper, rolling it up and tucking it into the torn lining of his coat before Harry could protest.

"I reckon I might do some digging around, just to see if there's any story there." he smiled. "My article on great health food supplements you must try before you die can probably be postponed. This sounds like it'll be much more interesting."

"Hey, you tight prick, that's a seventy-five pence newspaper you've just lifted!"

"I told you, I ain't paying for it," Frank's smile turned into a smirk. "It's a shit-filled rag. I'm doing you a favour taking it off your hands, trust me."

He turned and left the shop, ignoring Harry's protests about the unpaid-for newspaper as the door swung closed behind him.

***

Harry hadn't lied, he hadn't even embellished the truth for a change. The story - if that was what it could actually be called - was buried eight pages into the paper, given slightly less priority than the usual gossip and full-colour close-ups of celebrity nipple slips. Some guy had died alone in his flat and lay, probably in a puddle of his own shit and piss for days without anyone so much as batting an eyelid. Because it was in The Reds, the most the guy deserved was a one and a half by three-inch sidebar in the local rag, with no real details, other than a vague cause of death. Someone had decided that he didn't even warrant being named. He was nothing worthwhile, just one more corpse in the most overcrowded, slum-like part of the city. It was as annoying as it was depressingly commonplace. The trouble was that Frank almost no

71

idea where to start. Sighing, he took the cigarette from behind his ear and placed it between his lips. Reaching into his pocket for his lighter, he sparked it against the tip, taking a drag as it flared into life.

He had little to go on, but it was better than nothing and he still had some contacts where it mattered, as long as he played his cards right.

His head was buzzing in a way it hadn't for a while, the way it did when he knew he could be onto a story.

SEVEN

Betty MacKinnon was having one of her moments, one of those snatched times when she could stop living a lie for just a little while.

She stood in the back of the diner that she had been running at a steady loss for the last nine years. Huffing on her sixth cigarette of the day as if her life really did depend upon it, she reclined against the dishwasher that she hardly ever bothered looking at, never mind using. A habitual chain smoker since the age of thirteen and now only just passed the right side of the big four-oh, one of the few privileges that came from the lack of customers was the ability to sneak off for a quick drag on a cancer stick whenever she wanted. And that was pretty damned often, especially during the spaces that dragged on between customers actually being in the damn place. If it wasn't for fat cunts like that Brad fucking Whitman, she really would have had to call it quits years ago. Perhaps things might have been better if she had, instead of putting herself through the daily self-punishment of actually facing people, bastards that they were, every last one of them.

She ran both her hands over her greasy, red hair, scraped back into its usual bun, keeping the cigarette clamped between her lips as she did so. The LCD display of the grime-stained oven showed it to be a little after half-past eleven, the last of her regular breakfast customers - even Whitman, without Rosa this time - had cleared out almost twenty minutes ago. That had left her with more than enough time for a couple of smokes. The dishes and cutlery soaking in the sink could wait. Given enough time, the steady drip of water from the leaking tap would probably clean them well enough anyway.

Good old Betty MacKinnon, a chip off the old block, running a business to be proud of. If only people knew how things *really* were, how they had always been.

Betty sighed, leaning her head back and exhaling a cloud of smoke into the stale, grease-stink air as she did so. She hated running the place. She absolutely *hated* it and always had. She hated everything, the cooking, the cleaning, the same routine, day after day after miserable day. Most of all, she hated being around the people, sick of pretending to be a cheerful friend to everyone who sauntered their way in and out of her life over and over again with clockwork regularity. When her old man had opened the place up, all those years ago, he had managed to build it into a small, but respectable enough business. Never really too busy, but just enough to keep things ticking over, a group of regulars dropping by for coffee, a quick bite to eat and a bit of loose talk with good old Mackie. Yeah, George MacKinnon, or *Mackie* as the locals called him back then, was a real salt of the earth kind of bloke. Except that he wasn't salt of the earth at all, not really. George MacKinnon was a bastard, a through and through *bastard*. He had always just happened to be pretty good at hiding it from most people, a real expert at being a two-faced piece of work. Good old Georgie, who had managed to drive away three wives over a stretch of twenty years, with little to show from any of them, except for his own business and a daughter that he looked after out of a sense of obligation rather than any sort of genuine, honest-to-God feeling.

Between daughter and business, it had always been pretty obvious which of the two he cared about the most.

"You'll never amount to nothing, I'm telling you, you won't," he was fond of saying to her from an early age, so often that she ended up believing it for the most part. *"That's probably why your mother got herself up off her lazy, fat backside and left me,"* referring to the second ex-Mrs Mackinnon. Nothing at all to do with the way he used to beat seven bells out of her, in those rare hours when he wasn't hiding away from his little family in his little diner,

entertaining the locals with his made-up stories of what a great bloke he was.

Surely Betty must have just imagined all those times when he had cursed her out, each *useless, fat bitch*, every single *I'm not even sure you're really my kid* and, *you'll never get anywhere in life once I'm gone. You're an ugly waste of space, just like your useless cow of a mother.* And then, just a little over nine years ago, he had gone for good. Betty knew he was dead. After all, she had been there to see it happen. She had watched as he lifted a tray of fresh bread rolls from the oven at the back of the kitchen, the smell of baked bread hanging in the air like a thick, heady fog. She had stood by as calm as she ever had, watching as he clutched at his chest, his lips blue and slack like rubber, his face dewy with perspiration, with the sort of expression that a man like him might have had on his face if someone had just told him that his bollocks were about to roll out of his scrotum. She had stood there as he had sunk down to his knees on the linoleum, gasping for breath like a fish flapping around on a riverbank, twitching in helpless, breathless silence. She had seen good old Georgie die a slow and painful death, and she had done nothing but stand and watch, with an icy, numb sensation spreading through her veins. She had been unable to stomach the smell of fresh-baked bread ever since, the yeast odour always making her feel like she could throw up, right to this day. She always had thought it was far too much hassle to bake her own anyway, especially when she could pick them up much cheaper from the local shops.

First things first; she had made sure that he got the right send-off. A quick, cheap-as-possible funeral, with no one in attendance except for herself. She took great care to be certain that none of the old regulars got to hear about it and she only bothered to go herself so she could make sure that they stuck the selfish old cocksucker far enough into the ground for good. Against her better judgement, she had moved to a flat just a short distance from the diner, making sure that she got rid of pretty much every last thing that could possibly serve as a reminder of him. Photographs, books, vinyl records, anything that carried the nasty taint of George MacKinnon went the journey, either to the skip, or to Agnes Bell's second-hand shop just along the road.

Then came her final insult, as she set out to begin the deliberate process of trying to run his beloved business into the grave alongside him. To hell with the fact that she actually needed some sort of income. Some things, especially getting her own back, were more important than money. At least that was what Betty had told herself in the beginning.

She had allowed MacKinnon's pride and joy to slide into wreck and ruin, in as short a time as possible, standing back as paint chipped and blistered away, work surfaces became worn and dirty, menus remained unchanged for weeks, months, years. In the end, only the faithful few kept returning. Christ only knew why, she had done her best to get rid of them after all. Maybe it was their misguided sense of loyalty to good old Georgie that kept them coming back for more of the same old greasy slop. Most of the regulars were old farts who had been dropping by for their hot mugs of coffee and their bacon and egg sandwiches, year after year. Each one of them had some lame story to tell about their past with the great man himself, usually ending with some comment along the lines of how good it was that his daughter was keeping his memory alive. Yeah, if only they knew just how adept she had grown at keeping the truth hidden away. Perhaps she *was* growing to be more like him than she would care to admit after all.

She still kept a photograph of him hanging from the wall, directly behind the counter, the edges of its gilded frame blotched and tarnished, his piggy eyes glaring out blindly with that streak of smug nastiness that no one apart from her seemed to notice. Every once in a while, some old guy, like Eddie Caplin - he and George had gone back a *long* way, as he liked to constantly remind anyone who would listen - would make a point of looking up at the faded image and making some comment along the lines of, *what a great fella*, or, *one in a million. You must have been really proud of him, Betty.* The number of times, she had wanted to grab one of the geriatric pricks and shake them by their shoulders, spraying spittle in their face as she screamed herself hoarse,

No! He was a bastard! He took a huge shit on everyone close to him, most of all me and my mother! She never could though. Instead, she kept on hating him in silence, making sure to curse each and every one of them for their stupid ignorance, once the door was closed and the blinds were drawn for the day. Only then did she feel like she could lower her guard, safely tucked away in the shrine that she had dedicated to trashing his memory.

In some of her weaker moments, it made her feel sick to her stomach to think that she was probably turning into her own version of him. Sure, she was quick enough to smile and be nice to peoples' faces, only to call them all the names under the sun, no sooner had the door swung shut behind their backs. That fat bastard Whitman for instance, along with that stick-thin wife of his. There was a mismatch if ever she had seen one. How Rosa could even bear having the slob anywhere near her was anyone's guess. Jesus, it was a miracle that she hadn't broken in half the first time she let him clamber on top of her, if she actually ever did let him get close enough, not that she could ever be certain, the two of them having no kids. The thought of it was enough to make Betty want to throw up.

She had let the place fall apart long ago, anything along the lines of cleanliness just going ignored. But still the regulars kept on coming back. It said a lot about them, for sure, not caring how bad a thing was, just as long as it was still there at least. Gluttons for punishment, they were. Half of them could die of food poisoning and it probably wouldn't scare away the rest of them. She huffed on her cigarette again, the tip flaring and burning away a good half of the length in one go. The nicotine was one of the few things that helped her get through most days. That and the bottle of booze that she usually kept hidden away beneath the front counter, at least Eddie had never gotten wise to *that*, the alcoholic old sod. All the small things that contributed, making her life just that little bit more bearable. Smoking the cigarette almost down to the filter, she took the last of it between coarsened thumb and forefinger, and stubbed it out on the bench top, dragging it across the off-white laminate and leaving a tarry grey smear of ash in its wake. She allowed herself a thin-lipped smile of selfish satisfaction, something that never lasted too long, only until she remembered where she was. Exactly where her dear old dad had left her nine years ago: alone.

"Yeah, that one's for you, you miserable old prick," she said aloud, grinding the last of the stub into the work surface as she gasped out the last of the smoke with a hoarse cough. She stood up, the ache in her bones matched by the one that was building in her head, a dull throb, probably the onset of a hangover. It would probably take something more than caffeine to fix it. She cursed again under her breath as she glanced back at the clock. Time to open up again for a bit, before Eddie Caplin came banging on the door, looking for his cheese and beans on toast, just about the only thing the sour old fart could still chew on, with those rotten teeth of his. It turned her stomach every time she saw him out of the corner of her eye, pushing down on his food with the back of his fork, mashing everything together into a soft paste before shovelling it down his throat like it was about to go out of fashion, the filthy old cunt.

Right on cue, she heard the hollow rattle of the door, as someone pushed against it, before shaking it, as though in frustration at finding it locked.

"Okay, you old twat, I'm coming," she muttered under her breath as she shuffled towards the door, forcing her face into her usual glued-on smile as she did so.

EIGHT

Frank cleared his throat, hawking a mouthful of snot and swallowing it down while the 'phone was still ringing. That in itself was a bad sign. He usually loosened up just before a hangover kicked in. Really, he could have done with some good old hair of the dog, but as much as he dreaded any side-effects, he needed a clear head, for a little while at least. He was going to have to start digging if he was going to get anywhere. He could feel it in the pit of his belly, the sense of urgency that came the moment that he had an idea that he needed to follow up on. It was how he wrote most of the time, the spontaneity helping to keep things vital. Either that or the scrote itch had spread something nasty up into his belly. His hand gripping the telephone receiver felt sweaty, a sensation not helped by the rubber glove, stretched taut across his knuckles.

There was a crackle of static as the phone was picked up at the other end.

"Hello? Robert Martinson speaking, what can I do you for?"

"Good morning, Mister Martinson, or *Robert*, if I can call you that." Frank dropped his voice as low as it would go, slowing his words down. "I was wondering if you could help me with some-"

"You might as well stop messing about with the bad accent, Frank. You never manage to fool anyone, man. I don't know why you even bother."

"Really, Mister Martinson, I haven't the faintest idea what you mean."

Martinson's voice quieted down, almost hissing down the line. "Just knock it off Frank, man. I knew it was probably going to be you as soon as I saw your number was withheld."

"*Oh.*"

"Yes, *oh*. You'd make a pretty shite undercover agent, you *do* know that don't you? I bet you're wearing the gloves as well, eh? I *hope* that's what I can hear making that rubbery squeaking noise."

Frank laughed down the line, hoping that it didn't sound too strained. It was time to try and bluff it for a bit. "That would be telling, wouldn't it? I'm not exactly my sparkling best Bob - sorry - *Robert*. I've been a bit," he hesitated, "under the weather lately. Anyway, how's my favourite northerner doing these days, *pet?*"

"Give over, you tosser. We both know I'm only your favourite northerner when you want something. I've got a job to do, a proper, legitimate job, so why don't you just leave us alone, eh? Take your pissing OCD with you while you're at it."

"I'll pretend you didn't say that, or at least that I didn't *hear* you say it. You're an editor for a two-bit local rag Bob, not a national broadsheet. Most people wipe their arses clean on your stories five minutes after reading them. You're no better than me, you just get to sit behind a proper desk nowadays, that's all." Martinson grunted, as though Frank had touched a raw nerve.

"You've got two minutes," he mumbled, "and that's only 'cause Vicky's out of earshot. I still haven't forgotten what happened the last time you asked us for one of your *favours.*" Frank had to hold back laughter, remembering just what it was that had made him so reluctant, a story to be used another time perhaps, when he needed some real blackmail material.

"I don't know what you're complaining about," Frank said, "I ended up taking the rap for that. If it wasn't for me, you probably wouldn't even be sat at that desk." He paused for a moment, giving Bob enough time to realise where things were going. "Does Vicky know about it? Did you ever tell her the *full* story, I mean? Or did you give her the cleaned-up version, like the cherry-picking Magpie wanker that you are?"

"You *prick*," Bob's voice was still a whisper, but hoarse now, as if he really wished that he could start shouting down the line. The two of them went back a long way and Frank really didn't like the way that what he was thinking of doing made him feel, but he needed a starting point and, to get that, he had to use whatever leverage he had. There was a knocking noise in the background, probably Bob tapping his biro against the desk. He always used to do that when he felt under any sort of pressure.

"All right you sod, *all right*," Martinson grunted. "You win. What do you want?"

"It's nothing bad, honest. I'm just after some information about a story I read a couple of days ago. It struck me as the sort of thing that you might have been interested in. I'm looking for bit of background, that's all."

"That narrows it down. *What* story? If you say the one about the topless model auctioning herself over the internet, I'll bloody well have your guts for garters."

"No, maybe some other time, when my knob end doesn't feel like it's going to fall off and die."

"*What?*"

"It's a long story. No, I read a sidebar in one of the rags down here, two days ago now. Some guy in the flats over at The Reds, found dead in his kitchen. If the story was buried any deeper, it would need its own coffin."

"The Reds? Why the hell are you asking me about some bloke in *that* dump? You live there for Christ's sake. I'm right up the other end of the bloody country!"

"You *could* find out about it though? You know, if I wanted you to?"

"Yeah, I suppose I could. Why would you be bothered about something like that though?" Martinson sounded confused. "Why are you even interested in some random stranger karking it?"

"Karking?"

"You know? Dying."

"I just think it's a bit of a pisser, how someone can be lying dead somewhere for any length of time and, just because he lived in a dump, no one seems too bothered about him, at least around here." Frank raked at the side of his face, his fingernails, underneath the layer of thick yellow rubber, scratching against stubble before reaching up for a cigarette perched in the usual spot behind his ear. He cursed under his breath when he realised there was none there, he really could have done with a smoke as well as a drink.

"Yeah, and your point is?" Martinson sounded like he was getting impatient. Vicky would probably be back any minute, checking up on him to make sure that he hadn't gone back to calling those expensive phone lines again, the ones that he liked to say were educational.

"I want to know anything you've got on the guy, that's all," Frank knew that if Vicky did come back, Martinson would probably clam up. What was worse was that he would be wise to the trick second time around and would probably know better than to answer the telephone again. "A name, an actual address. Hell, a cause of death would be pretty useful. Anything you can turn up on him."

"Yeah, just following up on a story Vicky, I'll not be a minute," Bob's voice was muffled, as if he had clamped his hand over the receiver and moved his mouth away from it. There was a rattling sound as he repositioned it again. "I don't know anything about it, Frank. Really, what are you thinking of doing like, even if you do find anything out?"

"I'm not sure yet," Frank shrugged his shoulders, a pointless gesture. "Hopefully to find out how it happened, how it was ever allowed to happen. That, and make sure that people get to know about him at least. You know how much I hate it when people are forgotten about just because their social circumstances aren't up to scratch."

"I really don't think that you should be getting involved," Martinson said, before pausing.

"Is she there, next to you?" Frank asked. "She *is*, isn't she?" He took a deep breath and bellowed into the mouthpiece, "*Vicky!*"

"*Owww! You bloody tosser!*" Martinson gasped, the receiver rattling as he almost dropped it onto his desk.

"Come on Bob, give me something to go on. I'll owe you for it later, you know I will."

"I don't, like-"

"I could always shout of Vicky again."

"Okay, *okay*, Jesus Christ," he took a deep breath. "I think I know the story that you're talking about. There hasn't been much said about it though. I heard that the dead guy's name was William Marks, or something like that, and he wasn't from around your neck of the woods. Either German or Austrian, I can't remember which. One more thing."

"Yeah?" Popper had the phone tucked in the gap between his ear and his hunched shoulder, trying to scribble down what he was hearing onto the corner of a takeaway menu.

"Apparently, it wasn't too pretty."

"Thanks Bob. Anything else, you get in touch, yeah?"

"Whatever. That's your lot, now piss off and don't bother us again," Martinson slammed the receiver down before he could be questioned any further, leaving Frank even more intrigued than before.

NINE

He was more nervous than he was comfortable with. It had been a while since he had even tried to turn on the charm, especially when he was still sober. Throw in the fact that he hated waiting rooms and things already weren't looking too optimistic. The places were little more than enclosures, usually lorded over by some uppity old cow of a receptionist who acted like she had a medical degree of her own, demanding to know all of the gory details of your ailments before she would even consider making you an appointment. He couldn't really see why anyone in their right mind would think badly of him for wanting to get away.

Then of course, there were the OTHER PEOPLE. It couldn't be a good to have to spend any length of time sitting in easy reach of so many sick people, listening to the coughs, sneezes and constant hacking up of mucus, while you tried your best to ignore the faint odour of old person, a stomach-churning combination of perfume and stale urine. Half of them were probably just there because they wanted someone to talk to anyway, the other half because they were worried that spot, the one that they found on their arse cheek, was going to turn out to be a tumour after all and swallow them up while they slept.

Frank was thankful that he wasn't there because of his indiscretion from a few weeks ago. The itching had gone at least, the combination of out-of-date antibiotics, alcohol and crossing of fingers seeming to have done the trick. No, he was after information about some dead man that no one seemed to know or care about, and while there were probably better places to begin fishing, it had to be a start. It was the best idea that he had come up with so far.

The woman sitting behind the reception desk looked like she was in her late forties or possibly early fifties, her choice of clothing, permed grey hair and thick, horn-rimmed glasses didn't exactly help her appearance. She was wearing a floral print dress and smelt of spearmint chewing gum and lavender in a nauseating mixture. For a change, he felt thankful that he hadn't had a drink, the stink would probably have tipped his stomach over the edge if he had. He rested one hand on the desktop and cleared his throat, some old bloke sitting at the front of the waiting area looking up from his crossword at the sound and glaring at him for having the brass neck to break his concentration.

"How may I help you?" The receptionist stared up at him from the glare of her computer screen, her pale eyes gleaming ice cold over the top of her glasses. "If I can actually help you, Mister..." she paused, expecting an answer from him.

"Popovich," Frank fumbled in the inside pocket of his jacket, "Franklin Popovich. But I prefer to be called Frank Popper," he chuckled. "I find that it rolls off the tongue easier. I'd like to start by saying how lovely you look. That dress really suits you, if I may say so."

"No, you may not," she sniffed, her voice clipped. "I would prefer it if you just told me why you're here, since you don't seem to actually *have* an appointment." She looked at her computer screen, as if to confirm what she was saying, before turning back to him, glaring across the top rim of her glasses. "In fact, I never forget a face and I don't believe you're even registered here, Mister Popovich." She paused, letting the air whistle between her remarkably white front teeth as she exhaled a long, slow breath, Frank finding himself wondering whether or not they were dentures.

"Yes, well, I suppose you've got me on that one," Frank waved his hand as though in dismissal, like it was no big deal. "I don't usually bother with medicines and doctors, you know, no time for any of that nonsense." He tapped the side of his head with his forefinger, "I prefer to rely on my positive thoughts. I'm as healthy as they come, well, usually I am anyway." With perfect timing, he thought he could sense a tingling sensation starting in his crotch at the recollection of how different things had been just a few weeks earlier.

"Positive thoughts. Yes, yes, of course. I bet you do." She leaned forward, pushing her glasses further up the bridge of her nose. "But none of that actually explains why you would be here when there's nothing remotely wrong with you."

"I was hoping that you could tell me a little bit about a certain William Marks," Frank cleared his throat, trying to ignore just how awkward he suddenly felt under her owl-like glare. "I believe he's registered to this surgery."

"What on earth makes you think that I would give you any information about one of Doctor Hesketh's patients?"

"So, he *was* a patient here then, *eh?*" He saw the briefest flash of something that might have been annoyance flicker across her face, as though she knew that she had already said too much, before she resumed that same stern mask.

"Like I said, I'm not obliged to tell you anything about any patient, whether they are registered here or not. Are you actually familiar with the concept of confidentiality, Mister Popovich?"

"Look, I'll confess, okay? I'm a journalist-"

"A *journalist?*" Her eyes flared, suggesting that he had said the wrong thing.

"Yeah, you know, an *investigative* journalist-"

"Now it all makes sense. Really, people like you are nothing more than leeches, trying to pick over the details of a person's life before he's even cold in his grave. Evil, money-grubbing vultures, the lot of you." She looked back towards her computer screen, dismissing him. "Well, there's nothing for you here."

"Look," Frank drummed his fingers on the desktop, inches away from her keyboard, really wishing he had a cigarette. "Mister Marks died recently, in suspicious circumstances. It bothers me that no one seems to care about it, whether it's because of who he was or where he was from, I don't know. I just want to see that people at least get to hear about him. That's not a bad thing, surely?"

"Oh, so you're one of those so-called *social crusaders,* setting out to put the world to rights - without any least bit of benefit to yourself of course." There was a sneering edge to her voice now that Frank didn't care for. He looked around the waiting room, where people were starting to look visibly irritated by the delay that he was probably causing. The old guy with the crossword grunted as he glared up, shaking out his newspaper with an air of impatience.

"Well, if you're going to take that attitude, I'd like to make an appointment please," Frank smiled, the effort starting to make the sides of his face ache.

"You want to make an appointment?" The receptionist repeated, suspicious. "You can't. As I've already said, you aren't registered with this surgery.

"Yes, I know, but I've been pretty sick recently, and I think I might need checking over. Preferably by a nice lady doctor with warm hands," he winked.

"You really are rather disgusting, you perverted little man. I don't think many doctors know of a cure for sick people like you, Mister Popovich. There are people in this room with *genuine* illnesses, people who haven't come here today with the intention of prying into the life of a dead man. As I've said several times, you really should leave. Now." Frank looked around the waiting area, sensing a growing atmosphere of hostility. The crossword guy shook out his newspaper again with a flourish, his brow knitting as he stared in Frank's direction, looking like he was willing him to do as the receptionist said, before he felt obliged to stand up and start throwing his fists around. To his left sat an elderly woman who looked like she was probably at least somewhere in her late nineties. She wore a thick woollen coat and matching hat, clutching a tartan shopping bag on her lap as if it was a pet dog that had just been put to sleep. She was looking through Frank with pale, milky eyes, probably willing him to just disappear for long enough for her to get her haemorrhoids checked out.

"I will ask you politely one last time to leave, Mister Popovich, or Popper, or whatever you're called-"

There was a sudden murmur from near the back of the waiting area.

"*Popper?* I recognise that name. Did someone say *Popper?*" The speaker stood up, a woman, probably in her early twenties, dressed in a loose-fitting grey hooded top and matching tracksuit bottoms, her blonde hair pulled back into a loose ponytail. "I know you, don't I?" She looked straight at him, and Frank saw that she actually did look vaguely familiar. "*Fucking hell - you're the rotten sod what infected me! I'll have you, you prick!*" Her bushy eyebrows knitted across her forehead in a heaving bar as she pushed her way past an old man and a woman with a young baby swaddled on her lap. She didn't look anywhere near as accommodating as she had that night in the toilet cubicle, and she sounded like she didn't intend to be very friendly either. "*Stay right where you are, and I'll kick your arse for you!*"

"Miss Walters, take your seat please. Mister Popper is just leaving now and I'm sure that the doctor will see you shortly," the receptionist rose to her feet, which was far more than she had done for Frank, suggesting at least that perhaps her actions spoke for his less than threatening nature.

"*Bugger the doctor! That tosspot gave me a disease!*" The old lady with the milky eyes turned a slightly different shade of grey at the choice of words being used. "*You stay right where you are, you lying shitweasel!*"

"What? *Me* lying?" Frank started to back away, the exit suddenly feeling much further away than it had some twenty seconds earlier. "*You* were the one who said you were clear."

"*Why, you nasty cun-*"

"*Miss Walters!*" The receptionist snapped, her voice shrill and piercing, like an old schoolteacher. "If you insist on upsetting other patients with that sort of language, you'll have to leave." She turned to face Frank's direction. "As for you, you've caused enough disruption and need to leave right this second, you-" Not needing to be told, Frank was already halfway through the exit before he risked a backward glance at what was going on. His previous cloakroom conquest - he still couldn't remember her first name - had stopped in her tracks, the expression of anger on her face replaced by one of shock, almost of fear as she brought both of her hands up to try and catch the torrent of blood that had suddenly exploded from both nostrils. His last thought as he let the door swing shut behind him was that she really did need to get herself checked out, although for the life of him, he couldn't think of any sexually transmitted diseases that caused nosebleeds.

***

Fumbling, she squeezed herself into the padded chair, the cotton of her tracksuit bottoms squeaking against the green vinyl as she did so. Both of her hands were still cupped in front of her face, the blood pooling and trickling through her fingers as it still dripped from her nose. With a slow calm that seemed almost deliberate, Doctor Hesketh pulled several sheets of thick blue tissue from a roll on the wall, handing them to her, before snapping on a pair of latex gloves.

"There you go, Miss Walters," he said, his voice a soothing lull as he stepped forward. "That's it, just remember to pinch it as tight as you can. Lean your head forward, not back, that's right."

"This is why I thought I'd better come to see you," she said, her voice muffled beneath the wad of tissue. "I don't usually get them, not until a week or so ago. It ain't right."

Hesketh took his seat, peeling the gloves back off as he saw that she appeared to have the bleeding under control, leaving them on the side of his desk, just in case.

"Hmm, you've probably done the right thing Susanne," he said. "Or remind me, do you prefer Susie? Either way, it can be worrying when you suddenly start experiencing heavy nosebleeds, especially if you're not usually prone to them, which I guess you're not, judging by what you've just said?" She shook her head, being careful to keep the sodden tissue in place. She grimaced as the sour taste reached the back of her throat, trying not to cough it out in a bloody spray. "What was all that commotion about in the waiting area, anyway? Do you have any idea?" Hesketh asked, leaning forward in his chair just a little. His voice was low, almost kindly while still maintaining an air of authority. "I do hope that you weren't involved in it."

"There was some bastard - I mean some *man* - at the reception. I recognised him." She looked down as though embarrassed, realising that her voice must have sounded more like a duck call with her fingers still pinching her nostrils closed. "I met him in a club a couple of weeks ago, I reckon he caused this to happen."

"Don't worry Susanne," Hesketh smiled, flashing teeth that looked almost too perfect for someone of his age. "I don't think one-night stands are usually a cause of nosebleeds, if *that's* what you're concerned about." She nodded sheepishly, without saying anything, trying not to gag against the cloying taste. There was something about the doctor's manner that made it seem impossible to keep anything from him. No matter how embarrassing the situation, she could tell him, and it seemed like he would just understand, like he would listen calmly without judging her. Talking to him almost felt more like speaking to a favourite uncle, and was certainly better than trusting that gossip-hungry cow of a flatmate with anything, especially with the way things had been lately.

"If you're worried of course, there are tests that we can do. Have you noticed any other symptoms, Susanne? *Susanne?*"

"Sorry Doctor Hesketh, no, I guess not. I don't know really," she looked up at the ceiling and narrowed her eyes, trying to think what to say next. "My flatmate keeps saying that I'm a bit snappier than usual, but then again she *would* say that. Things have been annoying me lately, a lot of little things that just seem to build up, you know what I mean?"

"It sounds like stress perhaps. Has anything been bothering you lately? Anything at all?"

"When do things *not* bother me?"

"I mean seriously, really bothering you," Hesketh chuckled, managing to somehow make her feel like he was laughing along *with* her, rather than *at* her, until she almost felt like she wanted to join in. "Have there been any recent changes that maybe you're not happy with?"

Her eyes, still narrowed, swivelling from side to side around the room, as though looking out for something that wasn't there. Hesketh noticed that she was trembling as she sat, pale, almost clammy looking. Perhaps it was just the shock of the nosebleed, but she looked almost as if she was afraid of something.

"I don't know," she said at last. "I can't explain nothing. I just get a bit wound up, you know, over stupid things sometimes. I don't even think about it until afterwards though." She chanced moving the tissue from her nose, taking it away slowly to avoid disturbing the newly-formed clot. A thin crust of already-drying blood remained on her top lip and, without even realising, she reached out her tongue and probed at it with the tip. With her pale, oatmeal-coloured skin and bulging wide eyes, Hesketh thought she still looked as though she was moments away from fainting.

"Are you on any medication at the moment, Susanne? Anything that you haven't told me about, shall we say?" he asked, reaching into his desk drawer for a notepad. He produced a silver-plated ballpoint pen with a flourish, the polished barrel catching the fluorescent glare of the light and making her eyes ache as she looked straight at it. "Anything at all? If you are, now is a good time to tell me."

"No," she said, "nothing. But I *did* have quite a bit to drink the night I, you know," her voice trailed into a mumble as she thought back to her drunken fumble with that lying Popper bloke. Just out to see how quickly he could make a girl drop her knickers. Typical bloke.

Hesketh raised an eyebrow, is though he knew exactly what she was too embarrassed to say out loud. "Well, I don't think that a night of drinking is likely to be the cause of your symptoms either." He leaned back and knitted the fingers of both hands across his lap. "Even if it does end up in some sort of indiscretion, come the end of the night." He tapped out a rhythm on the pad with his pen and Susanne couldn't help but get the feeling that she was being told off without actually being told off. *Indiscretion.* That was a clever-sounding word, the sort of thing a person would say if they really knew what they were talking about and could be trusted.

Susanne nodded slowly, still wary of setting her nose gushing again. "I'm trying to think...there's *something* that happened, but I can't quite remember." She smiled, the action feeling forced somehow, making her jaw ache as her back teeth ground together.

Hesketh sat back in his chair with a squeak. "Try to do so. Anything you can think of that might help. Any stress or anxiety, that's the sort of thing that can cause some of your symptoms, for sure."

"No, nothing like that," she said, Hesketh almost wincing at the way she said *nuffink*, her slightly muffled voice exaggerating the effect. "There was one thing, but it's a bit stupid really."

"Go on."

"The night that bloke outside *fuc-* sorry, had sexual intercourse with me, I felt embarrassed after. Really embarrassed, so I left the club right after. I live in the flats over in The Reds, and it can get a bit rough sometimes at night, so I took my time. I walked down by the stream, you know, to try and clear my head a bit."

"Okay," Hesketh leaned across his desk, to show her that he was paying attention.

"Down by the stream," she repeated, as though concentrating on the memory. Forgetting, she rubbed the back of her hand across her nose, smearing a fresh trail of blood across her upper lip. "Oh, it's started again." Not wanting to interrupt, Hesketh reached across, passing her another tissue. "On the way to the lake, there was a horse. It looked old, you know, not very well. It was just lying there right in the middle of the path. It was odd, I've been there loads of times, but I hadn't seen it before. I don't even know how it could have got there." She narrowed her eyes, a faraway look in them as though she was still struggling to remember some half-forgotten detail. "It looked as lonely as I felt and I felt really sorry for it, especially with the mood I was in. I sat next to it just stroked it for a few minutes." She wiped at her nose again, the blood coming away heavier now. "The gravel was really uncomfortable for my arse – sorry, my *backside* – but it looked so sick, I thought it looked like it might die." Her eyes widened as a thought occurred to her. "Doctor Hesketh, you don't suppose I could have caught something from *that* do you, instead of from that pervert?"

"I doubt it, Susanne." Despite his reassuring words, his smile stopped just short of being warm, not quite reaching his eyes. "Again, I don't really see how there's much chance of you catching any of your symptoms from a horse. Not in so short a space of time anyway," he said, trying to sound comforting. "I think you're most likely just feeling overly anxious after whatever encounter you had with the man you spoke about. His chair creaking, he stood and held out an arm, ready to see her out. "I don't think that either sex, or a sick horse, are to blame, let's put it that way. Sex doesn't often make your nose bleed, even if it *did* take place in a toilet cubicle." What little colour there was in her face rushed to her cheeks. "There's no need to be embarrassed," he said, still with that same thin smile. "I'm a doctor and I've heard it all before. I've heard much worse, in fact, I promise. Although I do hope that you'll learn from it and be a little more careful in future."

"Yes, Doctor Hesketh, I'm sorry," she said, not even knowing why she felt the sudden need to apologise to him. "Thanks," she stood up and allowed herself to be guided towards the door. "You don't think I might need any tablets or anything like that?"

"I'd rather not rush into anything" Hesketh rested his hand on the door handle, pausing to speak. "Although there are medications that we can try you out on if things don't get better."

"You mean antidepressants, don't you?"

"Yes, but there's nothing to worry about. They're just a medicine like any other. There's really no shame in taking them if you have a problem and they help you."

"I suppose you're right," she shook her head, still worried that any sudden movement might set her nose gushing once again.

Hesketh tapped the side of his head with a bony forefinger. "It's probably best that you just get yourself home and try to get plenty of rest, for the time being, at least." He reached his free arm across her shoulders as he steered in the direction of the now open door. "Just keep an eye on how things go for the time being and make another appointment if you start to feel any worse. I'm sure that you'll be fine though."

He closed the door behind her and flopped back into his chair, exhaling the breath that he had been holding in for far too long. He leaned forward and flicked the switch on the intercom on his desk.

"Hello Anna, is everything okay out there now?"

"Yes, Doctor Hesketh," the receptionist's voice sounded thin and hollow as it seemed to squeeze its way out of the small speaker. "Things are fine now. Are you ready for your next patient?"

"Not quite. You'll have to give me perhaps fifteen minutes or so. There's something I just need to check out."

"Okay Doctor, things have settled down in here now anyway, now that loathsome little man has gone."

"Loathsome man? *Which* loathsome man?"

"He said he was a journalist, sloped his way right in here asking about that patient that you mentioned the other day."

"Patient? You mean Mister Marks?" Hesketh stroked his chin, feeling a sudden flutter in his chest.

"Yes, that's the one," the receptionist's voice brightened, as if she felt as though she was helping to safeguard a great secret. "I didn't tell him anything of course. Patient confidentiality and that sort of thing. He didn't half rile up a fair few people here in the waiting room. People like that really are awful, they would do *anything* to sell their newspapers, wouldn't they?"

"Yes, it sounds like that's just what he had in mind. You did well to keep him at bay though, thank you, Anna." He switched the speaker back off before she could answer, finding that forced clipped tone she always used annoying at the best of times.

He lay his head back again and looked up at the ceiling, the light from the frosted window dancing across the polystyrene ceiling tiles in a way that could almost be hypnotic. The problem with Susanne Walters, like so many other men and women a similar age was, in no small part due to their lack of morals. So often, he found that any number of ailments could be best explained away as being due to their proclivities. *You're a slut, what do you expect?* That was the sort of answer that he found himself wanting to give to people with an increasing regularity. Unfortunately, he really didn't have the damnedest idea what could actually be wrong with her. It was pretty worrying though, to think that a journalist was already sniffing around, asking questions about Marks. Especially considering the way things were.

Perhaps it was time to start worrying.

TEN

"Urggh...well, shit..."

His mouth felt as though it had shrunk at some point during the night, the insides of his cheeks feeling like they had sprouted hairs, along with a rough coating on his tongue and the back of his throat that made his breath taste like three-day old milk.

Rosa had long since left for work, as usual, without waking him. It wasn't that he was lazy, or anything like that. Most likely it was his thyroid problem acting up again. It always made him feel a bit sluggish, especially first thing in the morning. Of course, Rosa would probably argue with him about *that* as well, insisting that just because he had watched a television documentary about an illness didn't mean that he suffered from it. Then she would start with the usual name-calling. *Hypochondriac*, she would call him, *you're a bloody hypochondriac and you need to take better care of yourself and blah, blah, bloody blah.* She didn't know a damn thing and sometimes cared to understand even less. Today was no different to most others. He could never bring himself to admit it, least of all to her, but she was probably right, like she was about most things. There was still no need for her to be so bloody far up her own backside about it though.

He let out a sigh that sound far too loud in the otherwise quiet bedroom. He *was* sick of it. He was sick of feeling useless, sick of always sweating and running short of breath. He hated the way that he wheezed like an asthmatic before he made it to the top of a flight of stairs. He couldn't stand the way that people looked at him with one of two expressions: pity or disgust, including his own wife. He wanted to make a change, of course he did, but he didn't have the faintest idea how to. He just knew that he was going to have to do something about it. A weekly jaunt to the lake to sit on his fat backside and drink beer while he watched the end of his fishing rod bobbing up and down probably wasn't quite enough to make a difference. He tried to brush off half of the comments aimed at him, by her and everyone else, seemingly without a second thought, playing them down as a joke at best. The remaining half, he did his best to ignore completely, treating them like attempts at personal insults that warranted no real attention. But whenever Rosa questioned his habits, the look of concern on her face that she could never quite manage to hide just made him feel guilty if he thought about it long enough, which in turn just increased his appetite further. It sometimes felt like he was a fat old hamster stuck in its wheel, going around and around, day after day.

***

There must have been something wrong, a fault of some sort. Maybe the batteries were running out, that was probably it.

He had been weighing himself every Monday morning for the last two months, having found the electric scales buried under a pile of unwashed clothing in a corner of the spare bedroom. For his benefit, the digital display could have simplified things by having two possible readings, *obese* and *seriously - one at a time, please.* It had become almost like a punishment of sorts, a little morning reminder to wake himself up with the realisation that nothing had changed; he was still fat knacker, hiding all of his fears and insecurities behind a shield made up of a *couldn't-care-less* attitude, bolted on to a physical barrier of blubber. The problem was that, the worse he felt, the more Rosa nagged him, every time he pretended not to hear the latest wise comment or sly dig from the likes of Mitch Brennan - *his oldest friend, for Christ's sake* - he reacted in the only way he knew; by reaching for the junk food, the beer, or both. Sure, he had tried the old trick of re-weighing himself after a really big shit, just so he could experience how it felt to see a couple of pounds disappear. But the small comfort that came from seeing a digit or two drop from the reading on the scale wasn't enough to compensate for the rattling that started in his chest or the sweat that sprung up on his brow, every time he walked from one end of a room to the other.

He stepped off the scale, waited for the display to clear, then stepped back on again for the third time, the plastic plate sagging under the pressure as he did so. After a few seconds, the numbers blinked up again, flashing their insistence that he wasn't dreaming, he really had lost just over half a stone in a week.

"How the bloody hell did I manage *that?*" He asked aloud, as though expecting the answer to come from thin air.

Half a stone, more like three quarters in fact. In response, there was a rumbling sensation from the pit of his stomach as it let out a low, almost angry growl. Three quarters of a stone in a week. Rosa wouldn't believe it, if she even took the time to notice any change. It warranted a fry-up, surely. Just a small reward. Jesus Christ, he suddenly felt *starving*, even more so than usual.

He stepped off the scales again, picking them up and replacing them under the pile of clothing before the display had finished blinking out, his belly once more insisting that it was time for food.

ELEVEN

Frank Popper was beginning to think that he'd had better ideas. *Plenty* of better ideas. It had been about a week since he had tried his luck at the GP's surgery, trying to dig up some background information on William Marks, a dead bloke that he had since realised no one seemed to know, care, or even want to talk about. Instead, he had ended up pretty much legging it from the place, his ears ringing with the ranting of some woman he had gotten his end away with in a toilet cubicle. He would just have to chalk it up to a lesson learned the hard way. With hindsight, waltzing his way into the place thinking that a cheeky smile would get him what he was after had probably turned out to be a bit of a stupid move. Perhaps patient confidentiality still counted for something at least. The suddenness with which he had made his exit probably hadn't helped his cause or his public image either, ducking out before facing the beating that had been promised to him by whatever the hell crazy toilet sex woman was called. Her memory was obviously much better than his. A week and a half and he still had next to nothing useful to go on, apart from a few bits and pieces. William Marks had actually been British by birth, so that was one thing that Bob Martinson had been wrong about, although his parents had emigrated from Austria, probably sometime after the Second World War, and he had returned to live and work there for some twenty years before returning. As far as Frank could gather from what he *had* been able to dig up, Marks had lived alone, with no wife or kids to speak of. An ageing, single man, probably with a funny accent, who was all by himself in a piss-poor, squalid part of the city. It was little wonder that no one around the place seemed overly bothered about him popping his clogs.

The alarm clock display insisted that it was just past midday, even though the humming in his head made it feel more like it was still somewhere in the small hours. He couldn't be sure if the rumbling in his ears was the hiss of rain spattering against the window or just withdrawal from the alcohol that he had somehow managed to swear off. The low muscles in his back ached as he turned over to stare at the ceiling. He cupped his balls in one hand, as though cradling a glass of fine wine. The itching had stopped quite a few days ago now, but it still gave him a comforting sense of reassurance, to know that they were still there, having convinced himself until recently that they were sure to shrivel and drop off. He had even started to think at the time that it would probably be a good thing if they did, at least it would stop him from putting the damn things to use ever again. On the plus side, the ceiling wasn't whirling around some central point for a change. It was one of the rare occasions where the need to think really had proven greater than the need to drink. Either that, or maybe he was just slowing down with age. The potential for a story had made him feel like he had to get his shit together. At least it had to begin with, the sense of frustration soon building at the lack of available information. It was starting to feel like maybe he was losing his touch. He turned his head and looked towards the small desk by the window. The bottle standing next to his typewriter was still three-quarters full, the amber liquid inside making him realise just how dry the back of his throat felt.

There was a clattering sound from beyond the bedroom door, followed by the soft thud of something falling through the letterbox. As he shifted there was a dull ache in his lower legs, making him regret that he had never bothered to get a pet dog, or perhaps a partner willing to fetch the post for him. He paused, hoping that it wasn't the nightclub toilet girl - her name really *did* elude him - coming back for round two. She certainly hadn't seemed too happy with him the last time he'd seen her, instead making it clear that she was the type to bear a grudge. The last thing that he needed to see was a steaming pile of shit in his hallway, pushed through by some riddled mare who thought that he'd got her up the duff. He guessed that was probably why she had been paying a trip to the surgery herself. Either that, or to score some antibiotics for her own downstairs irritation. It had turned out to be a fuss over nothing in particular, but it had still given him a scare that would probably last until the next time he felt like he needed to get his end away. After a few minutes of deliberation there had been no sound of angry braying on the door, no tell-tale cloud of smoke carrying through to the main room, or faecal stink wafting through. At least things were all good on that front.

It wasn't until he convinced himself that it was about time that he got up to go for a piss that he saw what had made the sound. A thick manila envelope lay on the floor, the edges were dog-eared and wet from the rain outside. Curiosity getting the better of him, he stooped and picked it up, groaning as his spine popped with a sound like bubble wrap, but far less therapeutic. Kept shut with a small piece of Scotch tape, the contents slid around inside as he turned it over in his hands, looking for anything that might hopefully identify the sender. There were no stamps or an address, whoever was responsible must have chosen to deliver it personally, which perhaps should have been worrying. There was nothing other than his name, scrawled across the centre in spidery red ink, along with a few smeared blotches of the same. At least he hoped it was ink and nothing more suspicious.

***

He cradled the second mug of nuclear-strength coffee in both hands, just waiting for the caffeine to start to to kick in. He couldn't usually function properly unless he'd had a decent coffee fix, either with or without alcohol muting his senses. He stared at the envelope laid on the table in front of him, as though gazing down at it for long enough would somehow cause it to open by itself, safely at arm's length. It certainly didn't appear dangerous, quite the opposite in fact, unless it was a court summons or worse, a paternity test result. Biting the bullet, he set his mug of coffee down and reached across for the package. Weighing next to nothing, maybe it was just a letter of some sort. There was only one way to find out. He stuck his thumb into the gap at the sealed end and drew it across, wincing at the resulting paper cut as the flimsy paper split open. He jammed his thumb into his mouth, trying to suckle away the pain as he tipped the contents out onto the table. A slim, dog-eared reporter-style notebook, along with three Polaroid photographs, their glossy sheen glinting in the light that was just starting to filter in through the blinds. Suddenly, the sound of rain spattering against the window wasn't quite enough to relax him completely.

"Holy *fuck*," he muttered under his breath as he reached forward and picked the first one up.

The image showed what looked like a dead body, probably that of a man, but it was hard to be certain. Sat on what looked like a tiled floor strewn with rubbish, his legs were splayed out in front and his head slumped forward, *as if he had died trying to suck himself off*, Frank thought, aware of how bad it sounded. He was stripped to the waist, his ribs just visible at either side, the bones standing out as though he had gone without eating in weeks. One of his hands held what looked like a large knife in a death grip, and what could be seen of his lap looked as though his trousers were soaked through with blood. In the bottom left corner of the image, *Marks 01* had been scrawled across the white margin, in the same red ink that had been used on the envelope. The roof of Frank's mouth felt drier than ever, almost dusty as he picked up the next photo. This one was a close up of the torso, the ribs were clearly visible now, as was the crude, jagged slash that ran almost from side to side of his belly, allowing his insides to unspool onto his lap like an old cassette reel. *Marks 02 – close up,* the writing confirmed this time. He began to feel glad that he hadn't drunk the night before, the stale taste of fish and chip supper rising up to the back of his throat instead. The last picture was another close-up, showing the arm closest to the photographer, the one still clutching the knife. Coated in what looked like drying blood, the forearm was turned outward a little, showing what looked like three bite marks, bloody gaping holes where chunks of flesh were missing. *Marks 03 - arm bite marks,* the scribble proclaimed.

"Sweet Jesus Christ," he stared at all three photos with a hollow feeling in his gut. He had wanted to know just how William Marks had died and now he did, for better or worse. It looked as though his life had ended alone in his squalid little bedsit in one of the most run-down parts of the filthy, overcrowded city. Probably still sitting in a puddle of his own piss and shit, he had finally given up on whatever life he had, starved to the point where he had resorted to gnawing on the meat of his own arms and carving strips out of his own belly in order to survive. Frank had seen some pretty nasty stuff over the years, usually liking to tell himself that he was fairly unshakable. Still though, the pit of his stomach felt like he had swallowed a lead weight. *The haves and the have-nots,* he thought with a swelling feeling of rueful bitterness. *Just one more example of just how easy it's become for people to fall between the cracks and be completely forgotten about.* Reaching forward, he turned the photos face-down as the churning in his gut subsided a little. Someone had to answer for it all, to explain how it could possibly be seen as acceptable for anyone to be so poor, so empty of hope that they had to stoop to such desperate measures to try and stay alive. William Marks needed someone to tell his story, to make sure he was talked about and remembered. To make sure that he at least got some sort of justice.

He got up to make himself another coffee, still ignoring the bottle of bourbon inviting him to indulge, resisting the temptation. There was no time for booze, he needed to be able to focus, and for that he needed a clear head for a change.

William Marks needed to be remembered all right and, after seeing the photos of him lying dead in that squalid little hovel, Frank was even more determined to make it his mission to ensure that he was.

TWELVE

Mitchell Brennan was almost lost for words, something that most people, including himself, would say didn't happen very often. A skinny, weasel-like runt of a man, what he lacked in physical presence he more than made up for with his smart mouth. Always ready with something to say.

There were still rare exceptions of course.

"Bloody hell, *Brad?* What's happened to you? You look ill!" Brennan had almost walked by without a second glance at the man who could have easily passed as a complete stranger, but for the fact that he was sitting in Brad Whitman's favourite chair in Betty MacKinnon's diner, that green plastic one, with the once shiny seat sanded to a dull matte finish where it had been worn down by the chafing of his oversized backside over the years. The man had parked himself on that same seat so many times that it might as well have had a reserved sticker slapped across the backrest. Brennan had known Whitman for a long, long time, way back when they were both kids. In those days, the most important thing they had to think about was what sort of trouble they could cause around The Reds. Over the years of course, they had both settled into the trappings of middle age: a job, a wife, and a seemingly irreversibly expanding waistline, in that order. At least it had seemed to be irreversible. Whitman had never been the sort of bloke who gave a damn about whatever health advice anyone might have to offer him.

The Brad Whitman who sat clutching onto one of Betty MacKinnon's oversized mugs of coffee, as though for dear life, wasn't the same man that Mitch Brennan had last spoken to just over a couple of weeks before. Instead, he had been replaced by a gaunt figure who looked familiar and alien, both at the same time. It was as though his deflated head had been stuck onto the body of

111

someone else, someone who had never even sniffed a square meal, never mind eaten one.

That was Brennan's first thought. His second was that Brad Whitman looked very lonely and very afraid, both just as much out of character for him.

Trying not to let his shock show and knowing full well that he was probably failing, Brennan slid out a chair opposite with a scraping noise, inviting himself to sit down. As he did so Whitman looked up from the contents of his mug. His eyes, sunken and dull, seemed to light up with a faint spark of recognition, as though realisation was taking its time to sink in.

"Hey Mitch, how 'you doing?" As he spoke, he drummed his fingers against the surface of the table, as though agitated. His lips were dry and chapped and his gums looked as though they had shrunk back from his teeth, giving them a lengthened, almost vampire-like appearance. *He really does looks like he's gone without food in weeks*, Brennan thought, *it's crazy.*

"What have you been up to lately?" Whitman's fingers still beat out an almost frantic staccato in time with his words against the vinyl tablecloth. "I haven't seen you around for a little while."

"Just over a fortnight and I was about to ask you the same question, Brad. Jesus Christ, are you feeling okay? What's happened, has Rosa put locks on all of the cupboards or something?" Whitman almost seemed to look through him, a glazed, confused expression on his face, before he realised what Brennan meant. He forced a smile, his lips drawing back from pale gums in what looked more like a pained grimace than an attempt at a smile.

"Oh," he said. "Yeah, that. I've lost a bit of weight recently."

"A *bit* of weight?" Brennan repeated. "That's an understatement. Do you even know what's caused it?"

"I'm not really sure, I think I might be sick or something. It's probably nothing, just a stomach bug." Whitman stopped drumming and raised a finger to his temple. Brennan could almost see the shape of the bones outlined in the parchment-like skin. "I've been pretty ill for a few days now though, and I just can't seem to shake it off."

"Well, I know that Rosa's always complaining that you need to lose some weight," Brennan started to laugh, the sound choking off in the back of his throat as he immediately regretted what he had said. "Sorry," he mumbled. "I can be a bit of an arse sometimes."

"That's okay," Whitman smiled again. "I'm glad of the company, more than anything else. I just had to get out for a little while, I've spent most of the last week or two cooped up at home, talking to the bloody walls."

Brennan nodded, he had always thought Rosa Whitman to be a decent enough soul and he knew that Brad certainly loved his wife, but she had never struck him as the kind of woman whose company he would enjoy for more than a couple of hours at a time. She would probably be over the moon with her new-look husband, never mind that he looked as though he had been starving himself for at least a month.

"Where is Rosa anyway? I haven't seen her around for a bit, either."

"She's away," Whitman mumbled, looking down at the tablecloth in front of him as he spoke. "She's visiting her sister up in Manchester. That woman really hates me, we thought it would be best if I just stayed here until she gets back."

"She *is* coming back though, right?" Brennan tilted his head to one side. Always thinking that she liked to portray herself as some sort of a martyr, it wouldn't have surprised him too much if Rosa had just gotten out of bed one day and decided to walk out on her husband, ditching him to start over again somewhere else. Despite their longevity, they had always come across as a mismatched couple, Brennan could never understand what they actually saw in one another.

"So, what's going on? Has it just turned you off your food or something?"

"What?"

"Whatever it is that's wrong with you. Has it put you off your food? You know, stopped you from eating?"

"I wish that it had. It would make things a hell of a lot easier to understand if it had, wouldn't it?" As he spoke. Whitman pointed a bony finger to the next table, at a pile of dirty plates and bowls. "I really do wish that it had."

Brennan felt his jaw drop as he looked at the mess. "What the hell?"

"I've been eating pretty much everything in sight for days now. I can't fill myself up, I just feel so hungry all the time." He clutched at his stomach as he spoke and Brennan could have sworn that, right on cue, he could hear a low rumble coming from below the table. For the first time, he noticed a daub of something on Whitman's chin, a dark red-brown smear that might have been dried-on ketchup.

"Have you been to see a doctor? I mean, when did this even start?"

"I'm not too sure," Whitman looked up at the ceiling tiles, as though expecting to find an answer hiding in the mildew-spotted joins between them. "I think that it was probably the Thursday before last. Yes, I reckon it was, the day sticks out because that was the day that we lost the power." Brennan looked confused. "Some problem with the fuse box," Whitman continued. "It blew all the lights in the flat. It took me a good hour to fix, it was so damn dark that I couldn't see what I was doing, even with a torch. I don't know if anyone else was affected." He started drumming his fingers on the table again, the rhythm stuttering, as if to match the pattern of his thoughts. "*Strange...*"

Brennan shook his head. "Not that I've heard," he said. "Mine was just fine. I don't think that anyone else has said anything about it."

"Oh, like I say, it was probably just a blown fuse I suppose. Anyway, it sticks in my mind because of that. That's when I first started to feel funny."

"*Funny?*"

"Yeah, *funny*. Hungry, you know? *Really* hungry. It doesn't matter what I eat, how much I put away, the feeling just won't shift."

"Hey, do you think maybe you've got one of them tapeworm things?" Brennan's eyes widened. He had watched a television programme just a few nights before, about parasites, the graphic image of a ribbon-like, twelve-foot length of tapeworm being teased out from the guts of a cow was still fresh in his mind.

"No, I might not be the the brightest of sparks, Mitch, but even I'm not *that* stupid. A tapeworm doesn't make you lose weight, not really. Not how I've been losing it anyway. If I'm telling the truth, I'm getting a bit scared."

"Have you even told Rosa about any of this?" Brennan reached out, almost touching Whitman's shoulder, before thinking better of it. If he really did have any sort of disease, it could be catching, and it didn't look very pleasant. "Whether she's visiting her sister or not, if you're *that* bad, she should be back here with you."

"Are you taking the piss?" Whitman grimaced as he spoke, his expression making his cheeks and eyes looked even more sunken. "She'd probably be loving this. You know she's been nagging on at me to lose weight for years now." He paused, as if thinking of what to say next. "Besides," he continued, "she's been gone for several days, she's probably settled herself in by now. Maybe it's best I should just let her stay there. I could do with the peace and quiet, to be honest."

"I don't think so," Brennan tried to keep from leaning forward, again, just in case. "You two have your ups and downs, but I can't believe she would be happy to see you looking half dead. For God's sake Brad, give her a call."

There was a sudden noise, like a window being shattered as Betty dropped a stack of plates she had been trying to carry out to the kitchen, shards of white crockery exploding out across the linoleum floor.

"*Christ almighty!*" she cursed, "Eddie, it just isn't my day today!" Sat in his usual spot, old Eddie Caplin said nothing, just adjusting his cap and nodding his head in a silent agreement as she shuffled back the way she'd came to fetch a dustpan, still muttering curses beneath her breath as she went. Supposing one of the miserable pricks stood on a sharp bit of plate and did his or herself an injury, that would be the *last* thing she needed, even if it did serve them right.

"So anyway, that's all beside the point," Brennan continued. "Whether your missus is here or not, I reckon you ought to go and get yourself looked at." *Even if it's just to keep whatever's wrong with you from spreading*, he added inside his head, feeling a pang of guilt for even having the thought.

"It's okay you know," Whitman said, noticing just how far back into his chair the other man had shrunk. "I understand. If I was you, I wouldn't want to be getting too close to me either. No offence taken." He looked up from the tablecloth, to make full eye contact for the first time. Although sunken, his eyes were wide and round, the thin, gaunt lines of his face making them look even larger. "To tell you the truth Mitch, I'm bloody terrified of what any doctor might say. I told you I was a bit scared, but that was putting it lightly. I'm actually *really* scared. I don't know what's happening to me. I know Rosa's always spent her time nagging at me to be thinner, but Jesus, not like *this*." He shoved two fingers into his mouth, sucking away traces of tomato ketchup, before tapping them against the tabletop to emphasise his words. "I'm just so damned hungry all the time. I mean really, all the time. I eat and I eat, and I keep eating, but the more I put away, the more I want, and the thinner I seem to get."

"I read a horror story about something like that one time. You haven't done anything to piss some gypsy off, have you?" Brennan paused, seeing the look of confusion on Whitman's face. He cleared his throat, before starting again. "Maybe it *is* some kind of tapeworm, or something like that," Brennan said, "There's probably something you can get for that, you know? Some medicine, maybe."

Whitman shook his head, "I said before, I'm not stupid, Mitch. I know that a tapeworm wouldn't cause anything like *this*."

"What do you reckon Rosa would make of it, really?" Brennan spread his hands out in a gesture of appeal, "I mean, she would have to be worried, right? I wouldn't be surprised if she came back and packed you off to a doctor herself, if you just let her know about it."

"I'm not so sure about that Mitch. She thinks that Hesketh's an even bigger arsehole than I do."

Brennan shook his head. "It can't be that bad, surely. Nothing can be worse than just sitting in here, putting up with whatever's wrong with you."

"I don't know about that either. I-" As the words left his mouth, Whitman's face suddenly blanched, going from ashen grey to a doughy off-white. His spindly hands scrabbled at the table, ragged chewed fingernails raking and trying to find support like twin spiders as he tried to grope and claw his way to his feet. Too late, he whipped his head to one side with what looked like enough force to snap his neck, as he yawned his mouth open. With his eyes closed, he vomited a dark, almost solid void of blood that jetted across the table, spraying up like a fountain as it hit the edge and hosed the floor below.

"Jesus Christ!" Brennan shrank back further in his chair, almost toppling it backward as he tried to move out of reach of the bloody torrent. Somewhere behind him came gasps as what few other diners were in the place turned to see what was happening, drawn by the sudden noise.

"Oh, my sweet lord," Eddie Caplin mumbled as he looked up from studying the gingham pattern of his vinyl table covering, finally seeing something worth talking about. The fellas over at *The Dog and Master* wouldn't *believe* it when he told them about how Brad Whitman had just spewed half of his insides all over Betty MacKinnon's floor. No really, there were chunks of liver in it and *everything*, honest. No wonder he'd gone and lost so much weight. At that same moment, Betty turned around in the doorway to the kitchen, carrying a stack of greasy, half-empty plates.

"What the hell-" She dropped them to the floor again, where they exploded on impact, shattering across the linoleum. This time, no one seemed to notice, their attention focused elsewhere.

Whitman leaned forward across the table as he tried to keep himself upright, gripping onto the sides of it for support. A thin trail of blood-tinged drool still dangled from his lower lip and trailed its way down onto the cheap plastic covering. He quivered as he continued to hack and splutter, wavering as he brought one hand across to clutch at his belly as he did so.

"Christ, oh dear *Christ*," Brennan gasped again, still being careful not to touch the thick spreading pool as it dripped over the side of the table. "Brad - are you *okay?*"

"Bugger whether he's okay," Betty shouted as she bustled her way over to their table. Her voice was loud and ragged. "Just get him out of here, before he does it again. Oh, Jesus, it's fucking well *everywhere!*"

"I didn't bring him in here, Betty," Brennan protested, fearful of the possibility that he might have to make any sort of physical contact with Whitman in his current state.

"*I don't care how he got in here,*" Betty's face seemed to swell and redden with anger, as if it was moments away from exploding. She was almost on the verge of screaming and she looked as though she would physically pick them both up and bundle the two of them outside if she thought for a second that she was either big or strong enough.

"Just bloody well *get him out of here!*" she demanded again for good measure, oblivious to who might hear her. "God almighty, it's a mess and it frigging well *stinks!*"

As the words seemed to echo around the small room, Whitman lunged forward, with a drunken lurch that was as sudden as it was unexpected. He shoved the table aside with a loud scrape, almost toppling it over as he bolted for the door, pink-tinged spittle still trailing down from his chin. The door swung to behind him, the bell mounted on the door frame jangling in his wake.

Brennan felt unable to move, his legs like jelly as he sat mute, staring at the widening pool of blood as he tried his best to make some sense of what had just happened.

***

He had started running and just kept on going, for how long he didn't know and didn't really care. It didn't matter, all that he needed was to get somewhere safe, to close the door on everything. The air had whipped against his eyes as he went, stinging tears streaming across his face as he ran, dodging passers-by or nudging a few of them out of his way, usually to gasps of shock or muttered curses against him, aimed at *the clumsy arsehole who didn't take more care of where he was going.* He ignored them all, they weren't important.

He had no idea where his energy could be coming from. It was probably little more than blind panic that kept him moving, the same thing that now made all of his senses spin almost as much as the hollow churning feeling in his gut. Everywhere looked the same now, his surroundings mixing into one great big blur as he staggered along aimless, trying his best not to stumble, to outrun who or whatever it was that his imagination told him must surely be following him. His eyes felt as though they could bulge their way free from their sockets. His lungs felt like they were on fire and hot breath scorched the raw flesh at the back of his throat, still ripe with the sour taste of his own blood. Brad Whitman needed to be home, but he couldn't see where home was any more. If he closed his eyes, his vision swam with the faces of everyone who had been in MacKinnon's, their stupid doe eyes wide, gawping long and hard at his freakishness as they kept sufficiently close to have a good old stare at him, but far enough back to avoid being tainted by whatever it was that was wrong with him. *The hell with them,* he thought, his head filled with what he imagined their mocking laughter must have sounded like, laced with poison and false sympathy. That was what they were probably wanting to do really, have a good old laugh at him, at the freakish man who had just embarrassed himself in front of them. Well, screw them all. Every last one of them could go to hell for all he cared, he didn't need them anyway. What a bunch of nasty, two-faced bastards they really were.

He recognised the block of flats, uncertain of just how many times he had actually ran past it, feeling like he had been going around in circles for Christ only knew how long. The lift was out of order of course, instead he somehow managed to haul himself up the four flights of stairs to the home he shared with his wife. Yes, her, his sanctimonious, stick-insect wife who probably meant well, but was just as bad as all the others in her own way. Maybe it was for the best that she wasn't around, or at least he told himself. "I just fucking hope you're happy now," he tried to say aloud, the words barely wheezing out in broken gasps. "You wanted a thin husband, you got one. And now people can't take their eyes off me."

As his fingers wrapped around the door handle and he shook it, he was relieved to find that it was unlocked, saving him the precious time that it would have otherwise taken to search out his keys. There was a furious burning behind his eyes and in his head, matched only by the incessant churning in his belly. Hungry, so hungry, like he hadn't eaten anything in a month rather than less than an hour. Frantic, he almost collapsed through the doorway, stumbling as he tried to stay on his feet, not wanting to waste a second of precious time.

Food, there had to be some food somewhere, even if he had to resort to turning out the rubbish bin onto the floor, he had to find something, he thought, the gnawing sensation inside him maddening in its intensity.

THIRTEEN

It was quiet, just the way Betty MacKinnon would have preferred it any other time. Just about the only noises in the place were the steady *thrumming* of the refrigerator and the annoying *drip-drip-dripping* of the hot tap over the sink in the kitchen that still hadn't been fixed, thanks to that no-good, geriatric shitstain Caplin.

Yeah, any other time, she would have preferred it. But right now wasn't really *any other time*.

Everyone had cleared out of the place pretty damn sharp, thanks to the combination of that prick Whitman puking his guts out all over the floor, along with her own resulting outburst. She really had lost it good and proper, kicking off in front of everyone the way that she had. Not that she really cared what any of them thought of her. She could barely stand any of them anyway, in the same way that she hated so many other things in the horrible city. The sounds and smells, the people, all of it wound her up until sometimes it felt as though her head could explode with the pressure. Maybe *that* would make the place better, sharp bits of skull and chunks of brain sprayed across the grease-marked walls like a kid scrawling all over the place in crayon. She doubted that any of the regulars would even notice. She could walk away from the whole thing and leave a trained monkey behind and the likes of that old fart Caplin would probably still turn up for their fry-ups and their mugs of reheated coffee. Oh, there had been many an occasion when she had been tempted to hawk up a wad of phlegm and spit it into one of their mugs, irritating arseholes that they were, just to see whether they would even be able to tell.

Yeah, she hated it all right, she always had. Everything about the place, each and every single thing, little more than an irritating reminder of what it all stood for; a nasty, cold bastard who spent

123

years hiding behind a false mask of geniality. Thinking about it for too long always made her belly hurt, sour bile working its way up the back of her throat until she could vomit, trying to purge herself of it, whilst knowing that it would still be there afterward. Whatever she thought about the lot that she had been dealt, it couldn't possibly be much worse than where she was right at that moment, down on her knees, scrubbing away at a foul-smelling concoction of blood and puke. The dull ache in her calves was knotting her muscles up into a cramp, and she could feel her temperature rising as she worked at the stubborn muck without success. Trying to scrub it away, all she had managed to do was smear it around further, guiding it into the cracks in the old flooring, where it would take forever to clean back out. Christ, the stuff was almost like jelly, thick and dark, like an old blood clot that had been dislodged from somewhere deep inside Brad Whitman's rotten guts. She cursed again, the sound escaping in a wheeze of breath and the exertion taking its toll on her lungs. The effort was really screwing with her asthma.

"*Bloody hell!*" the already-sodden cloth skidded across a patch of gore, leaving a dark slug trail through it as she pitched forward under her own weight, striking her elbow against the floor, her mouth mashing against the meat of her forearm as her face followed forward. "Shit, that *hurt*," she spat, throwing the cloth to one side. It landed in a red, soiled heap with a wet slap against the linoleum. Grimacing she wiped at her face with her clean hand, a crimson smear lifting away on her fingers as they rubbed at her now-tingling lips.

Jesus, how could there be so *much* of it? The sod was probably lying dead in the back lane by now, he had to be surely, bleeding to death like some pale ghost. It was little wonder he had ended up so damned thin, spewing up all over the place like that. There was a sharp pain in her elbow where the bone had struck against the floor. She rubbed at it, trying to take the sting out of the grazed skin, wincing as her coarse fingers kneaded the uneven, raw flesh. Her fingers came away with a slick, oily sound, lifting away a glistening trail of red with them. She wrinkled her nose in disgust as she realised that she had planted her forearm into the bloody puddle as she had tried to keep her balance. She just hoped the dirty bugger didn't have anything that was catching. The slightly bitter taste playing about her lips reminded her that she had been lucky not to get a good old mouthful of the stuff, too.

"Dirty sod, he could've at least tried to make it to the bog instead of throwing up all over my floor," she muttered under her breath, her voice hoarse and ragged. "He needs to be told to stay the hell away from here if he's going to make a habit of *that*. Ill or not, that's just *rotten*. I'll make sure that Rosa knows about it too, if I ever see her again. She's probably upped and left him for good anyway, I wouldn't be surprised." She could do without the grief, already feeling under the weather. She hadn't felt too well for a little while in fact, a light throbbing in her head matched by a gurgling in her belly, as if she was on the verge of being sick herself. She rubbed a hand across the loose folds of her smock that covered her abdomen, trying to knead away the low rumble with her thick, stumpy fingers, the fabric catching against the raised welts of old cigarette burns above her hip, reminders of her past that refused to simply just fade.

There was a faint buzzing sound somewhere just next to her left ear, so slight that at first, she almost mistook it for another one of those damn headaches she always got when some stupid customer got her riled up. The fly circled around into her field of vision, settling down into the sticky pool in front of her. A greedy, bloated thing, it stayed there for a few seconds before taking off once again, resting right on her fat bottom lip.

"Ughh! You dirty *bastard!*" She swatted at it with her meaty hand, streaking more of that thick, almost gelatinous blood across her face as she did so. The droning noise choked off as it fell back down into the sticky puddle, spindly legs kicking and jerking to a standstill.

"That'll teach *you*, you *twat!*"

She settled back onto her haunches, the heels of her trainers making large dimples in the cheeks of her backside. Flinging the cloth to the floor again with a wet thud of defeat, she figured that she had better get herself cleaned up, as well as fetch a mop, before anyone felt brave enough to return. As she stood, she groaned as there was a creaking of the bones in her lower back. A quick wash of her hands and face would have to do. It'd be more than good enough for the customers, she could get a proper shower when she was done for the day, anyone who didn't like the smell of her could just go and piss off elsewhere. They'd be doing her a favour anyway.

Still mumbling curses to everyone and everything under her breath, she dragged her weak leg as she shuffled back towards the kitchen.

FOURTEEN

"You know, Frank, usually when a bloke asks a lady friend over to his place for the evening, it involves a nice meal or something. At *least* some decent drink, not this greasy, ordered-in slop and a can of supermarket brand cider. Why *did* you even ask me over here, anyway?"

"Maybe it's 'cause I was interested in hearing how you would define a *lady*."

"Fuck you. *There*, was *that* ladylike enough for you?"

One thing that had always been true about Kim Dzanic, for as long as Frank had known her; she wasn't shy when it came to speaking her mind. The two of them went a long way back, and not without good reason. Both of their parents had been first generation immigrants, Frank's from Poland and hers from Ukraine, or somewhere around there, at least. From the moment they had first met - the less said about *that* the better - they had always just seemed to *get* each other somehow, Kim being one of the few people who actually understood him and was still capable of getting along with him, in spite of his many faults. She had always known better than to put up with any of his bullshit, and she wasn't afraid to tell him so.

"You know," Frank said, trying to keep a straight face, "I *have* been clear for a couple of weeks now, tested properly, swabs up the pisshole and *everything*," he flashed her a knowing wink, just about managing to keep from laughing at the look of distaste that crossed her face. "Anyway, I always thought takeaway pizza was a known aphrodisiac. It usually works."

"Shut the hell up, Frank," Kim picked a piece of stringy mozzarella from her pepperoni slice and flicked it at him with her fingertip. "You know that if you were the last man alive, I'd rather stitch myself back up."

He wrinkled his nose. "That's an image that I'd rather not see in my head, at least not when I'm eating from a tray of kebab meat." He prodded the greasy mutton strips in the foil tray as he spoke, and she broke a smile.

"It sounds like I just out-grossed Franklin Popovich, that's got to count for something," she said, sounding pleased with the result. She raised a slice of pizza to her mouth and bit into it, cheese stretching free and falling down her chin in thick strings as she pulled it away. "Really though, why *did* you ask me over?"

"Oh, you know, just for a chat. A bit of a catch up."

"Bollocks," her voice sounded garbled, making its way through a mouthful of sloppy pizza mush. "The fact that you even called me in the first place is weird enough. I always thought that you had an allergy to telephones, anyway."

"Let me ask you something," Frank ignored the comment as he pushed his aluminium tray to one side for a moment. "Your parents are Ukrainian, right?"

"Moldovan, actually."

"Okay, whatever. Where did they get the name *Kim* from?"

Kim raised an eyebrow, throwing a chunk of pizza crust onto the paper plate in front of her. "They didn't, I was Karl to start with, remember? It wasn't until I got to my teens, you know when I started to realise just why things didn't feel right, I picked the name for myself."

"Why?"

"When we first emigrated here," she leaned back, as though readying herself to tell a story. "The three of us lived in this tiny, cramped place, not much more than a bedsit. Even back then, I didn't have much to do with them. It was," she paused, trying to think of the best way of saying what was on her mind. "It was like they didn't *like* me somehow, as though they thought there was something wrong with me." Instinctively, Frank reached out a hand in comfort. "*No, don't*," she said, "I'm okay with it. Seriously, I've had long enough to get used to the idea. Anyway, I spent most of the time huddled in front of an old portable television set, the damn thing could only get two channels, and one of them showed *Diff'rent Strokes* every fucking day." Frank let out a raspy chuckle, knowing what was coming next. "The girl in it was called Kimberley" she continued. "You know, the one who turned out to be a junkie in real life?"

"Dana Plato?"

"Yeah, that's her. Anyway, I shortened it to Kim. I thought that it sounded a bit more, I don't know, unisex, maybe." She picked up another slice of pizza between thumb and forefinger. "Way preferable to Karla, too, sounds a bit too much like something out of an old horror movie Kind of like *Karloff*. Anyway, that's me, what's your excuse, *Franklin Arno Popovich?*"

"No real reason," Frank coughed. "It was just the closest that my – probably drug addled at the time – imagination could get to sounding a bit more English."

"I suppose that explains why you've adopted the local accent, too," Kim smiled. "At least I haven't given up on my roots, you traitor."

Frank laughed this time. "Fair play, although it probably makes me a tiny bit less likely to be beaten up in the street, you know, not sounding like one of those *bloody foreigners*."

"Now that we've gotten the harmless, ice-breaking banter out of the way," Kim leaned forward, resting her hands against her thighs, "what did you *really* want to get off your chest?"

"Seriously?" he stroked his chin, feeling the tips of his fingers scrape against several days' growth of stubble.

"*Seriously.*"

"I think I've got a bit of a problem."

"I've told you before Frank, there are special doctors you can go and see for that sort of thing," she chuckled as she picked up her can of cider and held it up to her mouth, pausing to hear where he was taking the conversation.

"A problem with a story I've been working on. I said I was going to try and be serious, *remember?*"

"Sorry," she took a mouthful of drink before she could think of any further comeback.

Frank paused and looked up at the ceiling, thinking of the best way to explain what had been going through his head for the last few days.

"I've been trying to put something together for a couple of weeks now. Do you recall seeing any mention in the news recently about a guy called William Marks?"

"Marks? Nope. Why - *should* I have?" Kim grunted, her voice muffled through another mouthful of pizza.

"Not really, I suppose. I didn't expect you to say yes, for the simple reason that neither has anyone else as far as I can gather. Which has been pissing me off, if I'm being honest with you."

"Why?" she asked again. "Who is he? Some dodgy friend of yours that I don't know about?"

"*Was*, past tense, who *was* he." Frank corrected her, reaching for another piece of kebab meat and shoving it into his mouth, seeing Kim grimace as he wiped his greasy fingers down the side of his shirt. "No, I didn't know the guy myself, but I do know that he died a few weeks ago now. I've been looking into how it happened, but I haven't been having much luck. It's almost like he never even existed to start with, and that makes me curious. He had a flat over in The Reds. The place was a dump from the look of it."

"Well, there's your answer right there, isn't it? You know what the deal is with those places. No one gives a toss about them, they never have." She raised her hand up to her mouth and tried to mask a belch, Frank wrinkling his nose as the stale smell of cider and pepperoni wafted towards him. "I don't get why you're so interested though. I certainly don't understand why it would get under your skin at all. Christ Frank, you know the way things are around this place."

"Yeah, I do, that doesn't mean I should just turn a blind eye to it though. I'm sick of people doing that, it's about time they were made to take notice."

"Get you, you social justice warrior," she raised her can for another drink. "It sounds like your mind's pretty made up, so what does any of this actually have to do with me?"

"Well," Frank hesitated, still wary of sharing what little he actually knew, recalling what he had seen in those grainy, postmortem-like photos. "I've seen...something, probably to do with how William Marks died. It wasn't too pretty." Kim narrowed her eyes, usually a sign that her attention had been caught.

"What do you mean?"

"Let's just say that someone obviously knows that I'm looking for leads," he continued. "A few days ago, there was an envelope shoved through my front door. It had some photos of Marks, taken after he died."

"Like mortuary photos?"

"No, like taken pretty soon after he died, in the comfort of what looked like his own bathroom."

"That sounds pretty nasty," her voice dropped almost to a whisper. "Was it *bad*?"

"Jesus, Kim, what kind of question is *that*?"

"Sorry," another bite of pizza. "I was just asking."

"If you think that a dead guy lying in a pool of his own excrement in a dirty little flat is bad, then yes, I suppose it is. It gets worse though."

"How much worse?" the expression on her face suggested that she suddenly wasn't so sure that she wanted to hear the answer.

"From what I could see of him, he looked as though he hadn't eaten properly in weeks. He was wasted away, almost to skin and bones." Frank paused again, still able to see those pictures in his head, the sort of thing that couldn't be unseen. "His arms were bare and were chunks missing from both of them. Bite marks." Seeing the look of shock forming on her face, he reached for another strip of meat, cramming it in his mouth and chewing it loudly.

"Do you think...?"

"That he was starving to death in his own home?" Frank bit down on a mouthful of mutton. "That he was too weak to do anything about it and, as a desperate last resort, he bit chunks out of his own arms to try and stay alive? Yeah, that's what I think. I could show you the pictures if you like-"

"No, that's fine - thanks," she mumbled, pushing the remaining slices of her pizza to one side, her face a little paler than usual. "So you think you know how he died, what has it actually got to do with you? I still don't get that part, never mind what it has to do with *me*."

"I want to write about it," he said, his voice louder and more confident than usual. "It's something that I *need* to do. I reckon there's enough for the basis of an article at least," he spoke through another mouthful of meat, trying not to dribble mutton fat down his chin. Unlike Kim, he'd already had a few days to come to terms with the imagery without it spoiling his appetite. Besides it was the first he'd eaten all day and, at seven quid fifty, he didn't want to waste it. "Possibly a whole series of them. It could be a chance to highlight the problems in the area, hell, in the city as a whole. You know, call out the sort of people who like to bang on about how good it all is, while pretending all the shit doesn't happen, not to people that matter, anyway."

"You and your sudden fit of righteous indignation," Kim tried to laugh, the effort coming off as a little too thin and hollow sounding.

"It's always been there Kim, I'm just usually pretty good at keeping it hidden away beneath several layers of sarcasm and a general air of depravity."

"Your problem, *Franklin*, is that you're a good person, trying far too hard to be a bad one."

"That's because it's usually just much easier to be disliked," he raised a hand to his face as a mouthful of chewed-up kebab meat threatened to slop its way back out onto the table. "Expectation is never a good thing, I prefer for people to keep theirs low as far as I'm concerned."

"You just be careful you don't piss the wrong people off, yeah?"

"Since when has *that* bothered me in the past?"

"Point taken," she nodded, glancing across at the remaining pizza slices with needy indecision.

After a couple of minutes of stilted silence, Kim broke a smile, grabbing at her hips with both hands as she did so.

"Well, I suppose it's helped *me* anyway. I could do with losing a spare few pounds around the middle myself. That story of yours is the kind of thing that could scare me into doing something about it."

"Shut up," Frank snorted. "There's nothing wrong with you."

"Nothing that a few less takeaways and cans of booze won't fix," she said. "Don't worry, I'm not really about to starve myself, or get so bad that I need to chew holes in myself. Anyway," she reclined back in the chair and arched her back in a stretch, the movement forcing another loud belch. "Now you've gotten that off your chest, what's next?"

"There's one more thing," Frank said, still sounding far more serious than Kim was used to hearing. "There was a notebook in the envelope with the pictures."

"A notebook? What, was he writing down ideas for a novel or something?"

"Not exactly," Frank glanced across at the tray of meat, deciding against eating any more. "It was like he was keeping a diary or something. Recording the results of an experiment of some sort."

"An *experiment*? What kind of an experiment?" Kim leaned forward again.

"That's what I'm not sure about and it's been bugging the hell out of me. It was something to do with his weight, from the look of it. He was keeping a record of every single thing that he'd eaten, how much weight he had lost, that sort of thing."

Frank hesitated before speaking, as though he was still trying to piece together how what he was saying out loud to Kim tied into what he already knew.

"You mean like a clinical trial, or something like that?"

"No, not that I can see, and that's the funny thing," Frank's voice was almost a mumble now, as though he was weighing things up. "I asked Bob to take a quick look into it for me, and he hasn't been able to find any record of any clinical trials taking place, certainly not for diet pills or anything like that, anyway."

"Bob," Kim sneered, the tone of her voice not going unnoticed. "You know I wouldn't trust that Geordie cunt as far as I could throw him."

"He's still pretty good at what he does, Kim-"

"Once a prick, *always* a prick though," she waved her hand in dismissal. Still, can you imagine if your Marks bloke *was* involved in some sort of secret drug trial? *That* would be a story right there."

"No, I can't really see that being the case, Kim. I mean really, can you imagine what would happen if the bloke took some sort of tablet that made him chew his own arms off?"

"*But that's exactly what you're saying he did!*"

"Yeah, but it's the reason why that I can't get a handle on. *Why* would someone willfully get himself into that sort of a situation?"

"You don't know too many scientists, do you Frank?" Kim reached forward for her can, shaking it in her hand. "I'm out of cider by the way."

"Sorry, I only bought two. I'm still a cheapskate."

"Some things never change," she grunted, crumpling the can in her hand before setting it down on the table. "So, what now?"

"Well, I've got no immediate plans, unless you want to come through into the bedroom for a quick shag?"

"You're kidding, right?" she raised an eyebrow, glaring at him.

"Yeah, of course. I mean yes, really. *Honest.*" Frank cleared his throat. "Although, my wanking hand *has* been a bit achy for a couple of days now." Kim poked out her tongue, extending a middle finger in his direction as she did so.

"Well, if that's a *no*, then I'm going to just have to figure out how I'm going to dig out more information on some guy that the local press managed to reduce to a two-inch sidebar. I was kind of hoping that you might have some suggestions."

"So, you got me around here to wine and dine me with the best cuisine in the city, then to join in a brainstorming session? Great."

"Of course, the bedroom is just through there, if you'd rather reconsider offer number one?"

Kim leaned back in her seat with a sigh, not even wanting to go there, even though she knew he wasn't serious. Probably not, at least. "Okay, you need a sounding board, right? A bit like the old days," she raised a hand to her mouth to stifle another belch, Frank grinning in mock approval. "Okay you prick, what have you got so far?"

FIFTEEN

"I'd like four large trays of minced beef please, Huw. On second thoughts, you'd better make that five. I should be able to stretch them out a couple more days with any luck."

"Five? Large?"

"Yes please, five," she repeated, speaking the words clearly, as if he had suddenly been stricken with selective hearing. *You deaf cunt*, she thought to herself.

Hubert Danvers, or *Huw* as he was usually known, had been a butcher for almost as long as he had been able to hold a cleaver in his left hand. He had been cursed with fat, stump-like fingers of the sort that were no use for any musical instrument that he could think of, no good for holding a paintbrush, or anything similar for that matter. In his earlier years, it had even proven difficult for him to grip a pen or pencil, instead giving him a clumsiness that had made itself obvious to both him and everyone else around him a long time ago. *Club Fingers*, the other kids at school had called him, laughing right into his face as he struggled with so many things that they did as part of a normal day. *Dippy Danvers*, they would say, singling him out for his perceived slowness in learning to write, a situation not helped by a succession of unsympathetic teachers, eager to belittle him in front of the other kids, berating him for the incorrect way that his fat fingers curled around the slender barrel of his pen. Such comments only justified to the other kids, their belief that he was a freak of some sort, an oddity to be singled out and laughed at whenever someone decided that a joke was needed to lighten the tone. They all taught him, from an early age, that the best company was his own. The sign above the front door of his shop read *H Danvers and Son*, but he had no children of his own, no one to share in the business that he managed to keep running quite nicely. No, the place had once belonged to his old man, Huw Senior, having been passed down from father to son like some solemn gift, a birth right to which *Huw the Younger* had been entitled just as soon as he came of age.

He had given up on the idea of doing anything different with his life a long time ago. His parents had moved to the city from their native Welsh village before he had even been born, or so he had frequently been told growing up. So it was that life in the smog-ridden, overcrowded place was all that he knew, in pretty much the same way as he had long since accepted that he was good for little other than a job in butchery, having been exposed to it for so long that it *was* his whole life. At least he could finally claim to be good at something.

"Real working folk like their beef," old man had always made sure to impress upon his son from an early age. "They can't be doing with any of that, new-age salad and *cooscoos* stuff, or whatever it is those sissy boy hippies call it." He would spin his stories about how important the carnivore way of life really was, his favourite time for doing so being whilst he was poised above some fresh animal carcass, his cleaver newly-sharpened on the thick leather strop that hung close to the single door in and out of the back-room slaughterhouse. "Eating lettuce and cucumber didn't win any wars so far as I know, boyo, you just remember that. Ain't any sort of real heathy eatin' if you're askin' me, anyway. Bloody pasty-faced arseholes, most of 'em would blow away in a strong wind."

Huw would stand and watch wide-eyed, as his old man would raise the cleaver above his head, bringing it down over and over again, separating meat from bone and gristle in a way far more precise than it first appeared. He could still remember seeing the bone shrapnel pieces as they splintered and rained down on to the waxed wooden floorboards below. It was sometimes as though he enjoyed the work a little too much, as if he was venting a deep, hateful aggression against something that had no possible chance of fighting back. Huw's parents had separated by the time his third birthday came around and he soon learned that it was best not to ask too many questions about it. Not unless he wanted to see that cold, angry glint that appeared in his dad's eyes on the few occasions he had actually dared to mention his mother.

Days spent watching his dad swing the cleaver like he was taking aim at the head of someone with whom he was really annoyed had stayed with Huw long after his old man had kicked the bucket, passing the mantle down to him.

"Don't you be going and letting none of my regulars down, boyo," were pretty much the last words that Huw Senior said before he croaked. Huw the Younger had nodded like some wise old sage, fully intending to live his life by that instruction.

Betty MacKinnon had long been a familiar face at Huw's little shop. She had been buying from him ever since old George died. Huw liked to tell himself with some measure of pride that, in his own way, he was keeping the girl in business. He felt like he owed her that much. His dad and hers had gone way back after all, their regular poker nights something of which Huw Senior had often boasted back in the day.

Yeah, Huw was pretty used to the MacKinnons being around in one way or another. Their regular orders had been helping to keep the nearby folk in food for many a year. After all, it was true, those fancy modern salads sure didn't fill a belly too good. He had gotten to know a few vegetarians over the years, and most of them looked thin and pale, like they needed a couple of lamb chops down them and a few hours spent soaking up some actual sunlight. All of that aside though, he was pretty confident that he knew Betty and her meat buying habits pretty well, or so he had previously thought.

"*Five* trays?" he repeated a second time, still not quite sure that he had heard her correctly.

"Yes please, Huw, like I said. Unless that's a problem of course." One corner of her mouth twisted up into the smile that always ended up looking more like a grimace, something that she had always said was due to nerve damage, without ever elaborating any further. "Just make it the cheap stuff though. It's mainly for burgers, so it doesn't have to be too lean."

"No, no," Huw stuttered. "Of course it's not a problem, not at all, Betty. I'm just a little surprised, that's all. That's quite a lot of beef to get through." He tried to smile as he spoke, being careful not to show too much of his teeth. *Pyorrhoea*, the dentist had called it. An honest to God medical sounding name for why his breath smelled like a dog's rear end most mornings. "It's a little more than you usually buy. What, 'you gone and got through those four trays from last week already?" Huw remembered that just over a month ago, she had been on a real downer, talking about buying *less*, sounding bitter as she had complained about how business had been slowing right down, how she was sick of the whole thing anyway, and had been for a long time. She had seemed like she was just about ready to pack it all in at last.

"Yeah, well, things have been picking up pretty well lately, I don't know why but they have. I know the kids are back to school in a few weeks," she gave a sly smile. "It'd suit me just fine if the little bastards *stayed* there." Huw chuckled; typical Betty, making no secret of the fact that behind the tissue-thin front that she offered up for customers, she really had almost no patience for most people. She shifted her gaze away for just a moment as she spoke, looking as though she had dropped something on the floor, and Huw wondered if she was being completely honest, or if there was something she was keeping to herself. He dismissed the thought. He had known Betty for years, and she had no reason to lie to him or hide anything from him, he was sure. Besides, maybe she wanted to make a few more burgers than usual, so what? It was about time that business her old man had left her started to turn around a little. She certainly deserved it after all the grief the rotten old bugger had given her while he was still alive. Besides, at least she wasn't out buying lettuce and chickpeas to keep those politically correct whiners happy. He should have been grateful for *that*, at least.

"I'm sorry Betty," he said, "I really shouldn't be poking my nose in your business."

"Oh, don't worry, no offence taken, Huw," she smiled again, her expression a little more relaxed this time. "None at all." Her grin widened as she seemed to force out a chuckle. "I suppose it does show just how regular a customer I must be, for me upping my order to be noticed. You know, I've always admitted, to you at least, that I hate the place, I always have. But at least it pays the bills. It's a small step up from sleeping on the streets I suppose."

"Yes, it is that," Huw nodded. "It hasn't been your dad's for a long time, Betty. It's *your* place now, and you should remember that. Don't go letting his memory spoil things for you." He reached across the counter for a pile of large tin platters and a steel scoop, dragging a heavier tray from underneath the display counter, brimming with raw ground steak, the pink flesh glistening with an oily sheen in the fluorescent light from above.

"Anyway, that's five trays, coming right up." He dug the scoop into the contents of the large tray with a moist slurping noise, slopping load after load of raw meat into the platters with a loud slap. He liked to make sure that Betty always got her money's worth, more than aware of the way that some of his other customers had been known to have a joke at his expense, suggesting that he was sweet on the *grumpy diner woman*. Screw them, he couldn't care less what they thought. As long as the two of them were okay, that other stuff didn't matter at all.

He looked up from what he was doing, to see Betty wiping at the corner of her mouth with the back of her hand. For a moment he was sure he could see a silvery trail of saliva, trickling down her chin.

"Hey Betty, are you sure you're okay?" he asked, pausing. There was something in her eyes, a faraway look that he couldn't quite place. "You look like you're a million miles away. *Hey*, Betty?"

"I'm sorry Huw," she focused on him again, the distant expression clearing as suddenly as it had arrived. "I was just thinking of something, that's all. It's nothing for you to worry about." Her bottom lip trembled as she spoke, putting him off pushing things any further. He knew more than enough about her past to know that it was probably best that he didn't pry too much. Instead, he went back to filling the trays, making sure to add a bit extra, just for good measure.

"I'll have to stop by some time," he said, his voice sounding just a little too loud and hopeful. "You know, have one of your burgers. Good grief, it's been quite a while, hasn't it?" He smiled, forgetting his awkwardness for just a second until the bitter tang of his own breath reminded him. To his relief, she didn't seem to notice as he moved his free hand to the front of his mouth.

"It sure has," she nodded as he slid the filled platters across to her one at a time. "Yeah, why don't you do that? I'll fix you one up for sure. I might even make it extra-large."

"Are you okay to carry them back, or do you want me to fetch them over for you later?"

She smiled again, shaking her head, and Huw could see that when she did so, her face looked almost haggard. Her teeth looked longer somehow, as though the gums had drawn back from them. *She really ought to think about stopping by and seeing a doctor*, he thought. *She doesn't look too good.* He considered saying something, before hesitating again, as usual, worried that he would end up saying the wrong thing. Wrapping the last of the platters in its protective clear film, he pushed it alongside the others.

"Now you're *sure* you don't need a hand with these?" he asked again, just in case.

"No Huw, I'll be just fine, really," she dropped them, one at a time, into a large cloth bag that she had brought along with her, unconcerned by the possibility of them splitting or spilling. "I'd best be getting back now anyway. I've got stuff to do."

"Always the same, isn't it?"

"Always. I'll be seeing you around."

He waved after her. "I'll drop by in the next day or two, okay? That's a promise."

"You're welcome, any time," she said over her shoulder, without looking back. "I'll make sure that I fix you up something special." She flashed that drawn smile again and Huw tried not to look concerned.

Once she had left, he let out a sigh, trying not to wrinkle his nose at his own sour breath. To hell with what anyone else thought, but as far as Betty was concerned, her idea of *something special* and his were probably two completely different things. But he could always keep on hoping, damn it, so what if people thought he had a thing for her? Bloody well right he did, and he had for a long time, despite her sometimes-brash character that she had about her, as much as she tried to hide it from most people.

He hadn't wanted to say anything to her face, not wanting to mention anything that might cause any upset, but he still couldn't help but think that she didn't look very well. In fact, if anything, she looked pretty *unwell*, her usual full, just the right side of plump features looking pinched and drawn. It was almost as though she had been on a crash diet or something. It certainly seemed out of character for her. As long as Huw had known her, she had always seemed like the sort of person who couldn't care less what anyone thought of her, so the idea of her trying to lose weight didn't sit right somehow. He just hoped it was nothing too serious. God almighty, he knew that she'd had more than her share of her problems in the past, but she at least seemed like she had always managed to get through them. With any luck, she would go straight home, get some of that ground beef and fix up a bunch of those burgers of hers for herself. Huw smiled at the thought as he slid the large metal tray of ground beef back under the counter.

SIXTEEN

He sat on the edge of the folded-down sofa, still only half clothed. Kim had already slunk away shamefaced some half an hour earlier, mumbling something about *a bad idea* and *far too much to drink,* despite the fact that they hadn't actually done anything other than talk into the small hours, the discussion about William Marks eventually drifting into conversation about their past, as the bottle of bourbon from his writing desk had been cracked open and finished off. At any other time, he might have found her obvious discomfort funny, maybe even going so far as to try and lead her to thinking that perhaps they *had* gotten up to something. There was no time for that though, he had far more important things to think about. He looked over at his typewriter and cracked his knuckles, the joints flexing with a loud *pop*. He couldn't shake a thought that kept going around his head: What kind of person could William Marks be, that he would be so willing to keep a written record of whatever it was that was happening to him – whatever it was that was probably *killing* him? Not only that, but to see it through to its conclusion, without any sort of obvious contact with anyone. He walked across to the wall by the door, where he had stuck the photographs, each one held in place with a couple of pieces of Scotch tape right after Kim had left. There was an almost surreal quality to the images. He had seen death plenty of times before, it sometimes felt as though part of his job was to revel in the glorification of it. But whether it was the grainy, almost grindhouse appearance of the pictures or the knowledge he was starting to build about the story behind them, he felt a sour taste in his mouth when he looked at them. He would have torn them down and stuffed them in the bin, were it not for the fact that he needed them there, an aid to keep himself focused on what he needed to do; to find the truth and put it out there for others to see. His instinct for the seamier side of things giving him reason to think that there probably *were* more people involved.

Which meant, of course, that there was still plenty of time for things to get much worse.

SEVENTEEN

Then, closer to the start:

James Hesketh felt nervous, the fine tremors in both of his hands a little more pronounced than usual, thanks to the neurological disorder that he had somehow gotten away without disclosing for the last six years. He thought of the oath that he had sworn, back in the days when he was much younger, much more idealistic.

Back in the days when he still gave a damn.

It was only eleven-thirty in the morning, and he had already ignored two potentially-threatening telephone calls, as well as a plain envelope that had made its way through his letterbox, only to be shunted onto the growing pile of final demands. All of that had happened before he had even left his own home. Things showed no sign of improving any time soon.

He sat in the overstuffed, faux leather chair with his hands gripping at the armrests just enough to make his knuckles turn pale. For the few days previous he had turned things over and over in his head, thinking up so many smart things to say and so many smart ways to say them. Of course, all that cleverness evaporated away just as soon as he had taken his seat in the near-empty pub. Instead, he just sat in place, timid, as if all he was missing was a begging bowl placed on the table in front of him. It probably wasn't the best place to hold any sort of a meeting, but then again, since he couldn't help but shake the feeling that he was about to get himself into a whole load of trouble, then it was perhaps a little more appropriate. Besides, beggars like him couldn't really be choosers.

Just think of the money, he reminded himself yet again.

"I'm going to go out in a limb and guess that this seat isn't taken? Doctor Hesketh, I take it? I'm Benjamin Steele, you've been waiting for me," the line was delivered as a statement rather than a question.

Steele was more or less exactly as Hesketh had expected. On first impression, he looked like a person who belonged to a certain group, of whom Hesketh had always taught himself to be wary. Dressed in a pale grey suit and lilac shirt, unbuttoned at the neck, he was just a little bit too tanned, his teeth so white as to have an almost blue sheen. All manicure and glossy, over-oiled black hair, he just looked like the sort of man who could talk his way out of almost any hole. Or perhaps talk someone else *into* one.

"Umm, no, I mean yes, please sit down," Hesketh waved his hand, trying to feign control of the situation, not really sure why he was even bothering to do so. "I've been going over things in my head, about what you said previously, and I still don't understand what it is you could possibly need my help with-"

"It's a bad habit, to give too much consideration to things, really, it is. Trust me." Steele scraped out the facing stool from its position and sat down, hitching his expensive-looking trousers as he did so. He spread his arms out with his palms upward, like he just wanted nothing more than to be everyone's best friend, flashing those stupidly blue-white teeth of his in a fixed grin as he did so. "In simplest terms, my people need your help, and you need money, am I right?" Hesketh averted his gaze. Steele, or perhaps whoever it was that he worked for, had obviously done their homework before looking him up in the first place. They knew a lot more about his financial difficulties than he was really comfortable with. Once armed with that knowledge, it was easy for them to dangle a big enough carrot in front of him, and he had known from the start that he was in no position to turn down whatever it was that they wanted. Admitting as much still gave Hesketh a lump in the back of his throat that refused to shift. It didn't help that, in the absence of knowledge, his imagination had been allowed free reign to dream up all manner of situations for which he might be required. None of them were good.

"Oh, there have *definitely* been things to consider," Hesketh coughed, aware that his attempt to come off as assertive probably wouldn't even register with the man sitting within touching distance at the other side of the small table. "It's a worrying thing to a man of my profession, when a stranger gets in touch to say that they need my help, and they can make it worth my while. It's even more worrying when that stranger then starts to rattle off a list of my own problems, promising that they can make them go away."

"Already, I can tell that you worry far too much James. I *can* call you James, can't I?" Steele spoke the words in a way that suggested he would continue to do so, regardless of Hesketh's reply.

"I'm a *doctor*. People with problems usually have them dealt with in my surgery, during normal hours, not in some pokey pub before midday."

"James," Steele snorted, grinning again. "Do I *look* ill to you? Seriously?" He leaned forward, with that smile still on his face as though it had been carved in place. There was something about him that Hesketh had immediately taken a dislike to. Perhaps it was the cloying odour of his cologne, the almost mahogany darkness of his sunbed-enhanced tan, or the oily sheen of his dark, slicked-back hair that was just a little *too* glossy. "I'll be honest with you James, as far as profession is concerned, I'm probably more of a salesman than a scientist. Hell, I barely scraped my way through all of that stuffy, white coat rubbish. But I've always been able to talk my way through life pretty damn easily and I know how to fix things. You know, you scratch my back, and all that."

"What makes you think I've got anything that needs fixing?" Hesketh knew that he couldn't bluff his way out of it, but still, he tried anyway.

"I'm not stupid," Steele shrugged his shoulders, as if he was stating the obvious. "Neither are the people that I work for. They already know more than enough about you. Certainly enough for me to know that you *will* co-operate with whatever I say."

"Co-operate with *what* exactly?"

"Ah, finally, we're getting somewhere," Steele raised his hand. "Barman, two glasses of scotch over here when you're ready." Hesketh shook his head. "Sorry, make that one. Apparently, my friend here isn't drinking right now." He leaned forward again, folding his arms across the table in front of him. His breath had a garlic taint to it, which mingled with the aftershave to form a sickly odour from which Hesketh wanted to recoil. "You *are* my friend, aren't you James? You know what's on the table. We know just how desperate you were. How desperate you still are, for that matter. A demanding ex-wife, maintenance payments, and the slight problem of a gambling debt hanging over your head," Hesketh felt the blood drain from his face, along with a sudden sensation of lightness in his head. "All of which mean you have a price. A price that my clients are more than willing to pay. But there are a few conditions. You're an intelligent man, I'm sure you could make an educated guess at them if you really wanted."

"*Conditions,*" Hesketh cleared his throat, his voice turning hoarse. "Oh yes, I think I can imagine."

"Good. There is a patient registered to your practice who you last saw a couple of weeks ago. An expatriate, goes by the name of William Marks. He came to see you for an illness, I believe."

"I can't comment on tha-"

"Don't try and fob me off with your patient confidentiality. I *know* you saw him, and that he was ill. I would greatly appreciate it if you could tell me the nature of his illness."

"I really shouldn't," Hesketh felt a prickling sensation at the back of his neck, sweat springing up beneath his shirt collar.

"No. Trust me, you really should," Steele smiled still, but with a glint in his eyes that suggested a cold determination. "Let me make this easy for you. You can co-operate and be rewarded, or you can try and be stubborn, in which case I can have you taken around the back of this building and have the shit beaten out of you until you tell me what I want to know for free."

"Headaches," Hesketh stammered, nodding as he did so. "Headaches and frequent nosebleeds."

"Loss of appetite?"

"No, the opposite in fact. He complained of gnawing hunger pangs, with stomach pains if he went without food for more than a few hours." Hesketh reached his forefinger to his throat and loosened away his tie. "Why are you asking about him anyway?"

"My clients are worried. Herr Marks has *given* them reason to *be* worried, shall we say."

"Why?"

Steele raised a forefinger to the side of his nose and tapped it, tutting as he did so. "Don't ask too many questions. It doesn't become you." Hesketh nodded his understanding and Steele continued. "Suffice to say that our mutual acquaintance Herr Marks was one of a select few helping my clients with a, shall we say, confidential study." Steele raised his glass and took a mouthful of scotch, wincing as the drink burned its way down his throat. "His illness can perhaps be best summed up as a case of what becomes of the over-zealous. It's a shame really. Marks was quite the prominent scientist in his homeland, and his assistance so far has been greatly appreciated."

"So, what about him? Where do I come into this?"

"It's simple really. We have reason to believe that sooner or later, some curiosity might result from mister Marks' symptoms, whether or not they improve. The sort of curiosity that my clients can well do without."

"Again, where do I come into it?"

"Denial. *Full* denial. If anyone asks you anything, I mean *anything*, about William Marks, you deny all knowledge. You act like he never even existed."

"That's *all* I have to do?"

Steele shrugged again, his smile returning. "That's all. In return, we can keep our end of the bargain, make your problems go away, just like we promised. I'm not even asking you to lie, just to keep whatever little you *do* know to yourself. Hell, you'll be happy, we'll be happy. Everyone will be happy, so you can continue to leave your conscience at the door."

"I'm still not comfortable with it, not fully," Hesketh shifted nervously in his chair. Marks was still fresh in his mind. He could still remember him showing up at the surgery, just a couple of weeks ago. He had looked at death's door, little more than a delirious mess of skin and bone. Hesketh had wanted to refer him elsewhere there and then, but the man had struggled to his senses for long enough to refuse. *I won't see any sort of specialist*, he had insisted in a thick German accent, *if you send me, then I won't go, it's that simple.* Against his better judgement, Hesketh had ushered the man from his consultation room, clapping a hand across his shoulders and trying not to wince as he felt what might as well have been bare bone beneath the loose-fitting clothing. Doing so had made his stomach turn, losing him several nights of sleep in the process.

"Then I suggest you'd better *get* comfortable with it. Fast." Steele glared as his voice hardened, his smile thinning for the first time. "Look, you would probably fare a lot better if you stopped pretending that you're still in any position to give a damn." He was right and Hesketh knew it. That was the worst thing about the whole set-up: he couldn't *afford* to care. "William Marks is nobody, just another face in the crowd. We - *you* - need to make damned sure he stays that way," Steele's voice grew louder again, as if his sudden menacing outburst had never actually happened. The pub was almost empty, save for the token few old drunks propping up the bar at the far end, but it wouldn't have made a difference if the place was heaving, Steele no longer seemed to care who heard him. "The only way we're going to be able to do that is if we pull together, like a team should do. Everyone needs to play their part." He clapped his hands together, the rings on each clattering together as he made his point with a flourish.

"So, what if someone *does* start sniffing around?" Hesketh felt nervous again, almost confused by the sudden switch back and forth in character.

"It's easy," Steele laughed, his eyes narrowing, as if he thought the doctor must be stupid to even ask such a question. "You lie. You're a clever man, you should be able to manage that."

"*Lie?*"

"You're starting to ask too many questions, Jim - you don't mind if I call you *Jim*, do you? No, of course you don't. Look," Steele rolled his eyes, as if about to explain something straightforward to a child. "Your part in this is really easy. All you need to do is deny that you've even heard of Marks. You do that and you'll get paid. You *don't* do it and," he didn't finish the sentence, guessing that he wouldn't have to. Hesketh looked down at his hands, his thin fingers knotted together on the table the only thing keeping them from trembling again. He thought of his ex-wife, living it up with her new man, a lifestyle part-funded with money that should have rightfully been *his*. If it wasn't for her then he probably wouldn't have even agreed to meet this stranger who knew so much about him in the first place. He could almost feel a cold sensation knotting somewhere in his chest, icy vines radiating out from a small central point.

"We know more than enough about you to know that you can't afford to have reservations. Your problems can all be over, just as long as you take the money and keep your mouth shut. Now," Steele leaned forward, that same smug grin returning to his face. "Yes or no, do we have a deal?"

Hesketh looked down at the drink-stained dark floorboards, then back up again, his eyes narrowing as he felt his gaze harden. Steele was right, he had already fallen too far into the rabbit hole. He had almost nothing left to lose, thanks to his bitch of an ex-wife. Steele, or whoever he worked for, was at least offering a way out, whether it was legitimate or not. He was right, it was time to forget his conscience, and look after number one. Hesketh took a deep breath and held out his hand.

"Yes," he said, his voice sounding to him like something alien, as if it was coming from someone else, someone who had given up caring a long time ago. "Yes, you've got yourself a deal. If anyone asks, I'll make sure that I keep my mouth shut."

"Good man," Steele held out his hand and, after one last, brief hesitation, Hesketh took it. "I have every faith that you will. You won't regret it, doctor, trust me."

***

He splashed another handful of cold water into his face, his vision swimming as he did so. It dropped from his chin, soaking his shirt, not that he either cared or noticed. He clung to the metal rim of the sink for support, like he had for the last ten minutes since Steele had left him alone, even dropping a crisp five pound note on the table in front of him, *just in case he changed his mind about that whisky.*

He had been a doctor for almost twenty-eight years, in that time always doing his best to uphold the promise that he had made; to protect people, to do whatever was in their best interests.

So much had gone wrong since then. So very much.

He looked at his own reflection as he splashed his face again, doing so making his eyes burn this time, blurring his vision until it felt as though he couldn't even recognise himself anymore.

He shook his head, trying to focus, to tell himself that it was no big deal. He wasn't actually being asked to lie, or to hurt anyone. Just to keep his quiet, something that couldn't be too difficult, surely. No, he was being dug out of an almighty hole, and all he had to do was deny any knowledge of someone who had, the last time he had seen him, hardly seemed of sound enough mind to protest otherwise. It wasn't all that dissimilar to patient confidentiality anyway.

Who the hell are you trying to kid? An innocent man staggers into your practice looking like a warmed-up corpse and someone wants you offer you hush money to act as though he never even existed? That all but suggests that they're in on something not strictly legitimate somehow. Keeping silent about it makes you *just as guilty.*

He tried to ignore the voice of his conscience, to push it to the back of his mind, like the pathetic, dwindling thing that it really was.

Marks was nothing to him, not really. There was no reason why feigning ignorance should lose him any sleep, not if it meant his difficulties could be made to end. Really, what was the worst thing that could happen?

EIGHTEEN

Huw Danvers Junior tugged at the back of his collar with his forefinger, the movement causing a bead of sweat to trickle its way down the nape of his neck and run into the small of his back. The feel of it gave the sensation of a brief shudder along his spine. He had already popped the top two buttons of his new shirt, doing so making no real difference to what was going on inside his head.

"Dress like you're out to win," his old dad had always said, words that he had tried to live by himself before the ink had even finished drying on the divorce papers. "Ladies try to act like they don't care, but they still love that little bit of extra effort. Sure, all those layabouts with uncut hair and stubble, t-shirts and baggy jeans might think they look cool, but really, they just look scruffy. Trust me son, any woman that's even worth paying any attention to hates that whole slovenly attitude. Go out there like you want to win and you will, I promise." Huw could almost picture the old man, dressed to the nines in his best cut shirt, the one with the matching tie and handkerchief. Reeking of *Brüt* aftershave, his balding head gleaming in the light as though he'd gone and had it specially waxed for some occasion, he would frequently go out for the night dressed like he was himself up for a big score. On many an occasion, Huw had lain in his bed awake until the early hours of the morning, the dawn creeping against his bedroom curtains as the old man fumbled his key into the lock before staggering in through the front door, sometimes alone, sometimes with company. Huw had soon learned the signs. On those occasions when Huw Senior's slurred voice was accompanied by the higher-pitched tones of one of many lady friends, that meant it was time for young Huw to bury his head beneath his pillow for an hour or so, to drown out the noise that was sure to follow. The cloying, suffocating warmth was preferable to the sounds of the drunken fumblings of his father and whichever half-his-age tart he had thrown enough money at to actually entertain the thought of being with him. That was what it all boiled down to, however much his dad might have put his success down to charm and looks.

He had always promised himself that he would do things differently. It hadn't been too difficult, most girls that he had met not even willing to look twice in the direction of that *club-fingered arsehole, Dippy Danvers*, with his not-quite-from-around-here accent, clumsy movement and his face peppered with just the wrong amount of acne. Not that Huw really cared, he told himself that he was just biding his time, waiting for the right girl.

He was waiting for Betty MacKinnon, he always had been.

He had never gotten around to telling her of course, not in so many words at least, he didn't quite know how to. Every time he thought of doing it, he saw the image in his head of his dad, his bald head shining like a searchlight in the darkness of the bedroom as he slobbered over some strange woman who he had probably thrown a week's earnings at just to let him put his cock somewhere warm for the night. The image was vivid enough to cause a strange, twisting sensation in the pit of Huw's belly, something that still stayed with him years later, a mixture of repulsion, arousal and envy. A man who took pride in his freedom since his venomous falling-out with his ex-wife, at least Huw Senior *found* somewhere to dip his wick from time to time, whether he had to all but pay someone for the privilege or not.

Huw mopped at his brow with a piece of tissue that he had kept balled up in his trouser pocket. His heart was racing, leaving him with a feeling of light-headedness. For quite a few years now he had admired Betty from afar, his knowledge of her past only endearing her to him even more. He had often dreamed of taking her under his wing, of being the experienced man of the world that he knew he could never really be, the one to tell her that everything was going to be okay. He was going to watch out for her, she wouldn't have to worry about anything ever again, no one else mattered. Of course, he knew that such a fantasy could never exist outside of his head. Because of course, that's what it was; a fantasy, nothing more than the hopeful meanderings of a lonely middle-aged man. If he even dared to suggest any idea of togetherness to Betty, she would probably tell him where to go, in her usual colourful way. Still, it didn't stop him from dreaming though. When she had first raised the idea of his inviting himself over for some of her cooking just over a week ago, he had never thought that anything might ever actually come of it. Nor had he thought that it might be at her flat, rather than the café. Yet here he now was, standing outside the front door of her seventh floor flat, wearing his only half-decent suit with his heart beating fast enough to make him dizzy, able to feel the palpitations through the thin cotton of his shirt.

He looked down at the bottle of wine that he had bought from Batra's Convenience Store right after he had shut up his own shop for the day. He had set it down with care on the seventies style, dark granite-look floor, worried that it might slip through his sweat-slicked fingers if he held onto it for too long. He tried to breathe just through his nose, the back of his mouth tasting bitter with his own pyorrhoea breath.

He was torn between the idea of scooping up the bottle and running back down all seven flights of stairs into the cooling rain outside, forgetting that he had even entertained the thought of a dinner date, or sticking it out and trying to follow through on something of which he had dreamed for so long. Neither option helped to ease the hollow feeling in his belly that matched the sensation in his head. He was just about to wipe at his forehead again with his ragged tissue, when there came the loud scrape of a lock being turned from the other side of the door. Too late, the decision had been made for him.

***

"Well, hello there, Huw. You came." *Wishful thinking*, he had thought, trying not to chuckle at his own wit as he considered the obvious double meaning.

Betty MacKinnon had been standing in the doorway, dressed in a flimsy blouse and loose-fitting trousers, the light from behind her picking out the shape of her figure through the thin material. It hadn't been her choice of clothing that surprised him, nor had it been her smile, something that, as he had lamented many times before, she rarely had on her face nowadays. It was just how different she had looked, how much she had changed. In the short time since had last spoken to her, she looked as though she must have lost even more weight than before. It was like she had literally melted away.

"See anything that you like?" She had said when she first answered the door, noticing the shocked look on his face that he hadn't even made an effort to try and hide, caught completely off-guard. "Calm yourself down Huw, it's okay," she looked at him in a way to suggest that she knew exactly what he was thinking, what he had been thinking for a long time. "Perhaps we should at least wait until we've eaten though," she had continued. "I don't know about you, but I'm *famished*. Come on in," she had tilted her head in the direction of the short hallway behind her as she invited him into the flat. "Come on, let's go get something to eat." Still without speaking, Huw nodded, trying not to appear too shocked as he stooped to pick up the bottle of wine from the floor, unable to take his eyes off her.

"You, umm, look *lovely*," still he had struggled to think of something smooth to say and found that he couldn't, falling back on probably the weakest line imaginable instead.

"Thanks," she had said simply, her voice different somehow, in a way that he couldn't quite figure out. "I've actually had this old blouse for ages, do you really like it?"

"Yes...yes, it really suits you. You look great in it," he had stammered, trying to ignore the unusual straining sensation at his crotch, a feeling that he wasn't used to. She had glanced down just long enough to notice, her usual lop-sided grin playing about her lips as if to add to the awkwardness he already felt.

"There'll be plenty of time for *that*," she had said. "Maybe. We'll eat first though." Still smiling, she had taken his outstretched hand in hers and led him inside. "Like I said already, I'm *starving*."

***

It didn't take long, little more than half an hour.

"I've changed my mind." the words had escaped in a smothered mumble, her lips pushed against his as she spoke. With one hand, Betty shoved his chest, pushing him backward onto the bed.

Huw felt the collar of his smartest shirt tighten around his neck, a vein somewhere in his temple suddenly throbbing with a rapid *put-put-put* sensation. Despite all of the secret hopes that he had clung to for such a long time, the images that he had kept inside his head every time he'd tugged on his own cock like a guilt-ridden adolescent, discovering himself in the privacy of his own bedroom, he could never have thought that everything would start to move along at such a sudden pace. She was right of course, he knew that he wanted it, that he wanted *her*, but now that the option was right there in front of him, he wasn't so sure anymore, what he had always thought of as readiness was now, in the moment when it probably mattered most, replaced by a hollow, weak indecision.

"*Are you sure?*" His voice sounded like little more than a whisper, panted out on shallow breaths of apprehension.

"I've never been more sure of *anything*," her own voice was as strong as always, but with something underlying it that he couldn't quite place, a fresh determination as she scrabbled at his belt buckle like a crazed thing, the zipper of his best trousers breaking as she tugged them apart. He raised his backside up from the bed, allowing her to hitch the waistband over his hips and down to his ankles. Reaching her fingers into the front slit of his boxer shorts, she pulled out his already semi-erect cock, gripping it firmly and moving her hand up and down the full length of the shaft, massaging him to hardness.

"How about that? Do you like me playing with you, Huw?" Her voice was low, almost commanding, carrying a confidence that he couldn't remember ever being there before. "*You. Huw.* It rhymes," she stifled a laugh that he barely noticed, focusing instead on the pulsing sensation building up along his swollen length. "Have you ever dreamed about this? About *me?*"

"*Mmm-hmmm*," he murmured, arching his lower back to meet her stroke, savouring the slow, rhythmic throbbing and the growing tightness.

"I bet you've dreamed about it a *lot*." She kept her grip firm, the movement of her hand slow and steady, until he wanted to raise himself up, to thrust himself faster to make the teasing end, but she kept her other hand firm on his belly, staying in control. He felt like he could release at a moment only of her choosing, sending a jet of his warm, pent-up spunk into her face with a geyser-like pressure.

"There. I'm getting bored with that now." She released her grip as she moved back, his penis falling back onto his belly with a disappointed slap, the head throbbing, so close to release, leaking out a thin, dewy trail. His teeth sunk into his bottom lip, almost feeling like he could cry at the sudden rejection. *That's it*, he thought, his mind a whirl, *she knows how I've always felt about her, and she's been tormenting me all along. Now she's going to kick me out and tell everyone what a gullible idiot I've been. God, I've been so soft in the head.*

"There, there," her voice soft, almost coy-sounding, she picked him up again, pressing her thumb just below the head of his cock, making gentle circles that teased him to a hardness that he had never thought possible. "I don't want to play anymore. Like I said, I'm *hungry*." Before he could react to her words, she leaned her head forward again and took his full length into her mouth, the swollen head of his cock rubbing against the soft, fleshy back of her throat. His head felt hot and light and his heart raced as he looked down again. He raised himself up on his elbows, just enough to see her head bobbing up and down at his crotch, her red hair standing out dark in the pale light from the window, the rain against the glass sounding like it could have been a million miles away. There was a new tightening in his balls that matched the sensation in his belly, a feeling that he had only ever known in his own most private moments up until now.

"*Betty...*" He gasped, his voice sounding weak and strangled, forced out on the quickening, shallow gasps of his breath.

"Oh, I almost forgot, I *hate* the taste of spunk," she pulled her head back, grinning up at him, her mouth a cruel, toothy slash standing out from the darkness. He gasped in frustration again, so close to climax.

"Please," he begged, "*please* Betty."

"Tell me it's what you've always wanted," her voice was still quiet, but with an underlying air of control. "Tell me what you want me to do."

"*Just don't stop,*" he almost whimpered, the waves of sensation slowing down once again. "*Please...*"

"Oh, go on then," that almost wicked smile never breaking, she plunged her head down once again, taking his full length almost down to the base this time, making a muffled gagging sound as he pushed against the roof of her mouth. He lay back, his eyes closed as the pressure built up again, ready to burst.

(*she's*)

Then, so suddenly that it didn't even consciously register

(*o my god she's*)

at first. A pain like nothing he had ever felt before. Like how it might have felt to have white hot needles rammed up into his abdomen

(*bitten me she's*)

making him feel sick, his stomach dropping away into a dark, bloody nothingness.

(*bitten me SHE'S BITTEN ME-*)

He tried to get up and found that he couldn't, the movement sending molten hot jolts through his entire body, an agony, the likes of which he had never thought possible. With a choked snort, she leaned back away from his crotch, her cheeks bloated out, as though she had just taken a mouthful of one of those burgers she had promised him. Blood pumped upward in a geyser from somewhere between his legs, hitting her square in the face. Laughing, she smeared it around, the dark, oily sheen of it standing out on her pallid face in a ghoulish contrast, like something out of a nightmare. Chewing several times, there was a crackling sound as her teeth went through gristle, the same sort of noise that he was used to hearing when he prepared lamb chops for his customers. She turned her head to one side, spitting the contents of her mouth onto the floor, before turning back to him.

"Sorry Huw, I know that it's rude to speak with your mouth full. But I told you already, I'm *famished*." Her voice soft and mocking, he could barely hear her over the sound of what he imagined to be his own screaming as he looked down at the meaty, chewed-up mush that remained of his penis. "Now, what's for dessert?" Smiling again, she ran her tongue down the inside of his bare thigh, her teeth glinting out of the bloody darkness like twin rows of pearls, and he was sure that he could see a line of saliva hanging down from her chin, the same as he was so sure he had seen that day in his shop. As his vision began to fog, the last thing he felt was her hungry mouth tearing at the thick meat of his leg, pulling at flesh, muscle and sinews, stripping all away from the bone. He thought of his dad, cleaver raised above his head, ready to prepare the cuts ready for display.

"Eating lettuce and cucumbers never won any wars, son," he said over and over again, accompanied by Betty's unhinged cackle, echoing on forever in the background.

***

Later, much later, she felt safe in the privacy of her own flat. No one around to judge her, no one to see.

Naked, she stood in front of the full-length mirror that hung on the door, her focus drifting as she looked herself up and down. Somewhere behind her, she could see what was left of Huw Danvers, still splayed out on the bed, a tangled mess of raw, bloody flesh. It was a shame, but a person had to *eat* after all. Besides, it wasn't about him, not any more. In fact, it probably never really had been. She found that if she allowed her vision to wander, he shifted out of focus, like the unimportant thing that he always had been. So, she did that, reducing him to little more than a bloody smear in the background.

Moving her attention back to herself, she studied herself in the mirror, her eyes lingering for a moment as she ran her fingers over her ribcage, her touch gossamer-light, drawing goosebumps from her pale skin. She had lost weight - a whole *lot* of weight - despite eating more than enough for a horse lately. Her breasts sagged and the flesh between her ribs was sunken, the jutting bones casting shadows in the soft light. Brad Whitman, it was probably all his

165

fault, spreading some disease or other around the place. She was pretty sure that something similar had happened to him, although she couldn't quite be certain, it seemed like ages ago now. Closing her eyes, she could almost hear Georgie MacKinnon's voice, as if the nasty old bastard was still alive and in the room with her.

Well look at you there, you've gone and actually gotten almost pretty, ain't you? You look almost exactly like your slut of a mother. In fact, with those old saggy tits of yours, you look almost fuckable - just as long as you put a paper bag over your head anyway. Although, I suppose you don't usually look up at the mantelpiece when you're poking the fireplace, do you?

She kept her eyes closed as she tried to screen out that mocking drone of his, her breaths deepening as she gave in to the sensation of need growing within her. With a deliberate slowness now - there was no rush - she moved her hands down to the wiry tangle of her pubic thatch, spreading her legs wider to allow easier access, eager to explore the moist warmth beyond. She let out a low moan as two of her fingers sunk their way into that wetness then withdrew, before plunging in deeper again, with a greater urgency this time. Her breaths hoarsened as she held herself open, with the fingers of one, three fingers of the other jabbing in and out of the wet opening with a growing rhythm, far better than any cock as she fingered herself towards a climax.

She didn't need anyone else, least of all *him*. They were all the same. Bastards, every last one of them. Only their faces were different, nothing else.

Every nerve of her body tingling with electric fire, she withdrew her slick fingers and placed them hungrily into her mouth, her tongue lapping at them as she suckled, tasting the bitter sweetness of herself on them. Slowly, she traced a line with her tongue from the fingers, across the palm of her hand and up, along the length of her forearm, tasting the salt of her perspiration.

For one brief second, her eyes flickered open for long enough to see Huw, his bloodied corpse sprawled across the bed, right where she had left him. The sight sent another ripple of pleasure coursing through her.

Jesus, she was just still so *hungry*.

***

"*Hey, you in there! 'You okay?*" In just over three years of living in the flat below the strange woman, Lukasz Balierski had only ever crossed paths with her a handful of times. As far as he knew, she ran a café or something like that, somewhere near the city centre. It was something that surprised him when he thought of how miserable she looked those few times they had actually passed each other on the stairs. It must have been great, being served a mug of coffee by someone with a face like a slapped arse, or whatever the popular English phrase was for such an ugly, miserable-looking person. On the plus side, at least she kept herself to herself, never even making herself heard when Lukasz and his girlfriend had one of their many *moments*. No, whatever she was called, she seemed to be someone who liked to keep herself to herself, thank God for small mercies.

Which had made the noises from the night before all the more unusual.

"*Hey!*" Balling his hand into a fist, he hammered on the door for the third time. "*Is everything okay in there lady?*" Lukasz' head felt like it had been inflated with helium. Any other time, three quarters of a bottle of vodka would have sent him nicely into a stupor. Yes, it would have, except for it sounding like the crazy lady on the floor above was having a full-blown orgy. The selfish bitch had kept him awake for half of the night, making the sort of noises usually reserved for porno movies. Add to that his girlfriend having the sheer nerve to blame *him* for drinking too much and there was little wonder he was so pissed off.

"*Hey!*" He yelled again. "Crazy woman! 'You awake in there or what?" Not only was she noisy and inconsiderate, now it seemed like she was deaf, too. She would probably be the first to complain if she had been kept awake by the sound of him and Paulina fucking each other for half the night.

"I don't want to come in there, but I will if you don't get off your lazy fat ass and answer this door! I've had no fucking sleep thanks to you!"

Still nothing.

Muttering Polish curses under his breath, he backed away from the door, thinking about breaking it down. The things were flimsy enough, one well-aimed kick in the direction of the lock would be enough to send it in. He would have done it too, except for the fact that he was already under a police caution, thanks to his no-good girlfriend. Paulina was pretty good at giving as well as she got in their many frequent arguments. In fact, the only thing she was better at was playing the victim, no wonder he drank as much as he did.

No, he couldn't just walk away, not when there was his pride to consider.

He approached the door again, squatting down on his haunches and pressing both thumbs against the letterbox, lifting it in and upward. He put his mouth up close to the opening and yelled:

"Hey! You in there! I don't care how drunk or tired you are, you kept me awake half the night! You answer this door, or I'll kick it down, you hear me?" Still holding the letterbox open with one thumb, he moved in a little closer, trying to angle his eye against the narrow slit just enough to see inside. He could see straight through the front room and past the open bedroom door. He peered in, straining to make out some sort of detail inside the darkened room ahead. "Hey, you crazy woman, 'you in there? Why 'you not answering me, you mad bitch?" As his vision adjusted to the gloom, the first thing that he saw was the red. So much red. Everywhere, sprayed up the walls in stupid, shapeless patterns, so much of it that it took him a few seconds to process the fact that the bedsheets weren't actually meant to be that colour. Distracted by the sight of the blood, it was several seconds more before he noticed the bare legs, protruding over the edge of the bed, bloodstained trousers gathered around the ankles. Just off to the left of his field of view he could see what looked like a bare foot, the slender foot of a woman. His heart pounding in his ears, drowning out the sound of Paulina whining for him to come back downstairs and do something useful for a change, instead of trying to cause some trouble with the mad café woman upstairs who probably just decided to have a bit of fun for once. Besides, he had left the television on and wasn't watching it anyway, and was she really the only one who realised that was just a waste of electricity?

"Shut the hell up, woman!" Lukasz shouted, hardly hearing himself. He craned his neck to see just a little further, even though a part of him knew that he probably wouldn't want to see.

(don't look don't look don't-)

(too late you looked)

Suddenly nothing else mattered any more as, gagging, he ran downstairs, the stale taste of last night's vodka threatening to come back, and his screams sounding alien to his own ears as he shouted at Paulina to forget television, forget sleep, forget everything else and just call the fucking police.

-

NINETEEN

"Lukasz Balierski? That name sounds familiar. I'm sure that I've heard of him somewhere before. Has he been in some sort of trouble in the past or something?" Frank sat down on the step, wincing at the feel of the cold dampness through his trousers. He placed the tray with two wedges of leftover pizza on the ground in front of him, still holding a half-eaten third slice.

"Oh yeah, he's a wrong 'un for sure," Little Joe huddled in the doorway, his voice lisping through the gap where several of his front teeth had once been. "If you ever clapped eyes on him, you'd know. You can just *tell*."

"That's unusually judgemental of you, Joe. I think when those punters beat you up, they must've knocked the kindness clean out of your soul."

"Fuck off, you sarky cunt. Do you want me to tell you this story or not?"

"Yeah, sorry fella," Frank nodded. "Tell me about him."

"Well, he's Polish, he's built like a brick shithouse, he and looks as rough as a badger's arse. But that doesn't mean he was responsible for what happened. The pigs still interviewed him about it all the same though."

"What is it that the good old boys in blue think that mister Balierski might have done?" Frank took another bite of pizza, ignoring the elastic strings of mozzarella that hung down his chin.

"You really want to know?"

"I wouldn't be sat here next to some toothless wonder ex-dealer, freezing my arse off if I didn't, would I?"

"You had to go and mention my teeth, didn't you?" Joe huddled down a little further into his sleeping bag, reduced to sleeping rough since his regular source of income had dried up. At least his eyes and ears still worked. It was surprising just how loose some peoples' tongues got when they didn't think the homeless guy in the doorway was listening. He soon learned that he could use this to his advantage – something that Frank knew and was quick to put to good use himself.

"Balierki's live-in girlfriend - if that's what you can call the girl that he pimps out on a regular basis - told the police that he had been ready to have a bit of argy-bargy with the woman in the flat upstairs from them. She said that he'd been drinking pretty heavily the night before and gotten himself into a right old state over the noise."

"Noise?"

"The woman upstairs usually kept herself to herself, a café owner, or something like that. *A bit of a weirdo* is how the girlfriend described her, either way. Apparently, the night before last, while Balierski was tanked up on paint stripper or whatever it was he'd been drinking, she brought home some bloke and, well, the lady of the house said it sounded like they were getting up to a spot of something a bit kinky."

"Really," Frank chuckled. "You'll have to tell me what that sounds like. I'm guessing you're the kind of person who would know, or has it been a while for you, too?"

"Lots of screaming, apparently," Joe looked down at his gloved hands, ignoring the insult. "It seems that Balierski got himself pretty wound up by it anyway. His girlfriend said he can get a bit nasty if he doesn't get his beauty sleep."

"You know, you make a riveting storyteller, Joe," Frank cupped his free hand over his mouth, letting out an exaggerated yawn. "Remind me why those punters beat you up, did you try talking them to death?"

"The weird woman in the flat above Balierski is dead, along with her hot date," Joe continued. "Balierski reckoned he was being disturbed by their sex noises, it seems they were up to something a bit more than that."

"They're both dead, and Balierski's a suspect?"

"To be fair, it doesn't look too good for him right now. Even though his girlfriend is insisting that he wasn't upstairs for long enough to do it."

"And you believe her *because?*" Frank could tell by the sound of Joe's voice, he had a reason that he couldn't wait to share.

"I've got a mate in the flat next door. Well, when I say *mate*, I mean some bloke who's scored some shit from me a few times. Either way, he got a quick gander when the pigs were 'round. Said the place was a right mess."

"A mate?"

"Yeah, he's the same one what blagged that notebook and photos that you *still* haven't given back. Said he shoved 'em through your letterbox. He's getting a bit twitchy about it, Frank."

Frank flung down his pizza crust and pulled a notepad from his jacket pocket, twirling the pencil between thumb and forefinger, ready to scribble notes.

"Yeah, it took me a little while to suss where they could have come from. I should've known that you'd be in on it in some way or other. Tell him that it's for the greater good, Joe. The fuzz probably haven't even noticed that it's missing. Besides, it'd serve him right, the fucker almost gave me nightmares."

"Anyway, yeah, the place was a *mess*, like something out of a horror film. Skeevy – that's my mate – said there was blood everywhere and, in the middle of it all, a naked woman and a half naked man. Oh, and a chunk of the bloke's chewed-up dick was lying on the floor as well. Sorry if I'm putting you off your pizza."

"Jesus, it all sounds a bit familiar."

"Huh?"

"The story I told you about in the news a few weeks ago, you know, Marks, the dead guy your mate took the Polaroids of," Frank fumbled with the pencil between his fingers, wishing that it was a cigarette. "I've been looking into it, it was pretty similar."

"Oh," Joe looked at the pizza slices still in the tray, his belly giving out a tell-tale growl. "Anyway, Skeevy said that both bodies had bite marks and chunks missing from their legs and arms. He almost puked up just telling me about it. He *was* pretty stoned at the time though, to be honest."

"*Stoned*, right," Frank scratched at the side of his face with the point of his pencil, "as stoned as he must have been when he thought to take those photos in the first place."

"What?"

"You heard me, Joe. I'm grateful, don't get me wrong, but it takes a special kind of weirdo to sneak a few photos of your dead next-door neighbour and put them through my letterbox without even introducing themselves. Besides, who the fuck even *has* a Polaroid camera nowadays?"

"I might have let it slip that you were looking for leads on a story about a guy what did something similar."

"That's beside the point, it's still pretty fucking weird."

Joe said nothing more, still looking at the pizza, his usual alcohol-reddened complexion turning a little paler.

"What were their names anyway?" Frank ran his hand holding the pencil across his forehead, changing the subject as he tried to stave of the ache that he could feel building up. "I need to know their names, Joe. Like I've said before, every victim deserves to have a name."

"The woman who lived in the flat was called Elizabeth MacKinnon, a quiet one, but like I said, a bit weird. Her castrated man-friend was called Hubert Danvers. The poor cunt owned a little butcher's shop, not too far from your neck of the woods."

"Okay, thanks. I owe you one, Joe." Frank stood up, shoving the notebook and pencil back into his pocket before wiping both hands down the front of his trousers. They were dark, the grease smears wouldn't be noticed. He reached behind his ear for the cigarette that he usually kept there - his emergency smoke, he usually called it - only to mutter a curse under his breath when he remembered that he had chuffed away his last one two days ago, promising himself that he was finally going to pack them in. To hell with his lungs, he needed a cancer stick, and preferably a quarter bottle of something cheap and alcoholic to go with it.

"Are you gonna take the rest of that with you?" Joe pointed at the now-cold pizza.

"No, fill your boots," Frank smiled. "It tastes like crap anyway. The pepperoni smells like it's over a week old."

"Cheers Popper, you're all heart." Joe snatched up a slice and crammed it into his mouth, slurping congealed Mozzarella through the gap between his teeth. "Oh, before I forget," he mumbled, "have you heard anything about the protest?"

"Protest?" Frank repeated. "No, *what* protest?"

"There's a rumour been going 'round for a while now, there's a protest of some sort planned. The usual shit, you know, a bunch of people blaming someone else because they can't be arsed to get a job or find somewhere a bit better to live."

"It isn't always that easy, Joe," Frank said. "You ought to know that as well as most people. Any idea when this is supposed to be happening?"

"Nope," Joe smacked his lips as he spoke, chewing on another mouthful. Frank was right, it *did* taste bad, but he was just about hungry enough not to care. "Soon though, I reckon."

"Okay, fair enough," Frank answered, looking as though his mind was still fixed upon something more important. He reached into his pocket and brought out a crumpled twenty pound note, pressing it to Joe's grubby outstretched hand. "Keep a listen out, Joe, yeah? You do good work."

"Will do. Thanks for the pizza, by the way."

"Think nothing of it. I just hope it doesn't give you food poisoning. I'm sure I saw the guy in the takeaway picking his arse while he was making it." Before Joe could protest, Frank turned and walked away, scratching at the side of his face again in thought.

Three people dead, all in similar circumstances. Something was severely messed up somewhere.

It felt like he had some sniffing around to do.

TWENTY

They had been friends throughout school and for the first seven months they had both lasted in college, always assuming that they had far more in common than they actually did. The physical relationship side of it was something that they had simply drifted into over the passing of time, an on-off thing that neither of them had really ever taken too seriously. For a lesbian and a bisexual woman living together, it seemed like an obvious way to be, as long as they had an understanding that it was just casual. The idea that they might end up falling out if they were in one anothers' faces for most of every day had never even seemed like a possibility to begin with. *Oh, it'll be a right laugh*, they had both promised each other. *Getting bladdered every weekend, starting with Friday night, obviously. On the pull, it doesn't matter who you end up with, long as they can afford to call for a pizza afterward.* They had it all mapped out. They were going to have it made, the two of them.

They both soon realised that there was often a world of difference between expectation and reality.

Less than six weeks in and Susanne Walters had started to notice just how much she was irritated by Alex's insistence on having a cigarette dangling from her mouth pretty much constantly. Christ, she would have smoked them in her sleep if she was able. She had positioned ashtrays in every room of the small flat, except for Susanne's. Worse, she never bothered to clean the bloody things out, seeming to prefer it when the whole place drunk of stale fag ends.

Soon growing desperate to get away as much as possible, Susanne had taken to spending more and more time away from the flat, out most nights getting drunk and throwing herself at pretty much anyone with a pulse, as long as they had a bit of cash to burn and a place where she could crash for the night. She had never bothered telling Alex about Kyle, either. Susanne's occasional number two, Kyle was the one she went to whenever she felt like reminding herself what it felt like to get a shag from the same bloke more than once. He had told her before that the thought of her being bisexual turned him on. Thick as pig shit, the dozy prick had hinted at a threesome once, but she'd soon put him in his place over *that*, at least. Not that he seemed too bothered, just as long as he got to tickle the back of her throat with his dick every once in a while.

She had almost come close to messing up big time just a few weeks back when she made the mistake of getting completely rat-arsed and ending up letting herself get banged in a club toilet cubicle off some scruffy bastard who had the nerve to call himself a journalist. The whole sorry fumble had lasted about two and a half minutes and the bloke couldn't get away quick enough afterward. No offer of a bed for the night, no money for food or even a taxi, she had wound up taking off her high heels and trudging home alone, bare feet sloshing through the rain, before crawling into her own bed, covering her ears to block the sound of Alex fingering herself in the next room. The dirty cow was probably in a mood because she hadn't gotten a seeing to.

It was just a few days later that Susanne had first started to feel sick, with frequent nosebleeds and near-constant headaches. For the first time ever, she was actually scared that she might have pushed her luck a little bit too far, that those few drunken minutes had left her with something nastier than an unwanted pregnancy. It only added insult to injury when, a few days later, she had seen the cocky wanker at the doctor's surgery, strutting around the place like there was nothing wrong, looking like he was trying to coax gossip out of the snotty old receptionist. He had soon buggered off with his weasel tail between his legs when he'd spotted her though.

It had been what some people might have said was a wake-up call, enough to finally put her off men for life. She was twenty-three years old, it was about time she started looking after herself a bit better. Starting with the things closest to home.

"You cow! You proper fucking cow! You can't kick me out of my own flat - I pay as frigging much as you do!"

It was fair to say that it didn't go down too well.

"You know as well as I do that we get right on each other's tits, Alex. I reckon it's time for a fresh start." Susanne just spoke the words aloud as they came into her head, without really giving any thought to their meaning, worried that if she did so she would remember just how awkward it felt, trying to act like some sort of mediator.

"Besides, why should *I* move out? *You're* the one who spends most nights bunking up with some stranger or other! And don't you think I don't know about that thick wanker you've been seeing! If anything, *you* should move in with *him!*"

"Are you taking the piss?" Susanne could feel an ache at the top of her nose. Congestion, a hint that it was about to start gushing again at any moment. "Move in with Kyle? He still lives with his parents, for Christ's sake! I'm just surprised that he's never asked his mother for a tit wank - it's probably the only thing I do for him that she won't!"

"Maybe, but you're still the one who fucks off elsewhere most nights!"

"Yeah, only to get away from you!"

That had done it. Alex had stormed out, insisting that *at least she had found out what her best mate* really *thought of her* under her breath.

Susanne had tried to ready herself, but she still jumped as the front door slammed into place, the surrounding wall juddering as it did so. She had wiped at her nose with the back of her hand, trying to get rid of the maddening tingle that irritated the lining of her nostrils, gasping as the trail of red came away, smearing across her pale skin.

***

"So, what have you been up to all week?"

"Like you bloody well care," Alex tried to keep her voice level. She had been telling herself all the way to the flat that she was going to be the one to get the best parting shot in. "Like I said, I'm just here to collect a few things that I need. I can come by and pick up the rest of my stuff later." Despite her deliberately upfront talk, she hoped that she didn't look as though she was just playing at meaning what she said. The cigarette tucked behind her ear felt heavy, almost as if it could pull her head to one side, a millstone made out of paper and tobacco.

"Of *course* I care, you daft cow." There was the first surprise; Susanne's voice was softer than Alex remembered. More subdued, as if she was making a genuine effort to sound regretful. "And I'm sorry, really, I am. The place just don't feel the same without you. It's too, I don't know, just too *big*." She was dressed in a grey, misshapen sweatshirt that looked far too baggy, and a pair of black jogging bottoms. Her hair was pulled back into a loose ponytail and looked as though it hasn't been washed in several days. Her appearance was at odds with Alex's own, who had gone out of her way to make an effort, for no other reason than to show that she could cope just fine.

"It's a shame you didn't think of that before you decided that you didn't want me around anymore, that you prefer jumping in the sack with any man or woman who takes your fancy after the first few double vodkas." Alex wanted her to know that she had moved on, that she had no *real* reason to come back. As if she had read Alex's thoughts, Susanne took a step closer.

"I've missed you, Al," she said, "I've *really* missed you." There was something that Alex couldn't quite place, something different somehow. The last time Alex had been in the flat, Susanne had been sick, spending most of her time hugging the toilet bowl or trying to stop her sudden bouts of almost constant nosebleeds. A trip to the GP hadn't helped, only making her panic even more when it seemed like the doctor didn't have the first clue what the problem was. She seemed to have things more under control now, at least. If anything, she looked better for it, her usual plump face slimmed down, although only just on the right side of looking a little *too* thin.

"The place hasn't been the same without you, Al," another step forward, her voice low, almost soothing, like nothing Alex had ever heard from her before. "I wish we could just forget what happened, you know, just put it behind us."

Alex was caught off-guard. It was a world away from the full-on shouting match that she had spent most of the day mentally preparing herself for.

"Well, I suppose," she started, surprising herself with what she might have been about to say, her thoughts mixed up as she tried to think of something clever to follow up with, unable to do so. "I just hate it when you mess around with other people, especially when they're blokes or – worse - proper skanks."

"I can't help it. You knew what I was into before we got together."

"Yeah, I know it, but it doesn't make it easier when you're putting yourself about night after night." Alex shrugged her shoulders, looking down at the floor. "I know we agreed, an open relationship and all that. It's just not always as easy as I thought it would be."

"*Aww*, I'm touched. Do you remember?" Susanne looked straight at her, and Alex noticed for the first time, just how drawn her face actually looked, with the beginnings of dark circles forming beneath her eyes. *Christ, maybe she's not kidding*, she thought. *She looks like she's been losing sleep, as well as her appetite.*

"Remember what?"

"That night at Angie Bradburn's eighteenth birthday party? We'd both gone and got ourselves tanked up, I mean proper hammered." Alex felt a sudden prickling sensation at the back of her neck, moving her hand to the base of her skull to knead it out. The feeling was matched by a flush of warmth across her face. She knew exactly what Susanne was talking about. "Do you remember what we did?"

"We were drunk, Suze, it was just a fumble," Alex stammered, the words feeling almost sticky in her mouth. "It was *embarrassing*. It was just a stupid laugh, *stupid*."

"That's funny," Susanne took another step forward, then another. "It didn't feel stupid. Not to me, anyway. It was our first time together." She was inches away from Alex now, her breath felt warm and soft, with a faint underlying sweetness that felt familiar, something that she couldn't quite place.

"Susanne...you've been drinking."

"So have you." Susanne's lips met Alex's, brushing gossamer light to begin with, then pressing firmer, before relaxing again.

"It was...we were...we were just messing around," Alex tried to pull away, unable to do so, her thoughts whirling. She had come expecting a confrontation, not at all what she now found herself caught up in.

"Maybe I *wasn't* just messing around, I still remember it, every last bit of it. It was better than being with any bloke, even back then. Nothing else comes close, even now. Go on, tell me I'm wrong." Before Alex could form an answer, Susanne's mouth met hers again, more forceful this time. Alex gasped at the electric sensation as Susanne's tongue probed hungrily, parting her lips and

Alex found herself returning the kiss, stepping forward as she kicked the door closed behind herself.

***

"Well, *that* wasn't what I came 'round here for. It definitely wasn't what I was expecting."

Alex stretched out on the bed, propped up on one elbow, one finger of her free hand tracing a line from Susanne's breast to her hip and back again, feeling the goosebumps raise beneath the lightness of her touch.

"Good though, weren't it? I *told* you it would be." Susanne looked up to face her, a faint smile on her lips, that Alex hoped wasn't just her way of saying *I told you so*. She could still taste Susanne on her breath. It had all happened so fast; no fumbling, no build-up. Just the two of them in a race against time, pulling and grasping at one another, until their almost frantic need had swelled into a mutual, explosive climax.

Susanne shrugged a shoulder, moving closer again, "Admit it though, it *was* good, better than it has been with anyone else since."

"Christ, I didn't know I had it in me. Tell you what though, if that's what it's gonna be like after just a few *days* away from each other..." Alex shuddered as Susanne's hand reached across, tracing a line up her thigh with a single finger, before drifting almost lazily inward towards the thick tangle of hair between her thighs. "*Mmmm*, again already?"

"Oh, yeah, I could do this all night, if you want me to," Susanne pulled away again, a sigh that could have almost been disappointment escaping Alex's lips. "It sounds like *you* could, too." She said, placing her hand to her mouth. "You taste as good as I remember."

Before Alex could protest, Susanne placed a hand on each hip and rolled her onto her back. Sliding her hands down, she placed them against her inner thighs, parting them firmly to allow access, Alex's breathing already deepening in anticipation, as she understood what was about to happen, not wanting to fight it.

Burying her face in the dark thatch of curls, Susanne's tongue darted with feather-light strokes, pushing past the fleshy lips to lap at the warmth beyond. Alex's breaths became soft moans as she raised her hips, driving them both onward as the first ripples of pleasure began to course through her. Jesus Christ, she'd never experienced anything like it before. Anything else was forgotten about, all the previous arguments and fallings-out nothing more than distant memories as all that mattered were the sensations flooding through her, almost tormenting her with the promise of what was still to come. There was a new sensation, as Susanne's tongue seemed to become rigid, pushing its way deep into her, filling her.

Alex gasped, barely able to speak now. "Right there...that's it." Susanne mumbled something in response, her voice muffled as her lips clamped down harder, forming a seal around Alex's wet warmth, her hands pulling her ever closer as she plunged deeper. Alex arched her back until it felt as though her spine could break, crying out in pleasure, mixed with a pain that was as brief as it was exquisite, as Susanne's tongue felt like it was plunging deeper into her than she ever thought possible. Every nerve in her body felt on fire and she trembled, as if she didn't feel like she was just being tongued anymore, instead she was being fucked, filled to the brim by something larger and harder than any cock, sliding its way deep inside her, like some solid, serpentine *thing*. Then any thought was forgotten as the orgasm erupted from inside her, a sensation tearing through her that swamped everything and anything else not in that moment.

"*Shit, shit, shit!*" Alex sobbed, her whole body going rigid as she came again, wave after climactic wave washing over her, before she went limp, breathless and spent.

"Bloody hell, when and where did you learn to do *that?*" Several minutes later, Alex still struggled to catch her breath, the sheer intensity leaving her spent. "I mean, I've never felt anything like *that* before. *Jesus!*"

"I'm guessing you enjoyed it then?" Susanne sat up near the edge of the bed. She had flicked on the lamp that stood on the bedside chest of drawers, the pale glow thrown from the bulb accentuating the perspiration that sheened them both. "I dunno, really," she continued, "I just did the sort of thing that I would like to have done to me. Maybe you want to give it a try?" Her smile was faint, almost coy.

"I wouldn't know where to start," Alex said. "I mean, really, it was incredible. At one point, it actually felt like you were going at me with that strap-on we bought the Christmas before last. I don't know how, but it did." A look passed across Susanne's face, that might have been confusion or possibly concern, then it was gone again.

"Nope, I didn't use anything else, honest. Just my mouth and my tongue."

"In that case, I reckon I really have got some catching up to do." Susanne stood up and Alex looked her up and down.

"I thought so. You've lost some weight, haven't you?"

"Yeah, I don't know how. It's probably because I haven't been too well lately. Do I look okay though, yeah?"

Alex sat up. "You look just fine. Anyway, are you going to let me do you now? I can give it a go at least."

"Oh, you bet," Susanne said, smiling again. "In a few minutes though. I'm just going to get a glass of water, I'm parched."

"*Hmm,* I wonder why. Oh, I almost forgot, there's a bottle of wine in the 'fridge, from a few weeks ago, if you'd rather open that. Unless you already necked it while I was gone, that is."

Susanne laughed now, the sound soft, yet hollow. "Nah, I'm thirsty, really. Water will do, the wine can keep for another night. That's if there's going to *be* another night?" She winked as she half turned to face Alex, as though she had suddenly remembered something. *Bloody hell,* Alex thought, *she really has lost a lot of weight.*

"Come to think of it, you mentioning my weight has got me thinking, do you want anything brought back through? I'm *famished.* There might be some leftover pizza or something like that."

Bare feet padding against the floor, she headed for the kitchen, one hand rubbing at her belly as she did so, smiling to herself, as though in satisfaction.

TWENTY-ONE

"What's going on? Frank Popper turning down the offer of food – even when I've already said that I'll pay for it?" Kim Dzanic almost managed to look surprised, pulling a handful of ten pound notes from her pocket and waving them in the air as if to show how serious she was. "Pizza, kebab, anything, whatever. It's on me, I promise."

"I'm not hungry, thanks." Frank tipped the remainder of his coffee down his throat, placing the empty mug down on the table next to him and leaving a tarry, dark smear on the laminated surface.

"That's got to be another first right there," she grinned. "It's just past noon and you're actually drinking something non-alcoholic. Where's *my* Frank? What have you done with him, you impostor?"

"Where's *your* Frank? Careful, you almost make that sound promising. I don't know, maybe I've just grown a bit in character since the old days," he murmured, his answer making it sound as though his attention was fixed on something else. "I haven't had much time for booze. I've had a lot on my mind lately, and I've needed a clear head."

"Okay, okay, I didn't mean it, especially the bit about you being mine," Kim said, caught off guard by his seriousness. "Although I *am* a bit curious to know what could be so important that it's sworn you off the sauce. You're not still obsessing over that dead guy, are you?" He looked up at her and Kim thought that he should maybe have more important things on his mind more often. His eyes were pale and clear, and his voice had an edge to it, a sense of focus that she had all but forgotten he could be capable of when he stopped with the messing about and actually got on with something.

"Dead guy?" He looked up at her, as if considering what she had just said. "Oh, you mean *Marks?* Yeah, it's about him and more besides."

"More?"

"Yeah," Frank nodded. "Two more, just a few days ago. Some woman and a bloke. It wasn't pretty, from the sound of things."

"I'm not sure that I really want to know," Kim shuddered, drawing her anorak closer around herself. "Especially if the last one you told me about was anything to go by. Don't get me started on those *photos.*"

"Yeah, it's just as bad. These latest two were probably a little better known around the place though." Popper slid his hand into his jacket pocket, fumbling with something inside. The look on his face suggested that he was thinking of what to say next.

"You're fidgeting a bit there, Franklin. I hope you're not cracking one off, it's not a very nice thing to do while you're talking about that kind of stuff."

"You really are a dirty cow sometimes," Frank said, a grim smile creasing his face. "That's probably one of the things I liked about you back in the day."

"*Back in the day?* Now you just sound *old.* Old and serious Frank Popper. It could take a bit of getting used to, mind."

"That's a shame."

"Ain't it just?" Kim shrugged. "Anyway, I thought you were supposed to be talking about dead people, not lamenting about the good old days, if that's what you really want to insist on thinking they were."

"Actually," Frank coughed, "I was going to show you something and it's got nothing to do with my admittedly hazy recollections." He brought his hand out of his pocket, his spindly fingers wrapped around a large amber bottle.

"What's that?"

"I'm not sure yet," he placed the bottle on the table between them. It was half-full of what looked like large capsules, a white label on one side and a large, white child-proof cap. "It was found in Marks' flat." Kim looked at him, as if to ask just what the hell he was doing with something from a dead guy's place, was he really *that* desperate to get himself in trouble?

"Don't worry, no one'll find out about it. My insider might be a bit drugged up most of the time, but he's still pretty good. Friend of a friend and all that," Frank continued, as if guessing what she was thinking.

"You really are a one sometimes, aren't you?"

"Desperate times, Kim." Kim cocked her head to one side, raising an eyebrow as she looked at him in a way to suggest that she wasn't quite sure whether to believe him. "Marks was a bit of a loner by all accounts, but he did talk to his next-door neighbour from time to time, so I even managed to get a few words out of her. Some old girl by the name of Greta Sandberg, or something like that." Frank picked up the bottle again, turning it over in his hand. "She seems to think that he had a bit of an issue when it came to medicines. Said he once told her he wouldn't even take paracetamol for a headache."

"So what? I'm not sure I get where you're going with this."

"Blame Little Joe. He managed to set me up with the contact I was talking about."

"Little Joe put you in touch with a druggie? Fuck me, *there's* a surprise."

"Yeah, someone who's been inside the flat. He had a good old nose around the place and surprise, surprise, he found no trace of drugs or medication of any kind." He tapped his forefinger against the bottle top. "Just these."

"I bet he was *really* disappointed. Knowing any friend of Little Joe, he probably would've snorted anything he found anyway," Kim shook her head. "You ought to be more careful who you trust, Frank."

"Don't worry about me," Frank let out a dry chuckle, "I'm a big lad and I can look after myself. Besides, I've got to get my information where I can find it."

"That's the story of your life, isn't it?"

"Well played, Dzanic, well played."

"Well, what are they anyway?" Kim leaned forward as she spoke, picking the bottle up and narrowing her eyes to read the label. "I knew I should have brought my glasses, the contacts make my eyes itch too much. *Symbioloss?* What the hell is *Symbioloss?* It sounds like something out of a science fiction film."

Frank pointed to the small print at the bottom of the label:

With correct use, this medication can enable measurable weight loss without the need for a calorie-controlled diet. Medical supervision and caution are advised.

Then underneath that:

FOR EVALUATION PURPOSES ONLY.

"Evaluation?" Kim scratched her head. "What, like a drug trial?"

"It seems like it. They look and sound like some sort of diet pill." All trace of his usual snide humour had gone from Frank's voice, the seriousness sounding like something almost foreign to Kim's ears. "I've been trying to dig something up on these, since Bob was fuck all help," Frank shrugged, ignoring the look of distaste that crossed Kim's face at his saying the name. "Luckily, Joe's bloke came through a bit better. It looks like Marks was possibly involved with some sort of drug trial, for a new type of diet pill," he pointed a finger at the bottle still in Kim's hand as he spoke, his doing so making her feel suddenly uncomfortable. "A drug trial that I haven't been able to find anything else about. I can't trace it, which makes it sound like maybe there's something going on that isn't quite legal."

"Diet pills?" Kim repeated. "But you showed me the photos. He was like a rake."

"Yeah, he was when he died," Frank closed his eyes, trying to keep those images of the emaciated Marks out of his head. "By all accounts, he was a bit of a tubby bastard up until a few weeks before then. I thought he was so poor that he was starving to death," Frank paused, choosing his words with care now. "But all along it seems more like he was eating himself to death. It's just that something made it look like he wasn't."

"What does this have to do with the others?"

"No idea," Frank scratched at the side of his face, wincing as a ragged fingernail scraped against an old scab beneath his stubble, lifting it away. "Not at the moment, at least. I haven't been able to make any sort of connection between them, apart from the fact that they lived in the same block of flats," he paused, as if about to say something, before thinking better of it. "The woman's name was Elizabeth MacKinnon, Betty for short. An alcoholic nasty piece of work living in the flat below her, name of Balierski, was arrested. He was later released though, once it was obvious that he couldn't have done it."

"*How* was it obvious? And what about the bloke who died in the flat with her?"

"I don't know about *him*, either," Frank shook his head. "Some boyfriend maybe, or perhaps someone who at least thought his luck was in. Either way, he definitely got more than he bargained for." He decided to spare her the details about what Balierski had told the police he had seen through the letter box. "Trust me, Balierski might well be a thug and a prize arsehole, but there's no way he could have been responsible, not in the short time he had." He took the tablets from Kim's outstretched hand - she didn't resist - and gripped them in his own, rattling the contents.

Raising the bottle up, he gripped the white safety cap in his other hand and twisted it. After several empty clicks, he managed to loosen it away. "I've always thought that kids can manage these things far easier than adults," he said.

"What are you doing?" Kim asked as he tipped two of the contents into the palm of his hand, placing them onto the table side by side. The large, brightly-coloured capsules seemed conspicuous against the stained, tired-looking laminate of the table surface. "I don't know, just indulging my journalistic curiosity, I suppose."

"If you try and snort the contents I'm really going to worry. I'll leave, I mean it, I'll walk right out that fucking door."

"I doubt I'd want to give it a go," Frank leaned forward, hunching over the table as he picked up one of the capsules again, pulling apart the two halves of red, gelatinous shell. "My nasal lining is screwed up more than enough already, thanks."

"Don't you at least need a razor blade and a fiver for that?" Kim tried to laugh, the result sounding falser than she had intended.

"No," Frank said, "it doesn't look as though I do. Besides, what's a fiver? I'm skint, in case you haven't noticed." As he tipped one half of the capsule onto the table, they had expected to see fine powder, or perhaps a gel of some sort. Instead, there was a hollow sound as several pieces of what looked like large rice grains tumbled out onto the bench surface.

"You'd have a pretty hard time snorting that up," Kim said, looking down at the dried husks. "It doesn't look much like something that would help you lose weight though."

"It doesn't look too much like something that would make you want to chew your own arm off either," Frank said. "Or your boyfriend's cock, for that matter." A look of disappointment passed across his face, and Kim tutted, not understanding the reference.

"I don't know what you were hoping to see," Kim walked to the sink and picked up a coffee mug, the writing emblazoned on the side proclaiming the owner to be the *world's biggest arsehole*. She filled it with water from the tap before returning to the table, taking a drink as she did so.

"Sorry, I woke up with a bit of a sore throat this morning," she said.

"I won't ask how."

"I think I'm coming down with something. Get your mind out of the gutter." She placed the cup on the table alongside the opened capsule, water spilling over the rim and forming a puddle.

"Why did you have to go and do that?" Frank said. "You've gone and made a clean-" he paused, looking down at the table as though in concentration.

"What is it? What's the matter?" Kim asked, looking at him. "Oh, I'm sorry if I've gone and given you something to clean up."

"No, it's not that," he said, his gaze still focused on the same spot. "That stuff from out of the capsule, you got it wet."

"I said sorry."

"Yeah, but after a couple of seconds one of them moved."

"It was probably just when I put the cup down."

"No, not like that. I mean it *moved*. It *wriggled*."

"Wriggled?"

"Yeah," Frank said. "Wriggled. As if it was alive." Before Kim could say anything, he leaned across and picked up the mug, tipping it and pouring several more drops of water over the husks.

"What is it you're expecting to happen?" Kim asked, looking down. After a few seconds, the grains seemed to soften and contort, wriggling against one another, as though in a blind effort to escape the wetness.

"What the-" Kim stepped back from the table, a look of disgust on her face. "They're maggots! They look like *maggots!*" As they both watched, the things wriggled and writhed against one another, trying to feel their way around, their dry casings softening as they absorbed the moisture around them.

"Yeah," Frank repeated, still watching. "They do, don't they? Maggots, or something very similar. Definitely something alive. Whatever they are, I bet they're not the sort of thing that you'd expect to find inside a diet pill." Walking to the sink, he picked up a tablespoon from the draining board and used it to scoop the things up, dropping them into the mug of water with a plop, where they wriggled around, as though trying to find their way back out.

"Well, I guess that means I'm never drinking out of *that* cup again," Kim wrinkled her nose.

"But it suits you so well, *world's biggest arsehole.*"

"Shut up."

"I do own more than one cup you know," Frank looked down at the things in the mug. "Whatever they are, they don't look like good news for whoever has been in on that drug trial."

"Do you reckon they could be tapeworms or something like that? That would be all sorts of messed up."

"If I remember right, tapeworms don't actually cause much in the way of weight loss, not usually anyway," he hesitated, thinking. "But if there are three or four of them in every capsule, and then you take a capsule every day-"

"Before too long, you'd have a proper little family of them growing in your belly," Kim interrupted.

"Yeah," Frank tried to think of something more to say and realised that he couldn't. "Yeah, you would, wouldn't you?"

He reached across the table again and picked up a chipped saucer, laying it across the top of the mug like a makeshift lid, without another word.

TWENTY-TWO

"Mitch! Are you planning on coming down here any time soon, or have you gone and died up there?"

Carol Brennan didn't really expect a response, not a recognisable one at least. After four and a half months of his being in between jobs, she had grown aware of her husband's nasty new habit of trying to cultivate an increasingly lazy lifestyle. Stay in bed until midday, lounge around the place like a slob until he got sick of her threatening to kick him out, promise that he was going out to look for work when both of them knew that in reality he was going straight to the nearest pub to piss away money that they couldn't afford to lose. It didn't help that he was such close friends with that loser, Brad Whitman. The fat clown was an expert in the art of doing nothing, and it seemed like Mitch had been taking lessons from him lately.

"And get a shave before you come downstairs. No wonder no one will give you work, what with you looking like a right scruff!" No answer. "Are you even listening to me? Your breakfast's down here, although it's probably been cold for the last half as hour now!"

Doesn't the whining cow ever shut the bloody hell up? Mitch stood in front of the bathroom mirror, gripping the edge of the basin with one hand for support. With two fingers of the other, he pulled down the lower lid of his eye, studying the bloodshot threads running through. Next, he poked out his tongue, wincing at the sour taste of the thick, cream-coloured coating that furred the inside of his mouth. He had already brushed his teeth twice, the stubborn bitterness refusing to shift. That, along with the nagging coming from downstairs did nothing to help his mood. Carol had always been a judgemental cow, something that had only grown worse since he had lost his job. She didn't seem to understand that finding something new wasn't that straightforward. It took time, it wasn't something that could just be rushed into. She was just a typical bloody housewife who couldn't understand that. She probably wouldn't believe him if he tried telling her that he didn't feel well, either.

He stepped back and looked at his cheekbones, poking their way through skin that looked a little too tight. It had started about a week after he had sat next to Whitman that time in Betty's. At first, he'd thought that it had just knocked him sick, the sight of Brad spewing half of his insides all over the place. Jesus Christ, *that* had been something all right. Mitch had been amazed that the fella hadn't bled to death there and then. He hadn't seen him since, not that he was really bothered. He would do well to keep away from anyone *that* ill. It had shaken Mitch up pretty badly, although it had probably given some of the arseholes in there, Eddie fucking Caplin for instance, something new to talk about for a few days. He was just surprised that Betty MacKinnon's head hadn't exploded. He often wondered what the hell a miserable cow like her was doing running a place like that anyway. There was only that gullible wanker Danvers who had a good word to say about her behind her back, and that was probably because he was itching to get into her crusty knickers. The stupid, dog-breathed bastard thought that no one knew about it. Oh, Mitch knew plenty of people who had a right laugh behind *his* back, too. Old Dippy Danvers, always good for a laugh, acting like a lovesick puppy every time he caught sight of her.

"Mitch? Are you coming down here or not?"

For Christ's sake, didn't she ever shut up?

There was a dull ache at the base of his skull, as if someone was sinking their thumb into the nape of his neck. A stubborn sort of pain, it hadn't shifted for days, again, since shortly after that visit to the café in fact. *Fucking Whitman, better not have passed anything on to me, the riddled bastard,* he thought, trying to ignore the irritation behind his eyes. It's the last thing I need, with Carol getting on my back so damned much. *I told her I was ill, she never listens though. She's really been getting right on my tits lately. It's times like these I almost feel like I could kill her-*

He shook his head in an effort to clear it. At the same time there was a low rumbling sensation in the pit of his stomach. Running the palm of his hand across the greying, wiry hair of his belly, he turned to leave the bathroom, bracing himself for the tongue-lashing he was sure to get. Maybe he should make the effort to go downstairs and face the music after all, he was starving.

TWENTY-THREE

An earlier time, closer to the start of everything:

"Good afternoon, Mister Hesketh, we meet again."

"It's *Doctor* Hesketh, thanks, but you knew that already." James Hesketh held out his hand and Steele took it, the handshake as brief as it was firm, feeling like a formality. At least both men knew that it was little more than a token gesture, every bit as fake-looking as the too-white smile and oily tan that raised Hesketh's suspicions as much as they had first time around.

"I do hope you don't mind, Mister Hesketh," Steele smiled a forced-looking grin. "I know that you're a busy man, one with bills to pay and all that. I thought that it might be best if I came to see you as a patient, rather than our last meeting. It keeps things a little more, shall we say, discreet. You understand, yes?"

"Of course," Hesketh sat back in his chair, adjusting his collar and hoping that he didn't look as nervous as he felt. He motioned to the other man to sit, and he pulled out the seat on the other side of the desk, placing his small briefcase in front of his feet. Closer up, his tan accentuated the beginnings of lines around his eyes, and the black colour of his slicked-back hair looked a little less than natural. The smell of his aftershave was almost overpowering in the small room.

"You struck me as the curious type and, rather than have you hassle me with question after question, the sort of thing that could soon grow tiresome for me and pretty risky for you," he made the words sound like a threat without having to raise his voice, "I decided that it wouldn't do much harm to let you in on just one or two things."

"It's about time," Hesketh leaned forward, placing his hands on his desk, trying to project an air of authority. "I've kept my side of the bargain so far. I've kept my mouth shut, even though I've had no idea what it is I'm not meant to be talking about, apart from the fact that a patient who was overweight just a few weeks ago came into my practice last Tuesday looking like he'd been starving himself for a month."

"Really? He did? Excellent." Steele rubbed his hands together, the rings on his fingers clinking against each other as his grin widened.

"You said that everything would work out for the best and I had to do nothing. All the sort of words that a person likes to hear, it has to be said, but the kind of thing that carries very little substance, in my opinion."

"In your opinion?" Steele's grin looked as though it was fixed to his face, an unwavering, forced smile. "Fair enough, I suppose, but you haven't been told anything that isn't true." Hesketh tried to look past the mask, to see any glimpse of genuine emotion. "As far as I can gather, you should be more than happy, yes? We both know that you're up to your eyeballs in debt. Gambling, drinking, a wife who left you on account of her *extra-marital* activities?" His grin widened, as if he was enjoying watching Hesketh squirm. "Let's make no mistake here, *Mister* Hesketh," he emphasised the *mister* each time he said it, as though wanting to show who was really in charge, "you are still most likely in a situation where you can't afford to say *no*." Steele shrugged. "Like you've been told before, all I'm asking you to do is look the other way."

"I've already told you that I'll do it," Hesketh could feel the temperature rising under his collar. "You're right, I need the money, and you've got me over a barrel. But let's get something straight," Hesketh's voice rose in pitch, "I won't be bullied into anything, not even by you."

For the first time, Steele's smile wavered just a little.

"No one is bullying you, Mister Hesketh. You seem to misunderstand the situation. No one is, shall we say, holding a gun to your head."

"I've told you already, it's *Doctor* Hesketh. I'm a *doctor*."

"Yes, of course it is and of course you are," Steele cleared his throat and shuffled on his chair before continuing. "But I didn't come here to argue semantics with you, rather to explain some things to you so that you might be able to understand them a little better, like I said."

"Go on then, I have patients waiting. Say what you have to say and leave."

Steele leaned forward on the chair, reaching for the briefcase that he had placed at his feet with such precision. *He's leaving,* Hesketh thought, *just like that, he's going.* Instead, he brought the case up to his lap and rested it across his knees. He still smiled with a cold, almost cruel gleam in his eyes.

"Tell me Jim, I'm guessing that you must have some knowledge of biology, almost certainly more than I do, at least. How much do you know about parasitology?"

"Parasites? The animal or human kind?" Hesketh was uncertain what the point was in asking the question. "In either case, what does the answer have to do with any sort of medical trial?"

"Plenty, as it turns out. *Plenty.*" Steele flicked the brass clasp on his case and opened it, bringing out a slim folder of papers that he placed on Hesketh's desk. "A little light reading for you, when you have the time. You should understand it even better than I do. Like I told you before, I don't know much about any of that science stuff, I'm more of a salesman." He reached into the case again and brought out a small amber vial. Fumbling with the screw top, he tipped a single capsule into the palm of his hand. "Observe," he said. "I'm sorry, there really is something satisfying about saying that to a doctor." Holding the capsule between thumb and forefinger, he passed it to Hesketh. "Open it," he said. "Take the halves apart and tip the contents out, just into your hand. Tell me any thoughts."

Hesketh twisted apart the bright-coloured gelatine halves. Discarding one onto his desk, he turned out the other onto his waiting palm. Three grains of what looked like rice fell out, little more than dry husks, a pale straw colour.

"What are they?" He asked, unsure whether he actually wanted to know.

"Larvae," Steele's voice was flat. "I believe that's the correct term for them. *Taenia insinuii* larvae, to be precise."

"*Insinuii?*" Hesketh grimaced instinctively. "These things are *alive?*"

"Not yet, no, they're dormant. Although trust me, they'll thrive once they're in a suitable environment."

"A suitable environment?"

"Do you always just repeat whatever you hear? You must be a natural in conversation, Doctor."

"What exactly would count as a suitable environment?" Hesketh still looked down at the tiny husks, nestled in the folds of his palm. With no weight or substance to them, they looked as though they would probably blow away were he to as much as breathe on them.

"A moist, warm environment. Inside a host, for instance."

"And these things can help with weight loss? Your use of the word *parasite* worries me."

"It really shouldn't," Steele jabbed a finger at the papers. "The in-depth stuff is in there. Like I said, most of it even goes over *my* head. The thrust of it is that the organism-"

"*Parasitic* organism, just to be clear."

"The *organism*," Steele repeated, his still-flat tone masking any impatience, "migrates to the brain within a few days of introduction to a host. As part of its life cycle, it secretes a neurological inhibitor that blocks signals to a part of the brain believed to be responsible for appetite. Does that mean much to you?"

"So, it stops the host from feeling hungry?"

"No, there's nothing to suggest it does that exactly. However, it stimulates catabolism, leading to acceleration in weight loss. It should be quick and painless, with the end result that we're happy, the user is happy. Everyone's happy, even you," Steele tutted, noticing Hesketh's still-disapproving expression. "Although I'm starting to think that some people are never satisfied, regardless of their personal circumstances."

Hesketh stroked his chin. He hadn't shaved for several days, with so much weighing on his mind of late, whether or not his patients were put off by his unkempt appearance hadn't been his top priority of late. Something still didn't feel right, something that he couldn't quite put his finger on, but was there all the same.

"What has the stuff been tested on?"

"Lab mice, monkeys, the usual. It hasn't been trialled on humans...yet." Steele shrugged his shoulders again, as if the line of questioning was something of which he had already grown bored.

"Yet?"

"We live in a modern society where people constantly want more," Steele sighed as though he was being asked to explain something obvious. "More entertainment, more money, more food. More...information," he nodded. "Such as yourself, for instance. The problem being, that the gluttony of the average person, coupled with an increasingly sedentary lifestyle, has led to the obesity rates skyrocketing for the general population."

"Nothing that a focus on healthy nutrition and exercise can't put right. Short cuts aren't always the best way forward."

"If you'll pardon my bluntness Mister Hesketh, that's naïve horseshit and you know it. Short cuts are *vital* in this day and age. People don't have the time to count their calories, or to engage in an hour of cardio every day. They're far too busy wondering whether they'd be better off walking to their nearest takeaway or just ordering from their phone while they struggle to wrench their gaze away from whatever stupid reality show is blaring out from their television set at that particular time. That's the truth and you know it, I bet you see plenty of them every day. Fat, lazy people, looking for a quick fix to their problems." Hesketh mumbled something under his breath and Steele just smiled, not bothering to question him. "*Symbioloss* will provide the answer to the prayers of such people. It stimulates actual biological weight loss. It is the perfect solution, and we will market it as exactly that - once we have the evidence to back it up."

"Which is where I come in?"

"No, you don't even have to do anything about that."

"What am I actually being paid for then?"

For the first time, there was a change in Steele's tone, a shift from the calm flow of his sales pitch, as though he was starting to find the whole conversation irritating.

"As keep telling you and I'm actually growing sick of repeating, you're being paid to look the other way and to keep your trap *shut*."

"The fact that you're being so secretive about the whole thing is enough to make me suspicious."

"When will you get it into your skull? You can't *afford* to be suspicious, but if you'd rather keep playing the stubborn prick then we'll just find someone else and you can go on being up to your neck in debt. I do believe prison sentences have been handed down for far less than what you've been getting up to."

"I never said that I wanted out," Hesketh's head felt light now, almost as if he could be sick across the desk. That would be sure to go down well, if he were to vomit last night's belly full of vodka across Steele's expensive looking trousers. "It would just be good to know how you expect me to keep quiet abou-"

"*For God's sake man, you're supposed to be intelligent, use your imagination!*" Steele snapped. He adjusted the collar of his jacket, regaining his composure. "All you have to do is keep turning a blind eye."

"A blind eye to *what?*"

"To *everything*," Steele grinned again, his white teeth gleaming under the harsh, fluorescent glare of the consulting room lighting. "You know that at least one subject has already agreed to test the product of their own free will, with no coercion whatsoever. At some point down the line, we *do* want people to know about *Symbioloss*," Steele's smile broadened even further, those teeth contrasting against his oiled tan, looking almost too big for his mouth, like he could just reach across the desk and chew off Hesketh's head in a single bite. "But hey, that's why we have marketing people, right?" He rose to his feet, picking up his briefcase as he did so. He reached his right hand out and, after a brief hesitation, Hesketh took it, trying not to wince at the firmness of his grip. He's probably *a Freemason as well as a snake oil salesman*, he thought.

"Anyway, I'm glad that we've had this little chat. We've hopefully cleared a few things up. I hope we can count on your continued help, you won't regret it, *Mister* Hesketh," Steele winked, drawing a wince from Hesketh, who decided against saying anything more. "I probably won't be in touch with you again any time soon, and I sincerely hope that you don't feel the need to ask any more questions," his voice carried a faint air of menace now. "Trust me, you wouldn't benefit from doing so."

With a slight nod, Steele turned and saw himself out. Exhaling a long, drawn-out breath, Hesketh leaned back in his chair, gazing up at the ceiling tiles, the imitation leather creaking against the seat of his trousers as he squirmed back into a semi-comfortable position, using the palm of his hand to wipe away the sweat that had sprung across his forehead.

The problem was that he couldn't shake the feeling that comfort was something he wouldn't be able to experience for very much longer.

TWENTY-FOUR

Kim Dzanic knew that she was dreaming, just as much as she knew that she couldn't force herself awake. Maybe it was the alcohol that her and Frank had sunk just a short time earlier, making sure that she was slumped across his – probably flea-ridden – sofa in a drunken stupor, at the mercy of whatever thoughts were swimming around in her subconscious mind.

She was alone in a large room somewhere, sat at a large table, in what was probably the least comfortable chair imaginable, some rickety wooden thing with a plastic padded seat that made her sweat until her jeans were gummed to her arse cheeks. In front of her was a pint glass, filled to the brim with earthworms. She could hear a soft, rasping, like the sound of paper being crumpled into a ball, as their bloated bodies chafed against one another. Every now and again, several of them would try to slop over the top of the glass, their oily brown sheen glistening in the light. Her mouth and the back of her throat felt painfully dry, and her breath carried the vague taste of something stale and alcoholic. She sat in that chair, her backside glued in place as she looked at the glass, thinking of how thirsty she was, how she needed something - *anything* - to take away that foul, dry taste. Her hand felt like a lead weight as she stretched out her arm towards the glass, gripping it with numb, unfeeling fingers and sliding it across the table towards herself. Her throat felt like it was on fire, cracked and dry as she lifted the glass up in front of her face, up to her mouth, her nostrils filling with the cloying odour of damp earth and worm meat. Clenching her eyes shut until if felt like tears could squeeze their way out, she tried not to gag as the first of the creatures slid across her tongue, their fat bodies making sucking noises as they slipped against one another, wriggling and probing in search of the back of her mouth, choking off her breath as they clogged her throat-

207

She jerked awake like always, almost jumping from the sofa as she did so. Still fully dressed except for her shoes, her anorak had been draped across her as a makeshift duvet, probably by Frank. She remembered a bottle of vodka, a familiar conversation about the *good old days,* and not much else, her position suggesting that she must have flaked out at some point in the small hours. Looking down at her watch, Mickey Mouse was trying to tell her that she couldn't have had more than three or four hours sleep. It should have been worrying to know that Popper hadn't lost his talent for leading her into regrettable situations. Speaking of Frank, he was nowhere to be seen, suggesting that he must have at least made it to his study-cum-bedroom before either dying or crashing out. There was a dull sensation in the side of her head, she reckoned it would be another good hour or two before the hangover kicked in, for now she would have to settle for just feeling overly tired.

Taking her time, she dangled her feet over the edge of the sofa, feeling for the floor below. Her arms and legs still had a slightly too flexible, rubbery feeling to them, *I reckon I'm still pissed,* she thought, realising that she was voicing what was in her head out loud. Knowing that she probably wouldn't be able to get back to sleep any time soon, the next few hours were shaping up to be fun.

"How much did I put away last night?" She asked herself, expecting a little voice to whisper the answer from somewhere over her shoulder and into her ear. Stifling a yawn with the back of her hand, she pulled her anorak across her shoulders like a shawl, shivering as she shuffled towards the sink to get herself a glass of water. Her mouth and throat were parched, and she was sure that she could faintly taste damp earth, mingled with the stale vodka flavour. She reached the worktop and went to lift the saucer covering the chipped mug, before she remembered what was inside, the memory making her wince in distaste. Yeah, she wouldn't be drinking from *that* in a hurry. Shifting the saucer at arm's length, she leaned over, craning her neck to look at the contents.

"Frank," she shouted, then again, *"Frank!"*

"Someone had better be dying for you to be yelling my name like that," his voice drifted from the direction of the bedroom, low and hoarse. "My head hurts, and my mouth feels like a bear's had a shit in it."

"That's your own fault. Get up, you need to see this."

"Okay, okay, what's so important?" He crept into the kitchen area on tiptoe, as if walking on hot coals. Kim didn't speak, instead she just pointed down at the mug, shaking her head in disbelief.

"You probably need to just take a look for yourself," she said at last as he wiped sleep from his eyes, looking into the cup.

"What the-?"

The dried-up rice grains from the day before were gone, having swollen in size to three worm-like creatures, almost filling the available space as they wriggled and thrashed around in what little water was left, as though searching for a way out.

"The water must have reconstituted them somehow," he said, staring down at the bloated things moving about in the mug. "They definitely look like maggots, or slugs, or *something*."

"Big bloody dildo-shaped maggots. *That* can't be a good thing, right?" Kim still looked down at the mug and its contents. "Someone takes what they thinks is a diet pill and they end up getting a bellyful of worms. Some people might call that a rip-off." Frank didn't answer, instead he stared down into the cup, a faraway look on his face as one hand raked at his crotch. "Do you have to do that?" Kim said, "I hope you're going to wash your hands before you come anywhere near me."

"They're itching," he said simply. "Why? Is there a problem with that?" He pulled his hand from out of his shorts and lifted his fingers up to his nose, sniffing.

Kim winced. "You scruffy twat," she said, her face wrinkling in disgust. "Seriously, you really *are* filthy, aren't you?"

"Nah, you're just jealous 'cause you don't have a pair."

"Fuck right off, Popper," Kim grunted, Frank looking sheepish as he realised what he had just said. He picked up the mug, looking closer at the things inside, changing the subject.

"It's all a bit strange though, isn't it? It's like they're freeze-dried, maybe. Then, once they're inside the body..." His voice trailed into a murmur.

"Are you thinking that they really are some sort of a parasite, perhaps?"

"*Hmm*, I'm not sure. I'm not a scientist, but like I said yesterday, I remember reading that tapeworms don't usually cause massive weight loss in people with them."

"I always thought they did?" Kim scratched at her head, on guard in case he tried to move the mug nearer to her than she would be comfortable with. "I thought that was the whole point?"

"What? To starve your food source to death? It's all about balance. They only take pretty much what they need, otherwise they would just end up starving themselves eventually."

"What would be the alternative?"

"I don't know. To move on, I guess. To find another host."

"How? If they take what they need then move on, that sounds more like a predator than a parasite."

"It's like a bit of both, I guess," Frank said. He picked up the amber tablet bottle still on the worktop next to the mug. Holding it up to his face, he read the label peeling away from the front.

"One a day, to be taken with food. Swallow whole, do *not* chew, their emphasis on *not*. I guess that would make sense. You wouldn't want to chew up the contents of these things, would you?"

"One a day," Kim said, "with three in each capsule. You'd have a body full of the things in no time, assuming you didn't just shit them straight back out."

"They'd be a pretty crap parasite if that was the case, right? Perhaps they just don't live for very long, or something like that. If that was the case then you would need to keep topping it up, maybe." Kim nodded her understanding.

"That might make some sense."

"Whatever's going on here, it sounds like it could be something pretty big." Frank's eyes gleamed with a spark that Kim hadn't seen in a while, in a way that didn't happen very often. "I'm betting that the whole situation stinks. Someone out there has tried these things out on some sap of a bloke who probably wouldn't have been missed by many people if he just upped and vanished. William Marks was probably nothing more than a guinea pig, and there could be more out there just like him. That he was barely even mentioned in the local rag shows that whoever arranged things didn't give a shit about him. Christ, when word of this gets out-"

"What do you mean, *when word of this gets out?*" Kim's voice was sharper than even she had expected, taking herself by surprise.

"It gives me the handle I'm looking for on my story, right there. A blind eye being turned to some guy, probably along with Christ knows how many other people as well, being used as test subjects in some experiment, most likely for little more than the price of a large pizza every week. Given these bullshit diet pills to test out on themselves, in the hope that they'll just be quietly forgotten about if and when things go horribly tits-up."

"And that's all that you're bothered about, seriously? Getting your story? Getting the most ludicrous fucking headline you can out of it?"

"Of course not," Frank answered, raking at the side of his face with a single finger as if she had slapped him across the cheek with the force of her words. "But someone's got to stand up and say something about it, to make sure that it isn't just swept under the carpet. You know as well as I do that's what usually happens with things like this. The people behind the scenes are always the ones who get away with it."

"And that's *your* job, is it? To hold the bad guys accountable?"

"Yeah, why not? Someone's got to do it."

Kim folded her arms across her chest. She had hoped that it would all end without any sort of a scene and suddenly, it was all getting just a little too uncomfortable.

"If half of what you're saying is true then we've already seen too much. We're knee-deep in shit, with just the barest idea about what could really be going on. There's not much we can do about it, other than go to the police. Let them sort it out, and keep a low profile in the meantime."

Frank snorted, using the sarcastic laugh that he knew always used to piss her off so much back in the day.

"Christ, Frank, I'm *serious!*"

"You're serious? Really? Kim, have you even heard yourself? The pigs don't give a damn about the people around here. It sounds like your time away from the place has helped you to forget that."

"Fuck you," she raised her voice now, her cheeks flushed. "Seriously, I mean it, fuck you. For Christ's sake Frank, you're not Hunter S Thompson, getting into the thick of it all while you're off your tits on a suitcase full of drugs, so stop trying to act like you are for once. You're not some gonzo man of the people. You're just a forty-something year old man-child, still getting pissed off at the world for no good reason other than you can't get your end away on a regular basis." She thought she actually saw him rock back on his heels this time, as though she had just punched him square in the face. "You write columns for local rags, Frank, for anyone who'll have you. It's the story of your life and it always has been. You're a

hack, not some crusader for truth and justice. If this is what you're saying it is, and you try to fight it, you'll just back yourself into a corner. It'll be a fight that you'll never win."

"Is that really what you think?" Frank ducked his head and looked up, as though anticipating being hurt by what would come next.

"Yes, it's *exactly* what I think, and it's about time you actually heard someone say it. It'll hopefully wake you up out of that journalistic fantasy land you seem to enjoy living in so much. For Christ's sake, what have you got? You still drink yourself into a stupor almost every night, counting down the days until you can fuck the next skank willing to look at you for more than ten seconds."

He almost succeeded in looking hurt, betrayed in fact. She felt a pang, a tugging in her chest. *Just ignore it*, she told herself, *he needs to hear this, and if I don't say it no one else will.*

"I do it," his voice was low and trembling, as though he really had just been dealt a huge shock. "I do it because it's the only thing that I've got, it's one of the few things - just about the *only* thing - that makes me feel useful, that makes me feel *alive*. I see this shitty place where I live and it feeds me just as much as it feeds *off* me, as much as it feeds off *everyone*. I hate it – Christ knows I fucking *hate* it - but I need it. I need to tell the truth, I *have* to. *Someone has to*. That might not mean a hell of a lot to you, but it's everything to me." He paused for breath. "At least you've got something real to go home to, I don't have that, and I probably never will."

Kim's shoulders dropped as she let out a long breath.

"That's what you think. Me and Seren, we split up. A little over three months ago now."

"Really?" Frank looked at her with a mixture of suspicion and surprise. "Why didn't you tell me before?"

"You never asked me. Plus, it's none of your damn business. Why do you think I even agreed to come back in the first place?"

"Because you couldn't resist my boyish charm and wit?" He cracked a thin smile and Kim found herself smiling back. "I guess there's one more illusion you've shattered. Why then?"

"Why *what?*"

"Why did you split up? And why *did* you come back? I thought you had it pretty good, the two of you."

"The usual stuff," Kim shrugged her shoulders, "I loved her, yeah, of course I did, and I think she loved me, no, I *know* she loved me. That turned out to be the problem." Frank scratched his head, confused. "I suppose I just got bored. I couldn't put up with it anymore," she continued. "The insecurity and questions every time I went anywhere, you know, the usual thing when you're fed up with each other, but neither of you wants to be the one to have to say it out loud. Seren couldn't get her head around the fact that wherever I went, I always came back. Eventually, I decided that I'd had enough and didn't *want* to come back anymore."

"I'm sorry," Frank shook his head. "I didn't even think. She can't have been as bad as that other one you were seeing though," he grinned, trying to play down the seriousness. "You know, the dwarf? The one that looked like Jimmy Krankie?" Kim's eyes widened as she realised what he was talking about.

"You mean Toni? Oh, *piss off* Frank! I was seeing her for like two weeks, you wanker."

"That's two weeks of your life you'll never get back."

"I wouldn't want them back. She was a whole other level of obsessive."

Frank tried to look sincere, almost managing to do so. "I *am* sorry though, for what it's worth. Seren seemed good for you, apart from the fact she was Welsh. It's a shame it didn't work out." He grinned. "Besides, lesbian or not, she was pretty *hot*."

"Whatever. Seriously though, don't worry about it," Kim wiped at her eyes with her fingers, almost managing to make it look as though she was nothing more than tired. "I didn't. Besides, you know how things like that happen. Love doesn't last forever, not always."

"At least you've had it," Frank said. "You should know why I've got to do something, why I *need* to do something. I need to do it, to fill the hole. This place keeps me alive Kim, I've got to pay it forward, or nothing else is worthwhile."

"I don't know why you can't just go out and get laid instead. It'd be a lot easier, surely, even for *you*."

"I've tried that, and it didn't work, it just made my cock feel like it was going to drop off."

"So, where do you go from here, Mister Gonzo?" Kim smiled, the effort still coming across as forced-looking.

"I'm getting there. It would help a lot if I knew of a few more people taking these things," he rattled the tablets as he spoke. "It would be even better if I could get a handle on where they came from, if whoever's behind them had some idea of just what it looks like they actually cause."

"What you *think* they can cause, you mean."

"What I *think* they can cause," he corrected himself. "Although it *does* look pretty suspicious." Frank looked again at the contents of the mug. The three bloated creatures slid back and forth over one another, wet and glistening in the confined space. "Besides, if they can grow that much overnight," his voice dwindled, as if he was reluctant to consider the possibilities. He walked around Kim to the kettle, flicking it on.

"Okay, here's how it's going to go, because I know how much you love things to be planned out. We're both going to have a cup of double-strength coffee, out of mugs that have never been used to hold anything alive, not to the best of my knowledge, anyway," he said, as Kim's nose wrinkled in response. "Next, I'm going to spend a couple of hours getting some thoughts down on paper, and then I'm going to make a few calls. There must be something I can dig up on these things."

"I won't ask," Kim shook her head, her forced smile going unnoticed.

TWENTY-FIVE

"Mitch! Mitchell! I don't know why I bloody bother sometimes, this breakfast's going in the bin in five minutes! It's already gone stone cold! Like we can bloody well afford to waste food with you pissing most of what little money we have up the bloody wall!"

Mitch Brennan had tried everything to make the noise quieten down, to make it stop, all of it. He just wanted everything to go away, to stop the ride and let him get the hell off. Anything to let him have even a minute of peace. That wasn't too much to ask, was it?

Stupid cow, stupid, stupid fucking cow, he thought, closing his eyes and gritting his teeth until they ground together with a sound that made his head feel numb and the muscles in his jaw lock into place in a tight cramp. *I should have known better, shouldn't have expected anything else really. She knows that things have been tough for a while. I wish she would just leave me alone, the selfish fucking bitch, just thinking about herself as always.*

He didn't know what was worse; the grinding of his teeth, like fingernails scraping themselves ragged across sandpaper down to the quick, the sound of Carol's incessant nagging rattling around the inside of his skull, or the constant angry churning of his guts. Each of them in turn tried to cancel the others out. When everything was put together, it felt as though they could drive him mad.

Something had to give, surely.

The duvet was stifling, tucked around his head to try and block out what little light came in from the rain-spattered window. The small space was warm and fetid with his own rotten breath, almost suffocating. A part of him wished that it would smother him, just to put a stop to all the madness once and for all.

Maybe I am *mad,* he thought to himself. *It would explain a whole lot. Maybe I've gone mad and haven't realised it yet. Or perhaps it's everyone else that's gone mad, and I just haven't realised* that *yet, either.* He hadn't washed, shaved or brushed his teeth in several days, his mouth felt ripe with the taste of spoiled meat. He tried not to gag, in fact he could have vomited, were it not for the fact that he was so hungry he felt the need to cling on to any nutrition that he could. *Fucking Whitman,* he thought, *he's given me something bad, I knew he would. I should have kept well away from him, the disease-ridden bastard.* He moved his swollen tongue around the inside of his mouth, feeling rough and dry against the tender surface. The tip found something, a soggy piece of stringy meat, lodged between his teeth. He pushed at it, dislodging it and moving it to the side of his mouth, chewing it before swallowing it down. He couldn't afford to let a single morsel go to waste. His survival probably depended upon it, although a part of him still wished that it didn't, that he could just close his eyes and breathe in the warm air in his makeshift duvet cocoon until he drifted to sleep and didn't wake up again.

It should have been easier than it actually was.

No one had been to the house for several days, or so he thought. Time had stopped meaning very much lately. No visitors, although he wasn't sure if he could even be certain of that anymore.

"Mitch! I'm going to scrape it in the bin if you don't get your lazy backside down here! More bloody waste!"

For Christ's sake, whining, annoying cow! Why couldn't she just shut the hell up for once?

He thought about it. He was sure that the last time anyone had been around was three days ago now, when the postman had knocked at the door with a parcel for Carol. Some sort of diet supplement, or something stupid like that. She certainly needed it, the old heifer. Jesus, she had some nerve, calling him all the names under the sun, when she hadn't exactly gone out of her way to keep herself in decent shape either. Of course, she would probably find some way to blame him, saying something stupid like it was his fault for stressing her out, or that she had no time or reason to keep herself in shape and he wouldn't even notice any change in her if she did anyway. Yes, it always ended up being his fault somehow.

"Mitchell!"

Shut up shut up shut up! He clenched his eyes shut and gritted his teeth until the sides of his jaw ached, trying to shut out that echoing harpy whine, but nothing helped. No matter how hard he tried, he could still hear it ringing in his ears.

The postman had looked too young to even be out of school, never mind capable of holding down a proper paid job. A peppering of downy hair above his upper lip that passed for stubble and a regulation satchel slung over his left shoulder, he had looked more like he should have been sat in his bedroom playing computer games, or having a furtive tug of himself over one of his friend's old porn magazines. His face had been a blank mask of shock when Mitch had summoned up the strength to answer the front door, eyes and mouth widening into saucers as he had tried to pry behind him, whilst trying to make it look as though he was doing anything but.

"If the wind changes direction, your face will end up staying like that, that's what I was always told," Mitch had grunted, echoing the phrase that his own parents had always used to him whenever he gave anyone or anything a look of which they disapproved. The kid had flushed as red as his *Royal Mail* uniform with embarrassment, stammering something about a parcel for a Mrs C Brennan as he held out a brown paper-wrapped package.

"Right, that's it, I've had enough! I'm scraping the whole bloody lot in the bin! I wish we had a dog, that way we wouldn't waste so much food that we can't afford to throw away!"

For fuck's sake, did she ever stop, ever pause for a breath?

Afraid of what was waiting for him on the outside, he gripped weakly at the top of the duvet, peeling it away from the top of his head and face. He sucked in a lungful of stale air as he blinked his eyes, trying to dull the burning sensation behind them. As he shifted on the bed, he felt the tingling of pins and needles as the blood rushed back to his arms and legs. The only sound was that of the spatter of rain as it beat against the bedroom window, almost drowning out the noisy rush of air against his sensitive ears. His head throbbed in a rhythmic pulse that matched the rapid hammering of his own heartbeat.

He couldn't stave it off any longer, he needed to get up; he *had* to get up.

But he was just afraid. So afraid.

He pushed the cover away from his body and dragged himself into a sitting position, still wearing the same clothes that he had lain down in three days earlier, he couldn't be sure just how long exactly.

He caught sight of his reflection in the full-length mirror that hung from the closed bedroom door, unable to look away, as much as he wanted to. His face was pale and drawn, his cheekbones sunken and his eyes bulging out from darkened sockets, as if he had held his head underwater for too long.

"Mitch! What the hell are you doing up there?"

He wanted to scream, to shout at her to be quiet, to stop yelling and just give him a few precious minutes of peace, but he knew that he couldn't, not really, not ever.

Because he knew that, just like the sound of her unrelenting voice, she was just inside his head, as she had been for several days.

There was a low rumble in the bottom of his gut, a horrible, churning sensation that refused to go away, no matter what he tried.

And he really had tried almost *everything*.

The pain behind his eyes was more intense now, he looked away from the mirror, away from whatever it was that he had become - whatever it was that Whitman had *made* him - and down at the shapeless thing in the corner. A mess of ravaged flesh, sinew and bone, identifiable only from the ragged red uniform and the discarded satchel, envelopes spilling out across the floor unopened.

"Jesus, God, it hurts so much..."

(*mitch what are you doing up there*)

"God help me, I'm so *hungry*..."

Sinking to his hands and knees, his arms and legs like jelly, he dragged himself, inches at a time, to the corner, the rumbling in his belly refusing to stop as his nostrils were filled with the thick odour of raw, rotting meat, to match the taste still clogging the back of his throat.

Closing his eyes again, trying to ignore the stinging tears welling up behind the lids, he bowed his head, burying his face into the gaping split belly of the dead postal worker. Like a pig into a trough, he sunk himself deep in until it felt like he would suffocate on the cold, greasy viscera. He sobbed as he sucked and chewed hungrily on bloody entrails, his teeth tearing eagerly into fat and gristle as he fed, desperate to fill the aching void inside himself.

TWENTY-SIX

He had tried to call Bob Martinson first, the problem being that he had already been on his way to being drunk at the time, certainly drunk enough for Bob to hang up the phone in disgust. It was probably around the same point where Frank had mentioned that Kim was asleep on his sofa. Maybe it was just as well that she hadn't stirred, the feeling was more than mutual. He had done so well, keeping off the drink for a few days, surely just one or two couldn't hurt, right? The problem was that *one or two*, had quickly turned into the best part of a bottle. Just a few, to help him unwind. That was the usual excuse, right? Staggering to his feet, he had shoved what was left of a quarter bottle of vodka into one jacket pocket, a notebook and pencil into the other and a cigarette behind each ear, before stumbling from his flat in search of Little Joe instead.

***

He hadn't needed to look too far. Joe had been camped against the back exit of an Indian takeaway, his usual nighttime retreat, away from the noise of the bars and clubs, the air thick with the heady aroma of spices. Why Joe chose there, Frank had no idea. The bastard did nothing but complain about how hungry he was most of the time, the smell couldn't have helped. Some guy was kneeling down alongside him, a thin, bald-headed rodent of a man with bad breath, wearing a stained anorak that stunk like week-old piss.

"All right, Joe. I'm guessing the ratboy here is Skeevy, am I right?" Frank spoke slowly, trying not to slur his words too much.

"If you've come here for no reason other than to insult my good mate, you can just fuck right off, Popper," Joe grinned, his eyes glassy and vacant.

"Popper?" the rodent chuckled, flashing yellowed teeth. "That's spot on that is. *Popper.*" He laughed out loud, as though he had just thought of the world's funniest joke. "It's like, you know, *Popper,* like *poppers?*" he spread his hands, confused as to why no one else was laughing at his wit.

"Pull up a chair Frank," Joe patted the palm of his hand against the cobbles alongside him with a hollow slap. "It's a bit cold and damp, but it might do you some good to feel how the other half live for a change."

"Don't mind if I do, Joe," Frank hitched his trousers before squatting alongside them both, wincing as his knee joints cracked. He dipped into his jacket pockets in turn, setting the vodka bottle on the cobbles, before bringing out the notebook, pencil, and a dog-eared twenty pound note. "I've got twenty quid that I'm willing to part with in exchange for any more information you might have on those tablets you swiped from Marks' place." Skeevy's eyes widened at the sight of the cash. *He's probably already cooking up his next crack rock in his head*, Frank thought.

"What kind of information 'you after?" Skeevy's left hand twitched as though readying himself to snatch the money away before Frank could change his mind. "Fuck's sake, I swiped you that book from the place, you know, the one you still haven't given back. The photos and the tablets as well. Pigs'll be breaking my fucking door down any day now. I'll make sure they know who's got them."

"Calm the hell down, before you give yourself an aneurysm, or whatever it is you smackheads get."

"Why, you cheeky *cunt-*"

"Lads, *lads,*" Joe raised his hands. "There ain't no need for any bad feelings. We're all friends here, right? Skeevy son, you want the magic beans, you need the means, yeah?"

Skeevy looked again at the crumpled twenty, still in Frank's outstretched hand. It wouldn't go far, but it would be better than nothing. "What do you need?" he grunted, the tone of his voice grudging as he shuffled back against the wall.

"Anyone coming or going from Marks' flat in the few weeks before he died," Frank said. "That's all. Especially anyone dodgy-looking. If you saw anyone else with the tablets, then that's even better." Skeevy snatched the money away from him, letting out a dry snort as he stuffed it into the pocket of his anorak.

"Give me a swig of your vodka there and you've got yourself a deal."

***

His eyes closed, Frank rubbed at his temples with both thumbs, trying to massage his thoughts out from beneath whatever hungover tangle they were caught up in. He had been sitting in the same position for almost an hour, stripped to the waist at his desk. The sex noises of the next-door neighbours had ended, now he was trying to ignore the internal clock that was counting down the minutes to the shouting and arguing starting up once again.

The notebook in front of him had painfully few words scratched onto the page, his drunken reminders to himself from the night before barely even legible. It was pointless even trying to read them. Looking for any sort of inspiration, he reached across for the glass jar next to his typewriter, turning it around in his hand. He had found a half-empty pickle jar in the refrigerator, making sure to eat the not-too-far out of date pickles first. Once empty, he had transferred the worms, or parasites, or whatever the things from the capsule were into it, topping it up with water and making sure that the lid was screwed as hard as his neighbours. At Kim's insistence, he had thrown the mug in the dumpster at the back of the flats. An overnight soak in neat bleach wasn't quite good enough, apparently.

The things looked as though they had died soon after he had moved them, their thrashing movement stopping, and their deep red colour dulling to a dirty brown hue. Still, between them they almost filled the jar. Thick and rubbery, they resembled sort of a cross between a worm and a slug, with a circle of what looked like tiny, curved hooks in place of a mouth, a bit like photos he had seen of tapeworms. *Kim seemed right about one thing*, he thought, scratching his head. Whatever they are, it *looks like they have a pretty short life cycle*. He couldn't be sure whether that was a good or a bad thing.

"What the hell are you?" He mumbled, staring at the creatures as though trying to force an answer from them. "And who would want to put a shitload of you into something being handed out as slimming pills?" With a grimace of distaste, he put the jar aside and returned his attention to his notepad, trying again to decipher what he had written down the night before.

Doctor.

Pills.

Hesketh.

He could remember that Skeevy had looked desperate to talk, beads of sweat peppering his spotty forehead as he tried to keep his teeth from chattering. He had probably already cooked or snorted up half the money that Frank had slipped him in exchange for the information that he could hardly remember now anyway. The three words written down in front of him didn't help that much, either, making him wish that he had stayed sober.

Hesketh. The name sounded familiar, although he couldn't quite place where he had heard it before. Something to do with that slapper, perhaps. The one that he had shagged in that nightclub bog. No, not her exactly, but something else. Something to do with the last time he had seen her, not in a toilet cubicle with her tits rubbing in his face, but-

He jumped from the chair, almost tipping it over as he ran to the telephone on the wall in the kitchen. He looked at it, hesitating before reaching for it with his fingertips. He stopped; what was he - *stupid?* The Marigolds, *where were the Marigolds?* Aware that he had started to shiver now, he looked around, panicking as he realised that the rubber gloves were nowhere in sight. He tried to clear his head, to not think of the soft touch buttons, crawling with all manner of bacteria. Sweat pricked up across his forehead as he imagined the sort of diseases that a person could catch. Bits of old dirt, sweat, and germs nestled in the crevices between the keys, all manner of filthy microbes, munching on rotten skin flakes, just waiting to cross over to his hands. *I think I can do this,* he closed his eyes, trying not to cough as he could feel his chest starting to tighten, as if his ribs were shrinking, pushing the air from his lungs and squeezing against his heart. *No, I* can *do this. For fuck's sake, Frank, think about it. It's not like you've never stuck a part of yourself somewhere worse.* The thought didn't help much. Jesus, what would Kim say, if she knew that her favourite paragon of filth felt sick at the thought of touching telephone keys? She would probably just tell him to stop being so soft and get a grip, right after she had done pissing herself laughing at the irony of it. *That* thought didn't help much, either.

He closed both of his eyes then opened one of them slightly, his sight blurry as he reached out with a single finger to jab at the numbers, the tip feeling like it could start to burn at the touch. He stood back as the ringing started.

"Hello," the familiar voice was clipped, straight to the point. "Doctor Hesketh's surgery, how can I help you?" He jammed the receiver back into its cradle, as if it had just caught fire in his hand. He had heard all that he needed to, there was no need to prolong his discomfort any further. He clutched his chest, waiting for his rapid breathing to slow down to normal once again. *I'm a fucking journalist*, he thought, *I can't go on like this, cowering every time I need to use the 'phone. It's just a lump of plastic, that's all.*" Still, he moved back, looking down at his hand the whole time, as if some crawling thing had just leapt from between the keys and burrowed its way beneath the fleshy part of his palm. *Hesketh*, he thought, *he's that doctor. The one that I tried to get in to see when I first started asking about Marks.* He walked back to his desk, wiping his hand against his trouser leg.

"What has *he* got to do with any of this?" He thought aloud, telling himself that the quivering in his voice was nothing to do with any residual fear. "Apart from the fact that Marks was more than likely a patient of his." There were blanks that needed to be filled in and there would probably be more calls to make. He looked across at the telephone again, shuddering as he did so. *"This is ridiculous,"* he muttered, *"I'm more than happy to stick my pecker in anything with tits and a pulse, but I can't even* think *about touching a telephone or computer keyboard without hyperventilating."*

He looked from the telephone back to his desk, at the half-empty bottle of scotch next to his typewriter. His sturdy, safe typewriter, with its chunky, germ-free keys. A sheet of paper still protruded from where it had been fed through the roller, tilted forward as though wilting under the weight of what few words had actually been committed to it. His thought processes had been slow enough to be painful of late. Perhaps Kim *was* right about him after all; a forty-something, drunk, still filled with what he liked to tell himself was righteous anger, looking for a vent, a way to express himself, to feel like he was still relevant somehow. He looked from his hand to the whisky bottle, then back, as if in readiness to reach out and pick it up. *Go on*, he thought, *just do it*. One swig wouldn't hurt, after all. That was probably the problem anyway, he just wasn't drinking enough.

Just one.

Then the bottle was suddenly in his hand. It felt sturdy, his grip strong, much stronger than the grip of someone with no willpower, surely? He couldn't even remember reaching for it, as if it had just moved into his reach using nothing more than the power of his mind. He couldn't tell how long he had been standing holding it, half-formed thoughts in his head, disjointed and unfocused, questioning why he was even interested in what had happened to William Marks. For God's sake, it wasn't like anyone else gave a damn, why should he be any different? Was it really so Marks would be noticed, or so *he* would? Noticed, *really* noticed, instead of having to pick up nightclub drunks, spinning them lines about his dazzling career in investigative journalism.

Drunken. Selfish. Prick.

Eyes closed, he raised the bottle to his mouth, feeling his warm breath hitting the glass and rebounding, making his lips burn in guilt-ridden anticipation.

Drunk. Fucking useless drunk.

He drank a mouthful, then another. Then another, barely noticing that he was sobbing as he did so.

TWENTY-SEVEN

He had always found that sobriety had a habit of making his hands worse. *Essential tremors*, as he liked to call them. Probably a combination of stress and age, nothing he could do or could have done to prevent them. All doctors were supposed to have spidery handwriting anyway, it was the golden rule, right? Those times when the shaking in his fingers made even holding a pen difficult just served to add an air of authenticity to the fact. He had mastered the art of ignoring the way that they seemed to improve after even just a couple of sips from the bottle that he kept hidden in the bottom drawer of his desk.

It didn't help that James Hesketh was scared. Whether he was afraid of what he would see, or perhaps what he wouldn't, he couldn't be quite sure. He used the bandage wrapped around his left hand and thumb to mop away the perspiration that had collected across his brow, despite his shivering – nothing but the cold, of course. It had been bad enough that he had spilt his morning coffee, the resulting scald now itching with that deep-seated rawness that felt like something burrowing beneath his skin.

It'll be fine, they had promised. *Do your bit, shut up and take the money. No one will be hurt.* He had listened, trying to assure himself that he had weighed up any pros and cons with his years of medical judgement. In truth, he hadn't listened at all, weighing up nothing except the possible answer to his personal problems versus the emptiness of his bank account. He could have blamed *her* of course. His ex-wife never did understand how stressful it was for him, with the health and wellbeing of so many people under his charge. She just couldn't give him the slightest bit of leeway when he unwound at the end of those long days with a few drinks.

Frittering our money up the wall, she used to say, *drinking far too much* and, *you're going to make yourself ill one of these days.*

It was funny how quickly the divorce had absolved her of any previous worry over his health, as well as taught her how easy it could be to piss *his* hard-earned cash right up the wall. With her young new boyfriend and her sudden expensive tastes, making the sort of effort that she'd never made for *him*, it was easy enough to blame her for driving him to it.

We can make your problems go away. Just take the money and keep quiet.

It had sounded so straightforward. Then William Marks had died and there was no escaping the likelihood that the tablets – whatever they actually were - were the cause. That *he*, the man who had been so quick to turn a blind eye in the first place, was the cause. Steele would be free to go on with any denials that he might have cared to make. It was easy enough for him to dissociate himself from everything. It would be far more difficult for *him*, if word ever did get out. That had probably been the point all along. Perhaps he had been little more than a fall guy. He didn't have a lot left to lose, but what he did have was still just about worth clinging on to.

It had to have been the pills. There couldn't be any other medical explanation for how a seemingly rational man could go from tipping the scales at just over seventeen stone to being little more than skin and bones, chewing lumps out of himself to try and survive, in almost a month. Hesketh had seen Marks for himself, when he had first attempted to remove anything incriminating from the flat. Just how long the man had been there in that state, he couldn't be certain. He knew that it must have been less than a week, the last time he had seen Marks alive. Anything after that however was anyone's guess. All that he was sure of was that

William Marks had died, a pathetic, emaciated mess, and it was thanks to him as much as anyone else.

He reminded himself again of what he was doing; trying, in his own way, to put things right again, as best as he could.

Susanne Walters was only twenty-three years old and, the same as so many like her, her lifestyle choices were already starting to catch her up. He had last seen her just a few days ago, unable to ignore how different she had looked. Not just different – *thinner, that* was the word he was looking for, there was no point in trying to dress it up as something else. His suspicions had been aroused. Whether he was expected to look the other way or not, she was just the kind of person that Steele had talked about, someone who wanted to keep on with their convenient, lazy way of doing things, but who didn't want to have anything bad to show for it.

A perfect candidate, she probably wouldn't say anything to anyone, just as long as she could keep getting wasted every Friday and Saturday and shed a few pounds while doing it. That didn't mean that she deserved the same fate as William Marks though.

It just needs to be a quick visit, he told himself, mopping at his brow with the bandage again. *Just like a house call. If she's suspicious of anything, I can just tell her that I'm checking up on her, it's fair enough. Hell, she'll probably be fine anyway*, he tried to convince himself.

The lift juddered to a halt and the door ground back with a sound like fingers dragging down a chalkboard. He released the breath that he had been holding to avoid the stink of stale urine and vomit. At least the thing was working, he wasn't sure that his legs could have made it up even just the couple of flights of stairs, not after the day that he'd had. Honestly, if he had been faced with one more lavender-smelling old lady asking for something to help her sleep, or another snotty, diarrhoea-riddled toddler, he could have gladly thrown himself under the nearest bus. God, it would have been the perfect answer to *everything*. However dubious the morality of it.

He walked, the soft soles of his Trojans whispering against the granite-look floor, his head turning from left to right as he looked for the flat number that he had found in Susanne's medical record. The whole place looked like some throwback from the early 1970s, an appearance complemented by the faint musty smell, giving the air of an old peoples' home. The ceiling had a yellowed, nicotine-stained look. All of the doors were painted the same shade of dull green, the paint blistered and flaking in some cases, the only thing distinguishing them being the large brass numbers on each.

"Just a house call, that's all," he reminded himself again. "I'm not even here as a doctor, not really. Just someone who's concerned." He turned into the last part of the hallway, a dead end, with three doors on each side. The light cover was missing, probably smashed, and the fluorescent bulb flickered, its weakening glare making the grimy, beige-coloured walls look even closer than they were. He suddenly felt wary, as though he was stepping into somewhere that he really had no business going. He shook his head, trying to dispel the mental image of Marks, slumped in a pool of his own mess, his last thoughts probably being of how alone he was, how desperate and close to death, and how he knew that no one was coming to help. What if Susanne Walters was the same? What if she was even *worse?* He should have figured out that something was up when she came to him with the stomach cramps and nosebleeds. He should have asked her outright if she was taking anything. He should have told her to stop, to throw the pills away, to just *burn* them and have done with it. But he hadn't done any of those things, because he was weak and selfish. No, his patients had stopped being as important as his own self-preservation a long time ago. *My bitch of an ex-wife drove me to it, that oily prick Steele persuaded me with the promise of help*; they

were all just pathetic excuses. There was only one person to blame
in all of it. The one that he saw whenever he summoned up enough
courage to look at himself in the mirror.

He stopped. The door was ajar, the narrow gap showing no sign
of light behind.

If she asks, I'll say that I was just worried, he told himself. *She
didn't show for her follow-up appointment the other day, and I was
concerned about her. It makes as much sense as anything else in this
whole mess.*

He pushed against the door with his unbandaged hand, the
tremors worse than he could ever remember them feeling. The door
had a solid, sturdy feel to it, the way that they used to, back in the
days when people used to actually still care about such things. It
swung back with an ease that was surprising.

As he crossed the doorway into the darkness, the first thing
that hit him was the smell. A damp, sickly odour, a little like food
that had been left out for too long.

Oh, Christ, he thought, the image of Marks flaring up before
his eyes once again, so real that he could almost see the corpse in
front of him. *What if I'm too late? What if she's sitting dead in a
corner somewhere, just a pile of decomposing skin and bones?* He tried
to suppress a shudder, his hands shaking worse than ever now. God,
he needed a drink.

"Susanne?" He called out, his voice reed-thin, even in the
cramped hallway. *"Susanne?"* He leaned forward, cocking his head
as he strained his ears to listen for any sounds of life, any clue as to
whether she was alive or dead. *"Are you in here? It's Doctor Hesketh."*

There was no answer. Perhaps it wasn't such a good idea after
all. Maybe Steele had been right with his suave yet forceful
insistence that he should just get on with what he was being asked
to do, just stay out of it. It wasn't like he actually *knew* her or
anything. To all intents and purposes, she was a nasty piece of work

anyway, the kind of person who wouldn't be missed by too many people if anything bad *did* happen to her. *"Susanne?"* He called again, trying to keep his voice low, worried that he might draw the neighbours' attention to himself. That wouldn't help, if word got around that he had decided to call unannounced. The soft soles of his shoes whispered like crêpe paper against the laminate floor as he stepped forward, almost resigned to the realisation that he wasn't going to see anyone.

"Susanne-"

(???)

He didn't actually feel the pain, not in the way that he might have expected, at least. Instead, there was a sensation a bit like a torch being flashed into his eyes, a brief, sudden brightness that flared before him, heralding what was to come.

***

"You didn't hit him too hard, did you? We can do without him crashing out or anything."

"Sorry."

Hesketh tried to lift his head, grimacing through the pain that was lancing through his temple. He had been pretty much blindsided, and who - or *what* - ever it was that had got him had belted him a pretty good one. The side of his face was pressed against the floor, and he narrowed his eyes, straining them to try and peer through the darkness.

"Susanne...?" Susanne Walters stepped out from what looked like the side bedroom, as if in reply at the sound of her own name. At least it *looked* like Susanne Walters. She was barely recognisable as the slightly overweight young woman who had sat in his surgery just a few weeks before, with a gushing nosebleed and worrying about chronic migraines and the scruffy journalist bloke who had taken her from behind. She was naked, and even thinner than

before, almost painfully thin-looking. Her breasts drooped, all the fat sucked away from them, and her ribs protruded, the skin between them sunken, as though even the muscles had been eaten away. *My God*, Hesketh thought, *it's too late.* Loose folds of empty flesh hung down from her upper arms and thighs. Unbelievably, she was smiling, her anaemic lips pulled back from her teeth, giving the incisors a lengthened, almost fang-like appearance, the cruelness of her grin matched by the cold behind her sunken eyes.

"It's okay Alex babe, he's still awake," she stepped forward. Her voice was a rough croak, as though coming through a mouthful of gravel. "He needs to be. He needs to feel what's going to happen." She stepped forward, crouching down close to his head, her breath carrying an underlying odour of something rotten. "What do you reckon, Doc?"

"Susanne, it's not too late," Hesketh tried to stifle a gag as he tried to move away from her face, inches away from his own. "You can still get help. I know about the tablets, you need to stop taking them, if you haven't already."

"Tablets? *What* tablets? I ain't been takin' no tablets. But me and Alex, we can't keep our hands off each other now, ain't that right, Alex?"

"Yeah," another female voice came from behind him, probably whoever it was that had hit him from behind. "At it like rabbits now, aren't we? I mean, just *look* at her. I know it gets me horny every time *I* do."

"What about you, doc?" Susanne reached out her hand, brushing at his crotch with the back of her skeletal fingers. "I mean, I know you're pretty old and that, but I bet you could still get it up if you *really* wanted."

"What's happened to you?" Hesketh moaned, the pain in his head spreading as it diluted into a numbness. "You need help." Groaning, he flexed his arms to try and push himself up, the pain in his bandaged hand all but forgotten now. "I can go and get you the help that you need-"

The air was forced from his lungs in a gasp as he was seized, a hand hooking him beneath each armpit and pulling him back.

"You don't get it, do you? You stubborn old sod," Susanne moved closer again, still smiling. He could see the lines etched into her face where the once plump cheeks were now drawn and haggard, and the sour smell of her breath was almost overpowering. "It's *you* what needs the help. I'll help you, then you'll know just how much better things can be."

"Help? Me? H...how?" Hesketh stammered, unable to move. "I really don't want to take them, and I don't think you should, either. I mean it, Susanne, it's not too late."

"What *are* you banging on about, you old git? *I haven't been taking any fucking tablets!* Don't worry, it'll all be okay, really." She leaned over him further, her sagging breasts brushing against him as she did so, the sensation filling him with a coldness, a mixture of fear and revulsion. "Just a few minutes and it'll all be done with."

"What...I...don't know what you mean-" he cried out as his head was grabbed from behind, Alex's hands clamping it at either side like a vice. At the same time, Susanne leaned over him, her mouth yawning open above as she held her face above his. She still looked like she could have been smiling. As he looked, he could see something, a movement somewhere at the back of her mouth.

"What the-?" he tried to form the words, his voice cut off as her bony fingers gripped the top and bottom teeth, prying his jaws open with a strength that didn't seem possible. Unable to look away, he watched as it wriggled its way up from her throat to the front of her mouth, a large, slug-like creature. Red and oily-looking, about four inches in diameter and almost phallic in appearance, what he imagined to be its head turned blindly from side to side as it pushed itself forward, the tip ringed by a circle of small, sharp

INSATIABLE

hooks. The thing slid over her lips in a trail of silvery mucus, slipping into Hesketh's waiting mouth below. He gagged as he felt it probing, choking him as it pushed down his throat and past the folds of his epiglottis as it burrowed its way down into his oesophagus. Tears sprang to his eyes as he felt the fleshy lump pushing down his gullet, choking him as it continued to slide its way down inside him. Still, his jaws were held open, stopping him from coughing the thing back up. Only once there was no chance of him doing so, Susanne stepped back, giggling as Alex let go of his head. Hesketh slumped back to the floor, retching and spluttering.

"Stop being so soft about it," Susanne said, rising to her feet. "You're like one of us now. In a few days' time, you'll be thanking me for that."

"*What have you done to me?*" Hesketh forced the words out between gasps of breath, his lungs burning as his stomach heaved. "What the hell have you *done to me?*"

"Passed it on," Susanne shrugged her shoulders, as if surprised by his reaction. "Repaid the favour, if you like." She smiled again, stepping back, as though she was done with him and had lost interest. She was silhouetted against the faint light that came from the side room, picking out the sharp angles of her bones. "You'll get what I mean soon," her voice had an almost faraway quality to it, as though she had discovered some great secret, and he should have been honoured that she had chosen to share it with him. "You'll realise how much better everything is." She raised both of her hands, to cup her deflated breasts. "When I say everything, I mean *everything*. Ain't that right, Alex?"

"Oh yeah, that's right," the other woman spoke, still out of sight behind him. "The best ever." He felt a prodding in his lower back as she nudged him with her foot. "What 'we gonna do with him now though? He's making the place look proper untidy."

239

"Yeah," Susanne laughed. "Right scruffy. We'll leave him for a bit - *all right Doc?* Don't you worry, you can just lie there for a little while, till you feel better, anyway." Still cupping herself, she backed towards the bedroom door. "Better not make it too long though. Me and Alex, we've got some stuff to be getting on with."

"I'm *hungry*," Alex stepped over him to follow, being careful to avoid him, as though he was infected with something nasty. "*Starving*, in fact."

"Hmm, me too," Susanne's voice carried through from the bedroom. "Not just for food, either."

They both giggled as Alex followed close after, closing the door behind her and leaving him alone in darkness once again.

TWENTY-EIGHT

"I'm disappointed in you Frank, really I am, man."

Hareesh Batra almost managed to look sincere, shaking his head slowly from side to side as he delivered the words in a way that was so overly-solemn as to be almost laughable. "It's all or nothing with you, ain't it? You swear off the stuff for weeks, claiming that it keeps you from thinking straight. Then you crawl in here looking like death warmed up and buy enough cheap booze to put Oliver Reed to sleep."

"Oliver Reed has been dead for a few years now, Harry."

"I'm not surprised, especially if he drank anywhere near as much as you."

"I'm just stocking up," Frank slid two bottles of the cheapest scotch from the shelf across the counter, wincing as they clinked together. "You should be glad you've got someone like me to keep you in business."

"That's as maybe, Popper. I still prefer my customers to stay alive." His smile didn't quite make it to his eyes, as if he had been expecting an argument of some kind. "You look as though you're a couple of days away from your liver crawling away to die alone."

"Thanks Harry, you're all heart, you know that, don't you?"

"It's all an act, really." Batra leaned forward across the counter, extending his hand to Frank's shoulder. "Seriously though," his voice was softer than usual, as though he was trying to sound sincere for a change. "What's bothering you, Frank? You're stocking up? I've seen that look on your face before."

"*What* look?"

"The look like a smacked arse, *that's* what look. The one you get whenever there's something bothering you. Don't tell me you still haven't managed to turn Kim."

"She's not into blokes, Harry, and she's not a crank handle. She's also one of my oldest friends, so I wouldn't even *dream* of going there. Trust me, you don't know the half of it."

"A bit like Thatcher, eh?"

"What?"

"You know," Batra smirked, "the lady's not for turning," he folded his arms across the front of his smock, looking pleased with himself.

"Ha, very funny," Frank reached into his inside pocket, bringing out several ten pound notes. "Now are you going to let me buy these, or are you just going to keep on proving how unfunny you can be?"

"Seriously though Frank, what's eating you?" Frank chuckled, the irony of Batra's words not lost on him, the sound was empty, hollow to his own ears. "Oh, you *do* remember how to laugh?"

"Yeah, if only you knew." Without thinking, Frank reached for a cigarette tucked behind his ear and flipped it into his mouth. He groped in his jacket pocket for a box of matches.

"Don't you bloody dare," Batra waved his finger. "The smoke alarm's right above your head. The couple up there don't need an excuse to kick off, I don't want to give them one."

"Screw the smoke alarm, and screw the couple upstairs. I need a smoke."

"*Frank...*"

"Okay, okay, I'm sorry." Frank yawned as he itched at the side of his face, his ragged chewed fingernails rasping against several days' growth of stubble. "I haven't been sleeping too well lately, and no, it's got bugger all to do with Kim."

"What then? Have you been on the bennies or something?" Batra's eyes widened. "Oh, this hasn't got anything to do with that bloke in the paper from a few weeks back, has it? 'You *still* trying to get your head around that?"

"It has and I am," Frank's voice was muffled as his lips still clamped the cigarette in place. "Although I'm a bit disappointed that you would jump to conclusions, thinking that I'm on uppers." He sighed, "I thought it was going to be easy, you know? Do a bit of digging, put together a couple of columns. Christ, Harry, the guy had basically wasted away in his own flat, chewing his own arms half off to try and keep himself alive. It just pissed me off to think that no one out there gave a toss about him."

"So, what's the problem? Apart from the fact that it doesn't sound too much like the sort of thing most people would like to read about over breakfast?"

"Well, it's," Frank hesitated, not really sure if he should be volunteering even the small amount he actually knew. "It's pretty complicated, you know? I've opened up a whole can of worms," he paused again. "In more ways than one."

"What have I said to you before, about pissing the wrong people off? You haven't, gone and done something *really* stupid, have you?"

"Not yet, not that I know of, anyway. I get the feeling though, that if I push too much further then I might end up doing just that. Trust me, it ain't exactly straightforward."

"For the sake of a story? An attempt to avenge some dead guy you didn't even know?"

Frank didn't answer, instead he just nodded, looking down at the counter. He tapped the neck of one of the bottles with a forefinger. "This is the alternative," he said. "At least it's familiar and safe."

Batra smiled, and Frank found himself wondering just how the man managed to keep his teeth quite so white. "Funny, you never really struck me as the play-it-safe kind, Frank. Not knowing some of the stuff you've gotten up to in the past, anyway."

"There's a first time for everything, I suppose."

Batra took each bottle in turn, sliding them back across the counter, just out of Frank's reach. "There. You see? I'm making a decision for you, an executive decision, if you like. Ditch the alcohol, worry about the consequences later and concentrate on getting your bloody story sorted, along with whatever else is bugging you."

"Trust me, you don't know all the details, Harry-"

"But I know what a miserable pain in the arse you can be when you're not getting stuck into things, in more ways than one," he let out a sly chuckle. "You *need* to do this, Frank. I know what you're like by now, you can't get by without it."

Frank pulled himself up to his full height and un-hunched his shoulders, the bones in his spine cracking as he did so. "You're probably right," he said. "I can't really afford two bottles anyway. Besides, I'd only have to keep Kim from finding it."

"She's still sticking around?" Batra raised his eyebrows. "Must be the longest stretch for a good while. How much is she in on things?"

"Enough," Frank said. He didn't really want to have to go into detail about the capsules or their contents. "She knows enough." He pointed at the shelves behind Batra, with a nicotine-yellow fingertip. "Pass me a couple of extra packs of King Size then, would you?"

"Swapping cirrhosis for lung cancer, yeah?"

"I'll take whatever's coming to me." Frank took a lighter from his jacket pocket and, ignoring the look of disapproval on Batra's face, he sparked it against the tip of the cigarette still in his mouth, inhaling deep as he did so. "I prefer to live in the moment, and they help me to focus."

Turning around, Batra reached up and took two packs of cigarettes from the top shelf, putting them down on the countertop.

"Here you go," he said smiling again as he held out his hand for the money. "Now, piss of out of my shop and get some work done." Frank handed over a couple of ten pound notes.

"Keep the change," he said. "I reckon you've earned it. You've talked some sense into me. Kim would be shocked I tell you, *shocked*." He turned, reaching for the door handle.

"Hey, Frank Popper," Batra called after him. "Try and lay off the booze for a bit, yeah?"

"I'll try," Frank smiled. "And hey, Harry?"

"Yeah?"

"Thanks." He turned and left without another word, allowing himself a faint smile as the door swung closed behind him, the bell above the door frame announcing his departure.

He took one of the new packs of cigarettes from his pocket and slid a ragged fingernail around the cellophane, before peeling it away. Taking a fresh cigarette and placing it behind his ear, he drew again on the one already in his mouth, smoking it down almost to the filter before exhaling through his nostrils.

"Well, James Hesketh," he said under his breath, "since a drink isn't an option right now, I reckon it's about time we found out what you've been up to."

.

TWENTY-NINE

He wasn't stupid.

Oh, he had made some stupid decisions, some *really* stupid decisions lately, but that wasn't a reflection on his intelligence, not by any means. He had gotten away with it all for a long time, mainly due to hard work and careful application, rather than any sort of raw talent. He had always tried his best not to mess up and, for the most part, he had managed okay, right up until he had made that one mistake. One stupid, careless mistake, that he had tried to cover up, only to compound it with another, then another, like brushing the tip of your finger against the first domino to set off the whole row.

No, he wasn't stupid, not at all.

But he *was* a coward.

James Hesketh knew what was coming, he had figured it out fairly early on. He had made a conscious decision to ignore his suspicions, choosing instead to keep on burying his head in the sand. He had continued trying to convince himself that if he couldn't see it then it couldn't really be true.

Yes, he was a coward all right.

He couldn't remember too much about how he had made it back home. He had no idea just how long he had remained in that dark hallway, listening to the two of them, chatting and giggling, as if they were doing nothing more than swapping dirty stories of their previous conquests. Once he had that thing inside him, it was as though they had lost all interest in whatever he did, happy enough to leave him to his own devices. Eventually, he had come to the realisation that they had no real intention of coming back to him, not even to check up on him. They had given him that impression already, when they had left him in a heap on the hallway floor, to go about their business as though there was nothing out of the ordinary at all. So, he had just lay there, waiting for it, for any sort of movement inside him. He let out a soft groan every time he thought he could feel it, the sensation palpable, like a baby kicking inside the womb of its mother. It was something that had been described to him many a time over the years, by wide-eyed expectant mothers-to-be, while he had sat across from them listening with his best practiced expression of concern, hoping that his eyes hadn't simply glazed over with boredom. He could feel it for himself now, he knew that it was there.

***

They had sounded like they were having sex when he left. Having *sex*, no more than two or three hours after they had violated him, pushing him down and forcing that *thing* inside him. It really was as though they were no longer interested in him at all. *You'll thank me for it soon*, Susanne had said. If he closed his eyes, he could still see it, like some parasitic slug, dropping itself into his mouth and squirming its way inside him.

He had made it home in a daze, with just one thought on his mind: he had to get it out of himself somehow. He didn't know exactly how it worked, but he still had a good idea of what it could do to him if he didn't. He had been so willing to look the other way, not even entertaining the thought of who could be hurt in the process. He had let his own bitterness and greed cloud his judgement. He looked at the photograph he held in both hands, his knuckles white as he gripped onto the tarnished frame like it was the only thing keeping him from tumbling down into some bottomless pit. The picture was of a younger self, standing alongside his wife on their wedding day. They both looked so young, almost idealistic somehow. The expression on his face was one of pride, mingled with what looked like a sense of optimism, of the idea that everything was going to be straightforward, that it was all going to work out all right. For a little while he had been able to hold on to that belief, both with his marriage and with his career.

"It's all your fault, you conniving *bitch*," he muttered, the face of his wife staring out, her eyes looking through him as though his accusations didn't even warrant a response. "All your damn fault," he said again for good measure. He knew that it wasn't though, not really, even though a part of him was sufficiently bitter to hope that if he kept on saying so then it might become the truth. She might have been the one to set the ball rolling, but he had picked it right up and kept on running with it, for far longer than necessary. She was the one that had called time on a marriage that was probably already dwindling, moving on to someone younger, while still happy enough to keep on taking his money, so she could go on living a lifestyle that she had grown accustomed to. It was his decision to stagnate however, to stand still and hold on to the bitterness that he felt, until his heart was hardened and cold. Whether he actually meant to do so or not, it was just the way things were. He had liked to tell himself that the offer made to him by – let's face it – a salesman, was one that he had to consider long and hard, but that wasn't really true, either. The very thought that his problems could be made to go away was one that had widened his eyes from the start with an almost clandestine sense of promise. It had almost struck him as having some sort of romantic appeal, the idea that he was rebelling against a system that had been rigged against him for long enough, forcing his hand as it were.

It was all a load of bollocks, of course. He had just been weak, as always. Too weak to keep his grip on his marriage, too weak to resist the allure of vacuum-filling vices like alcohol and gambling, far too weak to know better when someone that he didn't even know from Adam dangled a fat carrot right under his nose. Who really cared about things like background checks and product research, as long as the payout was good? Sure as hell that *he* hadn't. He was supposed to be a *doctor*, for God's sake. Oh, he was happy enough to turn a blind eye while one of his patients dwindled away to nothing, pretending that he didn't know the cause. Marks had been the easy one, he didn't really have anyone to tell anyway. A stranger in a strange country, with no friends. He had even come from a scientific background himself, so had approached the whole thing like an experiment, something with tangible results to be recorded. He had gone so far as to show his notes off to Hesketh on one occasion, ordered and tabulated, almost like a real, legitimate study. There probably would have been hell to pay if Steele had ever got to know about it. He had forgotten about that when he had first discovered the body, looking for anything that could possibly link him to the dead man when he had stepped into a scene like something you would expect to see in a horror movie. Hesketh could still almost smell the thick stink of that room. A nauseating mixture of rotting flesh, shit and piss, the only sound the soft yet incessant drone of flies. Marks had missed his regular diabetes check-up and must have lain in that same spot for a few days at least. Even then, any thought of doing the right thing was pushed aside by the urge of self-preservation. Hesketh had pocketed two vials of the pills, prying one of them from the dead man's hand. He had just hoped that there were no more. Something like that could land him in serious trouble. He had returned to his home in a frantic daze, drinking himself into a stupor, because he knew how good *that* habit was at making all of his problems go away.

He had waited another two days before calling the police with an anonymous tip-off about the strange, lonely man in the fourth floor flat. Two days of pretending that everything was normal, going to work by day and drinking not quite enough cheap booze to blot the images from his mind by night.

It had taught him a big lesson in his own sense of morality all right.

It was those same couple of days later, in the small hours when sleep wouldn't come, when he had remembered about Marks' journal keeping, how he had written up every last detail like he was recording some ongoing science experiment. In the wrong hands, something like that could have definitely landed Hesketh in a whole heap of trouble. Weighing up the risks, he had gone back to the flat under the cover of darkness. Apart from the blue plastic tape strung across the front door to render it a potential crime scene, the place had remained unchanged, looking just the same as it had that morning when he had first found Marks' emaciated corpse. The smell of decay, of old blood and rotten flesh had still lingered, hanging like a dull taint in the stifling air of the flat, as though it was ingrained deep in the cheap plasterboard used to build the walls. A thin layer of dust had coated most of the available surfaces, clinging to grime and grease, not that there was really anyone around to notice. He had tried to avoid looking down at the floor where the body had sat undiscovered for so long, the soft soles of his shoes making a shucking sound as they lifted away from the sticky, congealed mess on the linoleum. With a sweating, nervous apprehension, he had snapped on a pair of latex gloves from his surgery, the powdered rubber clinging to his clammy hands like a second skin. Trying to stay calm, he had looked everywhere that he thought the notes might have been hidden, only to come away empty handed. Marks had either destroyed them, knowing that the end was close, or they had been taken, someone beating him to it.

He really hoped it was the former. There was a pretty good likelihood that, even if he wasn't mentioned by name, someone with half a brain could put two and two together, at least enough to ask some awkward questions. If someone had taken them and decided to read them, then there was a chance that he could be done for. There was no amount of money that could save him from the kind of prison sentence he would get for any involvement. Even if he hadn't contributed directly, he hadn't tried to stop anything either, which was probably just as bad, especially if a man was now dead as a consequence. The oily assurances of Steele had felt a million miles away as he looked down at his hands and saw that they were trembling as bad as ever. He took several deep breaths, trying to ignore the sour death smell that tried to fill his lungs.

It's okay, he had tried to tell himself, wiping at his watering eyes with the back of his sleeve. *I'm getting ahead of myself. No one knows, apart from the people who need to. The Walters girl has been okay, apart from a few nosebleeds and stomach cramps. She's probably just got herself up the stick, nothing to do with the damn things anyway.* He had known, even then, that he was clutching at straws, but it was the best he had. Besides, if he kept telling it to himself, it might become true sooner or later. He had looked around the room one last time. Dim and sparse, there was a faint scratching noise, coming from a far corner. He told himself it was probably just a floorboard shifting, nothing more.

As for his nerves, it was nothing that a couple of drinks wouldn't soon put right.

***

He was still holding the photograph, gripping hard enough for the bandage to chafe the knuckles of his burnt hand. The pain had all but gone now, the least of his worries. He could have laughed at the thought of how important it had seemed just a few hours earlier.

He had seen what they could do, how a man on the verge of being clinically obese had been reduced to an empty sack of skin and bone in a matter of weeks. Not just that, but what they had made him do to himself in the process.

Then there was Walters and that other woman that had been with her, a girlfriend perhaps? The fact that she had acted the same way suggested that the things could spread from person to person. Of course, he had since found that out for himself. Closing his eyes again, if was as though he could feel it still; the small, phallic-looking slug, writhing its way out of her mouth and into his. The sensation as it burrowed and probed its way into him, looking for a warm place to hide and breed. He didn't know much about the details, having avoided being drawn into any real conversation about it, apart from the one with Steele at the bar. He hadn't even bothered to look at the notes that he had been given. Doing so probably would have made it harder to go on looking the other way, something that even Steele probably would have agreed with. However, he wasn't stupid. He had a good idea of what was in store. He knew that he probably didn't have too long. If he didn't act soon, he might no longer be able to.

But he was still scared.

He looked at the picture again, narrowing his eyes as tears squeezed their way from them.

"You...*bitch!*" He cried as he flung the frame away from himself, across the room and out of the door, where it smashed against the far wall of the hallway beyond. He had entered into things without a second thought for anyone else involved, without considering the possibility that someone could get hurt. Now he understood as he rested his head on the table and sobbed, all too aware that his tears were for no one other than himself.

THIRTY

"Hello Bob, how's it going?"

"Who is this? I don't believe we've spoken before," Bob Martinson turned his head away from the telephone, clearing his throat with a snort. He'd had a head cold for the last few days and his sinuses still felt like they had been pumped full of concrete that had been allowed to set.

"You don't recognise my voice? I'm hurt. Well, you always liked to make the odd snide comment that it hadn't quite broke yet. Maybe the hormones reversed it. They really are magical things you know, hormones." Kim gripped the receiver as she spoke, gritting her teeth. "Seriously though, I'd heard a rumour that some of you Geordie types were a bit dense, but I didn't think that covered having a bad memory, too."

He hesitated, "*Kim? Kim Dzanic?*" He said at last, his voice wavering, still uncertain.

"The one and only. You see? You *do* remember me. There was me starting to worry that I wasn't memorable enough."

"Christ, man, that was ages ago. Besides…nowt happened." Kim could hear a soft scraping over the line, as if he was cupping his hand to try and stifle the conversation. "I thought I'd heard the last from you when you buggered off to, *I don't know*, wherever it was you buggered off to."

"That would have made your life a whole lot easier, wouldn't it?"

"Not really," Martinson sighed, as though he would rather any conversation was over. "Because, like I told you, nowt actually happened, like."

"Not for want of you trying though, right?"

"Yeah, that was before I realised that you were two steps away from being a rug muncher." Kim felt her eyes narrow as she gripped the phone harder, the skin of her knuckles tightening.

"Same old silver-tongued bastard, eh? For the record Bob, I'm *trans*, that doesn't mean I chew carpet."

"It's a figure of speech, Kim-"

"*I know what it is, you dirty bastard*. Nothing might have happened, but that's only because I shot you the fuck down."

"For God's sake Kim, it was a bit of harmless flirting. I can't help that you took it the wrong way-"

"*You prick!*" She cursed herself for raising her voice, unable to keep from doing so all the same. "You all but had me pinned in the corner, trying to get your tongue down my fucking throat. If it wasn't for Frank-"

"Oh, of course, I forgot, *Frank*. The world's biggest Boy Scout. Give me a break, Dzanic, he's hardly a guardian angel, in case you haven't noticed. The rest of the world has moved on, it's about time you did the same." Martinson moved the receiver away from his ear, ready to hang up.

"You never *did* tell your wife what happened, did you?"

"What?" He moved the phone back into place, wanting to be sure of what he had just heard.

"Oh, you heard me. You never told Lisa about how it didn't bother you when you tried to grope someone who still had a cock at the time. I wonder if she would be interested in knowing about how her husband got bladdered and tried to force himself on another woman, while she was sitting at home, eight months pregnant with their first kid."

"You *wouldn't*," Martinson felt his voice weaken, unable to hide the feeling of nervousness that had crept in as his throat suddenly felt dry. "Why would you even want to do that? We've been married almost ten years. She'd leave us and take the bairn with her."

"It would serve you right, you dirty Geordie bastard."

"*Yeah Vicky, pet, I'm just following up on it now,*" he sounded muffled as he turned away to speak, before returning his attention to the caller. "What the bloody hell do you want, Kim?"

"Apart from a trip down Memory Lane? Nothing much, just some information. Tell me what I want to know, and I'll keep what you *don't* want Lisa to know to myself, I promise."

"Information? *What* information? Ha'way man Kim, stop talking in riddles, for Christ's sake."

"The kind of information that'll stop me from telling your wife what a nasty scumbag you really can be." Kim waited for some bravado comment, or typical insult. Instead, there was nothing, except for the sound of chatter in the background. "Well, I'm waiting. Some sort of an answer would be nice."

"What *do* you want?" Martinson's voice was hushed, his usual tone of irritation absent. "Hurry up and just get it over with, whatever it is."

Kim realised that she had been holding her breath, waiting for his response.

"I want the truth. Not just the bits of it that you *want* to share."

"I don't know what you mean-"

"There you go again. You really can't help it, can you? *Gobshite,* isn't that what they call it up in your neck of the woods?"

"Okay," Martinson sighed. "I'll tell you what I know, but it isn't much, I *mean* it."

"It's probably better than nothing. Now we're getting somewhere," Kim grinned, and she almost wondered if he could feel it somehow through the telephone line. "I reckon there's something about this story that Frank's been looking into.

Something you haven't been telling him, and it's been doing his head in."

"I told the stubborn wanker that I didn't think he should get involved, that he's best off out of it."

"Fair enough, but you said it yourself, he's a stubborn wanker. So, what else have you got?"

"I was only thinking of him, you know? I do actually care about him."

"Yeah, so much that you slinked away and let him feel guilty when he found out that you all but tried to fuck me. *That's* caring?"

"For God's sake Kim, it wasn't like that!"

"It was *exactly* like that," she was surprised at just how emotionless she sounded. She had always known that she would have to face up to it all at some point and call him out on what he had done. She had never thought that it would be used as a means of blackmailing him though. "Speaking of caring, you've got thirty seconds before I hang up and make another call. Guess who *that* one will be to?"

"Okay, *okay*," Martinson stammered, not wanting to call her bluff. "But most of what I tell you is off the record, okay? None of it's been confirmed and some of it's just me guessing, trying to put pieces together for myself."

"I'm really past giving a shit, Bob. Just tell me what you've got, and I'll decide whether it's useful or not."

Martinson took a couple of deep breaths before he spoke again. "The diet pills, the ones that Frank said were found in William Marks' flat? There's definitely something dodgy about them."

"No kidding," Kim said, "I reckon we already figured that one out. You don't usually find maggots in your paracetamol."

"What? *Maggots?*"

"Never mind. Go on, tell me something I *don't* know."

"After he asked us, I tried looking for anything to do with a clinical trial, anything that could've helped Frank with what he was checking out. He seemed really hell-bent on uncovering something. I haven't heard him get so riled up by a story in a long time. Anyway, I tried digging around and," he paused, as if for dramatic effect. "Nothing. Well, next to nothing, anyway."

"No information at all?"

"Nah, nowt," he repeated for emphasis. "It's usually possible to find something, if you know where to look and you dig deep enough. There's no record of any clinical trials, or even research. Not down your neck of the woods and certainly not on any sort of diet pills. That alone should have been enough to set alarm bells ringing."

"So, whatever these things are, there's something not kosher about them?"

"Hey, you're pretty quick off the mark, aren't you?"

"If I were you, I'd talk nicer to me," Kim snapped. "There's still time for me to change my mind."

"Okay, I'm sorry. Anyway, Frank did give us the names of a few people that he said were involved. He wanted us to try and see if there was any connection between them."

"And was there?"

"Yes and no," he paused again, and Kim heard the faint sound of him gulping something down. He probably kept a bottle of something strong hidden away in his desk drawer, if he was the same person she had once known. "William Marks and Elizabeth MacKinnon lived pretty close to one another, in the same block of flats, in fact."

"Hmm, go on."

"Frank mentioned someone else, too. Some young lass that he banged in a nightclub, called Susanne Walters." Kim winced at the words, actually surprised that Frank had been sober enough to remember the woman's name, the dirty bastard. "She lives in the same place as well."

"Why would Frank ask about *her?* Was he wanting to go back for seconds, or something?"

"Beats me. Maybe he had a hunch. There is one other thing though. I don't know if Frank knows about it, but-"

"But *what?*"

"For fuck's sake Dzanic, let us finish, will you?" Martinson paused. "Wait a second," he whispered, turning away from the telephone again. "Nearly done pet," Kim heard him say. "Aye Vicky, another couple of minutes."

"You were saying?" Kim didn't want him to change the subject, not now.

"They all had the same GP. Some fella called Hesketh. Frank mentioned him a few weeks ago. Said he had gone over to the surgery to try fishing for info on Marks. Apparently, the receptionist there was a right snotty old cow."

"Hesketh, you said, yeah?"

"Aye," Martinson took a deep breath, the sound whistling down the telephone line. "That's pretty much all I know, I promise."

"Well, I suppose we'll soon find out, won't we?" without saying goodbye, Kim put the phone down, jamming the receiver into its cradle before he could say anything more. He was probably telling the truth, or at least a pretty near version of it. He had more than enough to lose by lying.

She walked to the sofa and sat down, resting her head in her hands as she let out a sigh. She hated trying to sound aggressive, always carrying the worry in the back of her head that she would be found out. Martinson was right about one thing; in all the time she had known Frank, she had ever seen him quite so focused on anything. He had left some time before she had woken, a rare feat in itself. She had no idea when he would be back, knowing how things had been lately, he was probably off chasing his own tail, or drowning his sorrows in a pub somewhere by now.

She had waited more than long enough to use any sort of leverage against Martinson. What he had so many times dismissed as little more than a simple misunderstanding had driven a wedge between Frank and her for a long time. Once he had found out what had happened, Frank had chosen to deal with his sense of guilt in the same way he dealt with anything else that he didn't like, by clamming up and burying his head in the sand. He had clung to the prehistoric notion that he should have done something to protect her, his inability to do so leading to his just trying to convince himself that perhaps nothing *had* happened after all, serving only to make the tension between them even worse. She could never have held him accountable for what Martinson had tried to do to her, but she could definitely blame him for the way he acted like a complete prick afterward, refusing to get his head around the fact that, just because she hadn't been reduced to an immediate needy mess, didn't mean that she couldn't have needed a friend to confide in. In the end, rather than end up resenting him, it was easier for her to get far enough away to give herself some room to breathe. Frank Popper was well-meaning enough, but when it came to friendship, he could be toxic, whether he meant to be or not.

But he was still one of the closest things she had always had to a real friend.

Martinson had more or less implied that they had stumbled across something far worse than a clinical trial. He had also all but suggested that the pills, with their parasitic contents, were somehow responsible for more than one death, and that whatever was inside them could perhaps be spread from one person to another.

"Where the hell are you, Frank?" She asked aloud. "And what have you managed to get us both into?"

THIRTY-ONE

It one of the rare occasions where the drum roll bouncing around inside Frank Popper's head wasn't alcohol related.

The worst part of his neighbours' almost daily arguments were the attempts at making up afterward. Four-thirty in the morning, that was when the noise had finally stopped bleeding through the tissue-thin plasterboard wall. *Four-fucking-thirty.* In the end, he had gotten dressed and left the flat early, leaving Kim to fend for herself while he went for a walk outside. He could already feel that the magical effects of the three mugs of double-strength coffee that he'd downed first were wearing off, leaving him with a fluttering in his chest, a weakness in his legs, and the feeling that he would crash and burn before too much longer. At least the back of his throat wasn't furred up, caked with so much cheap booze that it felt like there were hairs growing on the roof of his mouth, so that had to count for *something.*

Finding James Hesketh's home address had been the easy part. The good doctor lived in a modest semi-detached house in one of the so-called nicer parts of the city, if such a thing as a nicer part of the city actually existed. As far as Frank was concerned, all that meant was that he had slightly less chance of being stabbed to death, or being propositioned by some dealer or prostitute while he stood across the road from the place.

He took a last drag on the cigarette clamped between his lips, before removing it and flicking it away with one finger. He watched it land in a puddle, where it fizzed and sputtered out. Kim had made no secret of her opinion that smoking was one more bad habit that he should quit. He had tried before, but he always needed *something* to fill the emptiness, especially when he was struggling as much as he had been. Besides, he liked to try and convince himself that every artist needed *one* vice, even a hack like him.

He had a whole bunch of questions, readying himself to see the good doctor squirm. He was prepared for the likelihood that Hesketh would probably just deny whatever accusations were thrown at him, but Frank could still make damn sure that he knew that he was onto him. He had always thought himself pretty good at bluffing.

It was just a little after eight o' clock and there was no sign of life from the house across the street. The blinds and curtains were still drawn, and the only movement was of the apple tree in the front garden, its branches bowing tired towards the ground as its leaves rustled in the light rain.

"Okay Doctor," Frank muttered under his breath as he crossed the road towards the small driveway. "Nice and polite, let's find out just what you've got for me."

***

He had knocked at the door several times first. It usually paid to at least try and be courteous, even if there was no answer the first few times. Even if all the lights were out. Even if the front door was unlocked. *The hell with it*, he had thought, *I've gotten away with worse. It's not breaking and entering unless you actually* break *something*.

"Doctor Hesketh? Doctor *James* Hesketh?" He called out as he stood in the front hallway, easing the door closed behind himself. "My name's Frank Popper. I'm an investigative journalist and I've got a few questions I was hoping you could maybe help me with?"

No answer.

"Yeah, just a few questions about a patient of yours, a guy by the name of William Marks. I've heard that you were maybe helping him to try and lose a bit of weight?" At the mention of the name,

Frank thought that he heard a faint sobbing noise coming from ahead, standing out against a silence that suddenly felt too stifling and uncomfortable. "Is there anyone there?" Frank felt the hairs on his arms and the back of his neck rise although he didn't know why. "Hesketh? Are you in here?" On the floor ahead of him, there was a picture frame, the glass shattered across the plush carpet, shards glinting in the light. The photograph inside was a wedding picture, the couple stood arm in arm, smiling. Frank noticed that the expression on the face of the woman looked forced, as if she was perhaps thinking of somewhere that she would rather be – or someone that she would rather be with.

"You leave that alone," the voice that drifted from the other side of the doorway ahead sounded weary. "It's got nothing to do with you, it's just one more lie. They all add up, sooner or later, until they're big enough to finally catch you out."

Stepping forward, Frank pushed against the door, wincing as it swung forward with a groan that broke the stillness.

"Doctor Hesketh, I presume?" *Jesus Christ*, Frank added inside his head, *the bastard looks like he's been put through the wringer all right.*

Hesketh had dragged a chair out from under the kitchen table, in which he was reclining as though drunk, his legs splayed out in front of him. Pale and haggard-looking, his suit was crumpled and dishevelled, his white shirt spattered with what looked like a mixture of blood and vomit. There was a smear of the same below his mouth and across his stubble-flecked chin. On the table in front of him was a large glass, half-filled with a slightly cloudy liquid.

"Who...who are you?" He asked with a sluggish murmur, as though he had just been awoken. "Did *he* send you?"

"My name's Frank Popper," Frank stepped forward, instinctively holding out his hands, as if to show that he was harmless. "I've got no idea who or what you're talking about. I'm an investigative journalist and I've got a few questions to ask you."

Hesketh chuckled, the dry sound cracked and forced. "Well, Mister Investigate Journalist, or whatever you said your name was, I'm afraid I'm not really in the right sort of mood for an interview." He paused, coughing up a wad of phlegm that he spat out on the table in front of him. Frank was close enough to see that it was tinged with pink.

"This might be a stupid question, but do you think you might need a doctor?"

"No, that's the *last* thing I need, believe me," Hesketh looked down at what he had just hawked from his lungs, an expression of dismay on his face.

"What were you hoping for," Frank asked already suspecting the answer, "trying to teach yourself to gob up fivers, are you?"

Hesketh wiped at his chin with the sleeve of his jacket, trailing more blood across the lower part of his face. He didn't look bothered. "Well, I'm wondering if you might have some idea already. Hacks like you usually pride yourselves on your *journalistic hunches*, don't you? I'm guessing that's what brought you here?"

"I'm here because of a patient of yours – a *former* patient, that is. William Marks." Frank noticed a brief look of what could have resignation flicker across Hesketh's face, as though he really had known what was coming, having expected it sooner or later. "He died in a room a little bit like this," he looked around as he spoke, trying not to let the bitterness he felt creep into his voice. "Not quite as...nice, though. Do you want me to describe how he died, doctor? I've seen photos of it and, believe me, I've hardly slept a wink since."

"No," Hesketh shook his head, the movement slow and deliberate. "I know *exactly* how William Marks died. *Exactly*. I saw it as well, first-hand."

"Care to enlighten me?"

"No. Fuck off."

Frank dragged a chair out from the opposite side of the table, scraping it noisily across the floor, before sitting. He spread out both his hands again. "That wasn't very professional-sounding of you, was it? Look, I might be a hack, but I'm a patient hack and I've got all day, believe me. I've certainly got more time than you, from the look of things." He pointed at the glass in front of Hesketh. "What's your poison?"

"It's salt water," Hesketh cupped his hand to his mouth this time as he coughed again, a slight retching noise escaping as he did so. "It's usually the best thing if you need to throw up. There's a healthy measure of vodka in there too, of course, just to take the edge off a little bit."

"Why would you need to be making yourself sick, I wonder?" Frank shifted on the uncomfortable wooden chair as he leaned forward. "I could hazard a guess, us *hacks* are pretty good at that, like you say. But it's always better to hear it from the horse's mouth, isn't it?"

"*Be...because I...bec...*" Hesketh's face contorted as he almost doubled over. He turned his head to the side and yawned his mouth open, disgorging a jet of clear liquid that sprayed across the light-coloured floor tiles. Frank watched unsympathetic as he heaved again, the pool of vomit widening as it spread its way across the floor. Hesketh's fingers hooked into claws and his eyes rolled back in their sockets, his face turning red and seeming to swell as he convulsed, as if in the grip of a seizure. His jaw opened and closed in a silent spasm, foam flecking the corners of his mouth as he gasped, choking. Still sitting, Frank was about to move when Hesketh's whole body seemed to arch backward, before lunging his head forward again.

Huuurrrpp!

As Frank watched, Hesketh's jaw dropped as something wriggled, straining to free itself. A large, slug-like creature, like one of the things that he had found in the capsule, but larger, was protruding from Hesketh's mouth, wriggling as though trying to escape.

"What the hell-" Frank had suspected what might have been about to happen, but he was still unprepared for the sight. An almost blood red colour, with a slick, oily sheen, the thing slid from its hiding place, landing in the wetness below with a *plop*. At the same time, Hesketh fell back in the chair, his chest heaving as he gasped for breath, like someone who had stayed underwater for far too long.

Frank stepped around the table. Looking down for a second, he saw what Hesketh had just coughed up from inside himself. A fat, bloated slug, about four or five inches in length, it writhed blindly, slithering around in the puddle, as though trying to search out somewhere warm to hide. Still without saying a word, Frank raised a foot, before bringing it down again on the thing. He let out a grunt of satisfaction as he felt it pop like an over-filled water balloon under the pressure, grinding his shoe against the floor for good measure, his heel slipping around in the resulting slimy mess. Keeping his foot flat against the floor, he pulled it back, dragging a trail of bloody mucus in its wake.

"There," he muttered. "I fixed your mess for you." He turned to look at Hesketh, who was still gasping and wheezing as he tried to suck air back into his lungs, wiping blood and slime from his face with the back of his hand. "Now, you arrogant prick," Frank said. "I think it's about time you told me something about what the hell you've been up to."

"Really?" Hesketh looked down at the smear of blood and flesh streaking the tiles, an almost rueful smile on his face. "You do realise that it's far too late for me, right? I've tried, believe me, but

I've probably left it too long already." He wiped at his mouth again, trying in vain to scrub away the taint of the thing. "I didn't even have the guts to follow *that* through properly."

"It might help if I had the first idea of what you're talking about." Frank slid a glass of water across the table towards him. "It's fresh," he said. "I've figured out a few bits and pieces, but there are a whole load of gaps, which, I reckon, is where you come in."

"Why are you so interested?" Hesketh looked up, confused.

"Because a man died, and he's been forgotten about far too conveniently for my liking."

"*One* man?" Hesketh laughed openly now, the sound cold and hollow. "You're bothered about one man? Who you didn't even know? You're right about something, you really don't have a bloody clue, do you?"

"Oh, I'm getting there. But feel free to enlighten me, all the same," Frank thought that he hid his sense of shock quite well. The last time he had checked, doctors were supposed to be bothered about those people under their care, not give less than a flying fuck for them. He leaned forward across the table, placing his hands in front of him. "Don't miss out any of the details. I like a tasty bit of gossip, me."

Hesketh pointed a finger at the tarry smudge on the floor. "How do you think I ended up with that thing inside me? I'm telling you now, it wasn't from taking any damn diet pill."

"Maybe not, but you all but fed them to William Marks."

"I did no such thing - *Marks took them of his own free will!*" Hesketh sounded flustered, his breathing still hoarse. "*I didn't pin him down and force them down his throat!*" He coughed, his voice still hoarse and thick with mucus. "That was never a part of the deal. I just looked the other way."

"That's as maybe," Frank insisted, "but I bet you didn't tell him any of the risks, either."

"I can't advise a person on risk when I don't know what the risk *is*," Hesketh said, his voice as matter of fact as it could sound.

"You gave someone an untested medication, without knowing what it might do to them? You're an even bigger shit than I imagined."

"For the last time, I didn't give him the damn things."

"Whatever, it's all semantics really, I'm sure. You still sat back and ignored what was happening while he took them, yeah? That's just as bad. How much was his life worth to you, Doctor?"

"Of course, I bet you're whiter than white. Mister Popper. Trust me, at this point in time I don't really give a toss what you might think of me." Hesketh let out a sigh, as though growing bored of the conversation. He shrugged, as if volunteering information that he knew he didn't really have to. "The point is, the problem goes beyond the pills. For God's sake, I only know of one person taking them, and he's dead, as you know. The person who did this to me, she didn't take them, not to the best of my knowledge, anyway."

"*She?*" Frank repeated. "What about her?"

"She's still very much alive." He nodded at the remains steaking the floor again. "Acting like some sort of a plague carrier." Frank looked at him, confused. "She pinned me down and forced it down my throat. You could almost say she *violated* me. There, I've given you a headline, are you happy now, *investigative journalist?*"

"So, you're saying that it can be spread from person to person?"

"Oh, you are a bit cleverer than you look," Hesketh smirked, struggling into a better sitting position. A trail of bright blood began to run from his nose, dripping down onto his vomit-stained shirt.

"Who else? How many others have been infected? Who knows about it?"

"So many questions."

"*Stop taking the piss and just answer me!*" Frank snapped. "You've already made a mess of things, it sounds to me like you've helped to cause a hell of a problem that needs dealing with properly."

Hesketh's eyes rolled upward as he looked at the ceiling, as though searching for an answer. "I honestly have no idea," he said at last, rolling his tongue as he spoke with deliberate slowness. "What I do know is that, like any parasite, the thing can spread quickly and easily. Even easier than I would have thought. Not that I'm an expert on such things, of course."

"What is it? What does it *do?*" Frank could feel himself growing agitated, almost certain that he wasn't going to like what he was about to hear. He glanced at Hesketh's bottle of vodka, still at the side of the table, the sight of it enough to cause a dryness in his own throat.

"It's called *Taenia insinuii*, or so I've been told," Hesketh nodded. "Although I'm not a parasitologist, so that probably means just as much to me as it does to you."

"Fair enough, it's got a fancy name. How does it work?"

"It secretes a chemical that is supposed to affect neurotransmitters to the brain," Hesketh rolled his eyes at the look of confusion on Frank's face. "Don't look at me like that, you *did* ask me. "He cocked his head to the side. "It's supposed to regulate - *switch off*, if that sounds better - the part of the brain that causes cravings, whilst increasing catabolism."

"Cravings for food?"

"Cravings for *anything*. Unfortunately, it looks as though it has the exact opposite effect. Fat and tissue are both broken down rapidly. But the desire to replenish that lost mass with feeding seems to increase considerably, along with," he paused as he recalled his own experience, the way Susanne Walters had been, before she had attacked him. He could still see the look of cold glee in her eyes as she had leaned over, her slack flesh brushing against him as she forced herself upon him. He remembered what she had said, the way she had spoken. "I don't know," he said, "a loss of inhibition, perhaps." He didn't bother to detail how much he thought that to be an understatement.

"So, it turns people into super-skinny, sex-mad cannibals?"

"And there you go, still trying to condense it down into your next tabloid headline," Hesketh smirked as if to say *I told you so.* "I'd hoped that you were a little smarter, but you really don't surprise me at all."

"That's far more than I can say for you," Frank muttered. "What kind of a man willfully puts the people that he's supposed to be caring for into a situation that he knows will hurt them, maybe even kill them?"

"I didn't know for sure that it would."

"That's horseshit and you fucking well know it," Frank snapped. "You knew damn well that it wasn't above board. You probably even knew that it wasn't *legal.* And for *what?* Money? A shot at fame?"

"Don't you try and judge me, you bastard!" Hesketh raised his voice for the first time, his attempt at appearing disinterested wearing thin. "I've got *nothing*, my life has hardly been worth a bloody thing for ages now. I've been stuck in the darkest place you could think of for months and when I was offered a way out, yes, you're damn right I took it. I won't apologise for doing so either."

"Then you're even more of a selfish, narcissistic cunt than I thought." Frank stood, scraping the chair across the floor as he did so. "And you deserve whatever's coming to you." He could feel a prickling heat spreading out from the base of his neck. "At least you had a chance. William Marks and, I'm guessing Elizabeth MacKinnon and her boyfriend as well, they weren't as lucky as you. Not by a long way."

"I wouldn't be so sure," Hesketh's voice cracked, betraying emotion for the first time. "That thing's been inside me for long enough to multiply by now. I have no idea how quickly it does so, but I know that it has a short life cycle. It's probably more than enough for it to be too late for me."

"Are you saying what I think you are?"

"What I'm saying is that I've got no chance of puking up all of whatever it's left inside of me."

"Try telling it to someone who gives a damn," Frank backed away towards the door. "Because I'm as sure as hell that I don't." He turned and walked away before Hesketh could come back with any more snide responses.

Hesketh slumped forward, his head resting against the table.

No chance of puking them all out.

"There'll be more of them, you know," he shouted, his voice cracking under the strain. *"More people, not just here, God only knows where else!"* There was no response, he really was alone again.

Not for the first time, he started to sob, as always, thinking of little more than how he had ever managed to get himself into such a stupid bloody mess.

THIRTY-TWO

"Honey, I'm home!" Frank called out as he slammed the door behind himself. He flung his key into a bowl on the side kitchen worktop. Doing so always made him feel like a swinger, someone who at least got some semi-regular action. "Kim? Hey, I'm back," he shouted as no response came. She didn't usually sleep in so late, she must have gone out somewhere, probably to the nearby pub. Fumbling in his pocket for any money, he thought about heading off to try and meet up with her, he could even maybe stretch to buying that couple of pints that he probably owed her. His fingers brought out a toothpick, a stuck of chewing gum, a ballpoint pen, chewed at one end, and a single latex glove, for emergency telephone use.

So much for *that* idea then.

He took off his old jacket and draped it over the back of the nearest chair. Walking to the refrigerator, he opened it. Gazing at the two bottles of beer still in the door compartment, he thought about how much he needed them, before cursing himself and reaching for the milk instead. It was nothing that a double-strength coffee probably couldn't replace.

He pulled a mug from the cupboard and switched on the kettle, waiting for the hissing of the heating water to start.

It wasn't until he had poured his coffee and turned towards the kitchen table that he saw the note. A scrap of lined paper, probably torn from one of his old notebooks and pinned beneath a porcelain salt cellar, a few sentences had been scribbled down in Kim's usual *spider-crawling-across-the-page* handwriting:

Frank,

I've been trying to do a bit of scratching around for info while you've been busy. I thought it was about time I got my arse in gear and helped you a bit - that is why you wanted me back down here in the first place, right? I called Bob. Don't worry, I didn't say anything that he didn't deserve. He gave me some ideas on where to look. He mentioned someone called Elizabeth MacKinnon, who lived in the same block as your Marks bloke.

I shouldn't be too long. Reckon it's your turn to pay for the food. I'll settle for pizza!

- K

Elizabeth MacKinnon? That was the name of the woman who had died with her boyfriend, or whoever else the half-naked corpse in her flat with her might have been. Tutting to himself, he reached for the coffee jar with one hand and picked up a tablespoon from by the sink with the other. Popping the lid of the jar, he dumped two heaped spoonfuls into the waiting mug as the bubbling of the kettle reached a peak before clicking off. Hopefully, a large dose of caffeine would be enough to keep his cravings for something much stronger at bay.

Picking up his coffee, he walked to the sofa and sat down, cursing under his breath as a small amount of the hot liquid slopped over the side of the mug, spilling onto his leg. Clutching the mug in both hands, he blew across the surface, dispelling a faint cloud of steam.

Kim had taken it upon herself to call Bob Martinson? *That* must have taken some doing. There was a whole history there, one that Frank didn't really care too much to remember the details of. He sometimes regretted the way that things had played out, not feeling particularly proud of the way he had treated Kim back when the shit hit the fan. He was surprised that she had ever agreed to come back after the way he had been towards her. Many a time, he had thought of doing the right thing, of telling Bob just where to get off. But the truth was that Frank was as selfish as always. He needed contacts, people with inside information. Bob Martinson was still one of the better ears to the ground that he had. It didn't hurt that Frank had plenty of leverage over him, either. He wasn't proud of it, but at least he got by. He probably would never have followed through on any of his many blackmail threats, but the less Bob knew about *that*, the better.

He took a sip of coffee, wincing as the still too-hot liquid burned the back of his throat. He still felt guilty that he hadn't been there for Kim though. It didn't matter whether she was tough enough to stick up for herself or not, he still felt like he should have done *something*. He always had. He wondered what time she had left and when she would be back. Maybe they would have time to stop by the pub for an hour. He could even get the first round in - that *always* went down well. Leaning back in his chair, he took another mouthful of coffee.

Then spat it across the table in a dirty brown spray.

He jumped from his seat and snatched up Kim's note, rubbing his eyes with his thumb and forefinger as he scanned the smudged scrawl, making sure of what it said.

He mentioned someone called Elizabeth MacKinnon, who lived in the same block as Marks.

MacKinnon; she was the woman who had been found in her flat with a dead male friend. The two of them had looked as though they had died in some sort of bizarre murder-suicide sex game, one where the winner ended up eating chunks from their own body.

Hesketh had said that Marks had lived in the same block of flats, in The Reds, one of the most run-down, socially-deprived parts of the city.

He had also mentioned that Susanne Walters was living there, too. Jesus fucking Christ, three of them in the same building, all of them carrying a parasite that had the ability to spread *really* quickly.

And Kim was heading right for it.

He dropped the note and ran across to the telephone on the wall, before stopping in his tracks. Kim didn't own a mobile phone, she never had. She'd always hated the things, blaming them for everything from cancer, to the government being able to pinpoint a person's location. She had always bought into all manner of conspiracy theories, she would probably love the idea of some secret person or group, plotting to carry out illicit drug trials on the most easily forgotten people in an overcrowded city.

At least she would love it, if someone or some*thing* didn't get to her before she heard about it.

***

"What's she told you, like? I hope you didn't listen to her, 'cause whatever it was is a lie."

"Shut up, Bob, I'm just trying to find her."

"Try one of them, you know, dog whistle things. She'll come back in no time, man."

"Will you just shut up and listen to me for a change, you prick?" Frank was quickly losing patience. "Kim might be in trouble. She said she called you for information. Where have you sent her?" The latex glove squeaked against the telephone receiver as Frank gripped it.

"Are you wearing a condom on your fingers to hold the phone again, Frank?"

"Bob-"

"All right, all right. Anything, if it means the two of you will just go away and leave us alone for a bit, like." Martinson paused, and Frank could imagine him cupping his hand over the phone, looking up and down to make sure no one was within earshot. "She was looking for something that might help you, probably hoping to give you a nice surprise tonight, I don't know." Frank ignored the suggestion. "Anyway, she wanted to know addresses, that sort of thing. Threatened us if I didn't tell her. I can do without her sort of shite, Frank. I've changed, you know? I put me wife and kids first and-"

"*Where?*"

"Charnville House. It's a block of flats in The Reds."

"I know where Charnville House is, Bob. I lived in it once, remember?"

He hung up the telephone before Martinson could answer, before tearing the latex glove away from his hand, snapping it away like a second skin and flinging it down onto the floor.

Charnville was a thirty-minute walk. Twenty if he ran part of it.

He rushed from the room, not bothering to lock the door as he slammed it shut behind himself.

THIRTY-THREE

As predictable as ever, the rain had started falling heavily more or less as soon as she had stepped outside from Frank's flat and into the open air. It never seemed to stop in the city, as though in some vain effort to swill the place clean, sluicing its way through dirt-choked back lanes and down muck-clogged drains. Years ago, her parents, both of them first generation Moldovans, had left their home in search of the Promised Land. What they found instead was a place where they were barely made to feel welcome. They soon fell into the ritual; show up every two weeks for your benefits cheque, then keep your head down as best you could for the rest of the time. Growing up never too far from the city, Kimberley Dzanic had seen her fair share of windows smashed, of hateful graffiti daubed on front doors, hoardings, and shop fronts, telling her and her kind to go home. She still remembered the time that some brave, anonymous person had gone to the trouble of collecting up a fresh dog shit and posting it through her parents' letterbox. It had taken almost a week of scrubbing the cheap, worn carpet for her mother to manage to finally get rid of the smell. A *week*. At least the rancid stink of dog turd was much easier to get rid of than the memories ingrained by the act itself. She had learned from a young age, that if she ever wanted to get along in life, she had to keep a look out for number one. She had to trust herself, because she couldn't trust anyone else.

And then she had met Franklin Popovich.

She had to admit, even she was curious at the first sight of the lanky, already grey-stubbled, slightly grubby-looking man who insisted that he was an *investigative journalist,* whatever *that* meant.

***

281

"I'm a bit like Hunter Thompson, but with slightly fewer drugs. Only slightly, mind," he had said, his face creasing into a lop-sided grin that somehow managed to be creepy and endearing at the same time. "People call me Frank Popper, most of them figure that it's a bit easier to pronounce," he had followed up as he dug into his jacket pocket and fished out just enough loose change to cover a round. "I'll get them in. The next one's on you, mind," he had said as he raked at the coins with slightly too-long fingernails, chewed ragged and stained nicotine yellow. Happy that he had the right amount of money, he had shuffled to the bar, shoulders slumped as though the world was resting upon them.

"Snakebite for the lady," he had placed the pint down in front of her, mumbling an apology of sorts as the liquid slopped over the top of the glass, pooling on the old varnished wooden table, probably to add to the several white water marks already eating into the cheap lacquer. "And a bourbon for the gentleman – that's me by the way. No expense spared." He had sat down, looking Kim straight in the eyes as he cut to the chase. "So, are you single?" He had asked, no messing about.

"Yes," she had answered, without flinching. "And I'm not interested in being anything other, so if you think that a pint of warm piss disguised as cider and lager is going to get you into my knickers, then you can fuck off out of that door right now. Ain't happening, no chance."

"Fair enough," if he had been shocked by her confrontational attitude, then he hadn't shown it. "I don't usually have time for any of that bollocks anyway." He had raised his glass to his lips, slugging half the contents in one.

"You mean you can't get your end away very often?"

"Yes. That's exactly what I meant," he had shrugged, chuckling with a dry, dirty-sounding laugh.

***

That was it, they had clicked pretty much right away, for a reason that Kim had never even really tried to put her finger on. Perhaps it was his sense of self-destruction that seemed to bubble just under the surface, or the way that he was happy enough to own up to his own shortcomings without judging her over hers. Or perhaps it was the fact that he had never even thought to question either her gender or her sexuality, even back in her pre-op days. It had led to some awkward situations in the past, as well as its share of name-calling, men whose advances she rejected usually assuming that she was obviously some sort of a *dyke*, or a *typical frigging lezzer,* put out by the fact that their fragile male ego had been threatened somehow. Frank Popper, or Franklin Popovich, or whatever the hell he wanted people to call him, had been one of the few who genuinely didn't seem to care a damn. Of course, that didn't stop him from being a dirty bastard, just not towards her, never towards her.

Maybe that was why he had taken it so personally when things had kicked off between her and Bob Martinson. He had blamed himself for not looking out for her closely enough, forgetting somewhere along the line that, although a few years younger than him, she was still an adult, and that it should have been possible for him just to stand by her after the fact. That he had been there for her so much in the past made it a lot harder to take when he reacted the way that he had.

"If you were that upset by the way he was, just go to the bloody police," he had argued, like it was the easiest thing in the world to do. "It's just Bob, just the way he is," he had even trotted out the most clichéd excuse in the book. The go-to *it's just the way he is* excuse that was favoured by so many apologists for every type of deviant. It was as though Frank Popper, the man with a smart answer for anything, couldn't quite get his head around the fact that someone he trusted could possibly have been such a deceitful pervert. She had been shocked by his reaction, *really* shocked, almost as though he had slapped her across the face.

She had left soon after, abandoning him to his life in The Reds, unwilling to stick around any longer while he continued to bury his head in the sand. She had promised herself that she was finally going to burn her bridges, that her life could be so much better without Franklin Popovich in it anyway.

But if there was one thing about Frank, it was that he was like ringworm, he knew how to get under your skin and stay there. It had been almost ten years, but once that telephone rang just several weeks ago, it had felt more like ten days. Admittedly, curiosity had kicked in once she had gotten past her initial urge to tell him where exactly to get off and hang up the call. He sounded exactly as she remembered, exactly as she would have expected. The type of man who wouldn't change for anyone, even if he could. He had all but begged to see her again. He must have been serious too, if he was actually using the phone. Perhaps he had finally gotten some help to cope with that annoying phobia of his, or whatever it was. Wearing *Marigolds* to pick up a telephone, bloody hell that was just *stupid* behavior, right?

Fast forward to her spending most of her time sleeping on his sofa, or sharing pizza with him, laughing every time he got stringy, near-molten mozzarella caught in the grey stubble that still seemed to permanently coat his chin. It was just like the old days, probably a little *too much* like the old days, something that she didn't really care to give too much thought to. There was still the worry that she would sweep what had gone before under the carpet. She didn't want to move on, she *couldn't*; she was too proud and stubborn for *that*. In the short time that she had been around him though, she couldn't help but think that it seemed like Frank Popper had changed somehow. Sure, the anger was there, the sense of injustice at everything, buried away behind the *anything-for-a-story* mask that he had always liked to wear for some reason. The almost self-destructive nature was just as apparent, too, although it didn't sit quite as well these days, the idea of some forty-something loner, getting drunk and railing against all that was wrong with society. She had said her piece about that already, and that was something that probably wouldn't change now. She couldn't help but notice what *was* different about him though. Since her return, he had seemed a little warmer than she remembered, a bit more humble, as though more willing to let someone in.

He still couldn't quite seem to bring himself to admit that he had been wrong though, stopping somewhere just short of actually saying sorry.

At least a slightly kinder, gentler Frank Popper was a start.

She probably wouldn't have called Martinson's wife, not really. She still felt a small measure of satisfaction though, in the knowledge that *he* thought otherwise. It had been a long time ago and she really had moved on, a whole lot having happened between the years. As much as he denied it, he *knew* that he was the one in the wrong, and perhaps he would spend a little more time looking back over his shoulder every once in a while. That had to count for something.

***

She stopped in her tracks. Lost in her thoughts, Kim had been walking oblivious to her surroundings. It was probably for the best when she considered where she was heading. When she had known Frank first time around, he had lived pretty much smack in the middle of The Reds. He had finally moved on from the place a couple of years before, or so he had said, without offering any explanation why. *The Reds* was a local name, short for *The*

Redevelopments, a pretty sick joke in itself. Unchanged since somewhere in the mid-sixties, it was the closest the city had to a slum. Huge blocks of flats, towers of dirty concrete and steel, looking down on filthy, over-crowded streets. Real Poverty Row accommodation, with as many people shoehorned into them as would fit. Things such as basic safety and fire regulations were openly joked about. There were still a few people lingering about the place as she turned her head from side to side, looking up and down the length of the road. Shadowy figures, protected by the darkness beyond the reach of the orange-tinged streetlights and the veil of rainfall. The building right behind her looked like some sort of old warehouse, the hoarding showing the outlines of a scrubbed-away signage, proclaiming it to be

S C MEAT PROCESSING

That sounded *really* legitimate. Just beyond that, on the corner stood a couple of girls, their silhouettes cutting out against the harsh glare of red neon thrown from a pub across the road. They were dressed in a way that left no room for imagining what they were up to. Probably out to score something, maybe their next fix, or enough money to at least pay for it. A burly figure walked towards them, his hands thrust deep into his pockets and his head bowed down against the rain.

"Awright darlin'?" One of them stepped forward, holding out a hand as though to stop him in his tracks. "Lookin' for a good time? I can do you for whatever you want." The man stopped, grunting something as he turned to face her. Without another word, he reared his head back and hawked a lungful, before spitting it into her face.

"Ewww! Ewww! You dirty fuckin' bastard!" She cried out, as much in resignation as in shock, wiping the mess from her face with the sleeve of her jacket. He turned and carried on his way, head

lowered again, bustling past Kim as he did so. *If you did that to me, I'd pull your bollocks off,* she thought.

Frank had once said that, as dirty as it was, smog-choked and crime-ridden, the filth of the place gave him a focus of some sort, fuelling his angry creativity like no other place could. For a long time, he had insisted that the only things that he needed to function coherently were a supply of cigarettes, a bottle of anything alcoholic, and his surroundings. That had been then, though.

Tensions were probably running even higher than usual. She remembered what Frank had mentioned a few days earlier. *Peaceful protest*, as far as she knew, that usually translated roughly into full-blown *riot*. Little else had been said, apart from a few hushed murmurs on the streets, and there had been no mention in any news that she knew of. It showed how little people on the outside thought of The Reds, or of those crammed into the area. Her memories of what it had been like back when Frank lived in the area made it far too easy for her to be cynical.

Bob Martinson had sent her straight to the dark heart of the place. Shuddering as she stepped a little more carefully, avoiding rain-filled potholes, she drew her thick anorak closer around herself as her eyes swivelled from side to side, on the lookout for the first sight of even the slightest threat. She remembered how the place used to be; for every person who would punch you in the face or slide a knife between your ribs as soon as look at you, there were a dozen or so more who would gladly rush by with their head down, unwilling to help, for fear of being dealt the same treatment.

"You'd better bloody appreciate this, Frank Popper," she whispered under her breath. "The things I do for you." She fumbled in her pocket for the scrap of paper onto which she had scribbled down the address, making sure that she was in the right place. "Charnville House," she read out loud, the same block that Frank had called home until a few years ago. Each block of flats was given a name, seemingly in an attempt to make them sound like something better than the slums that they really were. Martinson had mentioned that William Marks had lived in a flat in Charnville, which meant that it was as good a place as any to sniff for information. Knowing the general attitude of most people around the place, the police and anyone else had probably long since lost interest, the usual apathy kicking in roughly twenty minutes after Marks' emaciated, part-gnawed corpse had been carried away from the flat. At least that meant she should probably be able to look around without being disturbed. Most of the neighbours had probably grown into the habit of locking their doors and minding their own business, so much the better.

***

She hadn't wanted to chance taking the lift, despite there being no indication that it was out of order. Instead, she took her time climbing the stairs, gripping the cold, rusted metal handrail, those fluorescent lights that weren't smashed or blown out were grime-coated, throwing out a feeble, yellow-tinged glow that cast long shadows behind her. She counted the steps under her breath, one floor at a time. *Just a quick look around*, she told herself. *Martinson said that there were a couple died here, too, in a similar way to Marks, from the sound of things.* After some of the things that she had experienced in her life so far, Kim liked to think of herself as a person who didn't scare easily. However, there was still something a little disconcerting about being in that place, unchanged, probably since the day it was first built. Some sense of foreboding, perhaps brought about by the hollow slap of her tread against the cold, dark speckled granite of the stairwell. Or maybe it was the way that all of the doors looked the same, painted in the same dull, green hue, each one indistinct from the next except for the brass numbering, set just above the fish-eye peephole.

She reached the fourth floor, the one where Martinson had told her she needed to be. Stopping to look around, the small hairs on the back of her neck stood on end.

"Hello?" She called out, not really knowing why. *"Is there anyone there?"*

There was no answer, her voice faint and tinny-sounding in the emptiness. *Stop being such an arsehole,* she thought to herself. *There's no one out here. Most people with any sense would've moved out long ago anyway, the place looks like it ought to be condemned.* Maybe it was just because of the discomforting gloom of her surroundings, or that she knew that around half of the tenants had long since been re-housed elsewhere, leaving only the stragglers behind in the block, clinging to the place with a sort of *we-shall-not-be-moved* attitude that was almost as masochistic as it was pointless. She didn't feel overly convinced by any of it. The place was nothing other than a long-forgotten problem, a testament to ignorance and mistakes that was swept under the carpet with far too much ease. There was little wonder that Frank's hatred of what he perceived to be injustice was stoked so easily.

From out of the corner of her eye, she noticed that one of the front doors was open, swung part inward, the cracked green paintwork hinting at the darkness beyond. The number on the front door didn't match that on the crumpled piece of paper on which she had scribbled the information given by Martinson. *I should really keep going,* she thought. *Whatever's in there is none of my business. It might be some skanky bloke, banging a cheap prostitute, or a couple of down-and-outs shooting up into their eyeballs.* She could see Marks' door from where she stood. *But what if there's someone in there who needs help?* She reached out her hand and pushed against the door, wincing as the hinges creaked under the pressure.

It was *very* dark.

"Hello?" She called, no one answering.
She stepped in, closing the door behind her.

THIRTY-FOUR

The light was bright, far too bright. It burned, reaching somewhere into the back of his head with a glaring intensity. He found that closing his eyes made no difference, it only shifted the focus of the pain a little, doing nothing to actually numb it or make it stop.

I'll give it another five minutes, just to see if it settles down, then I'll try to move.

James Hesketh tried to remember, finding that he couldn't. Any attempt to do so just made his head ache even more. He couldn't even be sure how long he had spent huddled in the corner of the room. The last time he had bothered to look, the clock on the wall had claimed the time to be a little after four, just the same as it had for the last three months, ever since the batteries had given up, never to be replaced.

The time didn't really matter anyway, not really. He knew, even before that miserable excuse for a journalist had shown up, that it was far too late to even try and do anything. Popper had left him to his own devices, leaving him, in no uncertain terms, with the feeling that he was getting nothing more than he deserved. For a while he had sat, feeling the fizzing in his belly as it intensified, the muscles surrounding his gut squeezing in contraction-like spasms. He had stared at that damn clock, as if doing so would somehow be enough to force it to start ticking again. Some hours later, or at least what he *guessed* to be some hours later, it had occurred to him that if he sat in the corner, huddling himself up against the numbing cold of the floor tiles, he became smaller, far less significant. So that was what he did, his knees pulled up beneath his chin, rocking back and forth. The air felt stale with the sickly odour of blood and vomit.

Contraction-like spasms. He could have laughed at the irony, if doing so didn't make his chest hurt so much, bringing with it the feeling that he could throw up again. The analogy was still a sound one though, the morbid realisation that there was another life that had been swelling inside of him. He had tried to get it out of himself, but he knew that he had left it too late, that the thing had already grown. The back of his throat felt raw and scratched, the roof of his mouth hurting from where he had repeatedly jammed his fingers down his throat, trying to make himself sick.

He knew that there was only one way to be really rid of it. But he was too afraid of that option, even though he had a pretty good idea of what would happen if he didn't. He had seen it firsthand, after all.

Only one way.

From where he sat, he could see the photograph of his wedding day. He had brought it in from the hallway, soon after Popper had left, propping it face up, just a couple of feet in front of himself, in full view. The glass in the frame was missing now, the picture itself scratched but still visible. The look of smug mocking on the face of his wife was so obvious, he didn't understand how it had taken so many years to notice it before. It was the sort of expression that said, even then, that she just *knew* he would mess everything up one day, that she was better off rinsing him for all she could in as short a time as possible. He didn't even have to wonder what it was that she was doing now, she did a good enough job of rubbing his face in it. She was continuing to fund a lifestyle to which she had become accustomed with his money, while he scraped on by with his debts. It was little wonder that he drank as much as he did, with that cold-hearted cow milking him dry, flaunting herself while he was left with barely a pot to piss in. He had every right to be as bitter as he was.

We can make all of your problems go away.

He chuckled, surprising himself that he still had the ability to do so. There was a dry patch at the back of his throat that stung when he laughed, making him feel like retching again. The boastful promise had turned out to be pretty hollow after all. None of his problems had gone away. Instead, they had just shifted a little, mutated into something else, into something even worse than before.

The worst if it was, he had a pretty good idea of what was going to happen. With Susanne Walters, he had seen it for himself. He had seen the lustful, cold gleam behind her otherwise dead eyes as she had forced herself upon him, allowing that *thing* to transfer itself from her and into him. It had *changed* her somehow, and he knew that, sooner or later, it would change him, too.

Unless he did what he knew that he had to do to make it stop.

He looked at the photograph again. Money: that was what it had all come down to in the end. He had actually tried to convince himself that he had been doing Marks a favour, continuing to avert his gaze while he willingly got involved in something that he probably genuinely thought would benefit him. At one point, he had even almost come close to believing his own line of bullshit, buying into Steele's assertions that all would come good in the end. In reality, he had been little more than a selfish shit, jumping at the first chance to claw some cash back, enough to be able to give the finger to everyone who had put him where he was. His wife and her new toy boy, Chris Cyrus, the money lender that had bailed him out from the gambling debt that had hung over his head, as good as handing him the shovel that he needed to dig himself in even deeper. If the rotten prick hadn't agreed to lend him the money in the first place, he wouldn't even be in the situation he was in now. It was their fault, all of them, not his, it was *never* his.

He knew what he would have to do, but at the same time, he knew that he wouldn't be able to do it. It kind of ran contrary to his whole philosophy of self-preservation.

Still sitting, he leaned back against the wall and tilted his head to gaze up at the ceiling, the movement causing a faint taste of blood to rise into the back of his throat. He started to laugh, the resulting sound more like a wet gurgle, dull and empty sounding. He laughed until the tears came, forcing sobs with them, until he could no longer remember which had come first anymore.

THIRTY-FIVE

Frank could recall few times when he had moved so fast, with quite as much of a sense of purpose. He certainly couldn't remember ever doing it for another person.

But for Kim, he was prepared to make an exception.

He had decided that it would be quicker on foot. A taxi probably would have ended up taking twice as long, especially if the rumours about a protest were anything to be believed. So far, he had only seen a few groups of what looked like typical stragglers, the usual sort of hangers-on who thought that holding a banner with some badly-worded slogan on it somehow made them look more like they had something to prove and less like they were just spoiling for a fight. *Give it time*, he thought, *the troublemakers will crawl out of the woodwork, and they'll have their way, while the people with a real point to make will just get lumped in with them and no one will be any further forward.* As he glanced across, he saw a group of some half a dozen men who looked like they'd taken a half hour break from the nearest boozer. One of them was a squat, bearded bloke wearing a donkey jacket over a stained shirt with the phrase *F**K THE POLICE* printed across his chest. He glared at Frank from beneath his brow as if daring him to say something, anything to give him the only excuse he needed to start a punch up. Instead, Frank hurried on with his head down against the rain, his shortness of breath almost enough to make him wish that he'd quit smoking years ago. His eyes itched with a sensation that he had almost forgotten; the irritation of the lingering smog and fumes, something that he had once been accustomed to, in the same way that a farmer eventually becomes immune to the stink of horse shit. He kept blinking, trying to dispel the almost burning feeling. As he reached the corner of Morley, just a few minutes away from Charnville, he stopped in his tracks as he felt a tug at his sleeve.

"Hey mister, you're out at a pretty weird time. 'You lookin' for anything in particular?" He turned on the spot, to see a bedraggled-looking girl, barely into her twenties. "I'm good at keepin' blokes company, I am," she added. Her long, dark blonde hair was soaked through and plastered down, and her thin clothing was rain-moulded to her slender frame. The words that came from her mouth sounded far too rehearsed, as if they should have been spoken by someone at least twice her age.

"No, no," he stammered, caught off-guard. "Sorry, I've gotta go, I've got somewhere I need to be." He fumbled in his jacket pocket, bringing out a five pound note, crumpled almost into a ball. He unrolled it, trying to smooth out some of the creases before passing it to her, her slender hand already stretched out in anticipation. "Here," he said, his voice firmer now. "It's not much, but it's all I've got on me at the moment. There's a place called Krantz's, about a minute back up the road. The owner's name is Josef, a big guy, you can't miss him. He'll still be doing his specials. Soup and a roll, with a cuppa, for a few quid. He'll probably moan about it a bit, but he won't turn you away. That ought to cover it." He tapped the side of his nose with his forefinger. "He's usually a decent enough bloke, but if he gives you any grief, tell him Frank sent you."

"Frank? Right."

"Then after that, go home, lock your door and change into something dry. Stop hanging around on street corners, grabbing at random strangers, and promise yourself that next week, you'll start looking for a proper job."

"But I'm not good at any sort of job, 'cept blow jobs of course," she looked up at him, her pale eyes wide, as if to say, *are you sure you don't want to change your mind? I'll make sure it's worth your while.*

"That's the sort of attitude that'll get you in deep trouble someday. It might be sooner, or it might be later, but it *will* happen. Trust me, I know."

"What's wrong with you mister? Were you born without a cock?" She stepped forward, and Frank saw that she looked even younger than he had first thought, despite the heavy makeup and her choice of speech. The rain didn't seem to bother her, she had probably been out in much worse.

"I'll ignore that you actually said that," Frank stepped back, aware that he had somewhere he really needed to be. "Go and get yourself somewhere warm. There's a pretty strong rumour that there's gonna be some trouble here later on, in case you hadn't heard," he looked back from where he had just came, where a few more people had gathered now. He turned away from the girl, not wanting to make further eye contact.

"If I can't make anything off of you, I'll just score the next punter what comes along," she called after him, her voice already dulled by the rain. "You know I will, too. Ain't got no time for no good Samaritans."

Frank didn't answer. The hell with it, he'd tried and he really did have more important things to worry about.

***

As he rounded the last corner, a shiver rode the length of Frank's spine. He told himself it was nothing really, just a combination of the rain and cold, but he knew that he was just kidding himself.

Just up ahead on the right was Charnville House, a fifteen-storey block of flats that looked like something pulled straight from one of those old seventies public information films, the kind of scary thing that would have had someone like Donald Pleasance providing a plummy voiceover. A towering monolith of soot-ingrained concrete, from where he had stopped, he could look up and still see the same seventh-floor window that had once been his grime-filmed eyepiece on the world. Across the street was the old warehouse, the roller shutter still down, the same as it had been ever since that time. He could still feel the sour taste of bile rising up his gullet and into the back of his mouth at the memory of the last time he had set foot in the place. The paint was cracked and blistered, peeling away from rust-eaten patches on the shutter. Above it was an old signage, little more than a wooden board nailed in place, with rough painted lettering:

S C MEAT PROCESSING

The words were faded but still legible, only just, against the rain-darkened background. To the side of the shutter was a *To Let* sign, to which someone had added an *'i'* between the two words with white paint, to make it read *TOiLET*. *Clever*, Frank thought, mindful that he had been shivering while he stood looking at the place, with more than just the cold. If he closed his eyes, he could still see, still remember. It was true what some people said, nightmares faded, but sometimes they never completely went away.

Blinking his eyes to get rid of what he told himself was just rainwater, he turned away to face the flats again. He could see his old place, a feeble yellowed light showing through the same old tattered curtain that had hung in place when he had lived there. Whoever was the current landlord was obviously every bit as tight-arsed as the old one. He tried to move forward, his legs suddenly feeling heavy, as though his feet had sunk down into the paving slabs.

Kim's in there somewhere, he told himself. *I've got to push past it and get my arse inside, before anything* really *bad happens.* Shaking his head in an effort to loosen away the ghosts of his memory, he hurried across the road, ducking his head against the wind and rain. With a sigh of relief, he noticed that the front entrance was ajar, taking away the need to touch the intercom. All the same, he felt an almost electric ripple down the full length of his spine as he crossed inside the building.

THIRTY-SIX

Blood. So much blood everywhere. More than Kim thought was possible to be held inside just one person. She sat cross-legged in the middle of the floor, trying to ignore the already-cooling, sticky wetness as it soaked through the seat of her jeans. *Well, I guess it's fair to say that these are ruined now*, she thought, unsure whether to laugh or cry about her being able to even have such a pointless thought in that particular moment. *Crazy*. It was just *crazy*. *All of it*.

How the hell did I even get here? She asked herself, unable to remember the answer. Less than two hours earlier, she had been on the phone to Bob Martinson, extorting information from him like a seasoned blackmailer, getting a furtive kick out of hearing him fumble his words and squirm like a teenager who had just been caught masturbating by his parents. It served the prick right, after so many years of thinking that he was probably in the clear. Right now, those two hours felt more like they might as well have been two weeks ago.

She could hear voices above the sound of her own still-hoarse breathing. At first, she thought that they must have been inside her head. After what had just happened, it surely didn't make any sense to be able to hear anything real. She cupped her hands over her ears, trying not to retch at the oily sensation of blood smearing up both sides of her face, in an effort to block out the noise. The sounds dulled, to be replaced by the hollow *thud-thud-thudding* of her own heartbeat. *Perhaps they* are *real*, she thought, *and maybe that's a good thing. It means that I haven't quite gone mad just yet.* Reassured a little, she took her hands away again. She could hear shouts in the distance, then a sound of breaking glass, followed by the muted blaring of what was probably a burglar alarm. She could just about remember hearing talk of a protest in The Reds, what felt like almost a lifetime ago now, although it no longer seemed important. In this instance, describing something as *peaceful* obviously encompassed vandalism, along with breaking and entering, carried out by the kind of people who probably couldn't even really remember what they were protesting against. Frank, the wannabe anarchist that he was, would have more than likely been in his element. A little over a month ago now, a twenty-three-year-old woman had been found blocking the fire escape of a second-hand shop just along from Charnville. The first anyone realised was when the sixty-something year old owner of the place noticed a smell that he described as being like *the sort of stink you noticed on bin collection day*, when he went out to the back of the shop to make himself a cup of tea. When he finally got around to working the rusted bolts free enough to open the rear door, he didn't find his bin full of last week's leftovers. Instead, there was the slightly gas-bloated corpse of a young woman who, it was later determined, had been stabbed at least thirty-three times. Whoever was responsible had also slit her throat from ear to ear for good measure. At least the old bloke did the decent thing and called the police before sitting down to finish his cuppa and slice of buttered toast with raspberry jam.

As soon as it was found out that the victim was a working prostitute with two kids and a crack cocaine habit that she was struggling to afford, the whole thing suddenly became a non-story, forgotten about by almost everyone. Even Frank had barely mentioned it, his usual sense of righteous social justice most likely preoccupied with stories of diet pills and oversized, cock-shaped maggots.

The people of The Reds didn't forget about her though. They remembered everything, and they were pissed off to say the least. After a few days, the whispers started, murmurs of unrest, accompanied by a few hand-scrawled flyers taped to some of the less conspicuous places around the city. A gathering, a show of strength to make everyone on the outside take notice and see that they, the people, were sick of being shoved face-down into the pressure cooker and just forgotten about. Something real was called for, to dish out a reminder that the poor were still deserving of attention, regardless of what they had to do to survive.

Yeah, Frank would have been in his element all right.

***

"Hello?" She had called out for the third time since stepping into the hallway of the flat. "Is there anyone in here? If you let me know then I can try and help, or at least find someone who can. *Hello?"* She strained her eyes until there was an ache in the back of her head, trying to get a feel for the darkness. The air was cold and damp, as though the place had been standing empty for some time. There was the lingering odour of something almost familiar. A sickly sweet, unpleasant smell that she couldn't quite place. Stretching her arm, she reached for the wall, tracing her fingers across what felt like old wooden wallboards. Finding a light switch, she pushed down.

"*Shit,*" she muttered as the only response was an empty click that echoed around the short hallway with a cold sharpness. She shouldn't have expected anything else, really. Unsure if the bulb had blown, or if the electrical supply had been disconnected. The latter wouldn't have surprised her too much. Frank had told her some stories of the days when he lived in the flats, including frequent mentions of just how much of a useless pillock the maintenance bloke actually was. Perhaps that was one of the reasons why he had finally moved out of the place. She suspected that there was probably more to it, but since she had come back, he had never seemed as though he wanted to give an actual explanation, and she hadn't felt a real need to ask.

"Why am I even in here?" She asked herself aloud, even her own voice sounding not quite the same. "I mean, what the hell was I thinking? I'm sure there are plenty of better, more useful things I could be doing than skulking around in some grotty-looking squat with the power cut off." Besides, she had told herself that she was only going to check out Marks' place, other peoples' problems really shouldn't have been her concern. *Just a quick peek though*, she had told herself, *in case there's anyone hurt. Then I'll move on along the hallway to Marks'. After that I'll get the hell out of here. There's a pub nearby, and as long as it hasn't been firebombed or anything, they'll have a pint of snakebite with my name on it.*

She reached into the inside pocket of her anorak and pulled out a small torch on a keychain, flicking it on. She had won it on one of those coin drop games in an amusement arcade in London a few months ago, and had kept it in her pocket, you know, just in case she ever found herself in a creepy-looking building with no lighting. If anything, it made her surroundings look even more eerie, shadows lengthening and flickering as the weak light danced across every surface, picking out specks of dust whirling in the cold, damp air.

There was a soft moaning sound from just up ahead and she almost dropped the keyring as she flinched.

"*Hello?*" She called out again. "*Who's there? Can you hear me?*" Nervous now, she stepped forward on her toes, trying to move as quietly as the cheap linoleum flooring would allow. She traced her fingertips along the top of a chest of drawers as she passed it, a silt-like layer of dust lifting away onto her fingers. There was another groaning sound, like someone weakened or in pain, coming from a room just off to the left of her.

"*Who's there?*" She spoke louder this time, hoping that it would help to hide the nervousness in her voice and knowing that it probably wouldn't. "If you're hurt, I can help you-"

She froze as she moved into the doorway of the room from where the sound had come.

"What the *hell-*?"

As she turned to face the source of the sound, there was a strangled cry of pain as the glare of the torchlight picked out a shapeless mass in the corner of the room.

"Turn it off... please...turn the light off. Please...the light, it's burning..." The man raised his hands to his face in an effort to shield his eyes. Kim gasped as she saw him, his knees drawn up against his chest in an effort to make himself as small as possible. He was little more than skin and bone, the tattered sleeves of his shirt flapping in the stale air as his arms flailed around. *"Please...turn it off."*

"Okay, it's okay," Kim angled the torch away from him, moving forward again as the initial shock passed. She pointed the light up toward the ceiling. "I'm sorry, I just needed to see whether you were okay." She tried to stifle a gag as the smell hit her; blood, mingled with the stale, bitter stink of urine.

The man let out a tinder-dry sound that might well have been a dry cough. As he did so he craned his head forward and spat a trail of bloody phlegm onto the floor between them.

"What happened to you?" Kim asked, taking care to keep the light angled away from him still as she moved nearer. She felt a rash of goosebumps raising on the length of both arms. "We can get out of here, get you to a doctor and-"

"You know as well as I do, that ain't going to happen," he turned to look straight at her, and Kim felt her stomach drop away. "I reckon it's a...bit too late for that... don't you?" The skin of his face looked as though it had been stretched taut across his skull, so pale as to be almost translucent. His eyes were sunken deep into darkened sockets, his lips were dry and cracked. There was a dry smear of something dark and rust-coloured staining his chin, with more of the same mottling his loose fitting, off-white t-shirt.

"What happened to you?" she asked again, noticing that the lower half of his left trouser leg was tied off in a loose, ragged knot, somewhere around where his knee should have been, the material stained dark and wet-looking. "What have you done?"

"I was hungry...so hungry..." His voice rasped its way from his parched throat like he had swallowed a mouthful of sand. "Mitch thought it was a tapeworm, I told him it couldn't be...maybe he was right though...a tapeworm...something making me hungry all the time."

"Mitch? Who's Mitch?"

"Is my wife back yet?" He seemed to be looking through her, his dull eyes gazing out blind from their sockets, as though he was following the sound of her voice instead of actually seeing her. "She's been gone for *ages* now."

"Your wife? What's she called? I'll go and check."

He paused, groaning as he tilted his head back to look up at the ceiling, as though trying to remember something important. The bones in his neck creaked as he did so.

"Rosa...Rosa Whitman. I told people she was away visiting, but...but..." He slumped back against the wall, exhausted by the effort of speaking. Without thinking, Kim stepped back as she noticed that there were what looked like several bite marks on each forearm, a large chunk of flesh missing from the worst one, caked with dark, congealed blood. *Just like those photos Frank showed me,* she thought.

"I'll go and look for her if you like," she said, "you just try and rest. Where's your phone? I really think I ought to call you an ambulance."

"No phone..." He slurred, his voice growing fainter. "Cut off...we never use it anyway."

"It's okay," she said, cursing under her breath. "Right," she said, trying to hide any uncertainty in her voice. "What's your name?"

"Brad," he said, his voice drifting, as though he was slipping into unconsciousness.

"Stay with me Brad," that was what they always said on television, wasn't it? "I'll take a look around the place, see if I can find that wife of yours, Rosa, yeah? Do you think she might be hurt or anything?"

"Hungry," he mumbled, barely audible now. "Was just so hungry...told them she'd gone..."

"Okay, it's all going to be okay," Kim said, suspecting that it was probably going to be anything but. "I'll check, I'll be as quick as I can, and we'll get you both some help." She flicked the torch away from the ceiling, being careful to angle it away from his face this time, still he grimaced at the light, his eyes rolling back almost white in their sunken sockets and his lips shrinking back from teeth that looked almost elongated against pale gums. She chose to ignore the dark, rust-coloured stains around his mouth.

"Rosa?" Kim walked slowly, trying to hold her keyring steady as she moved, the bobbing of the light as it picked out the dust in the air giving away her nervousness. "Rosa, are you here? Let me know and I can try to help you." The bathroom door was open just a crack, a sliver of light showing through from the frosted window behind. "Rosa?" She whispered again as she gripped the cold aluminium handle, pushing the door inward with a creak like old bones.

(o god o god o god)

A flashback to when she was eight years old, Kim – or *Karl* as she still was back then - had got her first pet, a cat, a small, tabby thing that she had named Hannibal. Little more than a kitten, picked from a shelter, she had been allowed the creature on the understanding that she would have to take necessary care of it. *I'm not cleaning up cat shit, if you want a pet, that's* your *job, son,* her father had said on more than one occasion. She took her new-found responsibility seriously, feeding, petting and, yes, even cleaning up after the straggly little fluffball. It was worth it. After all, kittens gave all the best cuddles, right?

The companionship was short-lived however. One day, a little more than three months since she had picked Hannibal out from a lineup of prospective pets, he didn't come home. It had been autumn, the wind starting to bite at the fingertips just a little harder than before. She had stood for half an hour calling out his name, food bowl in hand, feeling the cold pinch at her cheeks, forcing herself to stay outside just one minute longer, ready for him to saunter back from around the corner in his usual arrogant way as she tried to ignore the stares from the suspicious-looking guy from along the road. She told herself over and over again that the heavy feeling in her eyes was just the wind blowing against them, making them water. That first night she didn't sleep, her parents reluctantly allowing her to keep the light outside her bedroom switched on, for the first time in years. Every night for the two weeks that followed, she would stand outside the porch of the flat block, calling his name into the growing night, hoping that he would stop being quite so mean and come back to her, purring as he rubbed his haunches against the side of her leg the way that he liked to do. Every night for the two weeks that followed, her growing sadness went unanswered.

Then, three weeks to the day that he had walked out of the house never to come back, she found him, along with a life lesson that would stay with her forever.

She had been picking berries from the thick tangle of bramble bushes that grew wild down by the stream, just a fifteen-minute walk away from the flats. Good for nothing except the dustbin, she liked to pick them all the same, picturing what she could do with them if she was a little older and actually knew how to cook, as she placed them into an empty margarine tub with a length of string threaded through it as a makeshift strap that hung from the crook of her arm. She hummed a tune to herself under her breath, one that she didn't even really know, just something that she had picked up from the radio earlier in the day. She was just about to head for home when she spotted the clump of wet, matted-looking fur, poking out from a thick patch of bramble just a few feet away. She didn't want to look, really, she didn't, but she did so anyway. Maybe it was for no reason other than to prove something to herself, although she didn't know exactly what. Placing her basket down in the dirt, still muddy after the rain of a few days earlier, she walked across to this new object of interest and parted the twisted vines of bramble, being careful not to shred her fingers on the thorns.

She balled her hand into a fist and jammed it into her mouth in an effort to stop herself from screaming. Even three weeks later, the bloated, decomposing mass of fur and flesh was still just about recognisable. The smell, at first masked by the surrounding bushes, was overpowering, making her feel sick. It was probably the lump of thin, grey intestine that had spilled out from the belly, torn open in a gaping, jagged slash. Hannibal hadn't just died, something had gotten at him. The sort of something that would then go to the trouble of hiding his mangled body in a bush and leaving him to rot away. She cried herself to sleep every night for a week after, learning in the process that sometimes, bad things don't need a reason, they just *happen*, as stupid and senseless as that might be.

Now she stood in the bathroom of some man that she had only just met ten minutes earlier, and she remembered that same lesson once again.

"Rosa...oh, sweet fucking Jesus, Rosa..."

This time around, she tried to keep from shoving her fist into her mouth. She was a grown woman, and screams didn't always come quite so easily nowadays.

(o god rosa what has he done)

The tiles of the small bathroom were beige, or at least they had been once. The thin light from the keyring was faint enough for her to at least try and convince herself that the dark Rorschach patterns sprayed up the wall were dirt, or maybe spatters of paint. Perhaps if she looked at it for long enough, then she might actually start to believe it herself. Knowing that it was stupid, knowing that it was the wrong thing to do, she stepped forward anyway, barely noticing that she was holding her breath, just like she had when she found Hannibal all those years ago.

"Oh, my God..."

She was pretty sure that the body was that of a woman, older than herself, although it was hard to be certain at first. Slumped in the bathtub, as though asleep, the head was thankfully turned away from her, to face the wall. Still wearing clothes, they were ragged and torn, pulled back to expose what was left of the body beneath. Most of the belly and lower part was missing, only a gaping, congealed cavity left. Flesh had also been stripped away from the chest, ragged, dried shreds of meat still clinging to the exposed ribs.

(he said he was hungry)

One arm still dangled limp over the side of the bathtub, as though she had maybe tried to climb out, only to give up.

There were several chunks missing from the fleshy part of her forearm. Bite marks.

"He'd told people that she'd gone away, but really...but really-" Gagging, Kim struggled to hold onto the torch as she bent almost double, retching and dry heaving until it felt as though her insides were being clenched and squeezed up into her throat by force. There was a burning up the length of her gullet and behind her eyes, tears springing to the surface unhindered. She cried out as she felt her foot slip on something wet, her leg almost giving out beneath her. Still coughing and spluttering, she turned and ran back into the room where Whitman still cowered, fearing the return of the light.

"*What have you done to her?*" Kim screamed, knowing full well what the answer was. "*What the hell have you done to her?*" She shone the torchlight in the direction of his face now, no longer caring if it caused him any pain or distress. "*Answer me!*"

"Hungry...so hungry...always," he sobbed, the sound parched and strained, as though it was taking all of his effort. "I just wanted it to stop...wanted to make it stop, but I was so *hungry*."

He's not lying, Kim thought, unable to look away from the wretched thing, balled into the corner as though still trying to make himself inconspicuous. *He didn't do it because he* wanted *to, he did it because he* had *to.*

"Did you take the tablets?" She reached out and shook his shoulder, almost retching again at the touch as she gripped at him. Little more than skin and bone, his shoulder blade felt tinder dry, as though she could crush it into dust one-handed, without even trying. "The diet tablets, did you take them?"

"*What*...tablets?" He turned his head, the bones in his neck cracking as he did so. His sunken eyes had a milky, dead sheen to them, as though he was looking through her. "Never took anything, no tablets, honest...nothing stronger than paracetamol...no diet tablets...just so hungry all the time..."

There's barely anything left of him, Kim thought, yet she couldn't shake the sight of what she had just seen in the bathroom, the ghoulish image burned into her memory, and she almost retched again. Then she thought back to when Frank had cracked one of the capsules open, freeing those worms, or parasites, or whatever they were. If Whitman hadn't been taking the pills, then what about his wife? How else could he have ended up in such a state?

"What happened to you?" She asked, wanting to grab those bony, brittle-looking shoulders and shake him for what he had done. She wanted to scream in his face until she was hoarse. She could have done it easily, apart from the fear that as much as touching him might snap him in half. "What have you done?" She said again. "Your wife is dead in that bathtub, looking like she's been chewed up and left to rot! How could you do it, you *bastard?*"

A confused look crossed Whitman's face, his eyes welling up as though he was about to cry. "I don't know," he sobbed, his chest quivering as he did so. "I can't remember, I just know I was so hungry all the time...had to keep eating, to make the pain go away. *But it never did,*" his eyes widened. "Just made it worse. So much worse. I saw Mitch Brennan in the diner...was sick in front of him, I was so embarrassed." *Fucking hell,* Kim thought, *I've just found the part-eaten corpse of his wife in the bath and he's more worried about how stupid he felt when he puked in front of his mate.*

"I haven't seen Mitch since. Is he okay?"

"Mitch? I don't even know who bloody Mitch is," Kim shook her head.

"Honestly, it was all just such a mess. I spewed everywhere, there was...blood everywhere. I ran out of the place. Betty was really mad about it."

"Wait a minute. If you didn't take any of the pills, how do you think you got like this?"

"Why do you keep asking me about pills? What, do you think...I'm some sort of a junkie or something?" *You bloody well look like one,* Kim thought, noticing the way his parchment-thin skin stretched across his face, his lips dry. There were sores around his mouth and up one side of his face. "I've got no...got no idea how this happened," Whitman mumbled, his voice faltering. "She always said I needed to lose some weight. Not like this though, no, not like this..." His eyes widened, and her torch picked out a silvery trail of saliva, drooling from the side of his mouth. "What time is it? Is it supper time yet? I'm *starving.*"

"So starving that you had to resort to cannibalism?" Suddenly uneasy, she backed away a step as the words left her mouth. He looked in no fit state to make any sort of a lunge for her, but there was still something about the whole situation that made her nervous.

"*Cannibalism? What do you mean, cannibalism?*" His voice raised in pitch, as if he was growing agitated. "What are you talking about? Where's my wife?"

He really doesn't know what's happened, Kim thought, he can't remember doing anything wrong. His whole body shuddered as though he was in shock. "Where's Rosa? *I want Rosa!*"

"You really don't remember?" Kim moved forward again. Squatting down, she reached out a hand, her fingers brushing against his forehead, clammy and dewy with perspiration.

"There was a horse," he mumbled, his voice wavering, as though he was trying to recall some distant memory. "We were going fishing...Mitch and me. It looked like it had starved to death, I could count its ribs, all of them. Each and every one." He laughed, the sound almost hysterical, echoing around the small room. "Just like you can count mine now!" He lifted his baggy, stained t-shirt, Kim unable to hide her disgust. Indeed, the flesh of his belly seemed to have collapsed inward, as though his innards had been removed, leaving just an empty, skin-covered cavity. "Mitch thought it was a tapeworm," he continued again, "but...but...just hungry, all the time..." Kim looked again at his forearms, at the wounds on both. *Not just wounds, bite marks*, she corrected herself.

"I can't be...can't be like this anymore," Whitman sobbed, as though some sense of realisation had suddenly come to him. "Nothing...got nothing left. Belly hurts all the time...so hungry..." He let out a sharp gasp, as though he had been stabbed in the stomach, and his eyes rolled back almost white. As Kim watched, he convulsed, his jaw dropping and clenching in an attempt at a scream, spitting a thick, almost solid black gob of blood. Kim started to move closer, before thinking better of it. Locked in a spasm now, his lips parted as something attempted to push its way through. Kim could feel the same deep, primal sense of disgust that she remembered from all those years ago as a huge, dark, slug-like creature writhed its way from out of Whitman's mouth, twisting and thrashing blindly as though searching for something, its slick body glistening like wet leather in the thin light from the torch. With a last push, it dropped down into Whitman's lap. Another followed, then another, the three of them sliding down and squirming in a spreading pool of blood. Like a puppet released from its strings at last, Whitman's body tensed one last time, before going limp as his head lolled to one side with a dry snapping sound, and he slumped back against the wall.

Kim looked down at the creatures, one of them only inches away from her feet. Raising her head again, she saw a fourth and then a fifth, still dropping limp from his slack mouth. *Jesus*, she thought, *how many of them are there?* The sight of the things slopping their way across the floor was like a spell being broken as one of them slid up onto the front of her shoe, a slimy, red slug trail in its wake. Screaming now, she staggered back, almost slipping on the blood spreading across the linoleum floor. Shaking her foot to try and shrug the thing away, she flailed her arms as she lost her balance, toppling backwards this time, her hands smearing their way through the muck as she struggled to regain her footing. Frantic, she kicked out, punting one of the things back across the floor as she struggled to gather momentum, sliding back in the direction of where she hoped the doorway was. She skidded in an awkward, crab-like movement. Glancing away from the parasites, she saw Whitman's face, pallid in the weak gleam of the light from the keyring that she had somehow still managed to hold on to. Thankfully, his eyes were closed. As she looked, another creature dangled from his mouth, before dropping free, followed by yet another. How many now? She had lost count. Still sliding in the direction of the exit, she managed to pick herself up and turned, running out into the hallway. Kicking the door shut, she collapsed on the floor in a heap, her breath escaping in ragged bursts that made her chest hurt. The seat of her jeans felt wet, soaked through with blood, already cooling against her skin and raising goosebumps, her hands and the front of her anorak covered in more of the same.

How did I get here? She asked herself, trying to stifle an inappropriate laugh. *Really, how the fuck* did *I get here?*

In that particular moment, she couldn't think of a sane answer.

THIRTY-SEVEN

"*Frank!*" She cleared the last four steps in a leap, launching herself at him and almost sending both of them toppling back down the stairwell.

"*Kim!*" He tried to regain his footing, his voice muffled as she collided with him. "What happened? Are you all rig-" he pulled back, a shocked expression on his face as he saw the bloodstains on her clothes. "What the hell happened to you? Are you hurt?"

"No," she gasped, trying to regain her breath. "No, I don't think I am, anyway. Nothing that a drink or five won't fix. I *am* knackered though." Although the words were as throwaway as he had come to expect, her face told a different story. Pale and drawn, as though she had seen something she would just as soon forget, her coat and jeans were caked in blood, one of her hands leaving a bloody smear on the front of his jacket as she drew it away.

"You look like you just walked away from a car crash. What happened?"

"Upstairs," she wheezed, still short of breath. "Some guy like Marks, just skin and bone...maggot things...lots of them."

"Did any of them touch you?" He looked her up and down with a look of concern that, any other time, she probably would have found amusing. "Seriously Kim, did they get *anywhere* near you?"

"No," she said, suddenly wary of the way he seemed to be staring at her. "I had to boot a couple of them away, the filthy things, but no." She paused, sucking in a lungful of air before continuing. "The guy died. They just kept falling out of his mouth, more and more of them," her voice trailed away, barely a whisper as she thought back to the man upstairs, Whitman, or whatever he had called himself. Rambling and barely coherent, he had been little more than a pathetic shell. What was worse though was what

315

had been left of his wife, in the bathtub, a bloody, mangled mess. "It wasn't pretty," she mumbled, afraid to say too much aloud, for fear of driving home the mad reality of it all.

"We really should get the hell out of here," Frank said, putting an arm around her shoulders and pulling her close. "It's probably not a good place to be, for several reasons."

"What do you mean?" Kim asked. "What do you know that I don't?"

"I paid a visit to someone today, a doctor who, it turns out, knows quite a bit about what's going on."

"Did he have any suggestions about what caused it? About where the pills even come from, or why someone thought it would be a good idea to deliberately infect people with parasites?"

"No." Frank thought about Hesketh, sitting at his kitchen table, deliberately trying to make himself sick, a look of resignation on his haggard face, as though he already knew that doing so was pointless. Or perhaps he was a believer in karma, and just knew that he was getting exactly what he deserved. "No, he didn't have a clue about any of that. He had just seen a couple of his patients showing up in his surgery with extreme weight loss." He couldn't bring himself to go into detail. When he had last seen Hesketh, he had the appearance of someone who was minutes away from deciding to take his own life. Besides, even if he didn't top himself, the chances were that he was a dead man walking anyway, and he knew it. "He was as much in the dark as anyone else, anyone that I know of at least." Kim looked at him, reminding him just how hard it could actually be to read her sometimes. He couldn't be certain if she suspected he wasn't telling the whole truth, or if she was just so shaken up by whatever had happened to her that she was happy enough to go along with anything he said.

"What's *your* story anyway?" Frank asked, clearing his throat to show that he wanted to shift the focus of any conversation back to her. "What made you even think to come here in the first place? I thought I'd told you before, I'd rather eat my own left bollock before setting foot in this place again."

"Bob Martinson," Kim coughed as she spoke his name aloud, waiting for a response that didn't come, "gave me a heads-up. Apparently, a couple of folks in here have been affected."

"Affected?"

"You know, like that Marks guy, or Elizabeth MacKinnon and her fella."

"So, you just decided to check it out for yourself?"

"Get off your high horse, Frank," she snapped, seeing the look on his face and instinctively stepping away from him. "You're not my keeper and I'm pretty sure that I'm not obliged to phone in my every move to you. I'm stronger than I used to be, certainly stronger than *you* think, and I sure as hell don't need looking after anymore."

"I never said that you did, did I?" His shoulders slumped as he looked at her with an expression that could have passed for one of regret, although Kim couldn't be quite sure. It was something that she wasn't used to seeing. "That doesn't mean that I'm not going to worry about you though." He attempted to smile, the thin-lipped grin appearing forced. "I don't have many friends, so I could do with at least one sticking around, yeah? That's you, by the way."

"Jesus, Frank Popper finally shows a shred of humility. What is the world coming to?"

Frank turned and wiped his sleeve across the landing area window, smearing a condensation and grime mixture across the glass, before narrowing his eyes and peering through.

"I'm not sure what it's coming to, but I could hazard a guess at where it's going," he muttered, clicking his tongue against the roof of his mouth like a teacher about to deliver a lecture.

"The protest?"

"Yep. There are quite a few down there now. They were starting to head in this direction when I was on my way. I was starting to feel like some sort of Pied Piper for the disenfranchised folks of these parts."

"Let's see," Kim moved up alongside him, elbowing him out of the way as she looked out. A crowd of about forty, maybe fifty people were milling around now, spilling onto the road outside the flats, with more still making their way from the surrounding streets. Already, in the distance they could hear the faint wail of a siren and, coming from around the corner where she had seen the prostitute earlier was a faint glow that might have been a fire. *Christ, they're starting early*, she thought.

"Should've stayed indoors," Frank said. "You know, grabbed a couple of beers, maybe a kebab?"

"Really? I would've thought that you'd want to be out there, talking to the masses about why they're so pissed off."

"I already *know* why they're pissed off Kim. The problem is that I don't think *they* know, not really. He turned away from the window to look at her. "Oh, I get that they're angry, but their reasons are misplaced."

"That actually sounds pretty patronising."

"Maybe it does, but it's true. The problems that they're railing against, no jobs, no money, crime, they're kicking off in the only way they know, struggling to articulate anything more constructive. But they aren't paying any attention to what *causes* any of those things. They're playing into the hands of the sort of people who sit and make the decisions. You know, the ones who say that they obviously don't deserve help." He spread both his hands out, trying to emphasise his point. "Meanwhile, on the outside of the goldfish bowl, people sit and watch this shit unfold on their televisions and think, *just look at those scumbags, they deserve everything they get.*"

"And you wish you could change that?"

"I try, in my own little way. But I'm just one person, Kim. You're right about me, I'm just a middle aged - usually drunk - bloke, still getting angry about far too many things that I can't possibly fix," he shrugged his shoulders. "Words alone just aren't that powerful, not these days." As he finished speaking Kim stepped forward again. Flinging both arms around him, she drew him close in a hug, long enough to plant a kiss on the side of his face, her lips warm and soft against the roughness of his stubble-peppered cheek.

"What was that for?" he asked.

"For being you," she smiled. "You can be an arsehole sometimes, Frank, but at least you're an *honest* arsehole. Your heart's in the right place, that's for sure."

"Thank Christ for that," his mouth turned up in a half-grin. "Wait a minute, are you hitting on me? As much as I'd like to, this isn't the time or place to-"

"Prick," she swung her hand at his shoulder. "You just had to go spoiling the moment, didn't you?"

"Yeah, just like always." Frank turned back to the window, cupping a hand against the glass to make it easier to see through. The sirens sounded louder now, as did the shouts. "On a more serious note, I really do think we ought to be making a move out of here."

"I won't argue," Kim said, already heading towards the stairs.

***

"Help me, somebody help me." The voice drifted from the direction of the first flat on the second floor, faint and thin-sounding.

"Did you hear that?" Frank stopped in his tracks, looking towards from where the sound had come.

"Hear what?" Kim cocked her head to one side, pretending that she hadn't heard anything. The pathetic images of Whitman and his wife were still fresh in her mind, she was in no real hurry to go exploring again. "I didn't hear anything."

"Oh my God, it's my girlfriend. I think she's dying."

"There it is again, a woman from the sound of it." Frank started walking towards the sound now. Kim, wincing in apprehension, tugged at his jacket sleeve.

"Are you sure you want to check it out?" She asked, hesitating. "You don't know, it could be anyone."

"It was a woman, Kim, in need of help." He smiled again. "Besides, she mentioned her *girlfriend*, you know what *that* means..."

"Yeah, it means that you're *still* a dirty bastard with a one-track mind."

"Whatever, if the cap fits."

"You filthy twat," she allowed him to walk in front, still reluctant to go anywhere unfamiliar, even as he strode ahead. "You know," she called after him, "I'm kind of starting to understand why you moved out of this place. It's a right shithole."

There was no answer.

"Frank?" She turned the corner where he'd strode ahead. "Cheers for dropping me." There was an open door, where the voice must have come from. Frank had probably gone inside already. *"Frank?"* She called again, a little more apprehensive. "For Christ's sake, where are you now?" She pushed against the door, opening it inward and stepping into the short, dark hallway beyond. Nervous, she counted her steps as she walked. *One...two...three...*she found the light switch on the wall. Reaching out her hand, she flicked it, a dim, naked bulb flaring into life and filling the hallway with a dim glow. *Four...five... six...*

(*!?!*)

INSATIABLE

She saw it out of the corner of her eye, a quick blur of movement, that didn't give her any time to react before there was an explosion of pain somewhere in the back of her head and everything turned black.

THIRTY-EIGHT

(?)

"Wayyykupppyouuubitch..."

(???)

"Fuckinwayyykuppp..."

A pain, like being stabbed in the temple with a fistful of needles, something that she knew would only feel worse if she summoned up the courage to open her eyes. She thought about just keeping them closed for as long as she could. With any luck, it would be possible to wait until the whole world stopped rotating around her.

"Iknowyoureawakeyoubitchopenyourfuckingeyes..." The voice came from somewhere above her. Whispering softly, it could have passed for little more than some idle pleasantry, were it not for the actual words that were being used. She didn't want to hear what was said, rather she wanted to ignore the demand, just knowing that whatever she would see, it surely wouldn't be something good.

"Come on, come on, it's not like I hit you too hard or nothing, open your frigging eyes love, yeah? I know you're awake, so you can stop pissing me about now." There was a gentle slap of fingers against the side of her face, not enough to hurt, but just firm enough to get her attention.

"Whuuuu..." Against her better judgement, Kim opened her eyes, moving them from side to side in an effort to clear the blurring. The already-dim light was partly blocked by the person kneeling over her.

"Awright, now that's *much* better, innit?"

"Who...who are you?" Kim mumbled, the dryness of her throat making her voice sound weak and strangled.

"You can call me Susie," the woman said, "since it *is* my name after all." She knelt back on her haunches and grinned a wide, toothy smile that looked like it could almost split her face in half. Despite this, Kim noticed that she was painfully gaunt-looking, her cheekbones jutted out from her pinched face, and her sunken eyes were dull, despite her apparent forced cheer. Her greasy hair was scraped back from her forehead into a loose ponytail, and she was wearing an unkempt, stained t-shirt, the looseness of which hinted at the skeletal frame hidden beneath.

"Lookin' pretty good, ain't I?" Susanne Walters said, still with that same strained smile. "You wouldn't believe it if you'd seen me just a few weeks ago. I'm less than half the girl I was. Anyway," she raised her arm, jabbing a bony finger in the direction behind her. "What's your story? What have you got to do with that seedy old prick over there?"

"What?" Kim cocked her head, trying to look over Susanne's shoulder, gasping as she saw Frank slumped in the corner of the room, his head tilted forward with his chin resting against his chest. *"What have you done to him?"*

"Oh, nothing that the dirty bastard didn't deserve," Susanne smirked, Kim catching the smell of something rotten on her breath as she did so. "He *does* deserve it, and more besides. Do you even have *any* idea what he's like?"

More than you know, Kim thought, deciding against saying so out loud. "He's...an old friend," she said. "We go back a long way."

"Yeah, that might be, but did he ever arse-fuck you in a club toilet? Then do a runner without as much as a thank you or goodbye?" A look of anger flickered across Susanne's face in a brief spasm, the smile faltering for just a moment.

"No," Kim shook her head. "But I wouldn't put it past him."

"So, you *do* know what he's like, yeah? In that case you'll know that he deserves everything that he gets." Susanne tutted shaking her head as though disappointed somehow. "To start with, I thought that he'd given me something nasty, that he had caused this," she pointed at herself, lifting up her top for long enough to give a glimpse of her ribs and sunken belly. "Then to cap it all, it had to be the worst shag ever. He shot his load in, like, twenty seconds. I mean, fucking hell, he barely even scraped the sides." Kim tried not to wince with distaste at the thought of Frank living up to the character he always liked to project for some reason. Screwing some stranger in a toilet cubicle, without even asking her name first, seemed pretty much his style. Thinking it didn't make the reality of it any better though.

"Yeah, at first I thought that I should really be thanking him for giving me some sort of weight loss disease. You wouldn't think it, but I used to be a bit chunky."

Oh, trust me, I'm learning to believe you, Kim thought.

"It wasn't too good to begin with, what with the nosebleeds and everything. I thought he'd gone and gotten me up the stick at first, but I don't think you can get pregnant taking it up the arse."

"My, you're a smart one, aren't you?"

"If I were you, I'd stop trying to be so frigging clever."

Kim looked over at Frank again, the tendons in her neck straining as she stretched to see him. There was a low groan as he stirred, turning onto his side, as though in an effort to get up. *Come on, come on, you prick*, she thought, willing him to move.

Noticing the focus of Kim's attention, Susanne turned around, looking towards the corner.

"You see? He'll be okay," she said, "for now, anyway."

"What do you mean, *for now?*"

"You'll find out in a bit, don't worry." Susanne rose to her feet, and Kim noticed for the first time that she was naked from the waist down, her legs little more than bone covered in a grey, almost translucent layer of skin, looked barely enough to support her, the shins mottled with bruises and thread-like blood vessels. She turned her head, as if reading Kim's mind. "Don't worry, I'm not letting him anywhere near me, not *this* time. I told you, he's hardly hung like a donkey. Or maybe you already knew that."

"Fuck you."

"He already tried that one," Susanne laughed, the sound cold. "Now it's time to pay it back with interest. *I'm* in charge this time."

Kim coughed, spluttering as she got a lungful the same pungent smell she noticed when she first came to.

"Christ," she said, "it smells like something's died in here."

"Oh, that'll just be Alex," Susanne muttered under her breath. "It was only yesterday, but it's been pretty warm in here. She should still keep me going for a little while though, at least." Kim turned her head to other side, even though she knew she really shouldn't have. It was stupid to do so, stupid to look, especially after what she had already seen in Whitman's bathroom. Stupid, so stupid. But she still did it all the same.

Distracted, she heard the soft padding sound of bare feet against floor, giving herself no time to turn back before there was a new sharp pain, followed by nothing once again.

THIRTY-NINE

"Let's see how you like it."

Frank was in the middle of a dream in which he was being held down and receiving personal attention from his favourite *Page Three glamour model,* when everything went horribly wrong.

Jarring back into consciousness, his imaginings unravelled as he realised that he couldn't move quite as easily as he would have hoped. There was a dull ache in the back of his head, and the pressure of something across his thighs, not too heavy, but sufficient to hold him in place, making it uncomfortable, as well as difficult for him to move.

The last thing that he could remember was the call for help. A cry, soft and frightened sounding. As cold as he had to admit that he could be sometimes, it wasn't the kind of thing he could just ignore, especially if the person hopefully had some way of showing her gratitude afterward. He had left Kim standing on the landing, rushing towards the sound without really thinking of the consequences, despite where he was, and what was going on around them.

A sharp pain, then nothing, at least until the vision of Samantha Fox straddling his old fella as she rubbed her big old titties right up in his face.

All things considered, he had been a bit of a dick, really.

"Owowowow..." His legs were definitely pinned in place, held by something that he couldn't really be bothered to try and shrug off. He turned his head from side to side instead in an effort to clear it, grunting as he felt a raw, damp patch to the back, beneath his hair, scraping against the floor with the movement.

"It wakes up at last," the voice was familiar, although dry and cracked-sounding, as though the speaker was in desperate need of a drink of water. "I was starting to think I really had smacked you one a bit too hard. You must just be a bit soft, as well as a lying shitweasel."

Oh fuck, Frank thought.

"Has the penny dropped yet? Well, you *can* look at me if you like," Susanne said, leaning forward until her face was just inches away from his. "It'll make things more fun, and I reckon that I've earned some fun, especially after letting myself get shafted by a scumbag like you."

"I'd rather not, thanks," Frank turned his head to one side, wincing as the bones in his neck let out a crack that jolted through his shoulder blade. He tried to ignore the rotten smell of dead things on her breath, not wanting to imagine what could have actually caused it. "What's your name again? Sammy? Becky? Tell me if I'm getting warm, okay?"

"You didn't even ask me at the time," her voice had a cold edge to it, as though he had touched a nerve. "You were only bothered about shooting your load. After that, you couldn't be away from me quick enough. You even had the balls to spin me some story about you being a journalist."

"That's because I *am* a journalist," Frank coughed, feeling a dull ache in his chest now. He really felt a bit too old to be playing at wrestling. "I just like to use my job to my advantage sometimes. What can I say? I don't usually get out as much as I would like."

"Still every bit as mouthy as I thought you were," Susanne rocked back onto his thighs, her knees burying themselves into the muscles. This time he gasped, forcing his eyes open in shock.

"What the hell?" The girl that he had had his way with in the toilet cubicle just a few weeks ago had changed. Instead of rolls of fat squeezing their way out from skintight clothing there was a loose-fitting, dirty t-shirt, the neckline of which hung down low enough for him to see her painfully emaciated figure, deflated-looking breasts and letter-rack ribs poking out from beneath her skin. "What happened to you?"

"I got better, no thanks to you," she grinned, her thin lips pulling back from pale gums, her teeth yellowed and looking too large for her mouth.

"How? What have you been taking?" Frank gasped, his eyes widening as he almost pleaded.

"*Taken?* I haven't *taken* anything." She paused, glancing up towards the ceiling, as though for inspiration. "What is it with you blokes, anyway? That doctor, he was the same. *Tablets, you must be on tablets,*" she mocked in a deliberately high-pitched voice. "Me, I reckon I'd call it a *miracle,*" she smiled, pleased with her answer.

"You're telling me that you think a parasite that causes its host to resort to cannibalism is somehow a *good* thing?"

"Yeah, yeah, I think I probably am." Her grin was thin and sickly. "I don't reckon it's a parasite though."

"That's exactly what it is-"

"No, *you're* the fucking parasite," she snapped. "I guess that it takes one to know one, right? Feeding off people like me, just out for whatever you can get your mucky paws onto or shove your cock into." She placed both hands on her hips, as though readying herself to tell him off for something. "I never forget a scumbag, and my eyes have been opened, good and proper." She sat back, resting against him as she ground herself against his crotch. He noticed for the first time that she was naked from the waist down, her bare, bony legs clamped against his thighs. "Does it feel the same as you remember, or had you actually forgotten it? I sure haven't, but that's probably just 'cause I have a really good memory." She grinned again, the smile looking a little more forced this time. "Especially for no-good arseholes who fuck me and then run away," she added.

"I don't see the problem," Frank tested the water, wincing as the effort of talking sent a flash of pain into the back of his head. "At least we both got something out of it, right?"

"This isn't about me," Susanne said, her voice deliberately quiet and in control. "It's about you, and how things can change, how *you* can change."

"Maybe I don't want to change," Frank said, trying to raise his head from the floor, the pain causing him to lie it back against the tiles with a groan. "Maybe I'm happy enough being everyone's favourite loveable rogue."

"Go on, keep taking the piss," she arched her back as she still ground against him, letting out a soft moan, as though she was enjoying herself just a little too much. "I'm still the one on top, still the one in charge here," she paused, opening her eyes and staring down at him. "I reckon I might have a little something for you, just like you slipped me a little something, yeah? Notice how I said *little* there?"

"You know," Frank winced as she pushed against him, still keeping a steady rhythm. "When I heard you calling for help and came over here, your dry humping me while you mock the size of my wanger wasn't really at the front of my mind." He felt the muscles in his belly clench as he tried to pull himself into a sitting position.

"Lie back down, you dirty cunt!" Her bony fist glanced against the side of his face, enough to send him back to the floor, pinpricks of light dancing in front of his eyes as the back of his head struck the tiles again. *"Still trying to be a funny twat, aren't you? You need to realise, like I just told you, I'm the one in charge here!"*

"Who...said anything about...trying?"

"Open your eyes," she slapped him across both cheeks, not too hard, but once again enough to get his attention. "I said *open your fucking eyes.* I want you to see what's going to happen to you." He felt her bony fingers as she inserted them into his mouth, probing around for a decent grip as she pulled down on his jaw, widening the gap until the sides of his mouth felt like they would tear. As she did so, she stopped grinding against him and leaned over him, tilting her head until her face was right above his. Her mouth seemed to stretch into an impossibly wide smile, a jagged yawn that ran almost from ear to ear. He could hear it, a wet, slapping sound, rising up from the back of her throat. He guessed what was happening before he even saw the thing, pulling itself up to the front of her mouth in a wet, bloody mound, its tip pulsating and moving from side to side as it slid forward.

Grunting, he tried to move his jaw, to bring his teeth together, kicking his legs out at the same time, in an effort to buck her away from him.

I wish I'd just given her the clap or something now, he thought, knowing just how stupidly pointless it was to do so. He tried to close his eyes, to look away, but couldn't. Instead, he watched as the parasite teetered on the edge, working its way over her bottom teeth and hanging down over her chin. *This is it,* he thought. *After years of screwing around, I'm going to be finished off by being force-fed a giant fucking slug-*

Crack!

There was a whistling sensation, a movement of air as something swung in an arc and connected with the side of her head. The impact knocked her to the side, the top half of her body collapsing alongside him, her spindle-like legs still trailing across his. As she fell, she spat the creature out, the large, almost gelatinous thing landing inches away from Frank's face. He opened his mouth to scream as, just for a second, it seemed to rear up and taste the air around it, before Kim's boot came down on it with a wet, squelch. Her foot still flat on the floor, she dragged it backward, pulling a greasy, bloody streak across the tiles.

"That's for catching me off-guard twice in a row, you bitch," she grunted, still gripping the handle of the iron that had doubled as a makeshift weapon. "Jesus wept, my head's ringing."

"What were you thinking?" Frank wheezed, his breath escaping in short, uneven bursts, "I was just starting to get turned on by that."

"Still trying to make out like it's all a big old dirty joke," Kim reached a hand down, and he took it. "It's no laughing matter, it looked like she was after something a bit more than your sloppy seconds."

"I'm just impressed that she even remembered me," Frank pulled himself to his feet, shaking his head in an effort to clear it. "Impressed, but not surprised, of course." He tried, but no smile would come. Instead, he looked down again at the sticky, tar-like smudge, trailing across the floor. "She was going to pass that *thing* onto me deliberately," he said, an unusual tone of disbelief in his voice that couldn't be mistaken. "She almost *did*. She's probably already done it to other people."

"Yeah," every time she blinked or closed her eyes, Kim could still see Whitman, slumped against the wall in his dirty, unlit flat. How he had broken his own neck, probably out of some desperate need to end his own life, those things just slopping out of his mouth one after another. "Perhaps it's how they survive, making sure that their host spreads them to as many people as possible." She tried not to shudder at her own thoughts as she spoke them aloud.

"That's probably right," Frank brushed himself down, ignoring the stale, deathly smell that filled the room. "Earlier today, I tracked down that Doctor Hesketh, the guy who I was trying to tell you about before. I reckoned that he might have been involved in all of this somehow."

"How?"

"He was-" Frank hesitated as he thought back again to the pathetic figure he had found, sat on his own, just waiting to die, knowing that it was his own fault. "A few of the people, including Marks, were patients of his." Kim nodded, not wanting to press him for further information. It wasn't too hard to figure out.

"Anyway," Frank walked across to the window. Parting the tattered curtains, he peered out. "What's going on out there now?" His eyes widened as he looked. "Holy *shit*."

"What's the matter?" Kim stepped forward too, moving alongside him as she too looked down on the scene below. "*Oh, hell*," she said. "There's your peaceful protest right down there." The gathered crowd in the street below was even larger now. A general store along the road that she had passed only a few hours before now looked as though it had been ransacked, its windows smashed and its door hanging from its hinges. Someone had started a fire in the middle of the road, blocking it from traffic, and the sound of sirens could be clearly heard in the distance. Shouts and chanting noises swelled up from the still-growing mass of people. A couple of brawls had broken out already, violence bubbling under the surface and ready to spread, as some people were just out to cause trouble from the start. They were probably the sort of people who didn't even pretend to know why anyone would want to protest in the first place.

"This has been a long time coming," Frank murmured, his attention focused on the scene below. "It doesn't matter who they are, people can only take so much before they lash out."

"That doesn't make it right though."

"I never said that it does. Ignoring the cause won't make the problem go away. That's the trouble with this place, too many people are just happy enough to go on looking the other way." He would never have admitted as much, but deep inside, Frank was worried. Guilt tugged at him, as he wondered just how much of what was happening could have been instigated by him. For so long, he had poured out his vitriolic outbursts, the calls to arms for the disenfranchised, those people for whom he had sought to set himself up as some sort of a mouthpiece. He had wanted people to sit up and take notice of the things that they so often ignored, never really pausing to consider just who might be taking notice of *him*.

"I just wanted people to see it for what it was," he mumbled at last, under his breath.

"What?"

"Nothing, I didn't say anything. Well, nothing too important, anyway."

"Frank?" Kim's voice was faint, as though uncertain about something.

"What's the matter?" He asked, still straining his eyes through the dirt streaking the glass, to see if there were any people actually holding some sort of meaningful protest. "What's wrong?"

As he spoke, he turned away from the window. The floor was bare, in the middle was an iron with its cord trailing out behind it, the same one that Kim had used to smack Susanne upside her head just minutes earlier.

"She's gone," Kim said.

FORTY

"Shit," Frank looked around the room, checking the corners for any sign of her. She had caught him off-guard once already, he didn't want to risk a second time.

"I think I heard her heading out the front door," Kim said, her eyes narrowed as she looked towards the opening leading to the hallway. "It was hard to be sure though, with everything going on out there."

"She probably wants to spread it now," Frank said, his feet ungluing themselves from the spot at last. "Like some sort of Typhoid Mary, she wants to pass it on."

"Why the hell would she want to do that?"

"There was something that Hesketh said to me. He said that it affects the brain somehow. You said the same thing yourself earlier, it wants to survive. The best way to do that is to spread as far and as fast as possible. You saw what she was like, right?"

"All those people down there..." Kim wondered how many other people had already been infected, hidden away behind closed doors, slowly wasting away like Whitman, driving themselves mad with a hunger that they couldn't even begin to understand. The sort of hunger that could make them turn on anyone; friends, loved ones, themselves. She looked down at the street below again. The fire had spread to the shop now, a small crowd had gathered around the entrance waving their arms and shouting. As she watched, a burly man ran from the exit, hunched over almost double with the weight of the items he was carrying. He was followed by a smaller, rodent-like figure, probably the shopkeeper. Staggering, he was wearing a bloodstained apron and had one hand clasped to the side of his head. It looked as though he was shouting insults of some sort that went ignored. After a few seconds, someone rushed

335

forward out of the crowd and punched him in the gut, dropping him to his knees.

"How many of them already?" She said aloud this time.

"What?"

"We've got to find her," Kim said. "No one down there will realise, not even the pigs, if they ever show up."

"Are you mad?" Frank stopped short of rolling his eyes. "The pigs won't want a damn thing to do with any of this. The way they see it, most of the people down there are better off just forgotten about anyway."

"Jesus wept Frank, you'll never change, will you?" Kim's cheeks flushed with anger, her eyes flashing. "When are you going to just let go of it for a minute and realise that some things are just more bloody important?"

"What do you mean?" He tried to look indignant, as though he was ignorant of what she was saying, knowing that he probably came across as anything but.

"You know damn well what I mean. Christ, it's about time that you changed the record. You just muddle on from one day to the next, acting like some anti-authoritarian prick, sticking it to The Man. You know that you're really getting a bit too old for that sort of bollocks."

"That's a matter of opinion-"

"No Frank, it's a matter of fact. And what's more, you *know* it is." She paused for breath, Frank waiting for her to speak again, as though afraid to interrupt her. "But rather than grow the hell up, you find it easier to blame the local council, or the police, or whatever other people on high you like to think takes a massive shit on everyone from way up in their ivory towers."

"Someone has to say something about it."

"Who decided that it had to be you? Who actually gave *that* sort of responsibility to some middle-aged drunk who still thinks nothing of fucking some dirty slag in a nightclub toilet cubicle?" Frank said nothing, instead he stood with his eyes wide, staring straight at her, as though she had just slapped him hard across the face, not for the first time.

"I'm sorry Frank," Kim said, her breathing laboured, as if speaking had taken her full effort. "Really, I am. But the truth hurts sometimes, you know? You've never changed, even if you think you have. Same old Franklin Popovich, ploughing through life without a care for whatever crap gets churned up in your wake. You go on pretending that you're some maverick crusader for truth and justice, something more than the two-bit hack that everyone else sees you as. Really, you're such a damned contradiction, and just look at the trouble it's caused this time, for both of us."

"But even you can't blame me for what's happened here," he spoke in a mumble now, the fight leaving him to chase its own tail in the corner somewhere. "Surely you can see *that?*"

"Yes, of course I can, but you could have easily just walked away from it all, instead of doing your bit to make things worse." Kim cocked her head to one side, narrowing her eyes as though looking for any further sign of emotion, repentance, anything. "You of all people should know Frank, when you push people too hard, they usually push back even harder, and this is the sort of shit that happens because of it."

Frank lowered his head. "I always knew I should have stuck to writing poetry," he said. "Can't really hurt anyone with a few dirty haikus."

"Come on, Bukowski," Kim grinned, "I reckon that's enough home truths for the next few days at least." She forced a grin as she placed two fingers beneath his chin, bristling against his stubble as she raised his head. He broke a smile too as he remembered just how welcome the gentleness of her touch could be sometimes.

"Okay," he said, "lesson learned." He spread his hands outward in a gesture of openness. "Fair enough, I know I can be an arsehole sometimes - *lots* of times - but I'll keep on trying."

"We'd better get going," Kim turned, looking around the room again as she spoke. "She could be out there with all those people."

As though in response, the noise from outside suddenly sounded louder than ever.

FORTY-ONE

I

It happens every day. So-called ordinary people, the kind that most others wouldn't even think to look twice at, pretty much ignored, allowed to simply drop out of existence. Meanwhile, everything else continues to rush on by, as no one seems to notice or even care.

Tiny little deaths.

***

Samantha Rivers had never liked the flat. It had been seven months and she still couldn't get used to the cramped atmosphere of the place. It had some kind of retro seventies feel to it, and not in a good way. She had protested in the beginning of course, but Peter had pretty much ignored her at every turn, just like he always did when he didn't care too much for what she had to say. She sometimes thought that, if he could, he would buy a remote control and switch her permanently on mute.

It'll get better, he would say, along with, *beggars can't be choosers, remember.* Two of his favourite replies on the rare occasions when he actually bothered to engage with her in anything even vaguely serious. All of the avoidance tactics were little more than blatant attempts to evade the truth though; it was all *his* fault that they were in such a damn mess to begin with. Stupid, careless pillock, losing his job in the first place. Seriously though, what was he thinking, looking at those bloody websites during company time, even if it *was* on his lunch break? What the hell was he *thinking?*

Without his income, hardly a king's ransom, but at least enough, they had been forced to wave goodbye to the house and car, along with a good few of their friends, especially once the truth started to come out, most people not wanting to know about or be associated with *that* sort of behaviour. Bloody hypocrites that they probably were.

A sound came from the special room, that might have just been a cough, or perhaps he was trying to actually say something worthwhile for a change, she couldn't always tell. Whatever, either way, let the stubborn so-and-so know how it felt, just for once, yeah? It wouldn't hurt him. Well, it *probably* wouldn't, not too much, anyway.

She really did miss the house. It'd had just so much more space to breathe, to go about your business undisturbed, rather than feeling like you had been squeezed into a shoe box.

She missed the *old* special room, their name for the cellar. So quiet and private, they could get up to anything they wanted down there, absolutely *anything*.

Another muffled sound came from the room, definitely an attempt at speech this time, choking off, as though there was something wrong with his chest.

"*Shut your mouth you useless, dirty bastard, I'll come through when I'm good and ready,*" she called through. There was a ripple of static down the length of her back and the small hairs stood on end. No matter how she felt about their current situation, she still got a buzz out of *that* at least, one of the few things that they still had in common. Yes, the cellar had been far better, so much more private, but the box room still did the trick. One door, no windows, the four walls and ceiling covered with old egg boxes, polystyrene and off-cuts of carpet, it was pretty much soundproofed as well as possible, except for when the door was open. At least they had managed to get into a ground floor flat, so there was no one below them to kick up a fuss. *Small mercies*, she reminded herself sometimes.

It still would have been better with a cellar though.

"'Mantha," the sound was choked, as though coming through a mouthful of rotten seaweed. Perhaps she had fastened the gag just a little too tight.

"Shut up, you pathetic old cunt!" She shouted, itching at a spot on her nose with a single ragged fingernail. There was a faint odour, warm and cloying, that she couldn't quite place. *"I hope you haven't gone and shat yourself, or I'll shove your bloody nose in it when I come through there!"*

***

Funny little games: that had always been her pet name for it, a means of normalising what would soon become a habit for them both. Before then, things had been much more mundane, just the right side of boring, in fact. A couple of casual dates before they even slept together for the first time, their initial hook up had happened just gradually enough to make things seem a bit more normal. The weirdest thing about her relationship, what few friends she actually had commented a few times to begin with, was the age gap. *I'm surprised that people don't think you're on a night out with your dad*, or something along those lines had been said more than once. She had shrugged off the feelings of discomfort, probably with more ease than she could have hoped. Their opinion didn't really concern her, all that mattered was that he made her feel loved and wanted, to begin with, at least. For the first time in the eighteen years since she had last seen her actual father, she felt what she supposed passed as *secure*.

Of course, whatever novelty there had been wore off soon enough. It started to get just a bit too predictable, a little bit boring. Pretty soon, she had started to feel uncomfortable with some greying, slack-bellied bloke slavering over her like a dog in heat. She had to concentrate in order to ignore the way her stomach churned when his jowls quivered as he thrust himself into her, with about as much emotion as he might show poking a fireplace, as he grunted his way to a noisy climax. She even surprised herself with the way that she just about managed to turn a blind eye to the silvery trail of drool that would dangle from his flabby bottom lip in a gelatinous, snot-like string every time he shot his load.

"I've got an idea," he had said to her one morning, spitting out breadcrumbs as his voice garbled its way through a mouthful of burnt toast. "Have you ever thought of ways of spicing things up a bit?"

"I'm not sure I get you," Samantha had lied, quite convincingly, she thought, given his usual almost Neanderthal lack of subtlety.

"You know, in the bedroom," his sunken piggy eyes lit up, gleaming out from his ruddy face with a twinkle that she hadn't seen since their early days together. *Christ*, she thought, *he's already made his mind up anyway. He looks like he could come in his old grey jogging bottoms just thinking about it.* Her stomach lurched as she found herself wondering just what was going through that dirty little head of his.

"*What are you even going on about?*" She snapped, feeling her cheeks glow with a sudden unexpected warmth. "*I hope you're not thinking what I think you are!*" Just like that, he looked down, focusing his gaze on a smear of raspberry jam on the side of his plate, the same way he looked whenever he felt cowed into submission. Keeping one hand flat alongside his empty coffee mug, he slid the other beneath the table. Still avoiding her gaze, his shoulder twitched, giving away the attempt at subtle movement.

"*What the bloody hell are you doing?*" Samantha's eyes widened in disbelief. "Are you playing with yourself under there or something? You filthy bastard - learn some self-control!"

"Sorry... I'm sorry," he mumbled. "It's just that-"

"Just that *what?*"

He looked up at the ceiling, as though searching for an answer that would make some sort of sense.

"It's just that, you know, it gets me worked up when you...take charge."

"Oh, does it?" She folded her arms across her chest. "In that case, get off your lazy fucking arse and get some vacuuming done, instead of tickling your sad old cock under the breakfast table!"

"I don't mean *that* sort of control," he said, his voice sheepish with a tentative edge to it, as though he wanted to say something, but wasn't quite sure how she would react. "I mean when you get, you know, *dominating*."

"What are you, some kind of pervert?"

"No, there's nothing pervy about it, lots of people do it, you know? What goes on behind closed doors and all that sort of thing."

"So, what you mean is, you want me to boss you about a bit before we have sex?" She stood up from the table, brushing toast crumbs away from herself before folding her arms. From a standing position he looked much smaller, almost insignificant. The thought of putting him in his place suddenly seemed easier, more appealing. "Is *that* what you're getting at?"

"Pretty much, yeah."

***

Her initial dismissal had turned out to be somewhat premature. Along with the aid of a few carefully selected props, she had taken to the role of a dominatrix like the proverbial duck to water, actually enjoying it far more than she would ever have imagined beforehand. That first night, he had carried a wooden dining room chair down into the cellar, grunting and perspiring with the sort of anticipation that she had sometimes thought that he had in him, but had never quite seen before in all of its sweaty glory. Looping one of his leather belts through the back spindles of the chair, as a makeshift hand restraint, he had stripped naked and let her tie him down, just tight enough to stop him from changing his mind. Bound up in all his naked, milk bottle-flesh glory, she paraded back and forth for half an hour in that pair of high heels she didn't like - the narrow ones that always gave her blisters - and a mismatched pair of knickers and push-up bra that he'd bought for her in the Boxing Day sales, old-school romantic that he was. Glaring at his flabby naked belly with a coldness that came to her with far less effort than she would have expected, she spent half an hour hurling whatever abuse she could dream up at him, trying to ignore the thread of spittle hanging down from his chin, just beneath the homemade ball gag of an old pair of socks stuffed into his mouth. As she continued, getting into the swing of things with an ease that she had never considered possible before, she couldn't believe just how large his cock had swollen, her taunts giving him a bigger erection than she remembered him having in a long time. Once she had ran out of mean things to say, she dropped to her knees in front of him and sucked him off with a hunger that she had forgotten she was ever capable of. She squeezed his balls with one hand, fingering her own wetness with the other until they both came, a hot jet of his spunk hitting the back of her throat with a molten force that almost made her gag. Still, she kept going for several minutes, lost in the haze of her own equally forceful orgasm as his length slackened and went soft in her mouth.

That first time had pretty much settled it. Samantha found that she was even able to get past the fact that his belly looked like the underside of a fish and his sagging man tits were almost as big as hers.

Several plain-wrapped parcel deliveries later, and they had kitted out the small cellar with everything they needed to keep things the right side of interesting; rubber things, odd-shaped toys with spikes, leather straps and restraints, underwear that was little more than scraps of cloth held together with string. Just a short time ago, Samantha would have balked at the mention of a butt plug, now it didn't bother her so much, just as long as it was Peter's arse it was plugging up, of course.

Funny little games. Yes, that was the name they had soon adopted for what they got up to in private. It was a means of being able to talk about it without giving too much away. An almost comedic, joking title, it masked the increasing extremity of their behaviour, as what had started out as mild domination grew into something else. Samantha soon found that her own need to avoid the return of staleness, of boredom, led her to want to explore increasingly extreme avenues of excitement.

Then the careless prick had only gone and lost his bloody job.

It wasn't the fact he had been looking at porn online that bothered her so much. If anything, the thought of it made her tingle, giving her just one more reason to berate him in their next session, while secretly getting turned on by the thought of just what it was that he could have possibly been looking at. That he had been doing so on work time though, whilst doing a job that they needed him to keep if they wanted to stay living in the manner to which they had become accustomed, that wasn't so good.

"It'll do us for now, just until we get back on our feet," Peter had said, trying to make his voice as casual-sounding as possible, as though it was already a foregone conclusion. "It'll have to."

"You mean until *you* get back on your feet," Samantha had snapped. "None of this is my fault. *You* need to find another job, quick. Although I don't know who'll have you, once they hear about your viewing habits."

"Jesus, 'Mantha, that was a one-off," he said, looking down at the table. He might have been turned on by her displays of aggression during their sex play, but elsewhere, he still felt put in his place, and not in a good way. "It's not likely to happen again." Fingers interlinked, he twirled his thumbs, one around the other, trying to give himself something to look at other than her angry facial expression. "We just can't afford to keep the house anymore."

"Yes, thanks to *you*. Seriously, what were you thinking? Having a sly tug under the desk at the time, were you?"

"That's all by the by. We'll just have to rent something a bit smaller for the time being." He tapped the sheet of paper on the table in front of him with a pudgy forefinger. "It looks ideal. Ground floor flat, two bedrooms, one a decent size for sleeping and the other a box room for, well, *you* know-"

"We'll have to see about that," she said, folding her arms across her chest, as though already growing weary of the conversation. The dirty bastard, he still had a one-track mind. There was a time and a place, the kitchen table and breakfast time were neither.

That night, she had made sure that he paid for it with interest. Fastening the restraints a little tighter than usual, until the leather straps cut into the flesh of his wrists and ankles almost enough to draw blood. For over two hours she had drawn things out in an agony that was vicious, pacing back and forth as she called him every filthy name she could think of, pausing only to slap him across the face every ten minutes or so.

"Beg for it, you dirty prick! Beg!" Even as the tears of humiliation had welled up in his eyes, she had watched with the same sense of incredulity that had never quite left her as his cock swelled larger than she had ever thought possible. *Fucking hell*, she had thought, *it's like a Zeppelin. A massive, veined Zeppelin.* For the first time starting to actually worry that he might burst, his penis rupturing to spray a mixture of blood and semen across the cheap linoleum flooring. She had dropped to her knees in front of him and sucked him off there and then, almost choking as he shot his pent-up load.

There was certainly something to be said about taking charge, all right.

***

"Mantha," his voice sounded weaker now, almost strangulated. *Won't he just shut the hell up for a change?* She thought, pacing back and forth across the kitchen floor, the way she had been for the last ten minutes now. She still hadn't forgiven him for blowing most of his benefit money on the horses last Saturday afternoon. She had been pretty short on forgiveness for quite a while now, and she liked to make sure that he didn't forget it. She hadn't fastened the ball gag *too* tight, or so she thought, just tight enough. She had to admit that the thought of him being so completely helpless still excited her though. She would have been a liar if she had tried to say otherwise. Closing her eyes, she traced the fingers of one hand down her chest and towards her sagging, bra-cupped breast, her lips parting in a soft moan as the fingertip traced around the erect nipple straining at the flimsy fabric. She didn't know why, but she seemed to have lost a whole load of weight recently. Her hand continued its lazy journey, sliding across the ridged landscape of her rib cage and towards the central spot between her legs, to rub at the growing wetness down there.

There was a sudden noise at the window that made her jump. She still hadn't gotten used to the frequent commotions, as commonplace as they were. It was usually easier just to try and ignore them, having heard some of the stories of what could happen if they didn't. After-pub brawls, or fights over bad drug deals, that sort of thing. Or it was quite common for one of the regular prostitutes on the corner to get involved in some dust up or other, usually over how much money they were owed. Samantha was pretty certain that one of them lived on either the sixth or seventh floor above, and she worked her pitch right on the front doorstep, the thick bloody cow. More than once they had crossed each other going in or out of the block, the young girl sporting some visible fresh bruise or scrape. *At least I haven't had to resort to that,* Samantha would think to herself, worrying that there was still time, if Peter didn't buck his bloody ideas up, get off his lazy backside and find a job.

"What the hell is going *on* out there?" Whatever it was, it sounded like a proper ruck now, something much bigger than an average pub brawl. Screaming and shouting, carrying on the breeze, along with the familiar wail of sirens.

Then there was something else. The faintest smell of smoke, not cigarette smoke, but fire. The smell of burning.

"*Samantha...*" Peter's voice sounded even weaker now, more of a muffled croak, as he struggled to form words beyond the hard rubber ball stuffed into his mouth.

"Shut the bloody hell up for another few minutes," she mumbled, more to herself now rather than to him. The odour of burning was definitely stronger, masking the warm, chemical stink of petrol. She almost thought that she could hear the pops and crackles of flame, as though it was getting closer. Curiosity getting the better of her, she went across to the window and pinched the curtain, shifting it to one side to peer through the condensation-frosted glass.

There. Right between the-
(blackness)

***

(burning)
She forced her eyes to open, probably against her better judgment, the pain of doing so bringing tears to them. The rest of her face was numb, a cold sensation spreading out from the centre, as though she had been holding it against the inside of the

freezer door. Slowly, she managed to bring a hand up to where she imagined her nose to be, probing at it with two cautious fingers. The flesh was spongy, soft and wet beneath her touch, her fingertips stained red when she pulled them back again.

She could just about remember the shouting. Jeering, raucous taunts as she had looked out of the window. Struggling to gather her thoughts into something that made some sort of sense, it felt like things had lasted for several hours, rather than the split second that had actually been between her parting the curtains and the pane imploding, throwing her back in a spray of blood and glass shards. The brick - at least she *thought* it was a brick - had hit her square in the face, knocking her onto her back flat out, as well as spreading her nose into what was now so much pulp. There was a sharp pain in her left temple that sung out to her when she tried to move her head to one side. So instead, she just lay as still as she could.

The noise from outside was louder now, without the window to shield it out, and the smell of smoke stung the back of her tongue and roof of her mouth with an unpleasant tang.

It sounded like a riot of some sort was going on out there. Bloody typical, a bunch of pricks who couldn't get their own way, resorting to lobbing house bricks through the windows of ordinary people just trying to mind their own business.

Her legs refusing to move, she tried to roll over onto her side, letting out a howl of pain as the movement sent a lightning jolt down the length of her spine, the sensation ending somewhere around her pelvis. Sobbing, she fell back onto the floor tiles.

"Peter!" She shouted, her voice hoarse and cracking. *"Peter!"* She realised that she hadn't heard anything from him since she had first come to her senses. Of course, he was in no position to help, not unless he had managed to do a Houdini and free himself from the handcuffs and length of rope that she had used to tie him naked to the chair. The smell of smoke was stronger now, the choking dryness making her retch, and there was a sensation of scorching heat above her head, somewhere in the direction of the door. *"Peter!"* She called again, the smoke robbing her of her voice before she could say any more. She knew full well that he wasn't coming. *He's probably dead,* she thought, *and I won't be far behind. What a stupid way to die. Stupid.* Her, lying flat out in her silky underwear, the only matching set she owned, him trussed up like a turkey in some makeshift dungeon. What would the bloody neighbours think? Gritting her teeth and clenching her eyes tight shut to hold back the tears, she let out a scream of agony as she moved her upper body in an attempt at a log roll. Her numb legs followed behind limp, as she flopped around onto her belly like a dying fish. There was a dull ache in the base of her skull as she raised her head with a shucking noise as the mess that had until recently been her nose peeled itself away from the floor. Fortunately, the whole of her face had frozen into numbness. God only knew what sort of a state she actually *looked* like.

The first tendrils of smoke were starting to curl their way around the edge of the door, the orange glow-tinged greyness visible through the gap hinting at worse beyond. There was a sputtering, crackling sound that sounded almost quaint. It reminded her of the sort of childhood that she had always wanted but never had. It was the sound of campfires being prodded with sticks, getting them ready for marshmallows and hot chocolate. It was the sight of embers, skittering into the air in a glowing dance, like stars, never quite reaching their place in the sky.

It was the last thoughts and feelings of someone who had accepted that she was about to die.

"Nuh...no..." She gasped, barely recognising her own voice as she coughed in a choking spasm. *"Got to...get...out..."* Gritting her teeth again, she stretched out her arms, using them to pull herself

across the floor, grunting as the doorway inched closer. *"Puh...Peter...Pe-"* she gave up, as her attempt at shouting dissolved into another series of wracking coughs. The smoke was thicker now, a growing black cloud that seemed to swell and distort with a life of its own, and she could feel her hair starting to singe as blisters began to prickle on her scalp. Her eyes blurring, she could just about see the first tongues of flame, licking around the door frame. Dragging across the floor, shards of shattered window glass ripped into her exposed flesh, tearing out bloody chunks unnoticed.

She stopped, exhausted by the effort of movement. It was just so tiring, trying to drag herself along, and it was so warm where she was. It would do her no good to try and get outside anyway, certainly not in the flimsy underwear she was wearing. No, it was surely much better to stay inside, where it was warm. So warm.

Never-ending warmth and darkness.

II

Eddie Caplin was thinking, something that he did rather a lot of, despite most people believing otherwise.

Unknown to him, Samantha Rivers was five floors below, contemplating just how much longer she was going to make her husband suffer, before having her way with him. Even if he had known, he would have at least made a decent act of not being bothered. If there was one thing that Eddie Caplin believed to be true, it was that whatever went on behind closed doors was no one else's business. At least that was what he would say to anyone willing to listen. Of course, it never hurt to try and keep up to date with what was going on outside, just as long as no one realised how much you actually knew.

Eddie was worried, so much so that he held his third glass of neat scotch in his bony, liver-spotted hand, the cheap tumbler feeling almost heavy enough to weigh down his arm.

It felt like she had been testing him for months now. Pushing her luck, what with all the late nights, rolling in at God only knew what time, stinking of booze or cigarettes, or both. It had probably all started back when she went to that bloody college, falling in with a whole new crowd, *broadening her horizons*, as she put it on those few occasions when she actually still bothered to talk to him. *You wouldn't get it*, she would say, in that same sly, mocking tone that she would keep just for him. *Perhaps you're too old to realise, but it's what people actually do nowadays, you know? Some of us actually prefer to go out with friends, rather than hide away in the pub with a half of bitter like some crusty old fart from a seventies sitcom.*

If she was his daughter, he might have put her in her place a long time before now. But she wasn't and, boy, did Louisa Caplin know it. No, her real father, Eddie's layabout of a brother, had scarpered a long time ago, chasing after one of his many bits on the side, taking little more than a black plastic bin liner full of clothes, a bottle of vodka, and fifty quid in dole money. It was typical of the work-shy bugger, doing a runner and leaving Eddie to pick up the pieces. *You'll make a better dad than I ever could anyway*, Roger Caplin had said, the attempt at sincerity masked by his usual boozy slurring. The bloody bottler, he always had found it easier to wander from day-to-day half-cut, rather than focus on any sort of responsibility. The ticking of the clock sounded far too loud in the small room, a metronome reminder of just how alone he really was. That *was* why he had agreed to it after all, wasn't it? There was no sense of altruism there. He owed his brother nothing. Hell, the two of them had fought like cat and dog for as far back as he could remember. No, it was a combination of the need for companionship along with the ever-present desire to know that he had gotten one over the drunken old sod. So deep had the rivalry, the animosity been between them, that he had jumped at the chance to take Louisa under his wing, the niece that he barely knew. Looking back with the benefit of hindsight, it was easy to see that he had been more than a little arrogant, assuming that it would be easy.

He really didn't have the first bloody clue.

To make matters worse, with Louisa Caplin, the apple hadn't fallen too far from the tree. She was her father's daughter, for sure. It hadn't taken too long for Eddie to realise that. The choice had been a simple one; live with Uncle Eddie or go into care until you're old enough to fend for yourself. When faced with the options, she had chosen what she thought to be the lesser of two evils. Of course, why wouldn't she? At least shacked up with some ageing bloke that she openly couldn't stand, she still had the means to push the boundaries, taking liberties wherever she could. Bigger fool him for allowing her sufficient free rein to get away with so much, until it was too late to change anything. It was probably his own fault for being so damn soft with her in the beginning. He had been far too quick to turn a blind eye while she stayed out until all hours with those new-found friends of hers. He had pretended not to notice the smell of booze on her breath, or the stink of weed - or whatever the kids called it nowadays - that lingered on the clothing that she continued to dump in a crumpled heap outside her bedroom door.

"Dad wouldn't mind me going out, if he was still here," she would say on those few occasions when he had tried to challenge her. *"I'm not surprised he did a runner. It's probably easier to hide away and get permanently rat-arsed than it would be to have someone like you as a brother."* Then the laugh would come, an almost innocent sounding thing, only thinly masking the obvious contempt lying just beneath its surface.

Eddie blamed that bloody college. Although it had never seemed possible beforehand, her attitude towards him had worsened even more since she had started at the place. So much for getting an education, the first thing she had learned was how to find even more inventive ways to belittle him. Those new stuck-up friends of hers weren't much better, either. Encouraging her to stay out till all hours, wherever it was that teenagers liked to hang out nowadays, not that she needed a great deal of egging on to start with. The few times he had seen any of them, he could almost feel their stares digging into the soft spot between his shoulder blades, the backs of their hands barely masking their sniggers and insults. *Spineless wanker*, was a popular one, *soft touch* was another. The worst thing about it was the feeling that they were right, he *was* a soft touch. He had to be. It was the easiest option, when the only alternative was to risk losing her completely. He wasn't sure that he could resign himself to a return to the days where it was just him, with a mangy old cat for company. With a seemingly psychic realisation that he was being thought of in a less than pleasant way, Mister Donner glared out at Eddie from his spot on top of the old drawer unit at the side of the small room. The cat's once-keen eyes were now filmed with a milky layer that didn't quite filter out the stare that still carried a hint of something almost malevolent. Originally a stray, Eddie had first crossed paths with Mister Donner in the back lane behind Betty's diner. The scrawny thing, all poking-out bones and matted fur, had been hunched over what was left of another cat, tugging and gnawing at the greasy, exposed innards. In all of his years, Eddie Caplin had never seen or heard of a cannibal cat before, hence the name. Following him back to his pokey little flat, probably in search of something a little more fulfilling than his fellow feline, the cat had stayed, never quite losing that same look of distrust that sometimes unnerved the old man.

As should probably have been expected, he seemed to prefer Louisa. Bloody typical.

Eddie glanced at the clock: quarter-past eleven. He had lost count of how many times he had looked, watching as the minute hand crawled across the face with a slowness that seemed more drawn out than possible. He tightened his grip on his glass, his bony fingers flexing, almost enough to disguise his trembling, but not quite.

There was a sudden crash from outside, somewhere down below. A sound of breaking glass, followed by the wail of an alarm, a chorus of jeers swelling at the noise. Ear to the ground as always, he had heard the whispers of a protest of some sort for the last couple of weeks. To begin with, he had thought it little more than idle gossip. Bloody hell, most people in this part of the city were far too downtrodden to arrange a bingo meeting, never mind a protest of any sort. All mouth and no trousers, for want of a better way of putting it. Now though, in his front room, with his only company a whisky bottle and a cat that hated his guts as he listened to the swell of shouting, interspersed with sounds of breaking glass, he wasn't so sure anymore.

"*Fuck the rozzers! Fuck the council! Fuck the fucking government!*"

Alone.

And she was still out there somewhere.

Raising the glass to his thin mouth, he tipped the contents down his throat, wincing as he felt the satisfying burn, working its way down his gullet and spreading its warmth through his chest. It still wasn't enough to thaw the numbness inside him. The sort of numbness that stemmed from being old, alone and afraid. That was the problem, there was no denying it, he was *afraid*.

"*Fuck 'em all! Give us our fucking city back, you bastards!*"

It sounded close, *too* close. *Just lock the door,* he thought, hating himself for it. *Lock the door and hide yourself away in bed, old man. She's made her choice and she's old enough to deal with the consequences, so your conscience shouldn't even be ruffled. For God's sake, she's not even your daughter!*

Give us our city back. Back from *who* exactly? The problem was that the people who shouted the loudest about wanting things fixed were usually the same ones who contributed most to those things being broken in the first place. He shifted in his easy chair, one spindly finger tracing across the armrest, the worn felt patched up with yellow and green striped electrical tape. Yobs, everywhere you looked, foul-mouthed and spiteful yobs, mouthing off about what they wanted, not caring about anything or anyone else. Scum, the whole damned lot of them.

The noise from outside was louder now, and his nose wrinkled as he was sure he could smell smoke, faint but definitely there.

"What on earth is going on out there?" he said aloud. Sweet Lord, he would have something to talk about down the pub when all this protest nonsense died down, would he ever. If he survived the night, that was. The way things sounded like they were building up outside, surely it wouldn't be too much longer before his window came through, a chunk of brick or something ploughing its way through the single pane glass. The flat, like all of the others in the surrounding blocks, had been pretty much flung up somewhere back in the sixties. Dirty, *Stalag*-like things of pollution-soiled concrete, from an era when cheapness was the order of the day and safety mattered even less than it seemed to now.

***

He jumped at the sound, almost dropping the empty glass that had somehow stuck to the ends of his fingertips as though held in place with glue. He hadn't even realised that he must have dozed off, although quite how he had managed to do so with that racket outside was anyone's guess. Blinking the sleep from his eyes, he set the tumbler down on the side table with a gentle *clink* - it was the only glass that he had or needed - making sure not to let go until it had made contact.

He turned towards the window, half expecting to see the curtain billowing inward on the breeze that wafted in through his broken window, actually surprised to see that the glass was still intact, although still not enough to keep the noise at bay.

"Pigs! Pigs! Fuck off pigs - give us our fucking city back!" It had grown into a chant now, almost a mantra of sorts. People shouting and screaming over the top of each other, all vying to be heard with the result that none of them really could be. It was always the way of things, especially nowadays. The usual thuggish rabble, no one was ever prepared to actually sit down and talk anymore. No, they were much happier just to smash the place up, as if *that* would get them their own way. More was the pity that it usually *did*, the

powers that be too quick to fold under the pressure from the great unwashed hoodlums. There was just no discipline, no order.

There was another loud bang, and this time he recognised it as the front door slamming, followed by the familiar *clumping* of boots against the thin carpet of the hallway. He always *had* insisted that she looked and sounded like a thug in those things, probably every bit as much as the rabble outside. The sound was familiar enough, like clockwork. Eight steps and there she was, in the open doorway of the front room.

"Louisa?" he said, his voice wavering, as though he was still trying to convince himself that she was really standing there. "Where have you been? Have you *seen* it out there?"

She didn't speak. Instead, she just glared, almost through him, in a way that was even more sullen than usual. Her eyes were like dark pools of ink, a look that was further exaggerated by the sooty smears of kohl eyeshadow, giving her a skeletal appearance that would have looked comical, were it not for the seriousness of her expression.

"Louisa?" he said again, realising that his voice was wavering a little now, the constant underlying sense of uncertainty creeping to the fore. There was something almost intimidating about the way she stared from under her furrowed brows, her head lowered a little as though she was looking straight at him without actually seeing him. The small hairs on the back of his neck rose, and he could feel the temperature rising under the collar of his flannel shirt.

"What's wrong? Why are you looking at me like that, and where on earth have you *been?*"

Still no answer.

"Fuck all of you pricks! Give us our city back!" The noise from outside suddenly sounded like it was a whole world away but was still more than enough to counter the lack of a response.

"Are you listening?" he felt an edge creeping into his own voice, something that he wasn't used to, "or have you gone deaf?" He was aware that he was trembling – with anger, fear or both, he couldn't be sure.

"I heard what you said, you miserable old cunt."

He rocked back on his heels, as though she had stepped forward and slapped his face, to the point where he could actually feel a burning sensation blooming across his cheek.

"*What* did you just call me?"

"You heard me, you miserable old cunt. Or perhaps you're a *deaf* old cunt, too?" She raised an eyebrow, the first indication of any sort of emotion since she had walked in. "Either way, you're a *cunt*."

"How *dare* you." Eddie's voice rose in pitch, sounding like what the blokes down the pub would refer to as a mouse being stepped on. "How bloody *dare* you!"

"Oh, I dare all right," Louisa stepped forward, folding her arms across her chest as she did so. "I dare because I know full well that I can say whatever I want and you're too much of a spineless prick to do a thing about it." Another step closer. "Go on then, prove me wrong."

He wrinkled his nose in disgust. There was a faint odour lingering on her breath, something that was familiar, but that he couldn't quite place. Not alcohol, perhaps drugs of some sort. It wouldn't surprise him, not with those dropout druggie types that she liked to call friends nowadays.

"Why, you mean-spirited, ungrateful *cow*-"

"Is that the best you can do? *Really?*"

"I've been sitting here for hours, worried about you!"

"Horseshit. You couldn't worry about me if your life depended on it, so don't take the piss. You've always been a selfish old fuck, more worried about what gossip you can spew out to keep your miserable cronies entertained. You're like a bunch of fucking fishwives, the lot of you."

"Now just you wait a minute, you foul-mouthed little-"

"No," she interrupted him again. "*You* wait a minute. You wait a minute, and you listen to me." He felt his head rock back again, stung by the sharpness of her words. Usually so sullen and quietly anti-social, she had never as much as raised her voice to him before, instead going no further than muttering some muted insult under her breath, usually just out of earshot. Perhaps she had always thought that he would just convince himself that he was imagining each sly dig, each mocking remark at his expense. To be honest, he had sometimes even doubted himself, usually finding it easier to do so. He had always disliked her attitude, but he had never actually considered just how much worse the alternative could be.

"You listen up and you listen good, you sour-faced old fart," she stepped forward again, within touching distance now, itself unusual for someone who usually liked to make such a big deal of having her own personal space. Close enough that he could make out the faint rash of acne across her cheeks, masked by pale, layered-on foundation. "I've got something *really* important to tell you."

"*Wh-what?*" he stammered, trying to keep some element of firmness in his voice and realising that he was faltering. "What is it?"

"I've got a sister. Well, a *half*-sister at least."

"No, no you haven't," Eddie shook his head. Was that really what was so important? "You were an only child. That's one of the reasons why you ended up with me."

"Nope," she chuckled, something about the sound unnerving him even further. "I've got a half-sister. My dad told me, just before he pissed off into the sunset. I've never met her, but she's out there somewhere." She laughed again. "Go on, ask me how I know. Ask me where she came from, I *dare* you."

Eddie's head felt light, a fluttering in his chest that spread down to his belly, leaving a sudden hollow sensation there. He wasn't so sure that he wanted to hear whatever it was that she was going to say next.

"My half-sister – is kind of like your stepdaughter," she laughed openly now, the sound as cold and hollow as it was alien. "Let me spell it out for you. My daddy dearest, he fucked your whore of a wife and got her up the stick."

He didn't want to hear it, didn't want to believe it. Muriel Caplin had been cold in her grave for eleven years, but long before then, they had lived pretty much separate lives. Something had soured in their relationship, something that he could never quite put his finger on. He had always put it down to the complacency that came from a long-term relationship, the two of them treating each other like part of the furniture rather than as husband and wife. He had never even considered the possibility that she could have been playing away though. Perhaps it had been his own fault, taking her for granted the way that he almost certainly did. The very thought that she could have been in the arms of his no-good weasel of a brother was still something that he didn't even want to entertain.

"You're talking rubbish, young lady," he said, the hairs on the back of his neck bristling. "You spend most of your days skulking around the place with a face like a smacked backside, or making snide comments with your smart-Alec friends, then you have the nerve to march in here, spouting off dirty lies like some foul-mouthed little trollop. There are words for people like you."

"Like *what?*" she leered at him now, her mouth a cruel slash at odds with the darkness in her eyes. "Go on, make me laugh some more."

"You're a nasty little tramp, and I don't know why I've put up with you for as long as I have."

"That's funny," she said. "There are plenty of words for people like you, too." There was a dryness at the back of his throat, and he wanted to say something else, but the words wouldn't come. "Cuckold, that's one. Miserable, sad, pathetic old cuckold who could keep his whore of a wife from sneaking off and fucking his own brother behind his back."

"Stop it-"

"I bet he was better than you. Maybe he had a bigger cock, you know, the kind of meaty old dick that a woman could choke on. Like a *real* man."

"I said *stop* it-"

"I bet she screamed when he fucked her. I bet that he filled her dirty hole right up, better than you ever *could-"*

Whack!

"I said stop it, you dirty, lying little cow!" She reeled back, still grinning as the red welt bloomed on her cheek, the imprint of his hand clear. *"Stop it stop it stop it!"*

"Oh, *now* the old fart shows his true colours! It's a shame you never showed that much passion to your wife. It might have stopped her from looking elsewhere. From enjoying having someone – *anyone* other than you – sticking it to her!"

"I told you already, *stop it!*"

"You'd *like* me to stop, wouldn't you? It would be better than facing up to what an impotent, cuckolded cunt you really are!"

Whack!

His jaw dropped as he stepped back, shocked at himself for what he had done, the palm of his open hand turning numb from the force of the slap. He watched as a thin stream of blood began to run down from her nose, pooling above the smeared black of her lips. She still had that wide, almost idiotic grin, as though a manic smile had been glued to her usually sulky face.

"Are you done?" she ran her tongue across her top lip, wiping away the blood in a greasy smear.

"Louisa, I'm sorry...I...I don't know what-"

"Yes, you do. You've finally realised that behind all of that *lovable-rogue-gossip-down-the-pub* mask that you like to wear, you're nothing. You're just a weak, pathetic excuse for a man who turned a blind eye while he got side-lined by his own wife." She stepped away from him, backing into the corner of the room. His heart felt like a hammer, about to break its way through his rib cage, and his breath was ragged. By God, she had tested his patience for such a long time, and now things felt like everything had come to a head at last. At least he knew now just how little respect she had for him.

She was right in the corner of the room now, as though cowering from some schoolyard bully, both hands tucked behind her back.

(*that's where i keep*)

She raised her head up, still grinning as she looked him

(*my*)

straight in the eye.

"Now it's my turn, you spineless old prick."

In the corner where she had backed away, was a hat and walking stick stand. He never had liked it, but Muriel had insisted on it and now he felt somehow obliged to keep it. At least it had some use, a place for him to keep his walking stick. Solid and heavy, almost antique-looking, with a large brass handle, the sort of thing that could give someone quite a nasty injury if used as a weapon. There was a blur of movement as she rushed forward, and he realised that it was grasped in both of her hands.

"You...*prick!*" She swung sideways with both arms, the handle connecting with the side of his head, the resulting *crack* exploding in both of his ears as it did so. He felt himself lift off his feet, falling back against the easy chair and sliding down to the floor. His eyesight blurred and he raised his hand to his temple, pulling it away again with a sticky wetness, the same of which now drizzled down the side of his face.

"*Cuckold!*" The stick swung again, the light glinting against the handle in a flash. He barely even felt it, still numb from the first blow. Then again...and again.

"My dad fucked your whore of a wife. He fucked you over good and proper."

Again.

"Now *I'm* going to fuck you over, too."

And again.

Cowering in a feeble effort to defend himself, he managed to roll over onto his belly, both hands reaching around to protect the back of his head.

Again, he felt the cane come down, the heavy brass mashing though his knuckles and cracking his skull. Strangely, there was no pain, no real pain at least. Instead, there was a creeping icy sensation that spread down into the nape of his neck.

"Yeah, I'm going to fuck you over. I'm going to fuck you over *good*." She cackled, the sound cold and hollow, the stick whistling through the air as it rose and fell again and again. His final thoughts were a blur, filled with images of Muriel, laughing as his no-good drunk of a brother took her over and over again, satisfying her in a way that he had never been able to. *This is what it feels like to die*, he thought, with something that was almost a sense of relief, the back of his head little more than a wet pulp. It felt like she would never stop, that the end would be welcome, if it ever actually came. There was no sensation anymore, no pain or anything else, only the whoosh of the cane as it rose and fell over and over again, ending each time in a wet slap, as it struck what was left of his head. His thoughts drifted away into a bloody darkness.

***

She had lost track of just how long she had been sitting cross-legged on the floor, the noise from outside lulling her into an almost trance-like state.

She could still taste him on her lips. She hadn't been able to resist, unable to help herself. She had swung the cane until her arms hurt and her lungs burned, until the bloody mess in front of her was no longer recognisable and the air was thick with the raw stink of him. There had just been something about that smell, something that brought a low rumble into the pit of her stomach. It reminded her of how she had stupidly skipped both lunch and dinner. She had been trying to lose weight for ages, not that she had ever told *him*. He probably wouldn't have been interested anyway. It had been so much easier since she had blagged those pills from Michelle Farnby out of her English class. The two-faced skinny bitch was good for something at least, even if that something was scoring diet capsules from some skanky dealer off the street corner. *Twocked them from some dead guy's flat, she had said, or so I heard. That's why they're so cheap. Tenner for five. Apparently, they're really good.* The weird thing was that, since she had started taking the things, she had found it harder to stop eating, not easier.

She couldn't help herself, it was the hunger gnawing at her insides, combined with that rich, heady odour. He was lying there, stretched out defenceless, she was so hungry.

It had just tasted so *good*.

She wiped at her mouth with the back of her hand, a thin smear of blood standing out like a scarlet letter against her pale, parchment-thin skin.

Give us back our city you bastards!

It had soon descended into chaos out there. Like a pressure cooker that had been left to go unchecked for far too long, building up until it finally blew open, taking out everything and anything that got in its way. A glorious, beautiful chaos. She smiled, lapping at the salt taste that still clung to her dark-smeared lips.

***

Later still, minutes or hours, she couldn't tell, there was the stink of petrol, the crackle and searing heat of flame. She knew that she should get up and leave, but she couldn't bring herself to do so. Perhaps it had been deliberate, a Molotov cocktail shoved through the letterbox, or maybe the fire had spread from somewhere else in the building. The local news was always running stories of how the old tower blocks had been pretty much flung together on the cheap, built from the sort of stuff that would go up like tissue paper if anyone dared to strike a match nearby. There was one journalist in particular who liked to keep going on about how run down the place was at every opportunity, although if it was that bad, she had sometimes wondered why he seemed to love writing about it so much. She still hadn't moved, her legs long since having turned numb from staying in the same position. Even if she had been able to get up with any sort of speed, she probably wouldn't have wanted to. It was just so much easier to stay where she was.

Give us back our city!

The air was hot and dry, it burned deep inside her chest every time she took a breath. She looked at what was left of Eddie Caplin one more time, as if staring at him for long enough would be sufficient to make him get up and walk again, like some geriatric, cuckolded Lazarus.

Spineless old prick that he was, he had still tasted pretty good though.

As if in response to the thought, her stomach let out a low rumble. She traced a lazy finger down her side, counting off the ribs through the thin cotton of her top. It was funny how the more she ate, the thinner she got. Weird, *really* weird. What was *in* those pills anyway?

She blinked, trying to clear away the fog that was burning her eyes, only to realise that it wasn't fog at all, but thick, acrid smoke. The flames had made their way across the cheap, worn carpet and were lapping at Eddie's corpse, tongues of fire dancing across his overturned body. She inhaled the smell of charred meat and melting fat, grinning again as she did so, her eyes clouding over as they drifted in and out of focus.

The left side of her face stung, probably from where the miserable old fart had slapped her. Really, like that would have made a difference, pathetic old man. That had been his problem for as long as she had known him; too little, too late. Without even thinking, she raised a hand to her cheek. Tracing her fingers across the surface, she felt a blistered dryness as a layer of parchment skin sloughed away like old paper. *It's the fire*, she thought, *if I stay here much longer, I'm going to burn to death*. Despite the flames, now so close, the room looked darker somehow, blurry. She tried to take a breath and found that she couldn't, the air burning into her lungs in a way that hurt far too much. Perhaps it wasn't so different to how he had felt as she bashed his skull into a wet, pulpy mess, knowing that he was going to die. Maybe it was just poetic justice. She raised her hand to her mouth to stifle a yawn, suddenly realising just how tired she actually felt. Her fingertips touched against her face again, this time coming away coated in a greasy film of blood, mingled with what looked like soot. There was no pain any more, just a raw, numb sensation. *It might be better if I just lie down for a little while, just until this drowsiness passes over me.* She let herself fall back, closing her eyes as her head met the brittle, threadbare carpet. The last thing she saw were the flames dancing across her legs, the blackened skin cracking, and liquid fat dribbling its way through.

There was the sound of breaking glass as the window exploded inwards. She hardly heard it, just like she hardly heard the rush of flame, blowing the door off its hinges as it was pulled in by the backdraft and swallowing both of them up like the fires of Hell itself.

FORTY-TWO

"Kim!" Frank gripped at the handrail, leaning over it as his attempt at shouting ended in a wheezing spasm, the force of the cough feeling like it would push his lungs up and out of his mouth. His chest felt like a dog was sitting on it, the smoke burning its way down his throat, no doubt aided by the twenty-a-day habit he'd had since he was a fourteen-year-old. *"Kim! Where are you?"*

"What the hell have you stopped for?" Kim almost bundled him down the remaining steps to the landing, the smoke so thick now that she couldn't see more than a few feet in front of herself. She had wound her scarf around her mouth and nose in an effort to block out the worst of the fumes, but the stinging in her eyes still brought tears to them.

"Stopped to admire the...scenery, what do *you* think?" he brought a hand to his chest as if in an effort to steady his uneven breathing.

"I always did tell you those things would be the death of you, now keep moving!" she nudged him on his way, trying not to shove him to the floor. He looked over the handrail again, pointing down at the almost alien glow spreading its way through the choking, dark fog.

"We've got *that* to get through yet. Those stupid pricks outside, they must have firebombed the place!" Trying not to stumble as he moved forward, he groped for the handrail with one hand, pulling his jacket up and over his mouth and nose with the other. Suffocate or burn alive, some choice. As he looked away, he thought that he saw movement out of the corner of his eye. *It's probably not even her*, he thought, she's probably burned to death by now, or passed out in a doorway somewhere. There was still the chance that she *could* get through it though. She had fought like a wildcat earlier. If she managed to get outside into that crowd, with Christ only knew how many of those things festering inside her...He shook his head, the possibility too much to think of.

Regular man of the people, aren't you? Who died and made you into some sort of bloody hero? He thought to himself. *Just get back to your flat, neck a few vodkas and stop giving a damn about what happens on the other side of your front door, you'd be so much happier for it if you did.*

He knew that it wasn't really an option. It never had been. His life might have been a big mess, but at least he had always tried to do the right thing. *One hell of a price to pay for getting a quick shag in a club bog cubicle*, he thought. *For Christ's sake, she wasn't even that bloody memorable!*

"Keep moving, for fuck's sake!" Kim's voice cut through the noise, bringing him back to his senses. "You might have a death wish, but I'm pretty sure that I don't." He nodded his agreement. Maybe it was just the smoke, messing with his head.

"Look down there," he shouted, pointing down over the handrail with the hand that wasn't cupped over his mouth. "Someone must have lobbed a few cocktails into the place. It looks like at least the ground floor has gone up completely. We're not getting out that way." Kim turned her head, jabbing her finger behind them.

"With any luck, she didn't either then. There's a fire escape back over there. We'll just have to chance it."

Frank raised his head, narrowing his eyes to try and keep the stinging smoke at bay. The words *FIRE EXIT* had been daubed across the battered metal in faded emulsion, almost hidden beneath graffiti scrawls.

"Oww – shit!" he shouted as he shoulder-charged the door, bouncing back as though it was made of rubber.

"Why don't you just try the handle, like most normal people, instead of trying to act like some sort of macho, *Starsky and Hutch* twat?" Kim pushed down on the bar as she spoke, stumbling forward as the door swung out with a raw creaking noise. She almost recoiled as she stepped out onto the platform, the rusted old metal groaning beneath her feet. Gasping, she pulled the scarf away from her face, sucking in a lungful of what passed for clean air. The tell-tale glow, coupled with the noise, hinted at what was going on below them.

"Jesus," she said half to herself, "I thought it was bad, but *this-*

"It's been a long time coming," Frank stood behind her, his voice hoarse. "They're pissed off, sick of feeling like no one gives a toss about them."

"And they *really* think that setting fire to the place and shoving shit through a few letterboxes will make people sit up and listen to them?"

"Sometimes, anger is all that you have to hold on to. Trust me, I know it." As if in response, the sound echoed around the back of the building, like the hollow wails of ghosts as it bounced against the walls.

"It doesn't sound so bad from here, does it?" Kim leaned against the handrail, pulling back again as it shifted under the pressure. "It's actually almost soothing, in fact."

"Who are you trying to kid, Kimberley Dzanic? It sounds like a shit storm, and you know it."

"Spoken like someone who knows a good shit storm when he hears one, *Franklin Arno Popovich.*"

"Oh, I'm not so sure about that. It's been a while since I got involved in a decent ruck, I'm not sure that I could cut it anymore."

"Pussy."

"Yeah, you'd know all about *that*," Frank chuckled, the sound rasping as Kim extended the middle finger of her free hand up into his face.

"Let's get down there and find your damn story," Kim gestured towards the stairway. "It's only a couple of floors worth. After you."

Groaning, Frank hauled himself upright and started down the rusted metal steps. Kim followed behind, trying not to get too close, their combined weight feeling like it would be enough to bring the whole framework crashing down into a twisted heap of scrap metal.

***

The exit led them to the rear of the building, adjacent to a collection of dumpsters, jutting out from the wall at awkward angles, filling the air with the stink of rotten waste that was almost enough to overpower the smell of smoke and petroleum fumes. Frank leaned back against the wall between two dumpsters, ignoring the ammonia smell of urine and old fish guts making him want to vomit as he tried to catch his breath.

"I've told you loads of times," Kim couldn't help but smirk, despite everything that had happened. "Cancer or cirrhosis, whatever, pick your favourite. The fags or the booze, one or the other will be the death of you one of these days."

"They're still a better option than facing most days sober," he said, raising a fist to his mouth to stifle a hacking, phlegmy cough. Opening his eyes, he realised that Kim was no longer smiling. Instead, she was staring down at the base of one of the dumpsters just next to where he was leaning. What the hell is it *now?*"

"There's someone under there," she pointed down, to where a pair of bare legs jutted out from beneath the bin, the pallid skin gleaming with a dull amber sheen in the light from the streetlamp above.

"Maybe it's her. Maybe she crawled under there to die. Good riddance, I say. That's one less headache." Before he could say any more, Kim stepped forward and grabbed both feet, dragging the body out across the cobbles and into the back lane.

"Kim? What the hell-"

"Shit Frank, it's not her. It's some bloke." She raised her hand to her face to stifle a gag. The body was almost skeletal, mottled, tissue skin stretched taut across the ribcage, legs bony and freckled with dark ulcers. What was left of the belly had collapsed into the abdominal cavity, large chunks of the flesh eaten away. Eaten away by *what* exactly, Kim didn't want to consider.

"Bloke? What bloke?" Frank pulled himself away from the wall, craning his neck for a better view. "Kim? Wait – what are you-"

Resting her hands on her thighs, Kim leaned forward to get a closer look.

"Bwaaaaaaaaaa!"

"Shit!" She jumped back as the face lunged towards her, eyes still closed as the jaw opened and closed in a foam-flecked spasm. *"He's still alive! Shitshitshit!"* Spider-like hands hooked into claws and flailed blindly, trying to grasp at the source of this sudden disturbance.

"Get away from him, quick!" Frank grabbed her by the shoulder and hauled her back, the two of them watching as the head tipped back, the jaw dropping as the tongue flopped out, lolling from side to side.

"That's not his tongue," Frank sounded weary, as though recent events had left him numb to anything else that could happen. "It's one of those things." Sure enough, the slug-like creature straightened, punching forward in a blind effort to free itself, the man's spindle-thin arms flapping like twin windmills in response. The body stiffened, arching back until it looked as though it would snap in half, before going limp, the creature dropping free in a rush of dark blood and drool. It writhed and thrashed on the ground, looking for a new place to hide. Stepping forward, Frank raised his foot to stamp on it, pausing as he looked down at the wriggling, leathery mass of flesh.

So much trouble, he thought, *caused by such a small thing. Ugly, but harmless looking. Maybe I should just leave it, let it find its way somewhere. Christ, it might actually do some good. It's not like things around this crowded shit hole could actually get much worse.* He realised that his foot was wavering, still hovering in mid-air. *Perhaps it would be for the best if that Susanne slapper did escape after all. If she put it about a bit, so much the better. It might get rid of a few deserving people.* The thing was almost on his other foot now, slithering across the front of his shoe.

"No – *look!*" Kim pointed up, tugging him back as she did so. The ground shook as there was an explosion, the windows of the third floor blowing out on clouds of smoke. As though in slow motion, they watched as the fire escape ladder separated away from the wall and began to topple towards them. The two of them stumbled back, struggling to stay on their feet as they fell against the far wall, instinctively covering their ears with their hands to shield them from the crash of iron against concrete, a cloud of dust billowing up into the air.

"Shit," Frank coughed, still hacking on smoke and dust. "Looks like we're not getting back up there in a hurry. At least that poor bloke's out of his misery."

"Where do you reckon she got to?" Kim rubbed at her eyes with the thumb and forefinger of one hand, trying to dispel the blurring at the edges of her vision. "The scrawny little tart could have gotten anywhere, what with the head start she had."

"She's probably found some unsuspecting bloke to suck off in amongst the crowd," Frank muttered.

"You would know, I suppose," Kim glared up at him, her brows knitted as she rested her hands against her thighs, trying to hide just how short of breath she was. "Really Frank, I know you were always a bit desperate, even back in the day. But fucking someone you don't even know in a toilet cubicle?"

"Not now Kim, eh? You almost make it sound like I was proud of it. Trust me, I wasn't. Gave me a week's worth of ball itch, it did." He raked at his crotch at the memory, managing a sly grin at the look of distaste on Kim's face. "Jesus, it feels like a whole lifetime ago at the moment."

"You'll never change, will you Popovich?"

"You wouldn't love me anywhere near as much if I did."

"You absolute bloody arsehole," Kim tried to look stern, but still couldn't keep from smiling back. "You are the dirtiest, most obnoxious prick I know, but you always seem to – *hey* – are you even still *listening* to me?" She narrowed her eyes as she realised that he was looking behind her, towards the corner of the back lane. "Frank? What are you looking at?"

"Her," he mumbled, stepping forward, almost tripping over a chunk of concrete. "It's *her*, just ahead. *It's her!*"

"What? *Where?*"

He broke into a trot, looking straight ahead. "It's *her*," he said again. "If she reaches those people-" Kim followed him, looking down at the ground, half expecting to see one more of those slug things trying to make its way towards her. She glanced up for long enough to see him reach the corner.

"Oh, *shit-*" he paused in his tracks as he looked straight ahead. Kim came up behind him, looking over his shoulder towards the crowd ahead.

The glow was almost eerie, the light from the flames spreading through the thick haze of smoke, reducing the crowd to jostling silhouettes, coalescing into one almost solid mass. "It's her. Straight ahead, in the crowd, it's *her*," repeating himself over and over again, no other words able to come.

"Frank, no, *wait-*" Kim reached out a hand to take his shoulder, but he pulled away, still staring into the distance, as if oblivious to everything else. It was almost surreal, some raucous, hellish ballet of violent sound and motion, screams and crackles of flame.

"No time," he said, half to himself, unsure if he was shouting at the top of his lungs, or if the words were just inside his head. "Got to get to her." As though as in anticipation, she turned to look right at him from in the distance, a broad grin spreading across her face. The crowd around her, so wrapped up in their own agenda of violence, seemed oblivious to her skeletal semi-nakedness, just one more face in a crowd of ever-growing madness. She stood straight and stretched out her arms, closing her eyes as she did so. Frank felt rooted to the spot, watching as her lips parted, the glow of the flames licking against the oily sheen of the writhing blackness that protruded from her mouth.

"*Shit!*" As if the spell was broken, Frank stumbled forward again, trying to keep his footing as he broke into a run again. "*Move! Fucking move!*" he yelled unheard, shoving his way past people, some of whom he vaguely recognised from places and times that he couldn't even remember anymore. Harry Batra's store was right ahead, blurred by the haze of the flames, as though being viewed through a camera lens smeared with Vaseline. He just hoped that Harry had been smart enough to get the hell out of harm's way. Her head snapped upright again, and she stepped backward, almost tripping over debris behind her. Still grinning, her lips moved, forming words that might have been *come and get me, try and stop me, you bastard*, or something similar. She turned and almost skipped, the cheeks of her backside wobbling like something out of some seventies European softcore movie.

"*Get out of my way!*" Frank yelled, his face inches away from some old guy, bent almost double. "*I said get out of my fucking way!*"

"*Whatchusaytameyooprick?*"

He side-stepped, as two bruisers wrestled one another to the ground, one of them beating the other in the gut with what looked like a crowbar. It wasn't a protest anymore. Perhaps it never had been to begin with. It was nothing more or less than an orchestrated riot.

"*Frank...!*"

He thought that he could hear Kim, calling to him, as though from across an ocean, the sound of her voice almost swamped beneath a torrent of rage and chaos. *I'm okay*, he wanted to tell her, and he would have if she hadn't been so far away. *I'm okay really, I'm so close now. I can almost reach her, I can almost stop her*. He was, too, he really was. As though she could read his mind, she would stop for a few seconds, allowing him to catch her up just a little, before moving on again, always just out of reach.

"*Frank – look out!*"

It might have been Kim, or it could have been anyone else. All the voices, all of the noise blurred and dissolved into a single, never-ending sound, like the hiss and squeal of an old radio, stuck between stations, something to make the inside of his head itch if he listened to it for long enough.

(*give us our fucking city back you cunts*)

So much pushing and shoving.

(*pigs*)

He pushed his way through the crowd, blind to the people that he was thrusting aside in his efforts to catch her up.

(*our city*)

(*catch me if you can you lying shitweasel*)

She was so close now. So close.

(*frank!*)

"*Watch it you fucking fascist prick!*" Someone up in his face, someone that he'd never even seen before.

Grinning at him again. So close. Grinning.

LEE GLENWRIGHT

"What the-?"
Blinding white. Then black.

FORTY-THREE

-luckyyourestillaroundyoumadprick
   -whatwereyoushittingwellthinking

It was strange, the way the voice echoed quite so much, before it reached him at last. Even then, after bouncing and rolling around, it didn't feel as though the words were being spoken to him, so much as beamed straight into the back of his head. Maybe he was dead. Maybe he was dead, and he was finally finding out what Hell was like; a place where he was destined to be forever subjected to that same infuriating voice, reminding him of every stupid, decision that he had ever made.

"reallythinkitsabouttimeyouwerewakingupnowyousoftarsehole"

He just wished that he was at least allowed the luxury of ignoring the sound. Perhaps there were no earplugs in Hell.

"Okay Frank, I saw your eyes move that time. Wake up, you soft twat."

Better do as I'm told, I suppose. He focused on trying to open his eyes, the lids feeling as though they were being held down by lead weights. *Too much effort*, he thought, *much easier just to lie here and ignore everything. Better to just lie here like a lazy*

(slug)

thing, without a care in the world, instead of

(parasite)

waking up and remembering what it was that landed me here –
wherever here *is – in the first place.*

"Franklin!"

Kim, the voice was familiar, floating to him, as though still coming from some faraway place.

"Franklin bloody Popovich – open your eyes!"

Sunday name. It must be important.

"You *do* care after all." How the words escaped his mouth, he had no idea. His lips were parched and cracked, and the back of his throat felt dry and coated with whatever it was that was making his tongue feel like a chunk of old tyre rubber. He was desperate for a whisky or six. *Come on eyes, do what the Wicked Witch says, before she smacks me one.* Summoning what little willpower he actually possessed, he forced his eyes to open.

"*Owww...*" the light was far too bright, burning straight into the back of his head and drawing tears. "Why did you make me do that, you rotten cow?"

Kim leaned over him, her face filling his field of vision and her breath warm on his cheeks. She held the palm of her hand flat against his forehead for a few seconds, before moving it away again.

"To make sure that you hadn't gone and died on me. I don't know how I could ever cope without your wit and charm to keep me going, you silver tongued devil, you."

"Turn that bloody light off, it hurts."

"No can do. The ward sister is a proper mardy cow. She's already threatened to send me packing."

(ward sister?)

"Jesus, Kim, my mouth feels like I've been sucking on a badger's arsehole and my tongue feels like a dead slug. Wait a minute-"

(slug?)

His eyes snapped open, and he sat up, falling back onto the bed as the side of his head exploded in pain. He touched a finger to his temple, wincing as he pulled it away again.

"Where is she? What the hell happened to me?"

"What happened to you is that you're probably lucky to still be alive, you reckless sod. Chasing after some scraggy-arsed, half-naked slapper in the middle of a riot turned out to be a bit of a stupid thing to do, really."

"What?"

"You left me standing. I tried to go after you, but you just couldn't help yourself, as usual." Kim pulled a chair from the corner of the room, dragging it across the floor with a rubber squeal before sitting down at the side of the bed. "You were too busy trying to catch her up. I think you must have shoved into the wrong knuckle-dragger. He clocked you one good and proper, right on the side of the head with a half-brick." She paused, as though for dramatic effect. "You went down like a sack of hammers, and you've been in here pretty much ever since."

"Here?"

"For Christ's sake Frank, I reckon that smack must have rattled you pretty good. You've been in hospital for the last two days now."

"Hospital?"

"Yeah, you know? That place where they bring knackered old parrots who can't do anything except repeat the last thing they heard their best friend say?"

"Bitch."

"That's more like it," she smiled.

"So, I'm in hospital, because some old trog smacked me upside my head with a chunk of wall, right?"

"Bingo, he gets it at last." Kim leaned across to the table at the side of the bed, helping herself to a handful of grapes. She popped a couple in her mouth. "I bought them, it's allowed," she said through a mouthful of grape mush.

"It's okay, I don't like grapes. At least I *think* I don't."

"I know," she chuckled. "That's *why* I bought them."

Frank leaned forward, rubbing at his head again with a thumb and forefinger, wincing as the pad of his thumb pressed against a spongy lump of flesh. Something still itched in the back of his mind, something that seemed important somehow, but was just somewhere out of reach.

"What's wrong?" Kim asked.

"I'm not sure. It feels as though there's something important, but..."

Kim's eyebrows knitted, as though she was concerned. "What is it?" she leaned forward, "everything okay?"

"Susanne," Frank's voice dropped to a mumble, as his eyes narrowed with concentration. "I was trying to stop her. I *had* to stop her." He lurched forward, grabbing at the sleeve of Kim's anorak. "What happened to her? Did she get away? What *happened?*"

Kim shrugged her shoulders. "You were lucky, or maybe unlucky, depending on your point of view," she paused, narrowing her eyes in response to the confused look spreading across his face. "I'm not surprised really. You were knocked spark out when that guy decked you one. Tell you what though, for a scrawny rat, you're pretty heavy when you're a dead weight. It's just as well I dragged you away from there when I did." She leaned forward again, "Someone chucked a Molotov cocktail in the wrong direction. It hit an overturned van, one with a pretty full petrol tank, judging by the way the thing went up."

"And?"

"Fifteen people injured, three dead, including your slug-riddled slapper friend."

Frank fell back onto the pillow, letting out a sigh as he closed his eyes against the fluorescent light that was still just too bright to be comfortable.

"You saved my life," he said, "not for the first time, either."

"Yeah, well, you know I can be pretty stupid sometimes. We all do things we regret."

"So, what's the place like now?"

"No different really. If anything, the fire might have cleaned it up a little bit. The flats were gutted. Mainly Charnville, but the next one along took a hit as well," she looked away from him, even though his eyes were still closed. When she spoke again, her voice was softer. "They haven't got a final number for how many died inside yet. They reckon it was started by more than one Molotov cocktail."

"*They?*"

"The police. They finally put in an appearance about fifteen minutes after the car went up. The loud *boom* must have finally woken someone up."

"The cheap shit that those things were built out of, the whole place would've gone up like it was made out of cardboard," Frank's voice was subdued. *Maybe it's the stuff they've got him on*, Kim thought, *or maybe he's finally just about ready to give up*. When he opened his eyes, they had a glassy sheen to them. "She's dead? She's definitely dead?" It was as though he could still see her, almost skipping away from him like it was nothing more than a game, just looking for who she could possibly infect first. Hell, it was probably just as well that she was dead, it was certainly more convenient, for want of a better way of putting it. Perhaps that was the problem; the same old story, one of convenience. Something that could be swept under the carpet and forgotten about.

"Yeah," Kim said. "Definitely. I saw the explosion, I could still see her right before. She was only a few feet away from the car when it went up."

"You're sure it was her?"

"Christ, Frank. I don't remember there being any other skinny naked women skipping around the place," she sighed. "Yes, I'm sure it was her."

"Fucking hell."

"As eloquent as ever, Popovich." Kim cocked her head to one side, still gazing at him, looking like there was something that she wanted to say to him, but couldn't quite decide whether it was the right time. He didn't ask, he was far too tired.

"There could be others, you know?" he tried to focus in her direction, his gaze still wavering. "Not just here, but somewhere else. Anywhere."

"Yeah, I suppose there could be," Kim muttered, shuffling her feet against the floor with a squeaking sound. "Probably not though, not after what's happened, anyway. But we'll never get to know for sure." She leaned back in the chair. "And even if we did, what do you think you could *do* about it?" She paused waiting for an answer, surprised when one didn't come right away.

"Nothing," he said at last. He sounded weary, the resignation in his voice all too obvious, sounding like it was mingled with defeat as well as tiredness caused by the bump to his head. "I really don't know what else to say, but there's nothing I could do." After everything, he knew exactly what would happen. It would most likely make the national press for a few days, probably even get a spot on the evening news on at least one television channel. Meanwhile, the real immediate threat had probably been gotten rid of, without most people getting to hear about it. Nothing would change; those people on the bottom rung of the ladder would be blamed for everything and nothing would be done about it. He would have been the first to admit that he had been wasting his time, wasting his life, if it wasn't the only thing he knew. "*Fucking hell*," he said again.

FORTY-FOUR

"Really? But it feels like you've only just got here."

"That's bollocks. It feels like a whole lifetime, and you know it." Kim raised the glass to her mouth, draining the cider that she had tried to make last as long as possible. It had been Frank's round, reason enough to savour every last drop. "Besides, you've been out of hospital for over a week now. The last thing you need is me still taking up space on your sofa."

"You're welcome to it, anytime. It's old but it's still comfortable, as long as you ignore the crusty bits." He resisted the urge to smile at her grimace as he traced a lazy finger around the rim of his glass of whisky and Coke, instead fixing his gaze on a faded liquid stain on the lacquered table surface. The pain in his head had subsided to a dull throb over the last couple of days, and he was hoping that the first alcohol he had downed in a couple of weeks would help to numb it further. "Besides, I'm getting on a bit, you know. I really could do with the company."

"You mean you could do with someone hanging around you who has enough sense to reel you in whenever you feel like dropping your trousers in a nightclub toilet cubicle?"

"Yeah, there *is* that as well, I suppose."

Kim grinned, the smile playing about her lips somehow more bittersweet than usual, as though it was masking a seriousness of some sort.

"Thanks for the offer, but I've had more than enough of the damn thing throwing my neck out. Besides, I'm sure I've got bites on my leg. Christ knows what creatures I've been sharing sleeping space with."

"It beats me. I'm pretty sure that even the fleas gave up on that old thing ages ago."

"It's just a shame they didn't chew your cock off first. It would've kept you out of a whole heap of trouble from the start," she pointed to the two empty glasses on the table. "You want another?"

"You asked that like you thought I'd say no."

"There's a first time for everything, I suppose," she shoved her hand into the pocket of her anorak, bringing out a crumpled ten pound note. "I won't be a moment," she said, standing and moving towards the bar before Frank could speak again. He watched her as she stood, waiting to be served, looking for any signs of doubt, anything in her body language that could give her away. The barman took her money, sliding two more drinks across the bar before tipping shrapnel change into her outstretched hand. Shoving it back into her pocket without counting it, she picked up the drinks and returned to their table, dropping Frank's on the table in front of him.

"You spilled a bit," he pointed to a small puddle alongside the glass.

"Piss off," she mumbled though a mouthful of cider, moving her own glass away from her mouth as she took her seat. "You ought to think yourself lucky I bought you the damn thing."

"You've really made your mind up, haven't you? You're definitely leaving?"

"Yes," Kim said. "Yes, I am."

"For good?"

"I don't know, maybe." She took a swig of cider, downing half of the pint glass before continuing. "I needed that," she raised the cuff of her sleeve to her mouth to stifle a belch. "I just reckon that it's time, you know?"

"But I've only just gotten used to you being around again, especially after so long."

"No, Frank. What you mean is you miss someone – *me* – being around to sort out your mess, to keep you out of trouble. It doesn't have to be me, you just need *someone* to keep an eye out for you sometimes."

"Yeah, there *is* that, too," he raised his glass to his lips and tipped it back, ice cubes clinking as he downed the liquid in one, drawing a wince as is it burned its way down his gullet.

"You know, there are some people out there who would call you a heathen."

"Why?"

"Drinking scotch with ice."

"I can live with being called a heathen, I *have* heard worse," he lowered his glass. "You see? That's why I need you to stick around. I'd end up making a right arse of myself otherwise."

"Yeah, like I helped with *that*." Kim chugged the rest of her own drink, trying to buy time, to think of what to say. She sat back in her chair, trying to make just a little bit more space between them, while ignoring the spring that poked its way through the cheap velour fabric and dug into the small of her back. "Seriously Frank, it's not you, it's what *follows* you."

"Meaning?"

"*Trouble.* Trouble follows you everywhere, like a puppy biting at your ankles. You can't help yourself, you always bend right over to pick it up, just long enough for it to fu-"

"Okay," he raised his hand. "I get the picture." He looked down at the table, narrowing his eyes to focus on something that wasn't there. "I'll miss you," he said. "You *do* know that, right?"

"I know. I'll miss you, too. You're the only thing I *will* miss about this place though." Gazing at her glass to make sure that her drink really was finished, she stood, scraping the chair across the floor as she did so.

"My round?" Frank said.

Kim placed a hand on his shoulder, resting it there for a second. "Save your money, Popper. I'll let you off with it this once."

"Can't blame a bloke for trying, right?" he raised his eyebrow, willing her to look at him again.

"Goodbye Franklin Arno Popovich," she said walking towards the door without turning her head again. "Stay safe, keep out of trouble." She dropped her voice, almost to a whisper. "And if you've got any sense, maybe think about leaving this place too."

He resisted the urge to follow her as she left without looking back, feeling more than ever like he needed one more drink, just to take the edge off.

***

"All reet, all reet, I'm comin' for Christ's sake." Bob Martinson shook his head, trying to slough away the sleep that still clung to him. *Fucking hell*, he thought, *half ten on a Sunday morning. It'd better be someone with a topper of a story. Either that, or someone coming to tell us me ma's died.* He pulled his dressing down around himself, fastening the belt into a loose knot. With any luck it might be that fit lass from two doors down the street, coming to scrounge a cup of sugar. It wouldn't really be his fault if the belt came away just in time for her to see what he had to offer. It was all Lisa's fault anyway, buggering off for the morning with the kids and that cousin of hers, rather than letting him get his hole for the week. Jesus, it was a wonder that his knob hadn't withered and dropped off. Turning the key in the lock, he gripped the handle and opened the door.

"*Good morning, Bob!*"

"Frank? For Christ's sake man, what are you doin' here?" Bob felt the colour drain from his face, his semi-erection shriveling back into nothing just as suddenly as it had arrived.

"Christ knows mate. It's a right dump 'round here, ain't it?"

"Thanks," Bob looked up and down the street. "Lisa's probably gonna be back soon, mind you."

"So? I was passing by and I fancied catching up with an old mate. Ain't nothing wrong with that, is there?"

"No, there's nowt wrong at all. It's just that-"

"Exactly. Nothing wrong at all." Frank grinned, one hand fumbling with a cigarette, the other raking at his stubble with fingernails that were just a little too long. "So, are you gonna invite an old mate in or what?"

"Okay, okay," Bob stepped back, allowing Frank to bustle his way past him into the hallway.

"Stick the kettle on and fix us both a brew, yeah? Black, two sugars."

"Coffee?" Bob followed him, scratching at his head, hopes of further sleep and dreams of *two-doors-down girl* fading away even faster than his stiffy.

"Yeah, you know it. Got myself a bit of a headache. I ended up in a pub last night, right in the city centre. It was a bit of a dump, but the beer was pretty decent. Stayed well away from that fizzy Brown Ale shit that you always used to bang on about though."

"What 'you after, Frank?"

"The *Dog and Parrot*, or something, it was called. Are all bars around here that rough? I mean *really*, Christ on a bike, mate-"

"Frank!"

"What?" Frank cocked his head and lifted both of his hands out, as though being called out for some mistake that he didn't know how to fix.

"What are you even doing here, man?"

"I just wanted to speak to you about something."

Martinson rolled his eyes, pulling his dressing gown a little tighter around himself. "Something so important that you couldn't just ask us over the 'phone?"

"You know what I'm like with telephones, Bob. Besides, I've always wanted to visit up north, you know? Just to see if it's really as grim as people say."

Martinson looked down at the floor, averting his gaze as he rubbed his bare foot back and forth against the carpet. Lisa could be back at any moment. He had a feeling that whatever it was that Frank Popper wanted to say, it would be better said in her absence. "You didn't come all this way to take the piss out of us, did you mate? Why are you really here?"

"Because I wanted to try out that train system you have here – what do you call it – the *Tyne and Wear Metro?* Jesus, what a load of shit. It's hardly the London Underground, is it, fella?"

"It does okay, like."

"And some of the place names. *Byker?* Fucking hell, Bob, it sounds like a prossie hangout. But yeah, the beer wasn't too bad, I suppose. Certainly cheaper than back down home." Frank reached behind his ear, withdrawing a cigarette and twirling it between his thumb and forefinger.

"You can't smoke that in here, mind."

Frank flipped the cigarette between his lips. Pulling a lighter from his pocket, he sparked it against the tip of the cigarette, drawing as it flared into life. "I reckon I can do whatever the hell I want, Bob." He took hold of the cigarette and exhaled a plume of smoke into Martinson's face. "I reckon that I've earned it. Do you know, this is the first fag I've had in almost two weeks? You're still not allowed the things in hospital, you know?"

"Hospital?"

"Yeah. Didn't you know? I went and got myself into a bit of bother, shall we say? Anyway, no smoking allowed. Something about it being bad for your health."

"Aye, it's the same up here, you know? We're not total cavemen north of Watford."

"Yeah," Frank inhaled again, half the length of the cigarette disappearing as he did so, "It's still a filthy habit though. Kim tried telling me to jack it in. You remember Kim, yeah?"

"*Kim*," Martinson raised his head and took in a deep breath. "I thought so. I was wondering when we'd get around to your tranny marra."

"My *what?*"

"*Marra*. It means friend. You know, it's the way we-"

He rocked back on his feet, almost toppling as Frank's bony fist connected with the side of his jaw.

"*Ow, you fuckin' prick, what 'you do that for?*"

Frank winced, shaking his hand to dispel the pain of the blow, his knuckles turning numb. Martinson raised a hand to his chin. "You bell-end! Why'd you friggin' lamp us one?"

"Now I *knew* there was a reason why I came all the way up here. *That* was something I just couldn't do over the telephone."

"I wish you *had* just bloody phoned us up now!"

"I bet you do," Frank glared at him, rubbing his knuckles with his other hand. "Yeah, I *bet* you do, you prick. Now, you better listen to me and listen good and proper, okay?"

"Aye, okay."

"There's a good lad, Bob. Kim's told me everything, filled in some of the blanks from before."

"*Everything?*"

"Everything. She – emphasis on *she* – is worth ten of a shitwipe like you, 'you know that?"

"Frank mate, it isn't how it sounds. She's probably twisted things-"

"*Shut up and listen, or I'll smack you another one!*" he balled his hand up into a fist again, just to make it clear that he wasn't bluffing. "Christ knows, I should've done it years ago, and I would've if I hadn't been so fucking tunnel-visioned."

"Honest Frank, I was pissed at the time, she's probably took the hump, you know, blown it all out of proportion."

"*What?*"

"You know what I mean. People like her are all the same, with their sense of humour in their bollocks. Once they get them lopped off-"

Thwack!

"Oww! You bloody bastard!"

"You asked for that one, Bob. Tell me, how long will it be exactly before Lisa gets back?"

"*Eh?*" Martinson looked at Frank confused, rubbing the opposite side of his jaw now and feeling the knot already beginning to form "What's that got to do with owt?" His eyes already widened in fear as he guessed what Frank was going to say next.

"Well, I was thinking that it looks like a cosy little set-up you've got here. I reckon it'd be much nicer than spending a few hours in some shitty pub, listening to all those locals slurping Brown Ale through their gap teeth and going on about their mangy whippets." He grinned, spreading his hands and cocking his head to one side as he threw a wink. "I'm sure that your missus would be happy to see me. Especially when I tell her and your kid just how much of a prick you've always been."

"There's no need for that, Frank, man."

"There was no need for you to try and fuck around with a good friend of mine, either, but you still did it," Frank's brow furrowed with conflict. "You messed everything up, Bob. The best friend I had, and you went and messed things up between us."

"Nah, Frank," Martinson shook his head, his voice rising now. "You did that yourself, don't you bloody well go and blame me for your own shortcomings. She trusted you? Maybe she did, but you let her, him – *her* - I don't know, whatever the fuck she is – down more than I ever could. When the shit hit the fan, you couldn't be there for her. Don't you blame me for *that*, you holier-than-thou prick."

"Shut up."

"Besides, she was fucking *gagging* for it–"

Thwack!

Martinson's head snapped back as Frank's fist connected again, with his chin this time.

"I said shut *up!*" Frank clasped his fist into his other hand, rubbing at the knuckles as he winced. "Now you listen to me, you Geordie wank-stain, 'cause I ain't gonna repeat myself." Martinson glared up at him, his eyes bleary. His dressing gown had fallen open now, but he was too busy nursing his chin to notice.

"We are done, do you understand me, Bob? *Done.*" Martinson nodded his head. "Good. It only took a couple of smacks upside your head to make you listen. Now, if you ever, *ever* try to get in touch with me after today, I'll tell Lisa everything, do you understand?" Martinson nodded again. "I'll give Kim a couple of days to get her head together, then I'll get in touch, you know, just to check up on her. I might even brave it and use a phone, yeah?" Another nod. Frank took a step back, dropping his arm to his side and unballing his fist. "I'm sure Lisa would just love to hear about how you tried to force yourself on another woman while she was sat at home carrying your baby inside her."

"That's not how it happened, man. I don't know what that cow told you, but–"

"Shut up, before I smack you another one," Frank leaned his head forward, glaring up from under his brow in an effort to look more threatening. "You know I'll do it, too. The way I'm feeling right now, I could happily use your face as a punchbag for hours if I need to, for however long it takes until your missus gets back."

Martinson nodded his head again, saying nothing. "You keep away from Kim and you keep away from me. Once I walk out of that door, that's it. I don't want to see you, I don't want to hear from you. Ever. *Okay?*"

"Okay."

"Nice one," Frank clapped a hand to Martinson's shoulder. "You see? It might take a bit of effort, but even a tosser like you can be made to see how things are, sooner or later." He narrowed his eyes, his thin fingers biting down in a grip just tight enough to be uncomfortable. "I mean it Bob. I'll make sure that missus of yours feels like lopping your dirty cock off and throwing it into the nearest dustbin by the time she's finished hearing what I've got to say."

"You *need* me, Frank."

"I need my conscience to be clear more. I've fucked up too many times. I've already promised myself that I'm going to try not to let it happen again." He turned and walked away, not wanting to look back, only forward, ignoring the soft sobbing that came from behind him now.

He was halfway down the street before he remembered the second cigarette tucked behind his other ear. He twirled it between thumb and forefinger, before placing it between his lips. Dipping his hand into his jacket pocket, he drew out a lighter and sparked it before pausing.

Kim hated him smoking. *Doctor Blacklung*, she always used to call him, back in simpler times. *Those things will be the death of you, you Thompson wannabe. Cancer or cirrhosis, take your pick.*

Holding the lighter against the tip of the cigarette, he flicked it again, drawing as it glowed into life. Six hours before the next train home. Plenty of time for a couple of swift halves. Besides, there was still time to get lucky. He'd heard stories of the local girls. *Lots* of stories.

"Either, I don't care. Besides, I'll quit tomorrow. Promise," he said, his mouth curling up into a crooked grin. Sucking on the cigarette, he smoked a good portion of the length in one go, already reaching into his pocket for another, smiling in contentment as the warm smoke filled his lungs.

"I *promise*," he said again, looking forward as he went.

EPILOGUE

I

The smell of cologne was overpowering, even now.

James Hesketh didn't want to close his eyes. There was no real need to do so anyway, not anymore. He had no idea of the time, no clue as to whether it was day or night. Time had no real meaning anyway; it wasn't like he had much of it left.

At least he wasn't alone now.

He had been awoken by the sensation of pricking at his back, probably just a shard of glass from the shattered photograph. He had tried his best to ignore it, but it kept on irritating him, just one more thorn in his side, until he felt like he had to at least try and get away from it.

God, everything had happened so quickly.

Bracing his arms, he struggled into a sitting position, forcing tears to his eyes as he willed them to open. The room was in near darkness, suggesting that he had probably been asleep for several hours undisturbed.

He swivelled his head to look over to the corner of the room, the leather soles of the expensive-looking shoes the first thing that he saw. The damn things had probably cost a couple of weeks-worth of his salary, but what was the real value of shoes to a dead man walking? The thought brought a smile to his face, a small comfort, and something that would have seemed impossible even a few hours ago.

He could still remember what had happened, even though it felt as though it had happened to someone else, with him taking the role of idle spectator, watching things unfold from a safe distance.

"Is there anyone in here?" Steele had almost managed to sound concerned when he had first broken into the house, the softness of those expensive-soled shoes not quite enough to mask his presence completely. Hesketh had heard him as though echoing from somewhere far in the distance, waking him from what he was sure must have been a point close to his own death. *Go away and let me die in peace*, he had wanted to call out at first. Then he had somehow recognised the measured tone, and it had stirred something within him. It was the person who had put him where he was now. The person who had preyed upon his desperation, promising him something that he was never going to get. That same person had now shown up in his house, reeking of expensive aftershave and hair oil, creeping around the place in an expensive suit and shoes. He was probably intent on saving his own skin and cleaning up any loose ends. Even the sound of his voice hinted more at self-preservation than any sort of genuine concern.

He had lain as still as possible – something that wasn't too difficult anyway – as Steele had found him at last, standing in the doorway, still looking every inch the smarmy salesperson.

As Hesketh looked at him through half-closed eyes, he had seen his face, the paled look of what could have almost passed as worry fading, to be replaced by the familiar tanned expression of smugness. He had actually seen Steele crack a lopsided smile, probably of relief, as the bastard had allowed himself to believe that things had taken care of themselves. He had stood there in the open doorway, an intruder in *his* home, grinning like a Cheshire cat at the thought that his problems were fixed, that he had gotten away with everything.

Hesketh didn't even realise that he had it in him.

He had screamed, not even recognising the sound of his own voice as he had sprung to his feet, launching himself at the person who had put him where he was. Everything a blur, like an old movie reel, he could remember the way that the look of smugness on Steele's face had so quickly vanished, melting into an expression of shock, his jaw dropping his mouth into an elongated 'o' of surprise. The force had carried them both clear of the doorway, Steele colliding with the drawer unit against the far wall of the hallway, his neck snapping back as his head cracked against the wall. Weakened as well as shocked, he had crumpled to the floor in a heap. Before he could recover, Hesketh was upon him, raking at his face with his fingers hooked into claws, drawing blood as he swiped his hands from side to side.

"*You prick!*" he had screamed as he gouged at Steele's face with his ragged fingernails. "*I'm going to die because of you. It's all your fault – all of it!*" He hadn't given the other man a chance to answer, swinging his arms in a crazed, windmill motion, afraid that if he stopped for long enough then Steele might seize the opportunity to regain control of the situation. "Let's see how you like it!" His hands still rigid, he had gripped at either side of Steele's face, clutching twin handfuls of his flabby cheeks to hold him in place. Ignoring the dawning look of realization, he had squeezed his palms together, forcing the other man's mouth open wide before clamping his own against the parted lips, ignoring the cologne stink.

"*Mmmmphh! Mmmmphh!*" Steele had bucked in vain, trying to shake Hesketh away, the smaller man forcing his full weight upon him, pinching Steele's nose between scrawny thumb and forefinger as he did so.

Hesketh had focused, clenching the muscles of his gut, as though willing himself to vomit, his mouth spreading into a mad grin as he felt the movement starting at the back of his throat.

Here it comes, you smug bastard, he had wanted to say, instead keeping his lips clamped in place, despite his leering smile. He had wanted to laugh as Steele's eyes had bulged under the pressure of the thing working its way from mouth to mouth, burrowing down his throat as it sought a new place to nestle, scraping past the back of his tongue and tonsils, almost choking him as it did so.

"Now, let's see how you like it," Hesketh had leaned back, releasing his grip at last as he wiped bloody drool from his lips with the already-bloodstained cuff of his jacket. Steele had said nothing, instead gasping and spluttering as he tried to cough up the thing that was now inside him.

"You...*idiot*," he had said at last, forcing the words out on weakened breaths. "*What...have you done to me?*"

"I reckon I've just given you a taste of your own medicine," Hesketh had chuckled as he slumped back against the opposite wall, still grinning idiotically, already feeling himself weakening under the strain. "You can kill me now if you want, but it won't change anything for you, not now. Trust me, I'm a doctor." Still smiling, he had leaned back and closed his eyes, waiting for the end as he thought of how things could have been so much different, ignoring the sobs from the man opposite him, along with the gnawing pangs of hunger in his belly.

II

The sun was already dipping its way below the horizon, rays of crimson bleeding through the tree line in jagged shards. The first stirrings of an autumn breeze rustled through the undergrowth that flanked the edge of the river, the ripples on the surface of the water scattering the light like fallen stars.

An oasis of tranquil peace, little more than twenty minutes walking distance from the madness of the city, but at the same time almost a world away.

The horse carcass had lain undisturbed for weeks now, save for the flies that rested upon it, seeking to feed upon what little rotting, desiccated meat still clung to the weather-bleached bones.

Glossy, dark fur gleaming in the fading sunlight, a lone rat scurried out from the undergrowth, whiskers bristling as its nostrils flared, filling with some strange new scent that stood out from the stink of spoiled flesh. The bushes rustled as another joined it, followed by a third. Needle-like teeth bared, they squealed at each other, each of them drawn by the same odour, some new, rich thing, inviting them to try and find it.

The first rodent, the largest of the three, saw it first. Protruding from a withered, dried coil of intestines, piled in an exposed, untidy heap, a bloated, slug-like thing, glistening with a wet, oily sheen. It skittered across the gravel path, throwing up dust clouds in its wake to bury its snout deep into the viscera, groping for its prize. Too late, the other two followed, high-pitched screeches voicing their dismay at their missing out. With a sharp tug, the large rat fell back as it gripped the slug between its powerful jaws, a jet of dark blood spraying forth under the pressure. Raising its head, it opened its mouth wide, the slug sliding down its gullet whole with surprising ease, almost as though it had intentionally burrowed its way inside. The smaller two rats lunged forward in unison as another of the things poked up from the fleshy mound, swaying blindly from side to side as if tasting the night air. There was a flail of claws as the faster of the two swiped the other aside, before clamping the slug between its teeth, victorious. Defeated, the losing rodent turned about and slunk back into the shadows of the undergrowth.

Crouching alongside one another, the two remaining rats reared up, testing the air for any sign of more food. They both turned their heads in the direction of the city lights, glowing in the distance with a warmth that was as welcoming as it was inviting. Light meant people; people meant food. Their bellies growled with a new hunger, the sort that would take more – much more – to satiate.

As one, they scurried in the direction of the city, tails dragging behind them.

VECTORS

- Can't believe they had him then let him get away again-

- Just as well they stopped him in time. Who knows what he could have done-

- People these days, could be anything wrong with them and you wouldn't know until-

It just wasn't the sort of thing that many people would expect to see, certainly not in a crowded city centre on a Saturday afternoon, that was for sure. Eyewitnesses - several of them - had all said later that things seemed as normal as ever. Nothing out of the ordinary.

No one, they would all later admit, had been paying any particular attention to the man. After all, it wasn't the sort of thing that you did, was it? You just wouldn't think to take any notice of someone so inconspicuous, just in case they suddenly did something out of the ordinary, would you? One witness, a sixty-something year old who seemed more put out by the fact that his afternoon trip to the bookmakers had been interrupted, did recall it being a bit odd that the man wore a long, dark trenchcoat, despite it being a pretty warm afternoon, not even raining for a change. Each to their own though, even if it did make him look like one of those teeny-bopper goth things, or whatever the hell the kids liked to call themselves these days.

"I saw him a little bit," the same man would say, when quizzed about it afterwards. "He just looked like someone minding his own business. Walking along, glancing at people every now and then, before putting his head down again, maybe like he didn't really want to be recognised. Then, really suddenly, it happened."

- Can't believe how quick it was-

- One minute everything was normal, the next, there he was-

- Grabbing at the baby, like he was trying to snatch it away-

- Leaning over it like some bloody vampire or something-

- *Trying to lick its face. I mean really, you don't know* what *sort of diseases he could have had-*

- *Of course, the mother tried to beat him away. Tried to smack him one, right in the face. I mean, good on her, who wouldn't?*

- *The language was pretty choice, too. Not that I blame her. Some strange bloke shows up from out of nowhere and starts drooling all over her baby like a rabid dog, hell, I'd chin the bastard one for sure-*

- *Right in the middle of a crowded street, outside a busy shop. Unbelievable-*

- *So anyway, you would think that would have frightened the bloke off-*

- *But no, instead he grabs the mother, while she's still swinging her fists at him like Muhammad bloody Ali. Gets a hold of her throat, he does, hawks up a lungful and tries to spit it right into her mouth-*

- *Dirty bastard. Some people these days are just plain* filthy-

- *Next thing you know, someone shows up from out of nowhere, and makes a grab for him. Some big bear of a fella, yelling and trying to get him away from them both. But this guy, it's like he's completely flipped out now-*

- *Screaming and frothing at the mouth, like he's got Rabies or something-*

- *Probably what it was, Rabies. You can't be too careful, you know. Not in this day and age. People walk around with all sorts of diseases. The world's gone bloody soft, that's what it is.* Soft-

- *Still don't know how they managed to drag him away. Kicking and swinging his fists around like some wild animal-*

- *Strength of ten men, though you wouldn't have thought it from the look of him. Skinny bugger he was, nothing on him, with clothes hanging off him like a sack of spuds-*

- *Seriously though, what* was *he thinking?*

***

Sunday; the day of rest or, in Ethan Bennett's case, the day of recovery.

It started out pretty inconspicuous, although, even then he had a faint, niggling feeling that something wasn't quite right, was *different* somehow. He lay flat, trying to ignore the cold hardness of the coil spring, digging its way into the small of his back as it struggled to break free from the worn, confining fabric of the mattress. He found that if he watched the ceiling rotating around its central point for long enough, then it usually distracted him from the realisation that he really ought to get himself something a little more sturdy to sleep on. His spine was probably shot to shit, what with the way the bloody thing sagged in the middle, creaking every time he shifted his weight. And he didn't even *want* to think of the stains; sweat, probably old piss, along with other stuff of the sort that he didn't care to put a name to. He groaned, the thought of what he could be lying on enough to force a grimace as he turned onto his side.

He felt his head move, his arms and his legs, his torso. Every muscle fibre strained with the effort.

His belly stayed right where it was.

"What the-?" He craned his neck, ignoring the crick in it as he looked down at his exposed midriff. He had partly undressed, his best pulling shirt probably dumped on the floor somewhere, just out of sight. Everything looked just the same as it had the day before, dark curls peppering his chest, his lower abdomen, not too bad for his age, all things considered, despite the first signs of a growing paunch. He could see it, he just couldn't feel it. No tingling, no numbness, just *nothing*, as though it simply wasn't there anymore.

He wrinkled his nose in disgust, as the smell hit him; stale beer, vomit and the faint but unmistakable ammonia stink of his own urine. He must have really been pretty gone last night, no matter how he tried telling himself that he ought to know better. Slowly, as though bracing himself for pain of some sort, he ran both hands down the front of his torso. The rough skin of his palms bristled against the wiry curls of hair, before reaching his belly, then nothing. He might as well have been touching thin air.

It's like a chunk of my body has just disappeared, he thought to himself. *Like it's been cut away and moved someplace else. Crazy.*

How did it get to this? He closed his eyes, hoping that it would make the spinning stop, disappointed when he realised the inevitable, that it only made it worse.

***

The night before:

He really was old enough to know better, but, you know what? Fuck it, life just felt far too short to act your age sometimes. There were more than enough people in this world with their heads jammed far too much up their own arses, trying to act all respectable and, when he said respectable he actually meant really pissing boring. He wasn't quite ready for The Times *crossword, evening mugs of cocoa, and gingham pyjamas, not just yet anyway. You're only as old as the person you're feeling up, or some bollocks like that. And the younger the woman he felt, the better. The only trouble being that the younger, fitter models were getting increasingly hard to come by.*

Between the two of them, they had already vacuumed what felt like half a kilo of brick dust up their nostrils, before engaging in sex in several positions that he had never thought physically possible before, certainly not for him at least. His cock still hadn't subsided fully, and was still dewy with her wetness, the pungent smell of her something that he tried to ignore as it hung around, as though lodged somewhere in his nostrils.

"Damnit, Susan-"

"*Susanne, you prick! My bloody name's Susanne, at least get that right, yeah?*"

"*Sorry, Susanne,*" he corrected himself. Christ, it wasn't his fault that the words didn't spill out the way he wanted them to sometimes. "*My head's still buzzing, that was some decent shit.*" He threw what he hoped was a grin, as lop-sided as it was. "*And don't get me started on the tingling in the end of my prick.*"

"*You'd better get over it,*" she slurred, her voice every bit as thick as his. "*I've got plans for you. Trust me.*"

"*What sort of plans?*" his own voice sounded distant, as though the words were actually being spoken by someone else, coming at him on a drug-laden haze. "*It sounds intriguing, whatever it is.*"

"*Oh, I'm sure you'll love it, really you will.*" She sat up as she spoke, leaning forward as she did so, her breasts – nowhere near as full-looking as when they were stuffed into a bra that looked two sizes too small – swinging as they gave in to the lure of gravity. He just about managed to shift his gaze from their hypnotic sway for long enough to see that her eyes had an almost wicked gleam to them, at odds with the amount of gear that they had put away between the two of them. Christ, he really was getting a bit old for this sort of bullshit, not that he would ever admit it out loud.

"*Well, if it can just numb the burning in my cock for a little while, I'm sure it'll be okay for me,*" he rolled his eyes, as if to con her into thinking that he wasn't being totally serious.

"*It might,*" she smiled, licking her lips as she did so. Surely she couldn't want him to do her over the arm of the chair *again*? His come was still drying on her chest in pearly streaks, where he had shot his load when she had insisted that he pull out early. At least she had considered that much. "*Don't worry,*" she said, as if reading his mind, but probably more likely just noticing the pained expression that must have been on his face. "*You'll get to rest for a little while yet.*" He *frowned, trying his best to look disappointed, wondering if it looked more like a forced grimace of discomfort.*

"So what is it? This thing that you've got planned for me?" She pressed a finger to his lips to shush him, her grin widening as she did so. The light in her eyes gave her an almost otherworldly look, either that or he was still more high than he thought.

"Wait there just a minute," she stood up, her breasts flopping back into place with a faint slapping sound as she did so. "I'll go fetch it. It'll blow your mind, I promise. Then, I might blow something else, if you're a good boy." She turned to walk towards the door, and he noticed for the first time that there were faint stretch marks around her belly and the tops of her thighs, as though she had lost quite a lot of weight in a short space of time. I'm not really that surprised, *he* thought, *especially if she fucks other blokes the way we've just being doing. That'd burn the calories off for sure. He tried to ignore the faint sagging of her arse cheeks as she reached the door, gripping the handle.*

"Keep your voice down, my flatmate, she'll be back any time soon, she doesn't like noise," she smiled again, with a coldness that was at odds to the sound of her voice. "Stay right there, I'll be back in a minute. I promise, you'll love *it."*

***

"Owwww...fucking hell..." he lifted a hand to his temple, pressing his forefinger against it and wincing as the slightest pressure sent an electric shock through the front of his head. He had no idea of the time, although the shadows thrown across the room by the light from the window suggested that it was probably somewhere in the afternoon. "Far, *far* too old," he muttered, at that moment not really caring just how uncomfortable such an admission might have sounded. At least the numbness in his midriff seemed to have subsided now, although it had been replaced by a churning sensation, as though he hadn't eaten in about a week. Either that, or he was going to lose the contents in the not too distant future.

"This is what I get for enjoying myself," he mumbled to himself. "I'm not here for a long time, I'm here for a good time, right?" The words did little to convince him that he wasn't stupid. That was just how it always was though; he would fuck up, regret it and promise himself that he was going to take better care of himself, only to go back to fucking up all over again. *Nothing ever changes*, he thought. *Christ, I really should know better.*

Shaking his head as he struggled into a sitting position, he swung his legs over the side of the bed, wincing as the soles of his feet brushed against the cold flooring below. The daylight poking its way through a gap in the curtains suggested that he had been asleep for longer than intended. Not that it mattered too much; he liked to pride himself on the lack of responsibilities in his life. Responsibility was a sign of getting old, something that he could do without.

"I suppose I'd better try and eat something," he rose to his feet, feeling a tremor right through his body as he wavered unsteady, his head feeling like it had been inflated with helium and was floating somewhere just beneath the ceiling. "Need to put a lining back on my stomach, as well as get some coffee inside me."

***

"Just stop being such a pussy and take the damn things. You won't regret it, I promise."

His eyes still misted with a drug-induced blur, he narrowed them in an effort to focus upon the two capsules, resting in the palm of her outstretched hand. There they were, looking like the sort of thing that you might buy over the counter for a cold, nestled between the head and heart lines, as though to join the two together.

"I thought you said that your flatmate was due back," he tried to deflect her, suspecting that it was pointless, judging by the growing insistence, of near-urgency in her voice. "You know, the one who doesn't like noise?"

"Yeah, there are a lot of things Alex doesn't like," Susanne murmured, her voice almost coy. "Doesn't mean we can't still do some of them, we just have to try and be a little bit quieter." She pushed her hand further forward, until the capsules were almost under his nose.

"What the hell are they anyway? You haven't told me yet. I'm not about to take some shit if I don't know what it's supposed to do. For fuck's sake, I'm not that out of it."

She giggled, the sound wrong somehow, at odds with her appearance, almost alien. "Get this, it's actually pretty funny, they're supposed to be diet pills."

"Diet pills? What the hell-"

She raised her other hand, placing her forefinger against his mouth to shush him.

"Yeah, diet pills, you know, to help you lose weight."

"I don't need to lose weight, I just came here for a few drinks, some blow, and a good fuck."

"Yeah," she said, "and you've already had all three. Now I want you to do something for me. Like I said, if you do, then I might do something else for you." She waved the hand holding the capsules beneath his nose again, making a point. "You've enjoyed it so far, haven't you?" She smiled again, her grin widening. "Afterwards, I might even talk Alex into joining in. She can be just as much fun as me sometimes, if you get her in the mood."

"Why would you want me to take diet pills?"

"They're not just diet pills, you soft bastard, that's just what they're supposed to be. They do so much more."

"Like what?" His eyes narrowed in suspicion again, just wanting her to give him a straight answer. Even better, wanting her to take her *hand from out of his face and carry out her promise to suck him off again.*

"You'll find out," she said with that same icy giggle. "The best part is, they take a day or two to kick in, but when they do – whoosh!" Without breaking eye contact, she reached her free hand down to his crotch, wrapping her fingers around the base of his cock and stroking in an upward motion, massaging him back to stiffness. He let out an involuntary gasp as the movement sent a tingling spasm into the pit of his belly. "Just think, plenty more of this, along with anything else you want me to do. But you have to do this one little thing for me first."

Fuck it. You only live once.

He took the capsules from her hand and shoved them into his mouth without pausing to think of what he might be letting himself in for, reaching for a glass of vodka on the side table to wash them down.

"There's a good boy. That didn't hurt, did it?"

He lay back as she leaned into him, tracing her tongue slowly from his belly button down to the wiry thatch of his pubic curls. She mumbled against him as she took his erect length into her mouth, bobbing her head with a teasing slowness. "Now – mmmm – where were we again?"

***

He closed his eyes, squeezing tears from beneath the lids as he heaved, retching the contents of his stomach down the toilet bowl. A large gob of dark-stained drool trailed from his bottom lip as he grasped for the flush handle, trying to wash away the evidence of the night before without the chance to see it. Ever since he had been a kid, the sight of his own vomit just made him feel worse.

Diet pills my arse, he thought, coughing and spluttering in an effort to clear the mucus now coating the back of his throat. *What the hell has she given me?*

He sat back from the toilet, slumping against the wall in a limp heap, feeling the rise and fall of his chest in time with his hoarse panting.

"What the hell *did* she give me?" He asked aloud this time, as though expecting an answer to come from somewhere. He tried to clear his head, trying not to panic as he focused on his breathing returning to normal. *Try and be logical,* he thought, *it can't be an infection, there's been nowhere near long enough for* that. *Not yet, anyway.* He hadn't eaten anything to make him throw up so violently. Sure, he had put away enough cheap booze to sink a lifeboat, but he had most likely slept most of that off by now. The only thing left was those damn diet pills. Of course, that was what she had called them. She had been pretty cagey about the things from the start, she hadn't even told him what they were called or who she had scored them from, never mind what was actually in the fucking things.

"The best part is, they take a day or two to kick in, but when they do – whoosh!"

"*Whoosh*," he said under his breath, aware that his voice was still slurring. "You're not fucking kidding, *whoosh*. Doping bitch."

He rubbed at his eyes with his thumb and forefinger, trying to clear away his fogged vision. It was then that he felt it, a sticky wetness across his upper lip. He wiped at it with the back of his hand, groaning in dismay at the tell-tale red smear that appeared in place. Still unsteady, he hauled himself to his feet and turned to face the bathroom mirror. He moaned again at the sight of the nosebleed, not just a nosebleed but a fucking *torrent*, twin streams of crimson gouting from both nostrils and running down either side of his mouth to drip down from the greying stubble peppering his chin.

It had been at least thirty years since he'd had a nosebleed.

"What the hell did she *give* me?" He asked again, but there was no answer.

***

"Whuuuuu-" He was awakened by the sound of the doorbell ringing over and over again. He blinked his eyes, the glare of the lightbulb above burning into them. He was still in his dressing gown, the side of his face pressed against the bathroom floor tiles as though glued into place. He must have passed out soon after being sick. Groggy, he lifted his head, wincing as his cheek peeled away with a shucking noise as he did so, drying blood caking the side of his face, as well as in a small puddle on the floor.

"All right, I'm coming for fuck's sake!"

He lurched to the front door and slid back the bolt, trying to focus his effort into not being sick again as he swung the door inward.

"Parcel for you – *oh my!*" The postman averted his gaze, still holding out the small package in one outstretched hand. Looking down, Ethan realised that his dressing gown was hanging open, displaying all that he had to offer.

"Sorry...I'm sorry," he mumbled, gathering the belt around his waist and tying it. "I haven't been feeling too well, I'm still half asleep."

"It's not just that," the postman indicated, pointing at him with a stumpy finger. "You're not kidding, you don't look well at all. Have you had a nosebleed or something? You look ill. If I were you I'd go and see a doctor."

"Thanks. If I need medical advice from a postie I'll ask for it. Just give me my bloody parcel," he snapped. Then seeing the growing look of outrage on the other man's face, "I'm sorry, that was rude of me. I didn't mean it, I'm just tired and a bit under the weather."

413

"You can say *that* again," the postman's chubby face flushed red, betraying his offence at Ethan's abruptness. "Like I said, I reckon you need to see a doctor. For more than one issue, judging by the look of you."

Ethan said nothing, just nodding his head as he closed the door before the postman could say anything further.

"I reckon if there's anyone needs diet pills, it's you, you fat sod," he sighed as he walked back in the direction of the bedroom.

On the way he stopped. He hadn't really paid any attention earlier, but there was a low rumble in the pit of his belly, as though he hadn't eaten in days. *Probably cleared myself out with all my throwing up earlier*, he thought. *It might be a good idea to see if I can hold something down now.*

Walking into the kitchen area, he looked in the 'fridge. It was bare, apart from an empty milk bottle, two eggs and a pack of unopened raw beef burgers – probably out of date. As he stared at them, he was dimly aware that he was salivating as the rumbling in his stomach intensified.

***

He paced up and down the length of the kitchen floor, the way he had been doing for the last twenty minutes or so. The dressing gown had been discarded in a crumpled pile in the corner, sweat beading his brow and clinging to his torso with a dewy persistence. The previous fog had left him now, to be replaced by a nervous energy that refused to abate. He had tried to stand still for a moment, only to find that doing so made him twitch.

I'm skitzing out, he thought to himself. *She's doped me up with some bad junk, and now I'm skitzing out. It has to be that.* His eyesight was blurred around the edges and tinged with a pink hue. *Probably burst the blood vessels in my eyeballs*, he thought. *I'll be blind before the end of the day. I should call for an ambulance, but they won't do anything. Besides, they probably won't be able to figure out what she's done to me, either.*

Instead, he kept pacing back and forth, listening to the brisk, agitated sound of his own footsteps, matched only by the now incessant growling in his belly and a low droning noise in his head, like white static.

He paused in front of a cupboard, pulling it open to see what was inside. There was a box of breakfast cereal, unopened, the large, cartoon monkey on the front of the packaging proclaiming that they were just *sooooo chocolatey!* He remembered the empty bottle of milk in the 'fridge, before tearing the box open with spindly, nervous fingers.

So hungry. So fucking hungry.

He plunged his hand into the box and scooped out a large handful of the contents, shovelling the cereal into his mouth, dry chewing it as he ignored the sensation like sandpaper scraping the back of his throat. That monkey was right; they were very chocolatey indeed. Even better, they stopped the gnawing in his belly.

He reached in again and again, scooping out handful after handful and cramming them into his mouth as fast as he could chew, losing himself in the sensation of eating as though he might die if he stopped for long enough. *What are you even doing?* A small voice somewhere in the back of his head asked. He ignored it and instead, he ate.

After what felt like no time at all, he reached in again, feeling around with a growing sense of desperation as he realised that the box was empty. He slumped back against the cupboard, the door handle digging into the small of his back as he sobbed.

He was still hungry.

***

Dark. So dark.

He realised that he had been sleeping again, for how long, he had no idea. It must have been a while, given that it was night time. All that he had done was throw up, sleep, and eat. Of course, he had managed to piss off his postman as well, but that was the least of his worries. He had forgotten about the parcel. It probably wasn't important anyway, it could wait.

He had been dreaming about Susanne; about her sucking him off in her flat, with an eagerness that suggested she could gladly bite his cock off and swallow it whole, her deflated-looking breasts slapping back and forth all the time as she did so. He had dreamed about her slightly manic-looking stare, her cold laugh, the stretch marks across her belly and thighs. She looked like she had lost weight recently, he thought. She looked like she had lost a *lot* of weight recently. He knew that the thought should probably worry him, but all that he could think about was food, about how hungry he was.

Before he even knew what he was doing, he had opened the 'fridge door, his eyes watering against the light as it pierced through the darkness, making his retinas burn. Then the pack of raw burgers was in his hands. Then the cellophane shrink wrapping was crumpled up, discarded on the floor. Then he was chewing, a clump of raw ground beef clogging his mouth as he rolled it around, grinding it down to mush as he swallowed, the thick, cloying sensation making his throat ache. He ignored the raw, bloody stink of uncooked meat as he forced another handful down, followed by another, and another. He had to eat. He had to, it was the only thing that made the hunger stop.

All the time he ate, he could see her, her wicked grin smiling up at him from out of the darkness.

"The best part is, they take a day or two to kick in, but when they do – whoosh!"

Those same words, echoing through his head, over and over again.

***

Hungry. Still so hungry.

I can't do it. I *can't*.

(good food good meat good god let's eat)

He had been staring at his forearm for what felt like hours, but had probably only been a few minutes at most. He had never been one to pay close attention to his physical state, a part of him thinking that doing so might actually force him to consider the toll that his lifestyle choices were taking. All the same, he didn't remember there being that little meat on his bones. No wonder I'm so famished, he thought, it looks like I'm wasting away.

(food glorious fooooood)

I just need feeding up a bit,

(hot sausage and mustard)

then I'll be fine. Then the noise in my belly will stop, it'll have to stop.

(rich gentlemen have it boys in-di-gestion)

I just need to eat.

He looked down still, studying the fleshy underside of his forearm. A bit on the skinny side perhaps, but there was still a bit of meat on it. He was salivating like one of Pavlov's dogs now, a trail of drool running down the side of his chin and dripping onto the meat below.

Meat. Good food.

"*I can't!*" He sobbed, no tears coming, only a burning sensation in his eyes.

(man's gotta eat)

He lunged his head forward like a striking snake, burying his teeth into himself as he brought his jaws together, muffling his own scream of pain against himself as a white hot agony fired through his body, incisors tearing through gristle and muscle as his own hot blood pooled into his mouth with a rich salt tang.

He had barely finished chewing and swallowing before he passed out on the floor, pain replaced by a blessed oblivion.

Whoosh.

He must have only been unconscious for a few minutes at most. Still, as he opened his eyes, it was long enough to lose blood – a lot of blood.

Fuck, he thought to himself, shock stirring him into alertness, *I'm gonna bleed to death. Someone will find me a few weeks from now, maybe that fat postman. Someone will find me here, lying naked in a pool of my own snot, blood and puke. They'll look at me and they'll think, poor guy, looks like he ate himself to death.* The thought of it made him laugh, a dry, insane chuckle that hurt the back of his throat and made his ribs ache. For the life of him, he couldn't understand what it was that he found so funny.

He turned his head to one side and vomited, the action passive now, he didn't even strain. Groggy, he looked down at the fresh puke, pooling on the floor. For a moment, he could have sworn that he saw something move. A fleshy lump, dark red, about two inches in length and glistening with an oily sheen, like a bloated leech of some sort.

Probably just my imagination, he thought.

He struggled to his feet, clutching his wounded

(eaten)

forearm to his chest in an effort to stem the bleeding, blood smearing across his naked torso as he did so. He lurched into the bathroom and grabbed a towel from the rail, wrapping it tight around the wound and pulling it in place. Out of sight, out of mind. It did little to get rid of the aftertaste of raw meat on his tongue though.

As he turned, he caught sight of his reflection in the mirror of the medicine cabinet. Eyes that he didn't recognize glared out at him from sunken, blackened sockets. The skin over his cheekbones looked drawn, as though the fat had been sucked out of his face overnight, his lips pale, gums drawn back from his teeth, making them look elongated, almost like an emaciated vampire. He traced a finger down the length of his body, slowly picking out the beginnings of where ribs were beginning to poke their way through.

Diet pills, he thought, struggling to remember why he would think of such a thing. Perhaps something had happened, but he couldn't actually remember what it could be. All he could remember was an ever-present, gnawing hunger.

***

He had taken his time getting dressed, a combination of tiredness and a need to make sure that he looked as inconspicuous as possible. He tried to pick out something baggy and ill-fitting, in an effort to hide his shrunken frame. Doing so wasn't difficult; almost everything in his wardrobe seemed baggy and ill-fitting. He had been careful to bind his wounded arm tight with a bandage that he had found in the medicine cabinet, using the full roll, just to make sure. A person could catch all manner of nasty infections from an open wound, and he didn't want *that*. He dug out an old black trenchcoat from the back of the wardrobe. Something that he hadn't worn in years, it smelled stale, of damp and mothballs. A bit of fresh air would soon fix that. He slipped it on, buttoning it all the way up to just under his neck. There, almost normal-looking.

He was sure that he would be okay soon. After all, he couldn't stay cooped up in his pokey little flat forever. No, he probably just needed to make some effort to get out, to spend some time around people. That was it; he felt like he needed to see people, *lots* of people. That would help him to get better, lots of close, physical contact.

People, some fresh air and some decent food, and he would be right as rain.

Turning up his collar, he stepped out of his flat, closing the door behind himself.

ABOUT THE AUTHOR

Lee Glenwright's short fiction has been published in several anthologies and magazines, including *O, Unholy Night in Deathlehem* (Grinning Skull Press), *Deadman Humour: 13 Fears of a Clown* (Abstruse Press), *What Monsters Do for Love, Volume One* (Soteira Press), and *Trigger Warnings – Hallucinations* (Madness Heart Press). A collection of short fiction, *Ripe, and Others*, and a novel, *Mutt,* are also available.

Lee Glenwright lives in Sunderland UK with his family, far too many pets, and a dark sense of humour. He can be stalked on social media via BlueSky (@LeeGlenwright), or his Facebook page (@LeeGlenwrightWriter), or can be reached via his website *www.leeglenwright.weebly.com*

www.ingramcontent.com/pod-product-compliance
Ingram Content Group UK Ltd.
Pitfield, Milton Keynes, MK11 3LW, UK
UKHW041821110325
456069UK00002B/188